D1409846

THE OTHER SIDE OF DIVINE

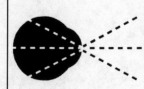

This Large Print Book carries the
Seal of Approval of N.A.V.H.

THE OTHER SIDE OF DIVINE

VANESSA DAVIS GRIGGS

THORNDIKE PRESS
A part of Gale, Cengage Learning

GALE
CENGAGE Learning®

Detroit • New York • San Francisco • New Haven, Conn • Waterville, Maine • London

LIBRARY OF CONGRESS CATALOGING-IN-PUBLICATION DATA

Griggs, Vanessa Davis.
  The Other Side of Divine / By Vanessa Davis Griggs. — Large Print edition.
    pages cm. — (A Blessed Trinity Novel Series) (Thorndike Press Large Print
  African-American)
  ISBN 978-1-4104-6279-4 (hardcover) — ISBN 1-4104-6279-X (hardcover) 1.
African American families—Fiction. 2. Family secrets—Fiction. 3. Ethics in the
Bible—Fiction. 4. Large type books. I. Title.
PS3557.R48954O835 2013
813'.54—dc23   2013032554

Published in 2013 by arrangement with Dafina Books, an imprint of
Kensington Publishing Corp.

Printed in Mexico
1 2 3 4 5 6 7 17 16 15 14 13

To you
The readers of my books

ACKNOWLEDGMENTS

To my Lord and Savior Jesus the Christ, the author and finisher of my faith; my loving mother and father, Josephine and James Davis Jr.; my husband, children, grandchildren, other family members, friends, publishing personnel, and all who have supported me and contributed in any way toward my dream in this magnificent writing journey I embarked upon so many years ago: I love you, thank you, and appreciate you more than words will *ever* be able to convey. If you're reading this right now, then my sincere and heartfelt thanks and acknowledgment are to you!

To those who may be new to my books (this being your first introduction to me and my works), thank you for choosing *The Other Side of Divine,* a novel that, like all of my others, was written with so much of my heart remaining inside of it.

As always, I do love hearing from you. You

can find me on the Web at: www.Vanessa-DavisGriggs.com and on Facebook at: www.Facebook.com/vanessadavisgriggs.

Once again: I truly, truly, love you and pray God's blessings upon you. If you know me at all, you know what I'm likely going to tell you next. And yes, I still continue to believe that the *BEST* is *YET* to come . . .

PROLOGUE

And take the helmet of salvation, and the sword of the Spirit, which is the word of God.

— Ephesians 6:17

When I tell you how beautiful, you're not going to believe *just* how much so. In fact, beautiful doesn't even *begin* to describe it or give it justice.

I'm sorry. Please forgive me. I'm getting ahead of myself here. I hate when someone starts in the middle of a conversation as though you've taken part in what was apparently going on in their heads before they began to speak and you have no *earthly* idea *what* they're jabbering on and on about.

To those who don't know me, my name is Esther Crowe. Those who know and love me best call me Esther, Aunt Esther, or Miss Crowe. A few folks even call me Zion from my days when I had a dance group called the Daughters of Zion many forgotten years ago. The miss part of Miss Crowe is actually a *miss* statement. There I go again: my attempt at a little humor and playing on words. I love words. For anyone who may have missed it, I was playing on the word misstatement.

I was born Esther Morgan, no middle name. I married into the last name of Crowe. My husband died young (much too young) early into our marriage, from complications of an illness called lupus, to be exact. I don't like talking much about it. Suffice it to say: I never remarried; I never got around to finding anyone special enough to fill his space.

Then there was that terrible automobile accident that pretty near claimed my life here on earth. I was spared, although barely. For ten years, it was as if I didn't really exist. But then my nephew, Dr. Zachary Wayne Morgan, stepped into that Chicago nursing facility, bringing with him someone near and dear to my heart: my dear, sweet Gabrielle Mercedes Booker all the way from Birmingham, Alabama and all grown up now.

Gabrielle dropped the last name of Booker and goes by Gabrielle Mercedes. That poor child has indeed lived a hard life. That wretched woman who was given charge over the almost four-year-old at the time was actually the cause of Gabrielle (eight years old when I first met her) and I becoming acquainted. I was out in the community on a summer jog and Aunt Cee-Cee (Mrs. Cecelia Murphy) was out there treating that sweet child like she thought her name was Cinderella (before the glass slippers). I laugh sometimes because Gabrielle has told me on more than one occasion that I was like her very own fairy godmother.

I suppose it's true what some folks say: What Satan meant for bad, God will use it for good.

I figured out a way to get that precious little girl some joy into her life while she endured being treated even worse than a redheaded stepchild. At least I'd like to believe I brought some good into that child's life. But Gabrielle could dance, oh my *goodness,* she could dance! The first time my eyes fell on her running around picking up after those four other children like she was their hired help, I saw the greatness in her. I often described her movements as like the seeds on the feathers of dandelions being carried in the wind: Graceful with a capital *G.* I saw the greatness in her future.

Gabrielle's aunt Cee-Cee tried to say I believed Gabrielle was the child I never had. She even said jokingly (or so she claimed after she didn't get the response she'd apparently hoped for) that I could have Gabrielle outright, for the right price, of course. If I could have gotten Gabrielle without the insult of seeming to buy her, I would have taken that child in a heartbeat, in a *heartbeat*. After I learned how badly Aunt Cee-Cee had done Gabrielle after my automobile accident — taking the money I'd paid for Gabrielle to attend Juilliard, then throwing her out on the streets with nowhere to go . . .

I don't even like thinking about that. Why couldn't I have been here? I wanted so much to see the look on her face when she received the information about Juilliard. But to think: That wretched woman took that money, stole it is what she did. . . . Well, needless to say, Cecelia Murphy's day of reckoning is coming. And you can believe *that.* Those that live by the sword shall die by the sword.

I didn't think of Gabrielle as the child I never had. What folks have to understand is none of us *truly* own anything or anybody here on earth. Everything belongs to God. Psalm 24:1 provides the title and the deed.

"The earth is the Lord's, and the fullness thereof; the world, and they that dwell therein." My father used to say, "If folks think they own it, then let them die and see just what they *really* own. You brought nothing into this world and for certain, you'll take nothing when you leave, not even these earth suits we fondly call our bodies."

I miss my father. Our parents taught us that if we saw someone in need, especially a child, we should try to do what we could to help. That's how things were back in my day. Yeah, I'm close to sixty years old, short by almost two years. Nowadays, if you say something to a child, not only might the child cuss you out, but nine times out of ten, when the parents find out, one or both of them will hunt you down and cuss you out.

Yes, I meant cuss and not curse. Having been a schoolteacher, I know the difference between the two words. Cussing is a whole other word and a whole other level than cursing. High-society folks, who make their subjects and verbs agree, curse. Folks who want to get you good and told cuss.

But back to what I was saying. I don't want to get off on that because that's a whole story in itself. I was in this horrific automobile accident. Everybody, including me, believed my life as I'd known it was over. Then Gabrielle stepped into my room and danced me back on my journey to recovery. There was such an anointing in my room that day, oh my goodness! I felt the glory of the Lord sitting . . . the weight of His glory on me. There's nothing like the glory of God to lift you up.

Yes, God raised me right up off of that sick bed. I heard Him speak to me just as clear as you hear me speaking now. "There is more that I require of thee. Get up, Esther! There's too much still left for you to do."

So I girded myself up. I began putting on the whole armor of God. I held up my sword, I'm talking about the Word of God, and I was ready to get back on the battle-field.

If God has ever told you to do anything, please know that God equips those He calls. He raised me up off that deathbed, and in a little less than a year's time, my speech has become ninety-five percent clear again. My dance returned, not so much in my legs and feet as in my heart. There's something glorious to be said about dancing from the heart.

People come up and say, "Esther, how are you doing?" And I say, "I'm still kicking, just not as high."

After God got me back on my feet, He told me I had to go help Gabrielle one more time. That there was a huge battle coming, and I needed to be there to assist. All I needed was one Word from the Lord. Over the objections of my family (mostly from my sister-in-law Leslie Morgan, also Zachary's mother), I packed my bags and told Zachary what time to pick me up from the airport. These new flying rules are horrible. I feel like Rip Van Winkle with everything that changed while I was out. What's all this taking off your shoes and folks with purple plastic gloves patting all over you? I'm almost an old woman. What exactly do they think I'm going to do?

There I go again: another subject for another time.

In mid-November 2010, I left Chicago and arrived in what had been my hometown for a few years. When you obey God, things fall into place even if to us it doesn't appear that's what it's doing. God knows what He's doing. I thought I was coming to Birmingham, Alabama, to help Gabrielle plan a wedding she and Zachary were taking much too long to move on. There was also that little unfinished legal matter between me and Mrs. Cecelia aka Cee-Cee Murphy, better known now as "the defendant."

So after a beautiful Christmas with Zachary and Gabrielle (not to leave out my biggest surprise of all, little Jasmine Noble, who can dance just as wonderfully as her mother Gabrielle), who would have guessed that at the beginning of 2011, all Hell would break loose. No, I did not cuss here. When I say Hell, I mean Hell in every biblical sense of the word with the devil, his imps, and the fire and brimstone. Well, all of Hell broke loose. It's definitely what you would call the *other* side of divine.

God knows in advance of spiritual warfare when prayer warriors are needed to be called to arms and in place. God sent me to Birmingham (the home of U.S. Steel that helped give Birmingham its nickname The Magic City because of how fast the city grew, although some say it was because of the smog that caused the city to seemingly disappear then "magically" appear again), for such a time as this and . . .

You know what? Instead of me telling you everything, why don't I just let you see for yourself?

CHAPTER 1

The light of the body is the eye: if therefore thine eye be single, thy whole body shall be full of light.

— Matthew 6:22

"All right, Jasmine, spell, energetic," fifty-eight-year-old Esther Crowe said as she and soon-to-be-ten-year-old Jasmine Noble sat on the couch in the den wearing their matching red Minnie Mouse shirts.

Jasmine smiled as she correctly spelled the word without even the slightest hesitation. Her brownish/black hair was pulled up into a cute little ponytail, her hair having grown tremendously in the thirteen months since her successful bone marrow transplant. Jasmine giggled. "Okay, Miss C," Jasmine said, calling her by the special name she'd given Miss Crowe as she'd done with Zachary, in calling him Dr. Z, and Gabrielle, whom she'd once called Miss G before calling her

Mama. "Now it's your turn."

Miss Crowe placed her hand on her chest. "My turn? How did I end up getting a turn? I'm not the one who has a spelling test tomorrow."

"Are you ready? Because this is going to be a long and tricky one that *always* seems to mess me up."

Miss Crowe nodded. She'd been a middle school teacher many years ago and there was nothing that put a smile on her face more than watching a child with an uncontained hunger for learning. "Hit me with your best shot, Miss Jazz."

Jasmine giggled again. "Okay, your word is Mississippi."

"Mississippi?"

Jasmine grinned and tilted her head to the side. "Yep. Mississippi."

A big smile spread across Miss Crowe's face. She repeated the word again, and then began. "Mississippi. M-i-crooked letter-crooked letter-i-crooked letter-crooked letter-i-humpback-humpback-i."

Jasmine was cracking up with laughter as she tossed her head back, falling back onto the sofa. "What?"

"You said Mississippi so I spelled Mississippi," Miss Crowe said. "Have you never heard it spelled that way before?"

Jasmine rolled onto the floor, kneeling as she giggled madly. "I most certainly have not. Crooked letter crooked letter, humpback humpback-i?"

Miss Crowe was laughing now as well. "Yes. Crooked letter-crooked letter" — she drew the letter S in the air with her index finger twice — "humpback-humpback" — she then drew two letter P's — "i," she said while cocking her head to one side and folding her arms like a rapper who'd just successfully delivered a rap.

Jasmine got up and sat back on the couch next to Miss Crowe. "That was *too* funny."

"Well, that's some of the things we did in the old days to help people learn to spell difficult words. The next time you have a need to spell Mississippi, you can sing that song in your mind, and you'll get it right every time, no problem."

Gabrielle Mercedes walked into the den. "Hey, you two. How are you feeling, Jasmine?"

Jasmine ran to Gabrielle's opened arms and hugged her. "Mama!"

Gabrielle smiled. There was nothing like hearing those words, especially after all they'd been through in the span of just a little over a year.

There was Jasmine's lifesaving bone mar-

19

row transplant at the end of December 2009. Then Jasmine's adoptive mother, Jessica Noble, died of cancer on March 30, 2010, which of all days was also Jasmine's birthday.

Jessica had desperately wanted to tell Jasmine that she *was* adopted. Sadly, she ended up taking her last breath before getting a chance. And as if that wasn't enough, in May of that same year, Gabrielle finally told Jasmine she'd been adopted by the Nobles before Jasmine learned in July, in the most horrific way, that Gabrielle was not merely a friend of the family as she'd been led to believe, but instead, her birth mother. "The mother who didn't want her and had given her away," as she overheard it carelessly blurted out from the mouth of the beautiful Paris Simmons-Holyfield.

Yes, it had been a journey all right, all coming to a climax November 2010 with the court's final approval of Gabrielle's adoption of Jasmine just as Gabrielle's beloved Miss Esther Crowe waltzed back into her life, vowing not to leave until she'd physically witnessed wedding vows exchanged between her very own nephew and the one some liked to call "the daughter she never had."

And now, it was a new year, 2011 — a

new season in every sense of the word. Engaged and come June 11, 2011, Gabrielle was set to wed the most amazing man: Dr. Zachary Wayne Morgan. For once, things were finally coming together . . . finally starting to look up.

Gabrielle strolled over to the couch and gave Miss Crowe a hug. "How did things go with the two of you today?"

"I told you that Jasmine and I would be fine. This baby is never a problem."

"I keep telling you I'm *not* a baby!" Jasmine said vehemently but with total respect toward an adult in her tone.

Miss Crowe pulled Jasmine over to her and hugged her. "I know, baby. I know. You're not a baby. Got it!"

"You just did it again!" Jasmine laughed and hugged Miss Crowe back.

"Sorry, baby. I know you're growing up into a big girl." Miss Crowe rocked her several times before letting her go. "But you'll always be my baby. Just like Gabrielle will always be my baby." Miss Crowe slowly shook her head. "It's amazing. I first met Gabrielle when she was around eight years old. And the first time I met you was when you were just a little past eight. That's something, isn't it?"

"Actually, I was nine and a half when we

first met," Jasmine said.

Gabrielle placed her hand on Jasmine's head. "Close enough. That would be considered a little past eight."

Jasmine grinned. "Me and Miss C had a great time today."

"Miss C and *I* had a great time today," Miss Crowe corrected.

Jasmine rolled her head in a circular motion. "Well, whichever way, we had a great time today." Jasmine looked at Gabrielle. "She helped me with all of my spelling words, so I'm ready to ace my test tomorrow."

"So you're feeling well enough to go to school tomorrow?" Gabrielle asked. "Because if you don't —"

"I'm fine," Jasmine said. "Now ask me how to spell Mississippi."

"Mississippi? Was that one of your words?" Gabrielle asked. "I don't recall seeing that one on your list."

"No. But go on. Ask me how to spell it."

"Okay," Gabrielle said as she glanced at Miss Crowe, who was also grinning like she'd eaten Tweety the bird. "Jasmine, please spell Mississippi."

Jasmine promptly spelled it the way Miss Crowe had shown her. She flopped down on the couch and giggled hard.

Gabrielle placed her hand on top of Jasmine's head. "That was good. I've heard people do that before. So I see you're learning all kinds of tricks from one of the best teachers around." Gabrielle glanced Miss Crowe's way and winked. "Well, I'm going upstairs to change."

"Dinner's ready. Miss C and I cooked," Jasmine said.

"Is that right? Well, I see you two have been quite busy today."

"May we eat in the dining room?" Jasmine said with her hands in a prayer mode. "Please, please, please."

"Sure," Gabrielle said. "Why have a dining room if we're not going to use it?"

"Yay! I'll set the table." Jasmine ran toward the dining room.

"Being around her is making me so much younger," Miss Crowe said. "I'll be back to my twenties at this rate. But she's such a precious and such a beautiful child, inside and out."

"Thanks. And I concur. She really is, although I can't take much credit for the terrific little girl she's become. Her adoptive parents laid a wonderful foundation with her. I'm merely maintaining and building on that."

"Now don't cut your contribution short.

Jasmine has a lot of your genes running around inside of her. That child reminds me so much of you," Miss Crowe said, shaking her head. "Especially when it comes to dancing. I've nicknamed her Happy Feet after that penguin in that movie." Miss Crowe did a few tap dancing steps.

"Well, I'm going to go and change into something more comfortable so we can have dinner in the dining room. I appreciate you so much for keeping Jasmine today. She wanted to go to school, but that shot she received yesterday caused her to have a fever. And I knew, even if I *had* let her go to school as she was begging for me to do, they would have sent her right back home. Besides, I don't want to take any chances, not when it comes to her health." Gabrielle shook her head.

"You don't have to explain anything to me. I've told you that I'm here to help out in any way that I can," Miss Crowe said. "It didn't make sense for you to take off work when I'm at your disposal."

"But I don't want to be imposing upon you, either."

Miss Crowe waved Gabrielle's comment away. "Child, please. I was laid up for over ten years. I've gotten all the rest one old woman needs for at least the next ten years.

I'm ready to be useful again. And being here with the two of you is the best medicine any doctor could prescribe."

"I don't know why you keep calling yourself old. You're not old," Gabrielle said.

"I know late fifties isn't considered old these days, but believe me: I really am getting close to being a senior citizen — there's no two ways about that. And in case you didn't know, you can get an AARP card at fifty. But being here, surrounded by you and Jasmine, makes me feel young again. You can't buy what the three of us generate. We're three true dancers from the heart."

"I'll be back in a few. I'm going to put on my Minnie Mouse shirt so then we can be the three *mouse*keteers." Gabrielle went upstairs.

Five minutes later, the doorbell rang. "I got it!" Miss Crowe yelled, mainly for Gabrielle's benefit. She quickly made her way to the door and cracked it open about the size of her small framed body. "Yes?"

"Good evening, miss," the older gentleman with a small patch of white, off centered in the top of his black hair, said. "I'm sorry. I'm looking for a Ms. Gabrielle Mercedes. Is this the right house?" He looked down at the index card that trembled slightly in his hand.

"That depends," Miss Crowe said. "Who are you?"

The man smiled. "My name is Benjamin. But everybody calls me Bennie."

"Bennie?" Miss Crowe said with a frown.

"Yes, ma'am."

"And might you possess a last name you'd care to disclose while you're passing out your first name?" Miss Crowe gave the dressed-down gentleman (wearing light brown pants and a crisp long-sleeved white shirt, incidentally with no coat, even though it was the dead of winter) a slow, methodical once-over just in case she might need to give a police description later.

Bennie flashed a full grin, showing that he wasn't missing any of his teeth as far as his grin extended. "Yes, ma'am, I most certainly do. It's —"

"Booker," Gabrielle said as she stepped up behind Miss Crowe and opened the door wider. She looked him dead in his eyes. "Hello" — she took a long hard swallow, one that could be heard as it went down — "Daddy."

CHAPTER 2

I am the man that hath seen affliction by
the rod of his wrath.
— Lamentations 3:1

"Gabrielle," Bennie Booker said as he stood
outside the door. After only mere seconds,
he nodded and wiped at tears that were now
falling.

Miss Crowe looked at Gabrielle, her attempt to gauge what Gabrielle might be
thinking and, in turn, what she should do,
since (for now anyway) she was the only
physical object separating father from
daughter.

Gabrielle took a step back from the doorway, visibly shaking now. Miss Crowe wasn't
sure whether Gabrielle's trembling reaction
was from seeing her father after all these
years or from the cold, January 20th
Birmingham air blasting through the still
opened door.

"Is it okay if I come in?" Bennie asked, wiping his eyes with a white handkerchief he'd taken out of his pants' pocket.

At first, Gabrielle said nothing. Miss Crowe was just about to politely tell him good-bye and close the door when Gabrielle placed her hand on her shoulder. "It's okay," Gabrielle said. Miss Crowe could feel the trembling in Gabrielle's hand. "You can come in." Gabrielle opened the door fully to her father.

Bennie turned back and waved to a waiting cab driver. The cab immediately backed out of the driveway. Bennie stepped inside the house. Miss Crowe closed the door and Gabrielle once again took a few steps back as though she wanted to maintain a certain distance between her and her father.

"I can't believe this," Bennie said with a huge grin on his face as tears continued to roll down. "Will you just look at you? Look at you. You're all grown up. My sweet little baby girl is not a baby anymore." He shook his head slowly as he simultaneously wiped his face with his folded handkerchief.

"So you're out? You're really out?" Gabrielle said. "They released you from prison."

He moved his mouth from side to side a few times as though he was trying to be certain of the words he chose with a few attempts obviously not making it past the vetting process and being turned back for another. "Yeah." He finally seemed to settle on. "I'm out. On parole, but for all that matters at this point, I'm a free man for now." He stared hard at Gabrielle. "Wow." He shook his head. "You look so much like . . . you look just like your moth . . . you look a lot like her." He nodded.

"Dinner is ready!" Jasmine said, bursting into the foyer. "The table is set and I even put some of the food on the table." She stopped where everyone now stood.

Bennie looked down at Jasmine. "Oh, my! Who, pray tell, is this? Wow, you look just like —"

"Jasmine, why don't you go to the den and watch TV for a little bit?" Gabrielle said, turning quickly to her daughter.

"But I thought we were about to eat." Jasmine looked over at Bennie. "I can set another plate if you like." Jasmine alternated her look between the man she hadn't been introduced to yet and Gabrielle. "It's really no trouble."

"Suppertime, huh?" Bennie said with a smile. "That sounds nice. It's been forever since I've actually sat down at a real table —"

"Jasmine, please. Go to the den like I told you, okay?" Gabrielle softly pressed Jasmine's little cheeks between her hands, then kissed her lightly on her nose.

"Okay," Jasmine said, turning on her toes like a ballerina doing a pivot move as she left to do as Gabrielle had instructed her.

"Miss Crowe, would you mind going with Jasmine for me? Please."

"I can, if you're sure about that."

Gabrielle nodded.

"Well," Miss Crowe said, giving Bennie a stern look. "I'll only be in the den if you need me. And don't forget about the food. We don't want it to get cold."

Gabrielle nodded again.

Miss Crowe started making her way out of the foyer, slower than normal to ensure that her exit was the right thing for her to be doing. After all, this was the same man who had killed his wife (bone of his bone and flesh of his flesh seeming not to matter to him), in the presence of his little daughter no less, only months from turning four years old. The same man who lied to the police about what he'd done. Going as far as to slander his wife's name and character by indicating she had a man on the side and that her secret lover was likely the culprit who'd murdered her. If they would find that man, they'd likely find their murderer. This was the same man who tried to intimidate his little girl into keeping her mouth closed about the truth she'd witnessed using the threat that she'd most assuredly be taken away and given to another family by these evil people who were merely out to trick her if she said one word.

So in the beginning, Gabrielle became mute.

Because of what Benjamin "Bennie" Booker had done, Gabrielle had been forced to grow up without the benefit of being cradled in the loving arms of a mother (or a father for that matter), and was mistreated by an aunt and uncle for more than fourteen years along with their four bratty children. And the one laudable out Gabrielle had going for her, the one thing that could have saved her from even more heartache — attending The Juilliard School dance division — and Cecelia Murphy, good old "Aunt Cee-Cee" had effectively managed to even steal *that* from her, right before kicking Gabrielle out onto the streets with no place to go.

Because of what Benjamin Booker did, setting off a chain reaction of all that was to come, Gabrielle had gone to stay with someone who really wasn't a friend, but more a user, named Paris Simmons. And Paris's father was a lowlife scum who'd taken advantage of Gabrielle's innocence, sleeping with her and getting her pregnant. Then he sat back and watched as Gabrielle was kicked out of the only place she had to live while insisting she terminate the pregnancy so it wouldn't mess up his marriage and relationship with his three children. The honorable Alabama congressman (now ex-congressman) Lawrence Simmons who didn't seem to care about anyone else other than himself and, in the end, his appearance to others.

Lawrence Simmons who, upon learning that Gabrielle had *not* aborted their child but instead had given the baby up for adoption, wouldn't immediately step up and do the right thing when that child was dying, in desperate need of a bone marrow donor. Oh, eventually he did the right thing (with a little push from Gabrielle). And Jasmine dancing around the house now was living proof of that today. But still . . .

So now here stood Bennie, the man who started the whole ball rolling, a man who had been sentenced to prison and had been incarcerated for two and half decades. A man who likely had his own sympathetic tales of things he'd gone through over these past brutal years.

But Miss Crowe didn't really care about him. It was his actions that had brought on the afflictions he'd had to endure. However, Gabrielle . . . Gabrielle was her heart. And even though she might not have been there to protect her from Aunt Cee-Cee and the others who'd done Gabrielle wrong, today was a new day, a different day. Today she *was* around. And Bennie Booker had better not even *think* about trying any funny business.

Not today. Not here. Not while she still had breath circulating in her body.

CHAPTER 3

Our fathers have sinned, and are not; and
we have borne their iniquities.
— Lamentations 5:7

"How are you?" Bennie asked Gabrielle.

"I'm fine."

"You are . . . absolutely beautiful." He
shook his head. "I'm standing here in
complete awe. I can't believe I had a hand
in creating something so beautiful."

"God created me," Gabrielle said in an
icy tone.

Bennie chuckled. "You're right. You're
right. I just meant . . ."

Gabrielle folded her arms. "I know what
you meant."

"I don't want to upset you or anything. I
promise I don't. But I'm just at a loss for
words or the right words at this moment.
It's been twenty-five years."

Gabrielle frowned at him. "And whose

fault is that?"

Bennie nodded as he folded his hands into each other. "I know it's all my fault. And I take full responsibility. Believe me: If I could go back in time and change things, do things all over again —"

"But you can't. So talking about it doesn't mean a hill of beans at this point."

He nodded again. "You're right. I can't argue with you about any of this. I just want you to understand from my heart that I have complete remorse for what I did. I want you to know that I'm sorry. And Gabrielle, whether you believe me or not: I really did love your mother. I loved her *so* much. That's what I think sent me over the edge that day. Maybe I loved her *too* much."

Gabrielle unfolded her arms and stared at him. "If that's your kind of love then I never want to experience it." She wiped at a few tears that were now falling. "So why are you here?"

"You mean here or out of prison?"

"Both."

"Is there somewhere you and I can go sit and talk? The old man is not as young as he used to be. And prison hasn't been so kind to me."

"We were just about to sit down and eat before you came."

Bennie nodded. "Okay. I get it. So you're saying that you'd like me to leave."

"I wasn't expecting you. I didn't know you were about to get out, let alone *be* out," Gabrielle said. "Nobody told me. You have to forgive me, but I'm having a bit of a time wrapping my brain around all of this right now."

"I understand, and I'll cut to the chase. I was released earlier today and this is the first place I came. Gabrielle, I had to come find you . . . I had to come and see my baby girl," Bennie said.

"Please don't do that."

He tilted his head to one side. "Do what?"

"Don't call me your baby girl."

"But you *are* my baby girl, Gabrielle Mercedes Booker."

Gabrielle let out a short, deranged chuckle. "I dropped the Booker a *long* time ago. I'm Gabrielle Mercedes now."

"Yeah, your aunt Cee-Cee wrote and told me that in one of the rare letters I got from her. It's been lonely being away from family; you just don't know how much. I've missed you, Gabrielle. I used to ask Cee-Cee to bring you to the prison for a visit, but she always had some excuse why she couldn't. Somehow, in all the years you were living with her, she never got around to it."

Bennie walked over to the staircase and sat down on the next to the bottom step.

Gabrielle stayed where she was, merely turning toward him as he continued to speak. "I wrote and told Cee-Cee about a year and a half ago that there was a good chance, a mighty good chance, that I might make parole this time around. I told her I would need a place to come home to if that was to happen."

"Good old Aunt Cee-Cee," Gabrielle said, stepping closer to where her father sat. "The person I ended up with after you *murdered* my mother." Gabrielle practically spat the words at his dark brown, worn face.

"Why do you say it like that? Did my sister not do right by you?"

Gabrielle released a sinister chortle this time around. "You don't know the half of all I've been through these years." She wiped hard at tears that were making their way down her face.

Bennie stood up and placed his hands gently on her shoulders. "Gabrielle, what did my sister do? Tell me."

Gabrielle pulled away from his hand and took two steps back. "I don't want to talk about it. Not with you."

"But suffice it to say, your years with her were not pleasant. Her husband, Dennis . . .

did he —"

"I said I don't want to talk about them, any of them, okay?" Gabrielle's voice escalated.

Bennie nodded as he held his hands up to calm her. "Okay. All right. I guess this is starting to make a little more sense now. I told Cee-Cee I had a good chance of being released. And during a rare time of sending back a response, she sent me a letter giving me your address saying this is where I should come if I were to ever get out. I tried calling her last year, but the number was disconnected. A letter I sent after that was returned without a forwarding address."

"Yeah. They were evicted from their house. I'm not sure where they're living these days. They came here briefly. Listen, I really don't want to talk about this right now. I don't care about Aunt Cee-Cee or her sorry excuse for a husband or her children or grandchildren. I just don't." Gabrielle wrapped her arms around herself.

"I understand. But I had to come and see you for myself. I had to look into your eyes and tell you how sorry I am for all the pain and hurt my actions caused you. I'd love to give you a hug if you'll let me. In fact, I *need* to hug you, Gabrielle. I know it might sound crazy for a grown man to be saying something like this. But I need to hold you in my arms. I want to ask your forgiveness and have you to accept it." Bennie stepped closer to Gabrielle, who quickly took an equal number of steps back from him.

"I'm saved, you know," he said with a quick nod, standing in his spot without moving any closer to her. "I gave my life to the Lord a little over fifteen years ago. I've been walking with God for a long time. I'm not the same man you once knew. The Word of God says, 'If any man be in Christ, he is a new creature.' I'm a new creature, Gabrielle. Not that wretched, vile man you once knew."

Gabrielle looked at him, diligently searching his face. For what? She wasn't sure. "I'm glad that you're saved. I am. That's really good to hear."

"Yes, sir. I asked God to forgive me and He has. Now, I need your forgiveness. I want to try and make things right."

"Why?"

"Why what?"

"Why do you need me to forgive you?" Gabrielle said.

"I took your mother from you. I did a despicable act and murdered someone. Someone I promised to love, honor, and cherish. Someone I was supposed to protect, not put my hands on to hurt, and most certainly not to kill. I took her life and, in ways I can tell just by your eyes right now, I took away a part of *your* life. I never intentionally meant to hurt your mother; I didn't. And I never meant to hurt you. But I ended up doing both. They say I've paid my debt to society. And in my incarceration, I also found the Lord. And God changed me. Standing in front of you is a new creature who wants to make amends for the wrong done, starting with you."

"You need somewhere to stay, don't you?" Gabrielle asked point-blank.

He pursed his lips. "Well, yes, I do. But that's not what this is about. True, I don't have anywhere to stay right now. When they release you from prison, it's generally on *you* to make it out here. But I'm not here saying these things to you because I need a place to stay. I promise you that's the gospel truth."

"But you do need me or someone to let you stay with them, for now anyway."

"Okay, Gabrielle." His voice projected a slight edge now. "Yes, I was going to ask you if I could stay here, at least until I can figure out my next move."

"I don't know if I want you here," Gabrielle said, wrapping her arms even tighter around about herself.

"Look, you have this big old house here. You can lend your old pops a room. I promise I'll stay out of your way. I know you need time to process everything. And if you don't want to have to look in my face just yet, I can stay in my room and out of your way until you're ready. I've been in solitary confinement before. Being confined to a room in a beautiful place like this would be like Heaven for me. It's just . . . the two of us have things we need to work out. What better way to do that than for me to be here with you so when you *are* ready, I'm right at your fingertips?"

"Gabrielle, are you all right?" Miss Crowe said, stepping back into the foyer. "You know, the food is on the table. We're going to have to reheat it if we don't go in and eat it about now. Jasmine has the table set so beautifully. I know you wouldn't want to disappoint her or anything."

Gabrielle looked at Miss Crowe with tears in her eyes. "I'm okay."

"I'm sorry," Bennie said to Miss Crowe. "But I don't think we were properly introduced the first time around. I gave my name, but I didn't get yours."

Miss Crowe looked unyieldingly at him. She could see how much he'd upset Gabrielle in just his brief time with her. She wasn't sure she liked this man much at all. She didn't know whether he really could be trusted. "My name is Esther Crowe."

"And who exactly are you to my daughter?"

"She's like the mother I never had." Gabrielle looked at Miss Crowe now.

"Well, Miss Crowe. It appears you have been a blessing in my daughter's life. And for that, I'd like to *personally* thank you." He bowed his head to Miss Crowe. "Gabrielle, my bag is just outside the door. I only have the one bag. So what do you say? May I stay if nothing more than for the night?"

Miss Crowe looked at Gabrielle, who wouldn't look her way now. If she had been able to get her to look her way, she would have stealthily shook her head to let her know she didn't think that was a good idea at all. Not at this point. Gabrielle needed to think a bit more on this before saying yes, even to just one night. Miss Crowe knew how this worked. Gabrielle might not be able to get him to leave.

"You don't have anywhere else you can go?" Gabrielle asked Bennie. "You don't have or know any person other than me?"

"You're all I have in this whole wide world

right now. You, and of course, the Lord. Everybody else has forsaken me . . . turned their backs on me."

Gabrielle looked long and hard at him. He *was* her father. How could she turn her own father away? He'd confessed to being saved now. He'd asked God to forgive Him and God had done that. Whether she was at a place to forgive him was yet to be determined. But if she turned him away, where would he go?

"Okay. You can stay the night," she said. "Tomorrow, we'll see where we go from there."

Bennie smiled. "Thank you. And God bless you for this. Glory to God, I thank You for hearing my cry! Thank You, Jesus for being true to Your Word." He nodded toward Gabrielle. "I'll go out and get my bag." He hurried out of the door and came back in quickly with one small suitcase.

"I'll show you to your room," Gabrielle said, taking him to the bedroom the farthest away from all the other bedrooms. The house was full now; no more vacancies. Miss Crowe stayed with her often these days and had her own bedroom. Jasmine's room was next to Gabrielle's.

Bennie set his beat-up suitcase on the bed. He pulled out a small bag of potato chips.

"I'm kind of hungry. I haven't eaten since they released me earlier today."

"We're about to eat supper. You're welcome to join us if you'd like."

He smiled. "Bless you. Bless you. I'd like that very much." He nodded.

"There's a bathroom in your room there. Towels are already in it. I'll see you downstairs in a few minutes." She turned to walk out.

"Gabrielle, thank you. I really appreciate this."

"No problem," Gabrielle said, having turned back to him.

"Oh, and Gabrielle?"

"Yes?"

"I love you."

Gabrielle nodded, then stepped into the hallway. She stopped midway down the hall, braced her back against the wall, and covered her face as she silently cried.

CHAPTER 4

He hath hedged me about, that I cannot
get out: he hath made my chain heavy.
                                      — Lamentations 3:7

Darius Connors was at the end of his rope.
He and his wife, Tiffany, had been separated
for close to five months now. Though admittedly, he'd been shocked when she took that
extra step of having him legally put out of
their house, he'd never had any real doubt
when their troubles began that they'd make
their way back to resolving things just as
they'd always done. But her doing this
(something totally out of character for her,
by the way) made it more difficult for him
to work his magic as he'd been able to do
in the past.

Early on, Pastor Landris had offered him
housing where he could have also received
marital counseling while working things out
with his wife. But he'd been adamant that

there was no way he was going to reside in a place riddled with folks who had drug, alcohol, and who knew what other kinds of problems.

So for the months he'd been not only without a job but out of his house, he'd crashed at the homes of various folks, starting with his good friend Big Red, who'd promptly put him out after only three weeks when it became apparent that Darius wasn't trying to find a job *or* make any sincere effort toward making things right with his wife and family. Darius contended that was more of Big Red's wife's doing than Big Red's.

It hadn't been that Darius wasn't trying to find a job, but the 2011 economy was proving to be not much better than 2010. As for his marriage, he was working on Tiffany, who he could tell was breaking down. If it hadn't been for the friends that surrounded her, she wouldn't have lasted a week with him out of the house. He knew that. Tiffany loved him; of that much he was certain.

But at this point, he'd exhausted all of his options for a place to stay. He'd talked extensively with Paris Simmons-Holyfield back in early October when she wanted to talk to him privately. He didn't have any objections to that. After all, he considered Paris a friend from the time they'd worked together. And maybe she would put him up somewhere nice. But it didn't take him but a minute to see that she was tripping like all of the other women. She'd told him she was pregnant. Knowing how much she'd wanted a child, he'd been excited for her.

But then Paris had laid the revelation on him that she wasn't sure the baby she was carrying was even her husband's and that there was a real possibility the baby could be his. He wasn't trying to hear any of that noise *at all.* The *last* thing he needed right now while trying to get back with his wife (who believed he'd cheated on her with another woman) was to confess that he had a baby on the way, proving he had cheated on her even more recently than he was being accused of.

"Darius, they have a procedure that can be done to tell the paternity of a baby while it's still in the womb," Paris had said. "It's a bit risky, but there's a certain short window where it can be done without being as much of an endangerment to the life of the baby. I'd like to do that using your DNA to eliminate you as the father."

Well, that window came and went. Number one: Darius didn't believe the baby Paris was carrying was his. Number two: He didn't see any reason to do anything that could come back and haunt him later. He told Paris, unlike her, he didn't have an extra thousand dollars lying around for the two-thousand-dollar test (the cost Paris offered to split with him). And because the window was so short, Paris ended up having to drop the idea altogether. The last thing Paris wanted (after finally getting pregnant) was to do something that might cause her to lose the baby.

So Paris's due date was April 28, 2011. In three months, she would be having the baby and who knew what drama might come with *that* birth.

Darius, with his belongings in his gas-guzzling SUV, tried to decide where to go now that he'd exhausted his fourth and final living arrangement. He'd parked outside of his house, opting to sleep in his vehicle for two nights. He'd been certain if Tiffany were to see him out there, she'd break down and agree to let him come in and stay. It was nearing the end of January and dead winter. No one could be heartless enough as to allow the father of her children to sleep outside in that kind of weather. All he needed was one night alone with Tiffany and he knew he could win her back, and therefore his way back into his house and back into his nice warm bed.

But Tiffany stood firm on him not sleeping there the first night or the second, not even in the den on the couch. Darius had always hated when folks who lived in their vehicles claimed they were homeless. But now he saw that was in fact what they were when they did that: homeless.

It was morning. He watched Tiffany load the children up and leave. She was standing firm and not going to waver. It was then that he knew it was time for him to get right with God and put all this foolishness aside. Tiffany and God had won. He was ready to go see Pastor Landris and do whatever he needed to do to get his family back.

Darius was out of money, out of time, and almost out of gas, literally. On his way to the church to see Pastor Landris, he stopped at the gas station. He didn't even have enough money to get a full gallon of gas. He laughed as he recalled how some of the older men would tell tales of how they used to be able to buy a dollar's worth of gas and end up with three to four gallons. Not anymore. Those days were like fairy tales now.

He pulled up to the pump behind a woman who was stepping out of her car

49

talking on her cell phone. She continued to talk on the phone as she lifted the nozzle from its holding place, preparing to pump gas. Darius quickly rushed up to her and grabbed the nozzle out of her hand.

"Let me do that for you," he said to her. She had light brown eyes that were a beautiful almond shape. Her lips were full, blood red and glistening from lip gloss perfectly placed. She was wearing a wig, but it was definitely the expensive kind made of quality human hair. The black leather coat she wore was buttoned down to her waist, hugging her body thereby showing how much of her curves were hitting in all the right places.

She looked at him as she released the nozzle into his capable hands. But she didn't say anything to him. Not bothering to tell him how she could do it herself and that she didn't need his help, as he'd grown accustomed to being told at times by independent women, or how much gas she wanted. She merely stepped away and continued her conversation with the person she was talking with on the phone.

Darius decided to pump until it stopped. If she'd prepaid (which she most likely had), it would automatically stop when it reached the prepaid amount. Since she didn't tell him an amount and didn't object to him pumping, he decided she'd probably done that or was planning to fill it up. She had most definitely been on empty, as it stopped three cents pass sixty-dollars.

She put her phone in her coat pocket and walked back over to him. Looking at the electronic counter, she yelled, "What have you done?! I don't have but twenty dollars! I can't pay that!"

"What?" Darius said, looking from the pump to her. "You didn't plan to fill it up?"

"No! I don't have but twenty dollars. What have you done?"

"Then why didn't you tell me you only wanted twenty dollars' worth of gas when I offered to pump it?" Darius said.

"I didn't ask you to pump anything for me. You just came over and took it out of my hands like you were Mr. In Control. I hope you have enough money on you to pay the rest." She stared hard at him with her arms folded, her lips buttoned tightly.

"No, I don't have enough. In fact, I don't have enough for *one* gallon of gas, let alone . . ." He looked at the pump again and rubbed his hand over his entire head. "Didn't you see that I was going over? Why didn't you say something then to stop me?"

She continued to stare hard at him. "Well,

do you have a credit card or a debit card?"

"I'm not going to pay for gas that just went into your car," Darius said.

"Well, I'm not going to pay for it, either. I didn't pump it." She pulled out her cell phone. "I suppose we have a problem then." She began to press buttons on her phone.

"Who are you calling?"

"The police," she said. "You don't have the money to pay for this. I didn't tell you to do it. I'm definitely not going to jail for this. And we know if I drive off without paying, they're going to come looking for *me* not *you*."

"Put that phone away," Darius said. "I'm sure we can work something out."

She looked him up and down, still holding her phone but in a more relaxed mode now. "Okay. I'm listening."

Darius didn't have a clue what to do. His only credit card had been totally maxed out months ago and apparently Tiffany wasn't making any payments that were making a dent on the balance. He didn't have any cash money. He already owed money to anyone who may have been open or foolish enough to loan him money. He began to pace and rubbed his head. "You see. It just doesn't pay to try and do a good deed anymore." He looked at her. "I offered to pump your gas because you were about to pump while you were on your cell phone wearing leather, no less. Apparently you haven't heard how dangerous that combination can be. I was trying to keep you from blowing yourself up. And now I'm stuck with you wanting me to pay for gas that's in *your* tank, when I don't even have enough money for one gallon of gas to put in mine."

She twisted her mouth and put her phone in her coat pocket. "You know, you really are kind of cute."

Darius didn't know how to respond to that. "Thank you. I think," he said.

"So, what's your name, cutie?"

"Darius. Darius Connors," he said.

She smiled. "Well, Darius Connors, I appreciate you for caring enough that you'd do something so gallant and noble like that for me. Wait right here," she said, then strolled toward the store.

Darius thought about leaving as he watched her walk inside. She was definitely self-assured. He liked the way she carried herself. She now knew *his* name, but he didn't know hers. If he left, she could always give the police his name so it was to his benefit to hang around until she returned. Besides, she was really hot.

She grinned as she walked back over to

him, going around the back of his car. "I had to go get my change," she said. "I told them I was filling it up, but you never know how much it will take. And they make you pay upfront, especially these days." She laughed. "Got you!"

"Woman," Darius said, placing his hand over his heart. "You had me going there for a minute." He chuckled. "You're something. Just a little jokester, I see."

"Yeah. I just wanted to have a little fun with you. Listen, I paid twenty dollars on your pump. Why don't you put the gas in your car and you and I go get a little breakfast and maybe talk? That's if it's all right with your wife."

"You paid for me some gas? Twenty dollars' worth?"

"Yes, Darius Connors. It's the least I could do."

"Well, I can't thank you enough for that. And I don't even know your name."

"You can find out whatever you want to know about me over breakfast. So are you game or do we say our good-byes here at the pump?" she said.

He stuck the nozzle in his tank. "Breakfast it is, just as soon as I finish pumping my gas here."

She smiled as she walked back to her car.

She opened her car door, then stopped and looked back at him. "When you finish, you can just follow me." She got in and closed the door of her cobalt-blue 2011 Jaguar.

Darius finished pumping, then smiled. *Breakfast.*

CHAPTER 5

Wherefore doth a living man complain, a man for the punishment of his sins?
                                        — Lamentations 3:39

Darius had thought the mystery woman was planning to go somewhere like IHOP or McDonald's for breakfast. But they stopped at an iron gate to a mansion and he was left trying to decide whether it was wise to blindly follow the Jaguar with its mystery woman inside. His indecision lasted all of five seconds as he drove in after her. The electronic gate slowly closed behind him. She parked her car in the circular driveway, got out, and waited. He parked and stepped out of his vehicle, praying she didn't come where he was and notice all his belongings stuffed in the back.

She smiled. "Hope you're hungry," she said.

He grabbed her by the wrist and grinned.

"What's your name?"

She bit down on her bottom lip and scanned down to where his hand held on to her wrist. "Are you scared I plan on having *you* for breakfast or something?"

"Nope." He returned the favor, scanning her from her head to her waist, loving the old-fashioned Coke-bottle shape accentuated by the leather of her coat. "I'm not scared at all, not when it comes to you. No, ma'am. I just want to know what to call you in case I have a need to call your name."

"You can call me Dee Vine," she said as she smirked, pulling her wrist out of his gentle clutches, then glancing back at his SUV before turning and walking to the entrance of the house.

Darius jogged and caught up with her. "Divine?"

She stopped and turned to him. "Dee as in Delores, Demonassa, Devondra, Delilah —"

He touched her elbow. "So which one is it, Miss Vine?"

She grinned. "After breakfast, why don't you tell me?" She opened the door and stepped inside, holding on to the door as he passed by her. He loved the perfume she was wearing — subtle and a tad fruity, but not flowery.

"Aren't you afraid? I mean, I could be a serial killer or something."

"If you are, then you've done a great job of flying under the radar from the police. You've had two speeding tickets in the past two years with one outstanding parking ticket now." She placed her keys on a glass table perfectly centered under a gorgeous crystal chandelier in the middle of an elaborately decorated foyer.

"So you've already managed to somehow check me out?" Darius asked.

She shrugged. "Let's just say I had a friend run your license plate number through the system. Your tag is due for renewal the first of March, by the way."

Darius looked around. "So, is this your place or are you merely housesitting?"

She grinned, set her small black leather purse on the table next to her keys, and began unbuttoning her leather coat.

Darius was mesmerized by the way she went about doing it. As she began to slip off the coat, he hurried over to help her out of it. "Delilah," he said as he held the coat completely removed now.

She laughed.

"I'm right, aren't I? Your name is Delilah?"

She took her coat from his hand as she

grinned. "Do you like grits?"

"Whatever you want to do, I'm completely onboard with it." He smiled as he scanned her from head to toe once more, but this time without the coat. "I see you like the color black. Black leather coat, black leather boots, black dress that, if you don't mind me saying, was created to cling to apparently a perfectly created body."

"Well, Mr. Connors —"

"Oh, please, after all we've been though at this point, call me Darius."

She smiled. "Sure, Darius. But what you need to know about me is just how much I believe in color coordination. When I commit to something, I don't half step when I do it. I believe in going all . . . the . . . way."

"Go hard or go home, huh?" He rubbed his goateed chin that was definitely in need of some manicuring attention. "You, Miss *Dee* Vine . . . is that a miss? I most certainly pray you're a miss." He waited for her to answer.

"Yes, it's miss, although you failed to answer my question about your wife," Dee said. "What would she say about you being here with me right now?"

"She's pretty much already spoken. See, she put me out and we're legally separated at this juncture."

"But not divorced?" Dee went and hung up her coat in the foyer closet.

Darius waited for her to walk back toward him before answering. "Not divorced. But what it does mean is that it's perfectly all right for me to be here about to devour . . . breakfast" — he grinned — "with you."

She walked over and picked up her keys and purse, putting her keys in her purse and snapping it back shut. "If you like," she said, "you're welcome to get whatever you need out of your SUV and bring it inside. I'll show you to a room with a bathroom connected where you can . . . freshen up maybe."

"How did you know — ?" He raised his arm and took a whiff.

She laughed. "You don't stink. I just happened to see those things in your vehicle that suggest you're possibly in need of a place to crash. Besides, you look like a man who slept in his car last night. So I'll show you to a room, you can go get what you need to take a shower and dress, and I'll make us breakfast."

He nodded, scanning her once again from head to toe as she started toward the staircase.

She turned back to him. "You're going to have to stop gawking though. I hate when men gawk."

"I apologize. It's just I was always taught to appreciate the beauty and blessings of God. And believe me, I know when God finished creating you, He couldn't do anything *but* shake His head on His accomplishment and say, 'That's *very* good!' "

"Another thing: I'm not one of those religious zealots. So if you can, also *can* the God references, and we'll get along just fine."

Darius raised both hands in surrender. "Not a problem." He smiled. "I can see right now that you and I are going to get along splendidly. Absolutely splendidly."

She walked a few steps ahead of him. "We shall see, Mr. Darius Connors. We shall most certainly see."

CHAPTER 6

And God said unto Moses, I AM THAT I
AM: and he said, Thus shalt thou say unto
the children of Israel, I AM hath sent me
unto you.

— Exodus 3:14

Six months pregnant now, twenty-eight-
year-old Paris Simmons-Holyfield sat in the
morning service at Followers of Jesus Faith
Worship Center next to her thirty-four-year-
old husband, Andrew Holyfield, who
couldn't have been happier. After years of
trying, they were expecting their first baby.
From all indications, the baby was developing beautifully. Paris had put on weight,
which wasn't her favorite thing about being
pregnant. But Andrew made her feel like
she was the most stunning woman who'd
ever walked on the face of the earth.

"You wake up even more beautiful than
when you go to sleep," he never failed to

say to her every morning as she awakened.

Andrew was concerned that Paris was laughing a little less these days. He questioned her on why she didn't seem to smile much after learning she was finally going to have a baby. She played it off as hormonal. But the truth (which she knew but couldn't tell him) was that she couldn't fully relax and enjoy the pregnancy knowing that there was a good possibility the baby they'd prayed so hard to conceive may not even be his. In truth, she couldn't tell anyone, not her mother or any of her friends. At this point, the only people who knew were she and Darius. And it was eating away at her.

"Secrets can tear you up inside," Pastor George Landris was saying from the pulpit. "You see, people don't understand the tactics of the devil. They don't understand that when it comes to spiritual warfare, when it comes to where the battle is being fought, the battleground *actually* is in the mind."

"Amen," people in the audience said.

"Let me tell you something that you need to know," Pastor Landris said as he stopped and looked out into the audience. "The devil wants so much to be like God, but he's not. Yes, people believe that the devil has power. But do you know that God is omnipotent, which means He has *all* power. God is omniscient, which means He sees everything. And God is omnipresent, which means He's everywhere all at the same time. God knows your thoughts. But even more, God is sovereign, which means God reigns."

"Preach it, Pastor!" someone yelled out.

Pastor Landris nodded as he came closer to the edge of the platform. "What you need to know is the power God has given you. God gave you a mouth to speak. God has given you the power of life and death in your tongue. Satan doesn't have that power, but Satan knows where power resides. So Satan sends out his little imps to mess with you. They get all up in your thoughts, not that they know what you're thinking, but they whisper things to your mind." Pastor Landris walked over to the other side. "Oh, y'all had better *recognize*!"

"Tell it, Pastor!" a few folks yelled. "Preach!" others said.

"Satan's strategy is to get *you* to use the power God has given *you* against *you*. Did you hear what I just said?" Pastor Landris walked over to the other side. "Okay, I don't know if they're hearing me over on the other side so I'm coming over to this side and say it. I said that Satan wants to get *you* to use the power God has granted you *against* you."

"Pastor, we hear you!" people shouted. "Go on and tell us the truth up in here."

Pastor Landris smiled. "People of God: Why are you listening to the thoughts being planted in your mind, then putting power behind negative thoughts by speaking those things into the atmosphere with your mouth? Huh? *Why?* I know you may be saying that you hear things in your mind and you're not sure if what you're hearing is from God or the devil. Well, let me help you out here."

"Come on, Pastor! Help us out!" some people said.

"Remember I told you that the devil wants to be like God but he's not? Well, God can hear you when you have thoughts in your mind. The devil can't read your mind, can't hear your thoughts, doesn't have a clue what you're thinking until and *unless* you open your mouth and speak those thoughts out loud or your actions clue him in. You can think things all you want, but Satan doesn't know for sure until you give him a sign. And just like a fish about to bite into a fisherman's hook, some of you need to learn to keep your mouths closed —"

"Pastor, you'd better say that thang!"

someone yelled while others stood clapping and making their own comments.

"Some of you need to quit saying how tired you are of certain things because all you're doing is telling the enemy how to get to you," Pastor Landris said. "You're running around telling folks how broke you are and wondering why you're still broke."

Some people in the audience laughed. Others shrugged and nodded.

"You're speaking about *who* hurt you and *how,* then wondering why you continue to get attacked . . . to be hurt in that same area. It's simple: You told the enemy your weak point. You told the enemy how to bring you down. You're speaking words into the atmosphere, giving power to those words. I'm sick, you say, and then wonder why you're sick. Satan is in your ear whispering words to destroy you, and instead of you saying what God says about the situation, you're repeating what the devil is whispering in your ear."

"Preach! Preach! Preach the Word, Pastor!" Paris heard as she turned to see that the words exploding so loudly in her ear were coming from her own husband's mouth. Andrew was on his feet clapping, shouting, and pumping and waving his hand in the air in testimony.

Pastor Landris nodded. "Two things I'm going to say, and then I'm going to be through."

"Take your time, Pastor," someone yelled. "We ain't in no hurry! Not *to*day!"

Pastor Landris smiled as he shook his head and walked back to where his Bible lay on the Lucite lectern. "I need you all to know the power behind the *I am*. I need you to understand what it means to be, as my subject for today stated, 'On fire for the Lord.' Listen to me good because I need you to hear and understand. Before Moses became the iconic Moses we all like to talk about, he was the Moses who first encountered a burning bush that burned but was not consumed. A bush that I submit to you was *on fire for the Lord.* And when God told Moses to tell His people that He'd seen and heard their afflictions and for him to tell Pharaoh to let His people go, Moses knew the importance of names to the Jewish people. Moses asked God when the people ask of him what is God's name, what should he say to them."

Pastor Landris picked up his Bible and began reading Exodus 3:14. " 'And God said unto Moses, I AM THAT I AM: and he said, Thus shalt thou say unto the children of Israel, I AM hath sent me unto you.'

I know some of you probably missed it, but when asked God's name, God told Moses to tell them 'I AM' is His name. Now stick with me on this for a minute. God is Yahweh. God is Adonai. But God's memorial name is I AM, perfect present tense. That means anytime you use 'I am,' you're invoking God's name, and after using God's name to begin the declaration, whatever you say after I am, you're giving authority and power to it."

Some people began clapping and praising, standing to their feet.

"Therefore!" Pastor Landris said, pointing a finger into the air. "When you say I am healed, then you've used the 'I AM' name of God and the power now added to what you're proclaiming . . . what you're declaring, and healing is there. I am blessed! Glory to God, you're blessed! I am the head and not the tail. I am above only and not beneath. I am blessed coming in and blessed going out. I am more than a conqueror. I am the righteousness of God. I am victorious!"

The entire congregation was on its feet now, including Paris.

"Things may be rough on *this* side, what we may call the other side of Divine. But Jesus came all the way from Heaven to the earth, was born, laid in a manger, He walked on this earth showing us how to deal with the things we encounter down here, He left the Divine and came here to show us how to live while we're here on *this* side. He was beaten, hung on a cross, and crucified, not for anything He'd done, but for the sins of the world . . . for your sin" — Pastor Landris began to point randomly into the audience — "and your sins and your sins . . . and mine. Jesus paid the price on that cross and the veil that separated us from God . . . the veil that kept us out of the Holy of Holies was ripped from the top down. They took Jesus off that cross and buried Him in a borrowed tomb. But thanks be to God, who always causes us to triumph, Jesus didn't really need anything more than to borrow that tomb for a few days. Because on that third day Jewish morning!"

The noise level in the sanctuary was almost deafening with shouts and praises now.

"On that third day morning, Sunday . . . the first day of the week, Jesus arose with all power in His hands. And because He arose and is now sitting at the right hand of the Father, I am redeemed! If you've accepted Jesus as your personal savior, then you're redeemed. We may be on the other side of

Divine right now, but one of these days, in a moment, in a twinkling of an eye, we shall all be changed. This corruptible body shall take on incorruptible. We shall be like Him . . . we will be like Jesus! We'll be forever in paradise with the Lord! No more tears. No more you're right and I'm wrong. Every day will be divine and there will be no more good-byes." Pastor Landris moved his head from side to side like a boxer preparing for a fight.

"If you're not saved," Pastor Landris continued, "if you haven't confessed Jesus as your Lord and Savior, will you come? Will you come? You may be on the other side of Divine right now, but there's a day coming! Jesus said the same way He left, He's coming back again. Every now and then I look up to the sky, looking to see Him coming back on a cloud, coming back for His people. Will you be in that number when He comes back? If you want the peace of God that surpasses all understanding, then come. If you want the joy of the Lord, then come. If you want the love of God . . . a love that will lift you when you're down, make you laugh when no one is saying anything funny, be there with you no matter what you may have done, assuring you that when He said He'd be with you always, He meant always. I'm talking about through the good times and the bad, through your ups and your downs. Will you come today? It doesn't matter what you've done or how bad it is in the world's eyes, Jesus will forgive you. What can separate us from the love of God? Nothing! Nothing that you've done as long as you come to Him and ask Him to forgive you. Come to Jesus. Come!" Pastor Landris stood with his arms open.

Paris stood and almost ran down the aisle, taking hold of Pastor Landris's outstretched hand. She fell to her knees and cried. And Andrew was right there along with her. He kneeled down as well, placing his arm around her.

"Lord, forgive me!" Paris cried out. "Lord, please forgive me! I want to be saved! I want to be right! I want to be Your child! Oh, Lord, have mercy on me!"

CHAPTER 7

And we being exceedingly tossed with a tempest, the next day they lightened the ship.

— Acts 27:18

Paris had confessed Jesus when she was eight years old. But she didn't feel now that she'd done it with the right heart. In fact, she and her three friends had merely made a pact to go up together so they could get it over with. Even more, so they could finally take part in communion services with the little crackers and the small cute glasses of what the preacher referred to on first Sunday as wine.

She and her friends felt duped the first time as they braced for the impact of having wine during Communion, only to learn it was nothing more than Welch's grape juice. But it was okay because at least now (they were told) they were saved and would go to

Heaven.

Five days later, Paris sat outside the office waiting for her time to be called. She'd joined Followers of Jesus Faith Worship Center, Pastor Landris's congregation, that Sunday. The following day after joining, she'd felt led to call and make an appointment to talk with him about what was going on in her life. Pastor Landris had talked about secrets and how they can eat a person up from the inside. She could definitely give witness to that. When she called to make an appointment, she quickly learned it would be months before she could get on schedule to see the pastor. Admittedly, she wasn't used to being told she'd have to wait to see her own pastor as she generally could show up at her former pastor's office and get to see him the same day.

Paris didn't want to discuss her problem with anyone *except* the pastor. She was quickly (though politely) informed of how things were done at *this* church. She couldn't argue much with the woman; it was a known fact that there was a large number of attendees at the church. She also found out that her financial status, as well as who her father was (or used to be) and who her husband was, didn't make any difference to these folks. Johnnie Mae, Pastor Landris's wife, was a counselor and she was available Friday morning. So Paris had taken that appointment, feeling that the anointing on the wife of the pastor was close enough for her.

"Paris," Johnnie Mae Landris said as she stood before her wearing a light blue long-sleeved dressed that hung from her size-eight body perfectly. "You may come on in."

Johnnie Mae had her own office she'd just moved into at the beginning of the year. Originally, she'd come in and help out, using an available conference room when she was scheduled to counsel. But her responsibilities had increased so much that she'd been given her own office.

Paris glanced around the nicely furnished space. It wasn't huge by any stretch of the imagination. In fact, she was surprised it wasn't larger considering this was the first lady and most certainly someone with pull in the church. Paris sat down in the wine-paisley-cloth-covered chair at the invitation of Johnnie Mae, who sat in a teal executive leather chair.

"Is that a picture of your family?" Paris asked, giving a nod toward a family picture on the cherry wooden credenza behind Johnnie Mae.

Johnnie Mae turned and smiled. "Yes.

Although my children are much older now and we *really* need to take a new one. My oldest child, Princess Rose, just turned twelve December eighteenth. She's excited that this year, she'll officially become a teenager. My son, Isaiah, will be six in June. Time most certainly does fly."

"Oh my, almost a teenager. And teenagers certainly can be a handful. I know I gave my mother and father more than a *few* fits and their hearts a few starts. So your daughter's name is Rose and you call her princess?" Paris asked.

Johnnie Mae smiled. "No, her real name is Princess Rose."

"Oh, okay." Paris readjusted her body more comfortably in her chair.

"Well, I see you're a new member here at FOJFWC. So again allow me to welcome you to our family," Johnnie Mae said.

"Thank you. I certainly have felt welcomed and loved since joining here. My husband and I went through new members' orientation this past Wednesday. It was most informative."

"That's wonderful. So what can I help you with today?" Johnnie Mae said with a smile.

"Wow, we're just going to go straight into it, huh?" Paris sat back against her chair and released a slow sigh before leaning forward again. She was fully aware that this was also the home church of Gabrielle Mercedes. In fact, when she'd thrown down her threat to take Jasmine from Gabrielle, she'd done it right here at this very church on a Wednesday night. "I don't mean any disrespect to you, but is what we say in here kept strictly confidential?"

"Absolutely. We don't play *that* here at this church. Now, if there's something that needs to be discussed further with the pastor, then that's the only time something may be repeated. And Pastor Landris is not one who tries to hit people below the belt by putting their business out in public from the pulpit."

"No offense, but how do I know what I tell you will stay strictly between us, with the exception of the pastor, of course?" Paris asked. "And how do I know you've not already drawn an opinion of me or that you don't already know things about me and you . . . let's just say, don't care for me much?"

Johnnie Mae leaned in and nodded. "Paris, I'm not going to sit here and tell you that I don't know about you and certain things that have transpired between you and one of our members. I'll even go so far as to disclose that Gabrielle Mercedes is near and dear to my heart, like a daughter to me."

"Yeah, Gabrielle seems to evoke that kind of a response no matter where she lands." Paris placed her hand up to her mouth, then took it down. "I'm sorry. That wasn't at all Christian-like and it was uncalled for. I'm trying. But as you can see: I have a lot of work ahead of me, a *lot* of work." She released a nervous laugh.

"All of us are working on something at one time or another," Johnnie Mae said. "So don't beat yourself up too much. But I will tell you that whatever you've done in the past, *I'm* not holding it against you. When we know better, we should do better. I'm praying that you've learned to do better since that situation. We're not going to look back; we're going to move forward. Is that all right with you?"

Paris nodded. If she told what she'd come in here to talk about, she was most certainly stepping out on faith. She didn't know Johnnie Mae. She felt like she knew Pastor Landris better, but that was only because she'd heard him preach and felt at ease when it came to him. She knew about some pastors' wives, first ladies as many either liked to be called or were called. Some of them were okay. But a few she'd known were something else behind the spotlight of having to be constantly *on* for the "cameras." She knew many who were great actresses. Those were the ones who generally learned things about members of the congregation, pretending to actually care, then spreading it on the sly. So to trust Johnnie Mae without having studied her longer was a decision she'd have to make at this point, then stand on.

"Before we begin," Johnnie Mae said, "I'd like for us to pray."

Paris looked up and smiled. This was a good first step and one she greatly appreciated.

When they finished praying, Paris stared soberly at Johnnie Mae. "I'm pregnant," she said. *There, she'd begun.*

Johnnie Mae let out a small chuckle. "Yes, I sort of noticed that. So when is your baby due?"

"April twenty-eighth. It's my first baby. My husband and I have been trying for a long time, even longer than *he* even knows. He thought it had been two years when in actuality it was about four."

"That's a blessing from God for sure. Congratulations."

Paris nodded. "Yes. You would think it's a blessing." She placed her hand up to her mouth and held it a few seconds before taking it down, and then began to cry. Johnnie Mae pulled tissues from the box on her desk and handed them to her. Paris wiped her eyes.

"It's okay. Take your time. Is there something going on with the baby? Something you haven't told your husband?" Johnnie Mae said.

Paris dabbed at her eyes, pulled more tissue from the box, and nodded. "Yes." Paris was sobbing now.

Johnnie Mae got up and sat in the chair next to Paris as she rubbed her back. "Is it something with the baby's health?"

Paris shook her head quickly. "Oh, no. The doctors say the baby is developing wonderfully. I'm gaining the right amount of weight. And he seems to be perfect from the ultrasound and listening to his heart."

Johnnie Mae took Paris's hand. "So it's a boy?"

Paris shrugged. "I don't know. We did the ultrasound and they asked if we wanted to know the sex of the baby. My husband, Andrew, told them we don't want to know. He's sort of old fashioned and said he'd prefer being surprised."

"Is that your desire as well?" Johnnie Mae asked.

"Oh, it's fine with me, I guess. Although, I do like knowing things as soon as information is available. I guess I'm just nosey that way. I just like to know. I don't have much of a waiting gene in my body."

"So is that the problem? You want to know and he doesn't? Or is it that you already know but you feel you betrayed him by doing it when he said he didn't?"

Paris released a short laugh. "You're kind of getting there. But it's not about knowing the sex of the baby." Paris turned squarely toward Johnnie Mae and stared hard into her eyes. "You won't tell anyone what I'm about to tell you. You promise?"

"I promise. I'm here for you, Paris. We're family now. It doesn't matter *when* you come into the family; you receive all the benefits and privileges as those who've been here from the beginning." Johnnie Mae grabbed both her hands and squeezed them. "What is it? What's troubling you so?"

Paris glanced down at her basketball of a stomach, then back up at Johnnie Mae. "I'm not sure if the baby I'm carrying is my husband's." With her hands out of commission to stop them, tears rolled down her face.

Johnnie Mae released one of her hands and pulled tissue out of the box, dabbing

Paris's tears for her. "Okay."

Paris took the tissue and stood up, stepping away from Johnnie Mae. With her back turned now, she said, "I don't know what to do."

Johnnie Mae stood and walked over to her. She turned Paris to face her as she held her by her shoulders. "Is there a chance that the baby is your husband's at all?"

Paris nodded. "Oh, yes."

"So the problem is that there's a possibility your baby could be your husband's or someone else's?" Johnnie Mae said, getting complete clarification.

Paris nodded one time. "Yes." She shrugged as she went and sat back in her chair. "And just so you don't think I'm some kind of a floozy or anything, I only slept with this guy one time. It wasn't a long-term affair or anything like that."

Johnnie Mae sat down in her teal chair behind her desk and leaned in as Paris continued speaking with her head bowed down, looking at her folded hands.

"It was one stupid time. And the sad part is that I don't even remember it."

"So, did this man drug you or something?"

Paris shook her head with her head still in a bowed position. "No. It was all my doing. In truth he was really trying to be helpful.

I'd gotten plastered and was in no condition to go home. So he took me to a hotel room —"

"Excuse me? You got drunk and he took you to a hotel room and you see nothing wrong or manipulative about that?" Johnnie Mae said.

Paris looked up into her face and sighed. "No. Because the room was already there for me. I was drunk and really didn't need to go home because I was also upset with my husband about some information I'd just learned he'd done. He knew —"

"He?"

"The other man. He knew it wouldn't have been pretty if I went home drunk and in the frame of mind I was in at the time. So he was nice enough to take me up to my hotel room. I do remember coming on to him, so I'm not going to lie and try to make it seem like I was *so* drunk that I was *completely* out of it and blameless."

"But you *were* drunk. He should never have slept with you knowing that you were not technically in your right frame of mind." Johnnie Mae sat up straight in her chair.

"Oh, the kicker is the paper I drew up and signed stating that I was doing this of my own free will and volition. Sleeping with him definitely appeared to be something I wanted to do, although I was totally devastated when I learned the following day what had transpired between us."

"Look, I think you should talk to your husband and tell him this, all of it," Johnnie Mae said.

"If only it was that easy."

"Is this person someone your husband knows? A friend of his or something?"

Paris chortled a little. "My husband knows him only slightly . . . by name. They're not friends or anything like that. But I can't tell my husband there's a possibility this baby isn't his. You should see him, how excited he is about this whole process and experience. He takes off work to go to my doctor appointments with me. He waits on me hand and foot as though I were a queen or something. He talks and sings to my stomach saying the baby is going to know him when he or she gets here. He's already bonded with this baby, maybe even better than me."

Johnnie Mae sat back in her chair and nodded. "This is tough."

"I know. That's why, early on, I wanted to do this thing you can do to determine paternity while the baby is still in the womb. There's only a brief window where it can be safely done, and it costs about two thousand dollars, which is fine if you have that kind of money lying around since insurance companies don't pay for that sort of thing. I didn't have the money, no⁺ like where my husband wouldn't have noticed. My mother and father are struggling since my daddy is out of his position as an Alabama congressman. It's like the two of them are starting over. My mother even briefly took a part-time job, if you can believe that."

"Yeah. Your father is Lawrence Simmons."

Paris twisted her mouth a few times. "Yes. Although these days, as his family, it's not something you go around bragging about like in the past. I don't know just how much you truly know when it comes to my father and Gabrielle —"

"If you don't mind, I'd like to just keep the conversation on that which pertains to you," Johnnie Mae said without giving away what she may or may not know.

"Okay," Paris said. "Anyway, I talked with the other man about possibly doing this test, but that didn't pan out so well. In fact, he's pretty certain this baby is *not* his. In truth, that might seem plausible except for how long my husband and I have been trying without there ever even being a false alarm of success. Then the one time I happen to do something like this with another man and voila, I'm pregnant."

"So you feel then that most likely this baby is the other man's and not your husband's?" Johnnie Mae said.

"I pray this baby is my husband's. I don't know what I'm going to do if it's not. Honestly, my husband would likely never know if he's not his. I mean, I know. The other man has been told, but I can fix that easily by telling him he definitely isn't. And with the exception of me telling you right now —"

"Which you could very well come back later and tell me the baby definitely is your husband's and I would be none the wiser as well," Johnnie Mae said.

"Well, I'm not going to come back and purposely lie to a preacher's wife. I recall the story about those two people in the Bible who fell dead after they lied. . . ."

"You're talking about Ananias and his wife, Sapphira, who lied to Peter about how much their land had sold for when they were selling possessions and bringing the money to benefit the ministry," Johnnie Mae said. "The problem wasn't in them keeping back part of what they sold the land for, as the land was theirs to do with as they pleased. It was their flat-out lying about it. And Peter told Ananias that Satan filled his heart to lie not to them but to the Holy Ghost. He and his wife didn't have to lie. We do have to be careful because a lie is not necessarily to people, as we believe it to be, but to the Holy Ghost, which is a dangerous thing to play with."

"Yes," Paris said. "And from what I know about Pastor Landris and this ministry, there's no way I would go there. So for now, I don't know if this baby is my husband's or not. So you see what I'm dealing with here. I just need some godly advice on what I should do. Do I tell my husband now or wait until the baby gets here? In truth, I could do a normal DNA test, much less costly and without my husband's knowledge, *after* the baby is born. That way, if the baby is his, he never has to go through any pain concerning this. If the baby isn't, we can deal with that fact from there."

"So you're asking me whether you should tell your husband that you cheated on him, albeit only that one time, and that you're not sure if the baby you're carrying is his or not. Is that what you're asking?"

Paris bit down on her bottom lip. "Yes, ma'am. That's what I'm asking. Plus, I needed to get this secret out of me. It's been eating away at me, just like Pastor Landris preached on Sunday. The devil has been having a field day with my mind and I needed someone to confide in. I wanted to talk with Pastor Landris, but that wasn't doable at this time —"

"So you ended up with me instead," Johnnie Mae said with a warm smile.

"I wouldn't put it quite that way at this point. God knew what He was doing. He knew what I really needed. I would say He *blessed* me to talk with you instead."

"Praise God for that. This *is* what would seem to be a great dilemma. The question is: Do you keep this secret from your husband, believing it will maintain peace in your household at least until there's a reason to possibly tear things up? Or do you tell your husband the truth that he deserves and has a right to know, the fact that he may not be the baby's father."

Paris placed her hands up to her face and pressed hard as she waited on the answer this woman of God was about to tell her. But at least she'd made a step toward lightening her load on what had become a tempest-tossed ship.

CHAPTER 8

And if a stranger sojourn with thee in your land, ye shall not vex him.

— Leviticus 19:33

Zachary Wayne Morgan walked quickly through the door his aunt Esther held open for him. "I came as quickly as I could get here," he said to her. "Where is Gabrielle?"

"She's upstairs with her father. We're supposed to be sitting down to eat, but the two of them have been up there for a while now."

"Dr. Z!" Jasmine said, running into his arms. "I didn't know you were coming in time for dinner."

He hoisted her up into the air and smiled. "My favorite little girl in all of the world!"

"You always say that," Jasmine said.

"How are you feeling?" he asked.

"I'm fine. I told them I felt fine, but they still wouldn't let me go to school. I'm going tomorrow though. I absolutely love school,"

Jasmine said. Zachary set her back down. "I guess I need to set a place for you at the table. I'm glad I suggested we eat in the dining room tonight. It's just growing and growing bigger and bigger with more people by the minute." She illustrated the way it was growing with her hands.

"Sounds good, Miss Jazz. Go on and fix a place for me." Zachary watched as Jasmine skipped merrily away.

"Okay, Aunt Esther. What's going on?"

Esther walked toward the den as Zachary followed. She sat in a chair while he sat scooted on the edge of the sofa. "Her father showed up. Gabrielle's father is here. Twenty-five years and without warning, he just shows up on her doorstep."

Zachary sat back a little. "She certainly never indicated to me that she knew he was getting out any time soon, let alone getting out now." Zachary stood up. "I should go up and check on her."

"Zach, wait. I don't think you should do that."

"Why not?"

"Because I believe she's okay with him, for now anyway. They need some room to breathe . . . to talk if they want. If you go up there, she'll know I called you almost as soon as he cleared the doorway and I could

89

make my way to the phone," Miss Crowe said. "This is still her house. If she wanted him gone, she could have done that."

"But she didn't," Zachary said.

"Nope, she didn't. Instead, she's letting him stay, at least tonight."

"So what do you think about that?" Zachary asked.

Miss Crowe shook her head slowly. "I don't know. He doesn't appear to be a threat or a danger to her. He claims he's changed." She tilted her head slightly. "I was listening in when they were still down here. He says he's saved now, a new creature in Christ."

"That's what they all say when they go in," Zachary said. He began to pace in front of the sofa as he scratched his head. "I don't know, Aunt Esther. I want to protect Gabrielle. Do you know how much that man has hurt her so far?"

Miss Crowe nodded. "Absolutely I do. But Gabrielle is a grown woman. She's able to make her own decisions. All we can do is keep our eyes and ears open. And if we need to step in to protect her, we just have to pray we can and do and that she'll have the right mind to listen. But he's her father."

"Yeah. And I know how important a father can be in a little girl's life."

"Precisely. And it doesn't matter how old a daughter is. She'll always be a little girl looking for love and attention from her father if he appears to be trying to give it, sincere or not."

"Well, you met him," Zachary said. "Do you think he's a threat to her?"

"I don't know. All I know is even though he's like a stranger about to dwell among us — all of us really, because you know I'm not going too far from Gabrielle, not at this point — he's still her father in need of a place to stay."

"Thank you, Auntie. Because we're too close to becoming husband and wife now for someone like him to come in and mess everything up," Zachary said with a harsh edge to his voice.

Miss Crowe nodded. "I know, Zach. And you know I've been doing what I can when it comes to working on your mother. But she's still bound and determined that you're not going to marry Gabrielle."

"Well, my mother is not going to stop us. But Gabrielle's father —"

"Benjamin Booker," Miss Crowe said. "But he says everyone calls him Bennie."

"Well, Benjamin 'Bennie' Booker, whatever his name, is not going to get in the way of our happiness, either. I'll respect him as long as he's on the up and up," Zachary said. "But the first sign that he's up to no good —"

"Zachary," Gabrielle said, almost sprinting across the room toward him.

He hugged her tight. "I hope you don't mind," Zachary said. "But I just felt like coming over for dinner and eating with my family."

"How coincidental," Gabrielle said, looking at Miss Crowe with a sly grin. "You just *happened* to show up right after my father arrived. Isn't that something?"

Miss Crowe turned away from Gabrielle's stare.

"Are you all right?" Zachary asked, gathering her up by the shoulders as he looked into her beautiful brown eyes. At thirty years of age, the good doctor knew when he should be on high alert.

"I'm good," Gabrielle said with a smile. "I would have liked to have been forewarned about my father coming today. But what's done is done. We're moving on from the hand we've both been dealt."

"The table is set and the food is probably cold," Jasmine said, strolling into the den. "I've never had so much trouble getting people to do right in my life." She was being completely and purposely overdramatic.

"Coming right now," Gabrielle said, raising her index finger in the air. "And if we have to microwave our plates to reheat our food, then that's what we'll have to do."

Zachary was the last one to step out of the den. He and Bennie, almost having bumped into each other, were now face to face.

"Hello," Bennie said. "My name is —"

"Mr. Booker," Zachary said. "Pleased to meet you. My name is Zachary Morgan. I'm Gabrielle's fiancé. Please forgive me for not shaking your hand, but since we're about to sit down and eat, I'm sure you wouldn't want to contaminate your clean hand by shaking mine." Zachary smiled.

"It's okay. I'm sure whatever germs are there won't kill either me or you," Bennie said, holding out his hand to Zachary.

Zachary looked down at his hand, then at Gabrielle. He took Bennie's hand and gave it a quick pump.

Bennie nodded as he seemed to be sizing Zachary up as well. "You have a good grip on you there, young fellow," Bennie said. "Yep. That's a good solid handshake right there if ever I met one."

They went into the dining room and sat down. Zachary sat with Gabrielle on one side and Jasmine on the other. Miss Crowe and Bennie sat next to each other on the other side of the table. Unlike times past, no one, this time around, sat at the head of the table.

CHAPTER 9

Wherefore I also said, I will not drive them
out from before you; but they shall be as
thorns in your sides, and their gods shall
be a snare unto you.

— Judges 2:3

It was Valentine's Day and Darius was fully
moved into his new place of residence. He'd
gotten his unemployment check, but as
always, it was never enough for all he
needed. Every time he saw Tiffany she was
complaining that he wasn't giving her
anything to help out with the children.

"You were the one who put *me* out.
Remember? If I wasn't trying to pay for
somewhere to live on a daily basis, I could
be putting that money here and toward our
children," Darius had said to her a month
earlier. "If you'd let me come home, we
could work together instead of against each
other. This isn't good for our children,

Tiffany. I hope you know that. I apologized to you for what I did years ago. I don't think it's fair that you're punishing me *and* our children for something that happened some five years earlier. It's just wrong, Tiffany. And you're wrong."

It hadn't helped matters when he'd stopped by the house around Christmastime and met Clarence Walker, the minister of music from their church, coming out of his house. He'd blasted Tiffany, accusing her of playing footsy with Clarence. She'd laughed in his face as he went from one extreme to the other, first accusing her of having an affair with the once-upon-a-time exotic dance club owner before he gave it all up to serve the Lord, then accusing Clarence of being gay.

Tiffany told him he was wrong for stereotyping Clarence just because of his music position in the church.

"How can he be gay but having an affair with me, a woman, at the same time? You're just talking crazy, Darius." Tiffany was clearly frustrated with her husband. "You need help. Clarence came by to bring us some food and other things we needed. The church blessed me and *our* children with groceries, clothes, and some toys for Christmas. Clarence just brought the things over so I wouldn't have to carry them all by myself. The man was merely being a blessing, something you might want to try sometime yourself."

"Sure, Tiff. Sure. I *bet* he was just being a blessing. But you'd better be careful. I know how men's minds work. They see a woman in distress and that's their inroad to them. Clarence never liked me. I suppose he just wants what I have, and he'll do whatever it takes to make it happen, including making me look bad if he has to."

"Clarence is not trying to talk to me. He's just being a good Christian brother."

"Okay, Tiffany. Let your guard down at your own peril. I'm trying all I know how to make things back up to you and you won't give me the same chance you're seemingly giving this Clarence snake in the grass. I asked you to let me come home; I asked you to give me one more chance. We have history. . . . We have children together, Tiffany. And I can't even manage to get a decent audience with you. But good old Brother Clarence can. It's just wrong."

"Darius, you're not serious about working things out between us. You're not."

"I told you we can go talk to Pastor Landris together whenever you want. I told you that a little after I left back in September."

"But you're not serious, Darius. Didn't you tell me that Pastor Landris offered you a place to stay at that house they have — ?"

"It's a halfway house, Tiffany. I'm not going to stay at a halfway house with a bunch of drug addicts, alcohol heads, and known losers. I'm just not."

"But if it will help us —"

"This discussion is over," Darius said. "We need to get back together. You need to let me come home. You know I don't like this stupid separation. And I certainly don't want a divorce. But if you want a fight, then we can fight. But I'm not going to give up on us so easily. You might, but I'm not. How can we work things out if you're over here and I'm somewhere else? Communication is the key to any relationship succeeding. And we don't need some jack-legged preacher telling us that. I want to come home, Tiffany. My children need me and you know it."

"Your children need you to grow up and be the man and father God is calling you to be."

"I am that. At least, I'm trying. We fall down, but we get up. Right? Isn't that what the song says? You're the one standing in the way of progress here."

"No . . . you're not trying."

"Okay, Tiffany. I'm not going to stand here and argue with you. Okay? I'm going to pray for you 'cause you need real prayer."

Tiffany laughed. "You're going to pray for *me*? I'm not the one who was doing the wrong in this marriage, repeatedly doing it after you said it wouldn't happen again."

"What you're doing now is wrong. And you know what they say: Two wrongs don't make a right." Darius reached into his pocket and pulled out folded dollar bills. "Here's some money to help pay on the cell phone bill. I need my phone, especially since I'm out here busting my behind trying to find a job so I can do more for you and our family. *You* might not want to do right by me and *our* children, but I'm not going to let you drag me down in the mud with you. I'm going to pray for you, and I pray God will open your eyes to what you truly had in a man like me. If you need me or if my children need me, I'm only a phone call away. But I'm not going to run up behind you when you're not trying to do right yourself."

Tiffany shook her head. "You are truly a piece of work."

"Well, I'm going to warn you: Watch

yourself with that Clarence dude. And don't leave my daughters alone around him, either. Any man who will put women on stage to dance out of their clothes, there's no telling what he'll do if left alone with our daughters. For that matter, I don't want him around our son, either. Because I'm going to tell you, Tiffany: If I find out that man ever puts his hand on *any* of my children in the wrong way . . ." He balled his fist and held it with his eyes closed in the air. "Just don't be naïve when it comes to Mr. Wonderful. Do you hear me?"

"Are you *quite* finished?"

Darius stood back and grinned. "Yeah. I just need you to hurry up and come to your senses. I'm getting tired of having to find a place to stay while you're getting it together. You know you need me. You know you miss me. We belong together. You need to quit playing these little games. They're getting old."

"Bye, Darius." She walked to the door and opened it, tapping her feet as she waited.

He strolled over with an added swag, deliberately taking his time. "Tell the kids I'll see them next week. And as soon as I get a permanent place, that's if you and I are not going to get back together, I'll be getting them for some weekend visits. I pray it doesn't have to come to that and you grow up and we work things out."

Tiffany didn't say anything but continued to hold the door open.

Darius walked past her, took one step back, leaned backward on his heels, and gave her a soft peck on the cheek. "See ya, baby. I love you."

That conversation had taken place at the beginning of January before he'd shown back up again in late January asking if he could at least stay the night on the couch. Two nights of sleeping outside in his vehicle with Tiffany knowing it had not moved her in the least. The Connors magic was not working. He'd then made up his mind that he was going to see Pastor Landris and try doing things *their* way. And that was when divine intervention had just happened along, and he'd met Divine, as he called her, or Miss Delilah Vine as she was legally known.

He and Divine had hit it off from the first bite of omelets and grits before topping things off with chocolate-dipped strawberries they devoured for breakfast.

"I like the way you clean up," Divine had said when he stepped into the kitchen after showering and shaving.

"Well, thank you. And I *love* your home.

This is yours, isn't it?" he said. "You never did answer me earlier when I asked."

She smiled. "It's mine, all four thousand five hundred square feet of it."

"So is there a Mr. Vine somewhere?"

She laughed. "Nope. Just me. No ties, no strings, no headaches."

"So you consider a man to be a head-ache?"

She brought a plate with breakfast over to him and, cutting off a piece of the omelet with a gold-plated fork, placed it gently on his tongue. "Not at all. I just don't care to be owned or possessed. It's the possessive-ness that I don't care much for." She watched his mouth as he chewed the omelet, which was perfectly seasoned and perfectly cooked. "Are you a possessive man, Darius?"

He smiled as he swallowed. "You want an honest answer?"

"Always," she said with a slight Eartha Kitt–like purr to her voice.

He grinned. "I don't like much sharing what's mine. So I suppose you can say I am possessive in that way. I suppose that means you and I would never have a chance to-gether." He tilted his head slightly as though he'd asked a question and was patiently waiting for an answer.

"I hear that possession is nine-tenths of the law. You're here with me right now, eating my food, instead of home with your wife and children. So I suppose there's always a chance for *anything* in this life." She set the plate down on the table and sat down. Darius followed her lead and sat as well. She picked up a slice of bacon and held it up to his mouth. "Is pork okay or are you a turkey man?"

He laughed, then bit the crispy bacon that almost made him release a moan, it was just that good. "I'm pretty flexible and somewhat easy to please," he said. "And you . . . you; Miss Delilah, are certainly living up to your name. You keep doing what you're doing and I will be divulging all my secrets as to where my strength lies in no time at all."

It had been three weeks since that first day when he had been graced to meet Divine. He thought for sure he'd died from exposure outside his house and gone to Heaven, merely dreaming of the subsequent encounter with this woman called Divine. She was the most perfect woman he'd ever met. She didn't put requirements on him. She owned a mansion that he was allowed to stay in without having to fork over one red cent. There was always more than enough to eat. And after only two weeks, she'd given him a new iPhone with all the great things he normally couldn't afford with his and Tiffany's phone service.

Tiffany had called him after not hearing from him in two weeks.

"I was just checking to be sure you're okay," she had said.

He knew she was worried about him since he generally checked in with her at least twice a week. Seeing him sleeping outside their house those two days, and then not hearing from him anymore after that, must have scared her. He could tell she was shifting a bit. He laughed as he saw how much she still cared. But now it was too late. If she wanted him out of her life, well, she was about to get what she wanted. Because he felt he'd found Heaven here on earth and there was no reason to give this up now.

Divine worked in the pharmacy department of one of the chain stores. She would get up and go to work, seeming to love what she did. He still didn't know how she was able to afford all the things she possessed: the mansion, the Jaguar, the expensive clothes (which included a closet dedicated to just her shoes, most of which were the red bottom kind), the cost of maintaining the house, and eating at the most expensive restaurants the times they went out to dinner.

When he got his unemployment check, he tried to step up and give her some of it, but she told him to keep it. In fact, not only was she now paying for his cell phone, but also she had bought him clothes and shoes and given him a Rolex watch (although that could have been one she'd given another man and was now merely recycling, but still . . .). She even broke him off a few hundred-dollar bills when they went out.

"I like for my man to at least *appear* to be taking care of me when we're in public," Divine had said when she gave him five one-hundred-dollar bills that first time out two days after he was at the house.

Dinner for the two of them was only one hundred and fifty dollars that night. And when he tried to give her the change left over, she refused to take it. Yes, he could really get used to living like this.

So on Valentine's Day, he bought several boxes of candy and two dozen yellow roses. He stopped off at Tiffany's house with three small boxes of candy for his two daughters, Jade and Dana, and his son, Junior. They were so excited to see him and to get their own boxes of chocolates, especially since he hadn't given them anything for Christmas or Dana anything for her birthday that had just passed.

"I can't stay long. I just wanted to drop these off," Darius said, handing Tiffany one yellow rose. She smiled, seemingly relieved that he was still alive.

"You look to be doing well," Tiffany said, scanning him from head to toe. He was perfectly put together and he knew it: hair, face, clothing, and shoes all setting him off the way he liked.

"I am. All is well," he said with a smirk. "God is good, that's all I can say. And I thank Him for divine blessings that have come my way." He chuckled a little.

"Yeah," Tiffany said. "Look, I guess you noticed Friday that your cell phone was disconnected. You didn't bring me any money to pay it and I can't pay all of this by my —"

"Here." He handed her two hundred dollars.

"It's too late now. It's already been turned off. While you were out there throwing your money away on fancy clothes and shoes —"

"Please don't," Darius said. "I really don't care to hear the nagging today, if you don't mind. I just came by to bring the children something for Valentine's Day and to give you a little something to help out. The phone is off and that's fine. I have another phone now anyway so it's no biggie."

"You have another phone?" Tiffany said. "Well, do you think you'd like to give me that number? I don't have any way of getting in touch with you should I need you."

He laughed, then grinned big. "Yeah . . . right. Who cares if I need something, but we have to be sure you're taken care of should *you* need something. The phone gets turned off from your end and that doesn't bother you. But when I get a new phone to replace it, then you feel you should have the number in case *you* have a need."

"Darius, stop being silly. You have children. I was hoping you'd reached your bottom and were on your way back up to being sensible and reasonable. But I see I was wrong," Tiffany said.

"Yeah. Okay. Well, it was good to see you. I'm going to get out of here."

"And go where?" Tiffany said. "Where are you living these days?"

He smiled. "Since you didn't want me here, where you would know where I was living these days, I fail to see where that's any of your business anymore. You wanted me gone and out of the house. Well, guess what? I'm gone and out of the house. What happens to me after that is no longer your business or your concern. As for if you should need me, you can always call Big Red and leave a message with him. I'll check in with him from time to time and he'll be able to get me a message."

"You can't do that. I shouldn't have to call Big Red to get a message to you. What if it's an emergency? What if something happens to one of the kids and I need you immediately?"

"Tell you what: Do what you would have done if my only phone had been cut off and you needed to get in touch with me. Oh, wait . . . that's right. My only phone *was* turned off because you didn't pay for it to stay on. So let's see how that works out for the both of us. Got to go." He leaned down and tried to kiss her on the cheek. She moved her face just in time to cause him to miss. He laughed. "Bye, love. I'll be checking on you and the children soon."

CHAPTER 10

The best of them is as a brier: the most upright is sharper than a thorn hedge: the day of thy watchmen and thy visitation cometh; now shall be their perplexity.

— Micah 7:4

Darius opened the door to his new home, unable to stop smiling as he thought about how blessed his life was. Tiffany had reminded him of what he'd once had and, when he compared it to what he had now, he couldn't help but want to give God a shout of praise for his newfound blessings.

Divine was on the bed with her feet propped up on a pillow watching the fifty-inch flat-screen TV mounted on the wall. He walked in with a large box of chocolates (the fancy, expensive kind with nuts and truffles) and two dozen yellow roses (minus the one he'd given Tiffany).

"Oh my! How lovely," Divine said, standing quickly to her feet when she saw him come in. "A man after my own heart. You bought me candy *and* flowers . . . with my own money, no less."

He laughed. "No. Actually, I used *my* money for these. I used *your* money for other things."

She moved her lips in and out like a fish. "You are a most thoughtful man. I so love that about you!"

"So how was your day?" Darius asked as he watched her carefully snuggle her face into the roses.

"It was good," she said. "Ouch!"

"What happened?" Darius moved closer to see what was wrong.

She sucked her finger and shook it, then repeated her actions a few more times as she spoke. "I must have stuck my finger on a thorn. You would think they'd ensure all of the thorns are off before they thrust them upon the innocent public." She laid the roses down on the bed next to the box of chocolates. "So, did you go see your wife and children already?"

"Yeah. How did you know I was doing that?"

"I just figured you most likely would. You seem to be the type of man who would make sure his children got something on a

110

day like this," Divine said.

"You apparently know me all too well," Darius said. "In fact, it sort of scares me how well you appear to know me."

She stepped up close to him with a wicked smile. "Now I *know* you're not afraid of little ol' me." She put her finger in her mouth where she'd been stuck earlier by the thorn and sucked it again. She then held out her finger to Darius. "Kiss it and make it better."

He grinned, took her finger, and gave it a soft kiss. "There," he said. "All better now?"

She skipped back over to the bed and flopped down on it. "Darius, I need to ask a favor of you."

He nodded, going over and sitting down next her. "Okay."

"It's pretty simple, really. In fact, you can make some extra money if you agree to do it."

"Extra money? Sounds like you're talking my kind of language now."

"You know I work in the pharmacy department behind the counter. And I was wondering if you would consider doing me a teeny, tiny favor and coming in and purchasing a few items that we happen to sell behind the counter, with money I'll provide you, of course."

He laughed. "What's going on? Are you trying to win employee of the month or something?"

She shook her head. "No. Nothing like that. It's just I have these people who are willing to pay top dollar for things like Sudafed, if you can believe that. But you know we have these dumb laws passed in Alabama that make it harder to get your hands on them. You have to purchase them from behind the pharmacy counter now and they make you show an ID and stuff in order to get certain medications that used to sell on the counter."

"So what is it you're asking me?" Darius said with a stern, yet playful look.

"I'm asking you to come in and purchase some items when I'm there at the store. That's all. I'll give you the money, so it won't cost you a thing. In fact, not only will I give you the seed money to get it, but after you turn the items over to me later, you'll get paid pretty well for doing it."

"Hey, I don't see any problems with doing that. And I get paid, too?" He nodded his head. "Let's do it."

She grabbed his face and kissed him. "Oh, thank you! Thank you! You're so wonderful! And you treat me so wonderfully. I'm grateful to whatever providence caused our paths to cross that day back in January."

"You're grateful? I'm the one. However, I still call mine God Almighty."

She puckered her lips and rolled her eyes. "So you mean to tell me that you actually think God brought me into your life?"

"You're a blessing. And I was always taught that every good and perfect gift comes from above. These past few weeks with you don't get any gooder or more perfect."

She laughed. "Gooder? Gooder is not a word."

"Yes it is. I just used it, so it's a word," Darius said. "How do you think words become words? Someone says something, other people start saying it, and before you know anything, it's added to the dictionary with the meaning we assigned to it, making it officially a word. If we can get enough people to start saying gooder, I bet we can make it to the dictionary."

"Okay. But I dare say that God, yours or mine, which I like to just refer to as The Universe, had anything to do with me and you coming together. In fact, if your wife and pastor knew what was going on, I'm certain they would say this is anything *but* God, and in fact, the doings of the devil."

"Well, let's look at this objectively. My

wife had me put out of my own house because of something I did almost a half a decade ago. I tried my best to go back, but she, not me, was the only thing standing in the way of that happening. I went to talk to my pastor and he wanted to put me in some halfway house with a bunch of addicts and losers instead of telling my wife that she was wrong to put me out and to stop the games and nonsense. There I was sleeping in my SUV when there was no reason I should have been outdoors *or* homeless. I mean, these so-called Christian folks will help out folks they don't even know, but when it comes to folks they *do* know, like me, they turn me out on the streets and couldn't care less that I'm without a place to lay my head. I was just about to crack and what happens?" Darius said. "God sends me you. And *now* look at me: I'm here with a beautiful, caring, fine woman —"

She laughed loudly.

"And we're here in a house I hadn't even thought to dream of. All of my needs are met. Sounds like the blessings of the Lord to me. And now you want to offer me a way to make money and all I have to do is buy something I would normally buy in a store anyway? Say what you like, but let me get

up and get my praise on *right now!*" Darius
stood and began doing a praise dance while
Divine threw her head back in sheer delight.

CHAPTER 11

Boast not thyself of tomorrow; for thou knowest not what a day may bring forth.
— Proverbs 27:1

Deidra wrapped her arms around her daughter and gently pulled her toward her after she'd stepped into the house. "Okay, Paris, when are you going to smile again?" Deidra asked as she walked her oldest daughter into the den. They sat down on the couch next to each other as Deidra held tightly on to her hand.

"I *do* smile," Paris said. "I do. I don't know why you and Andrew say I don't."

"Because you don't. Not lately. Not from what I've seen. Every time I see you, you look like something is weighing on your mind. Do you want to talk about it?"

Paris had discussed this with Johnnie Mae Landris just two weeks ago. She still hadn't said anything to Andrew about the baby and

116

what was a possibility. "There's nothing to talk about, not really. My stomach is getting bigger, but I'm *definitely* not complaining about that. My feet swell so I'm not able to wear some of my favorite shoes. And you know how I am about my shoes." Paris laughed, hoping that little joke would set her mother's mind at ease. She held up one of her flats-wearing feet and twirled it in a circle.

"Well, you don't have too much longer before the baby comes and you'll be able to squeeze your little size-seven feet right back into your high-fashion high heels. Although I'm not so sure how the heels you like to wear will work when you're left carrying a baby in a pumpkin seat," Deidra said.

"Pumpkin seat? Really, Mom, no one calls baby carriers pumpkin seats anymore."

"Well, I do. And I can't wait until my grandbaby gets here so I can carry *her* in it when I take her to church."

"Who says the baby is a girl?" Paris said.

"You know you're having a little girl. As much as you want to put a little girl in pageants and things, this baby *has* to be a girl. You've never forgiven me for not allowing you to do those things on the level you wanted to. I can see you now: You'll have your little girl dressed in all those cute, frilly little things," Deidra said. "Tutus, lots of shimmy, net, and glitter. Me? I'm just looking forward to being Grandma or Granny, I haven't quite settled on which one I want to be called yet. And enjoying my grandchild while you get to do all the work, like changing diapers and waking up in the middle of the night."

"Well, I'm not having a girl."

"I thought you said you didn't know what you were having. So have you found out since the last time we spoke? Because if you know, then you need to tell me so I can start buying clothes and things in the appropriate gender and color. They have the cutest little things for little boys these days. You know I only had the one boy so a grandson would be absolutely delightful." Deidra winked. "On another note: You and Andrew have joined a new church. So I won't get to see all of you at church the way I'm used to doing. I'm still floored to hear that. I never thought, in a million years, you'd leave our church and join another."

"Mother, please, let's not go there again. Okay? We did it, it's done."

Deidra held up her hands in surrender. "I'm not, I'm not. I get it, and I'm fine with it. I was only bringing it up because it was a shock to me and your father when you told us. That's all. But we realize most of you young people seem drawn to places like Pastor Landris's church. In fact, Imani has been trying her best to get us to visit there for several months now."

"Well, I think you should visit," Paris said. "And now that Andrew and I are members, we would love for you to go with us one Sunday. But for sure, you'll be there when we have our baby dedicated."

"Absolutely we'll be there."

Paris laid her head on the back of the couch.

"Baby, what's the matter?" Deidra asked. "Come on; talk to me."

Paris sat up and looked at her mother. She wanted to tell her so badly. But if she were to tell her, what would her mother say?

Deidra grabbed Paris's hand and squeezed it. "Talk to me. I'm your mother. Whatever is going on, you don't have to go through it alone. That's what mothers are for. You'll see when your little one gets here. There's nothing that hurts a mother more than to see her own child in pain and not be able to make it better."

"I know, Mom. I just don't know if you'll understand or you may even decide you gave birth to a horrible person."

"A horrible person?" Deidra said. "You're

my child, Paris. A mother's love is a lot stronger than you know. No matter how bad, I'm still going to be your mother and your father is *still* going to be your father. And the Lord knows your father is not going to judge. Not with his history. You see what I've had to deal with when it comes to his past sins. But I'm still here, still hanging in there with him."

"You've been through a lot, that's for sure. I don't know if I would or could have handled it quite as graciously and forgiving as you. Tell me, Mother: How exactly *does* one forgive their spouse after they've cheated on them?" Just putting those words out there caused Paris to cringe a little. What she was actually asking her mother was: How was she supposed to get her husband to forgive her if she was to disclose to him her own truth of her *own* past sins? It was ironic how much she and her father were turning out to be so much alike.

"Is there something going on with Andrew? Is he not treating you right? Have you learned that he's cheated on you or something and you've retaliated?" Deidra said. "You can tell me, Paris. You know you can tell me anything."

"No." Paris chuckled nervously. "No. Andrew has been great. He truly has."

"Then what is it? Are you having second thoughts about the baby? Is that it? Because I can understand you being apprehensive about becoming a new mother. When I was pregnant with you . . . oh, my goodness, I was terrified that I would mess up. I wasn't sure what labor would actually be like. I mean, you can read about it, hear others talk about it, but once you're physically in it, you're in it. There's no turning back. But baby, I'll tell you this much: After you lay your eyes on that beautiful little bundle of beauty, your life will never ever be the same. You'll wonder how you ever lived without that precious little being in your world."

"I'm not worried about the baby, not in that way anyway."

Deidra began to nod. "Are you afraid something will be wrong with the baby? I know about that, too. But we *know* this baby is going to be fine. Do you have any idea how many people have been and are right now praying for this little one?" Deidra placed her hand on Paris's taut, almost seven-months-pregnant tummy. "Oh!" she said with a slight lift in her voice. "The baby just kicked me! I do believe that was a nice, strong, roundhouse kick."

Paris smiled as she placed her hand on her stomach. "Isn't it something? I'm still amazed at the wonder of it all. There's actually a little person growing inside of me." Paris glanced down at her black and white striped knit-covered belly.

"Well, just know that you're going to have plenty of help when this baby arrives. And *I* . . . am going to be *right* there with you every step of the way. I'll try not to smother you too much, but you're still my baby." Deidra grinned, then bit down on her bottom lip. "My baby is about to have a baby. I'm so excited!"

Paris nodded, wiping her eyes as she began to cry, upset with herself because she hadn't been able to hold it together.

"Baby, what's wrong?" Deidra pulled Paris into her arms and began to gently rock her. "I'm not going to let you go until you tell me what's wrong, so you might as well tell me."

Paris began to really cry. "Oh, Mom. I've got to do something, and I'm scared. I'm so scared of how it will all turn out. I'm scared Andrew will leave me."

"Leave you? Why would Andrew leave you? Andrew's not like that. There's nothing you likely can do that would cause him to leave, especially not at this point." She hugged Paris. "Do you have any idea how excited that man is about this baby? He's about to drive me crazy, talking about this baby all the time. He walks around with his chest all stuck out like a proud peacock, grinning like he just won the lottery or something."

Paris opened her mouth to tell her mother. If she could tell her mother, then she would be one step closer to being able to tell Andrew. "I-I-I —"

"Mom, where's my blue pullover sweater?" Imani said, practically running full speed into the den. "Oh! Paris! I didn't know you were here."

Paris sat up and quickly wiped her face with her hand. "Hi, Imani."

Imani went and hugged Paris. "What's the matter? Why are you crying?"

Paris shook her head and sat up even straighter. "It's nothing."

"It *is* something," Deidra said. "So go on, Imani and let your sister and me finish talking. I'm sure your sweater is in your closet and you just overlooked it as usual."

"No. Don't go, Imani. I'm all right. It's just hormones; that's all. Babies and menopause have a way of messing with women and their hormones, causing us to cry for no real reason." Paris chuckled although it was obvious she was faking it.

"That's true," Imani said. "Because when

Mom is crying for no reason, she has these sudden burst of anger moods that have the rest of us dodging for cover."

"What? I don't have anger mood bursts," Deidra said. "Do I?"

"Yes, Mother dearest, you do. That's why I stay in my room as much as I do these days," Imani said. "Daddy has been taking the brunt of it. Mom has been extra brutal on him."

"Well, Imani, since you don't know of what you speak, you probably shouldn't go around repeating things like that," Deidra said.

"Oh, I don't say a word to anyone else. But we're all family here, and I'm sure Paris already knows, and she's not going to broadcast it. We all seem to be great at keeping and hiding secrets, especially family secrets."

"O-kaaay. That's my cue to leave," Paris said, struggling to get up off the couch.

"But you just got here," Deidra said to Paris, trying to help her in her struggle to get up. "And it sounds like your father is home."

"I know. But I wasn't planning on staying long anyway. Andrew has plans for Valentine's Day today."

"I know, and you came by to get your box

of candy from Daddy," Imani said. Lawrence stepped into the room after coming in from the garage. "And right on time, here comes Daddy!" Imani ran and hugged her fifty-one-year-old father, who seemed to have aged ten years, actually looking closer to his true age since he'd ceased dying his hair after dropping out of politics last year.

"Hello, hello!" Lawrence said, placing the familiar large paper brown sack on the kitchen counter. He reached inside the sack and pulled out a red heart-shaped box and handed it to Imani. "For you, Imani."

Imani took the box and grinned, giving her father a quick peck on his perfectly positioned, awaiting cheek. "Thank you, Daddy!" Imani left in a hurry, headed back up to her room.

Lawrence picked up the sack and pulled out another red heart-shaped box, handing that one to Paris.

Paris took the large box and smiled. "Daddy, I keep telling you that I have my own man now and that you don't have to keep doing this every year."

"Yeah . . . well. I just want you to know that even when you have your own 'man,' I was the first *man* to ever really love you, unconditionally I might add, and that's never going to change *or* grow old. So deal with it," Lawrence said.

Already on her feet, Paris pulled the box close to her, then pulling herself just a little bit taller, gave her father a peck on his cheek just as Imani had done. "I love you, Daddy."

"I know," he said with a nod and a smile.

"And now, I need to make my way home." Paris hugged her mother good-bye.

"We still haven't finished our little talk," Deidra said.

"I know."

"And you're going to tell me what it is," Deidra said. "Right?"

Paris smiled and started out of the room. "Bye, you two. I love you."

"Bye, baby girl. Love you, too," Lawrence said, watching her as she walked away. The front door closed. "Love you," Lawrence whispered, before turning back to his wife, who was no longer smiling.

CHAPTER 12

Is there any thing whereof it may be said,
See, this is new? it hath been already of
old time, which was before us.
                    — Ecclesiastes 1:10

Lawrence reached into the sack and pulled out an extra-large red velvet box. Lovingly, he handed it to the woman he'd known now and loved for over thirty years, this year marking their thirtieth wedding anniversary.

"Thanks," Deidra said with as much enthusiasm as a dead fish as she set the box down on the coffee table.

Lawrence forced a smile, then reached into the sack again, this time pulling out a small red velvet square box and presenting it to her with a slight bow of his head. "*This* is also for you."

Looking down at the box, she frowned. "What is it?"

"Open it and see."

"Look, Lawrence, I told you when you left this morning on the pretense of looking for a job that I didn't want anything for Valentine's Day this year."

"You meant you didn't want anything from *me* for Valentine's Day this year," Lawrence said still holding out the box to her. "Please, Deidra . . . take this."

She let out an audible sigh and gently took possession of the box. Slowly, she untied the white ribbon and lifted the top. Her hand quickly flew up to her mouth. "Lawrence . . . how? Where did you get this?"

"I'll admit that it took some doing, but I was able to track it down." Lawrence took a step closer to Deidra.

She took the necklace out of the box, setting the now empty box down on the table next to the box of candy. "Is this really it?" she asked, questioning Lawrence about the heart-shaped semi-diamond-covered necklace with the diamond-looking pink rose on the inside made from what she now believed were, if this was the actual necklace, Swarovski crystals instead of diamonds.

He nodded. "It is. One and the same."

Tears began to do a free-fall from Deidra's eyes straight to her hands that lovingly held the necklace. She slowly turned the necklace over to the back and saw the slight cut mark on the gold in the exact same place, certain now that this was the necklace her beloved grandfather had given to her on her eighteenth birthday. A gift he'd originally given to her grandmother decades earlier but, wanting to make it into a family heirloom, had passed on to his little "Binky" as he called Deidra (in honor of the brand name of the pacifier that had never been far from her mouth when she was a toddler before they took it away, which then caused her to start sucking her thumb). Lost to her forever, or so she believed, after someone took it from her dorm room when she was twenty.

Composing herself after several huge swallows, she again asked, "How? Where?"

Lawrence took her by the hand that still held the necklace and guided her to the couch, where they both sat down. He angled his body toward her, refusing to take his hand away from a hand she was for once in seven months allowing to rest in his. A hand she had religiously and consistently pulled out of his when he'd attempted to merely reach for it.

"I tracked it down," Lawrence said.

Deidra looked down at the necklace, lovingly settled in the palm of her hand.

Lawrence smiled and carefully picked up

the necklace by its chain. Holding it in the air, he looked into Deidra's eyes, which were now looking into his. "May I?" he said, holding the two sides of the chain apart now.

Deidra nodded and turned her back to Lawrence, who, with shaking hands, managed to clasp the necklace around her neck. Deidra turned back to him as she touched the heart pendant lying next to her chest, once again close to her heart.

"Beautiful," Lawrence said with a satisfied smile.

"Where did you find it? How were you able to get it back?" Deidra asked again, more completely this time.

Lawrence nodded. "I knew who took it."

Deidra leaned back slightly away from him. "You knew who took it? You mean when I was frantically trying to find it that day all of those years ago, you knew who took it and you never said a word?"

Lawrence placed his hands over both of hers. "If you'll recall, that was the first time you and I actually held a real conversation."

"So what are you saying, Lawrence? That you put someone up to taking my necklace just so you could talk to me," Deidra said, snatching her hand out of his. "Help me out here. Tell me the truth and I mean the whole truth because you know that I know when you're lying."

Lawrence smiled as he nodded. "Yes, you, of all people, know me better than anyone on this earth. And yet, you still love me . . . you're still with me. And I thank you for that. I thought I fell in love with you all those years ago. But these past few months, I can truly say that I love you even more than I ever thought possible."

"Lawrence, are you trying to change the subject?" Deidra touched the heart of the necklace again. "This necklace . . . did you know who took it and you've known where it was all of these years and you never said anything to me?"

Lawrence took both her hands again and squeezed them. "Yes, I knew who took it." Deidra tried to snatch her hands out of his again, but this time he held on tight. "No, no, don't try and run. I need you to hear me out on this. You owe me that much."

Deidra stopped fighting him. "Okay. I'm listening."

"This guy I knew enlisted his then girl-friend to take it. He wanted to give his mother a Mother's Day present —"

"And he thought stealing my necklace was the perfect gift for his mother?" Deidra shook her head.

"He got his girlfriend to take the necklace

after she was talking about how you kept it in some box but you never wore it," Lawrence said. "His girlfriend said she didn't think you really wanted it since you would pass it over whenever you were looking for a necklace to wear."

"Wait a minute," Deidra said. "This girlfriend . . . was this someone close to me? Yes, of course, it would have *had* to be a friend of mine since I wouldn't have been doing something like that around just anyone."

Lawrence grimaced a little. "It *was* your best friend."

"Lynette? You're telling me Lynette is the one who took my necklace?" Deidra pulled her hands out of his and stood to her feet. She placed her hand up to her mouth, took her hand down, and frowned as she slowly shook her head. "I don't believe that. I don't believe you, Lawrence. I'm not saying you're lying, but your buddy who told you it was Lynette is not telling the truth. Lynette was tearing up the room trying to help me find it. If she'd taken it —"

Lawrence stood and walked over to Deidra. "If she'd taken it, which she did, it's not like she was going to tell you she had."

"But she knew how important this necklace was. When we were frantically looking for it, I told her the sentimental value behind it." Deidra nodded quickly. "That's why she fussed at me for having it with me on campus if it was something of that much sentimental value. And then she stormed out of the room —"

"And she went to find her boyfriend to get your necklace back. But by then, he'd given it to his mother and said he couldn't ask for it back," Lawrence said.

"Well, why didn't he just steal it back from his mother the same way he stole it from me?"

"Baby, you don't really mean that like you just said it," Lawrence said. "His mother was sick. The necklace cheered her up so much that once she put it on she promised to never take it off."

Deidra looked into Lawrence's eyes. "If all that you're saying is true, then how were you able to get it back after all these years?" She lifted the heart pendant and looked down at it before gently laying it back down.

Lawrence took Deidra by the hand and guided her back over to the sofa, where they both sat again next to each other.

"When you and I connected, because of how upset you were about the missing necklace, I went to Reggie and told him I wanted to buy the necklace from him."

"My necklace? The necklace he stole? You offered to buy it from him?"

"Yes. But you have to understand, Reggie really wasn't a bad guy."

"A man who stole *my* necklace wasn't really a bad guy?"

"I know it sounds crazy, but you have to understand what Reggie had gone through in his life. His mother had sacrificed so much for him and his three siblings. She was very sick, not expected to live long. He wanted her to have something nice for Mother's Day for a change —"

"So he got my best friend to steal my necklace. Lawrence, please . . . spare me the sob story. I don't care how hard he may have had it. I don't care how wonderful his mother may have been. I really don't care how sick his mother was at the time, except to say I'm sorry she was sick. But you can't take someone else's property and still be called a good guy. You just can't. He was wrong and I don't know how he could live with himself knowing he'd given his mother a stolen piece of property. That's just it in a nutshell and no amount of spin is going to change that."

"You're right, Deidra. But I'm telling you, Reggie *did* feel bad, especially after he found out you indeed wanted the necklace. And after Lynette told him it was a gift your grandfather had given to your grandmother years ago and how your grandfather was passing it on to you as a family heirloom, he felt really bad about what he'd done."

"Yeah, he felt really bad all right. But not bad enough to make things right," Deidra said.

"It's like I said: In the beginning both he and Lynette believed you were this well-to-do college student who probably had more stuff than you ever cared about. Lynette decided, rightly or wrongly, that you didn't want what she believed you felt was an old piece of junk. She also didn't think you'd ever miss it."

"I wonder where Lynette is today. I can't believe she didn't open her mouth about what she'd done. She was one of my closest friends. But getting back to how you managed to get this back . . ." She touched the necklace.

"After you and I got serious, I went to Reggie and offered to buy the necklace from him. It cost me a pretty penny, but he did sell it to me."

Deidra held up her hand. "Hold up." She turned squarely toward Lawrence and stared hard at him. "So you're telling me that you bought my necklace way back then and you never gave it to me?"

Lawrence grabbed her hands; she snatched them away. "Deidra, let me tell you everything. Okay?"

"I'm listening. But you need to hurry up and get to the part I want to hear because my patience has worn thin with you, Lawrence." She folded her arms.

"All right. I did buy the necklace way back then. And at the time I was trying to figure out how to get it back to you without you thinking you were crazy if it just happened to show up out of nowhere after you tore up your room searching for it."

"How about you just coming to me and telling me the truth, Lawrence. How about having done that as a strategy?"

"In retrospect, that might have been *one* plan. But you have to keep in mind that you and I had just started dating. You and Lynette were still friends although on your way out as close. If I had told you the truth, there would have been a huge fiasco. Who knows? Something like that might have broken us up before we even got going good —"

"So as what has now become your signature pattern, you decided to keep the truth from me so you could get what you desired in the end. Just like with Jasmine."

"Deidra, let's not talk about Jasmine right now. We're having a pretty nice time right now and I'd prefer not to ruin it. Not now. I'd like to resolve this issue we're discussing if it's okay with you. Anyway, that necklace —"

She lifted up the pendant and rubbed it between her fingers. "You mean this necklace that apparently you've had all of these years but never told me until now? And why is that, Lawrence? Why didn't you tell me you had it? You knew how much it meant to me. You knew I wanted to pass it on to one of my daughters when I had one, which I did. In fact, I ended up having two."

Lawrence nodded. "I was trying to figure out the right time and the right way. I knew if I just gave it back to you, short of it just showing up on its own, I'd have to tell you either the truth or make up a lie."

Deidra laughed. "You could have gone with the lie back then. It's obvious that lying has never been beneath you, not even when it comes to me. In fact, how do I know you're not lying right now? I mean, *you* could have been the one who stole this necklace and you're just lying and pinning it on Lynette and her boyfriend Reggie. I mean, it's not like I can easily find them and ask them, isn't that right?"

"I'm not lying to you, Deidra. Not this time. I promised you I wouldn't lie to you anymore and I will keep that promise at whatever cost. I appreciate you for standing by me through all of this unfortunate mess —"

"Oh, you mean the mess you made," Deidra said.

"Yes, the mess I made. The mess I'm doing my best to clean up. I've talked to Gabrielle about Jasmine, but she still isn't ready to tell her that I'm her father. Paris and Malachi know the truth, even if Imani doesn't. But at least I don't have to worry about Paris going off and doing something destructive like she did last year, you know like taking Imani over and introducing them now as half-sisters."

"Lawrence, keep your voice down, unless you want Imani to overhear you."

"Imani has her music blasting. She can't hear us. But I know you want this thing with Jasmine to be resolved. I know you believe all of our children have a right to know their sister. And as soon as Gabrielle allows me to move forward, we'll take care of that. Gabrielle says she wants to wait until her wedding is over in June. After that, she promises we can tell both Imani and Jasmine the truth."

"My necklace, Lawrence. Why are you giving it to me now?"

"Right. A few months after we got married, I did put the necklace in with some of your other jewelry. But by then, you were pregnant and not interested in wearing jewelry much. After Paris was born, I took it back out to give it to you as a gift."

"And — ?"

"And then so much started to happen. You and I got into stupid arguments. I decided to hold off until another time because I didn't want to have to explain anything. I found myself right back to the same reason why I couldn't tell you before we got married. After Imani was born, I figured you'd have the problem with which daughter to pass it down to —"

"So you were *sparing* me the anguish of having to choose which daughter? Is that what you're saying? That's why you kept it for some thirty years?"

"Things were complicated. I then forgot about it. But today . . . today God brought it back to my memory and my heart. I wanted to do right by you. So the necklace is finally back with you where it belongs. And I've told you the truth concerning it.

Please forgive me, yet again, for the bone-headed things I've done. But please know that I love you, Deidra. And I'm trying to make things right, at least with those things that I can."

Deidra touched the necklace again. "Well, it certainly has been preserved well. It looks exactly like it did when Granddaddy first gave it to me. I don't agree with everything you did when it comes to this necklace. But Lawrence, I do appreciate that I finally have it back."

Lawrence took her hands and held them. "I'm going to make you love me again, Dee. I'm going to make up for all the wrong I've done when it comes to you and my family. I promised you that back in August, and I meant it."

Deidra removed her hands from his and stood up. "I hope so, Lawrence. Because I still have Gigi's number. And if I need her to find out anything on you, you and I both already know that she's good, really good."

Lawrence shook his head. "I still can't believe you and William crossed me the way you did. William, I might have expected, but not you," Lawrence said. "You hiring Gigi the PI to investigate me — now that totally took me by surprise."

"If there was nothing to report on you,

what I did in hiring Gigi wouldn't have ever mattered. You have only yourself to blame for what she discovered. And as for William: I guess you see that William had his own agenda. He definitely didn't have any problem when it came to selling you out if it advanced his own interest and pockets. Too bad he didn't realize he would push things too far and both of you would end up out and in the unemployment line," Deidra said. "Although in William's defense, I don't think he was trying to hurt you by having Gigi give Paris that information about Gabrielle having given her baby up for adoption while trying to be the one to adopt her after the fact. He truly was mainly trying to stop Paris from ruining both of your *good* things. William, as he can sometimes do, merely overplayed his hand with a Paris that was pretty much primed to blow Gabrielle out of the water if she found the right ammunition, which we now know that she did."

"Yeah, well, William has a new job now, the double-crossing snake, while I'm still trying to find what's available for an ex-congressman, other than becoming a lobbyist. But he's going to get his one day," Lawrence said. "You mark my words: William is going to get his."

"You mean the same way you seem to

have gotten yours?" Deidra patted him softly on his chest. "As they say: live and learn. Live and learn."

CHAPTER 13

Then I turned, and lifted up mine eyes,
and looked, and behold a flying roll.
— Zechariah 5:1

Three weeks had come and gone and Bennie was still staying at Gabrielle's house.
They hadn't talked a whole lot. When Gabrielle's aunt Cee-Cee found out her
brother was out of prison and at Gabrielle's,
she quickly rushed over to see him. Gabrielle was not there at the time, but Miss
Crowe was, and none too happy to have to
lay eyes on this despicable woman. Aunt
Cee-Cee mistreating Gabrielle as a young
child, then taking the money and opportunity Miss Crowe had provided for Gabrielle
through a well-paid, thought-out plan for
her to attend Juilliard was the last straw for
Miss Crowe.

And still Aunt Cee-Cee was trying to
defend her thievery in having taken that

money through fraudulent means and trying every avenue she could think of to get Miss Crowe to drop the charges against her. Still, Cecelia Murphy was roaming free, appearing to have so far beaten the system of paying for any of her misdeeds.

Miss Crowe had already told Zachary she wasn't leaving Gabrielle's house until Bennie was gone. Zachary didn't want his aunt getting in the middle of anything. In fact, he didn't want Bennie there at all. But Gabrielle had explained to him that Benjamin Booker was *still* her father. It didn't seem right to just turn him out on the streets without anywhere to go. He appeared to be a truly changed man, although when pressed about it, Gabrielle had to admit that she was too young to remember much about who he had been before he murdered her mother.

"But he says he's saved now, Zachary," Gabrielle said. "Who am I to argue that he's not? I can't judge him on where he stands with the Lord. But I will say that if at any time I see his actions lining up differently from that, I'll have him out of here faster than he can take a second breath. I'll not put me or my daughter in danger to discover whether I'm right or wrong about my father."

Zachary shook his head. "Okay. Then why don't you do this. Why don't you let him come to *my* house and stay? Aunt Esther is already here at your house anyway. She claims to help out with Jasmine and to work on the wedding plans, but I know my aunt."

"Yeah, I know your aunt, too. She doesn't trust Bennie. I told her I can take care of myself."

Zachary took her hand and held it. "You might as well not waste your breath on Aunt Esther. Once she's made up in her mind to do a thing, she becomes like cement that's been poured and hardened in whatever form it was poured into."

"Well, my father is my problem. I won't be punting him off on you or anyone else for that matter." Gabrielle glanced down at her hand and how gingerly he was holding it.

"You're just as bad as Aunt Esther. I don't know what I'm going to do with the two of you," Zachary said.

Gabrielle smiled. "Love us. That's what you're going to do with us. You're going to do just what you're doing now and love me, love Jasmine, and love your aunt."

Zachary raised Gabrielle's hand up to his lips and gently placed a kiss on it before lowering it back down. "You're right. And part of loving someone is to protect them, something your father apparently didn't know before and I'm not convinced that he knows now." Zachary shook his head. "I don't feel good about that man being here. I just don't. Call me overprotective; call me crazy, but I don't want him here alone with any of you. So give me a little peace of mind and let's move him into my place. He can come over here whenever the two of you want. In fact, I'll be more than happy to bring him after I come home from work."

"I don't want him at your house when you're not there, Zachary. And the truth is, you're not home most of the day."

"So . . . what? You think he's a thief? You think he'll rob me?" Zachary sat back against the couch. "If he'll steal from me, then that means he'll likely steal from you. I don't care about my stuff, but I do care about you."

Gabrielle smiled. "I know you care about me. And I'm not saying that I believe he steals. But Zachary, I don't know this man, either. You're offering to allow a perfect stranger into your home. When it comes to me, he's my father. If anyone has to put themselves out there for him, it should be me."

"Why? What has he done for you? You

don't owe him anything. He wasn't even here for you when you needed him. He was the one who took your mother from you. I don't mean to be cruel, but these are the facts."

"They are the facts," Bennie said, standing quietly in the den entranceway.

Zachary stood to his feet. "I'm sorry. I'm not trying to be hateful, but —"

"*But* . . . you love my daughter. You want to take care of my daughter. You want to protect . . . *my* daughter. You're doing what I've not been around to do." Bennie walked into the den where Gabrielle continued to remain seated.

"I do love Gabrielle. I love Jasmine. And I *don't* trust you. I'm sorry, but I don't," Zachary said. "You murdered her mother —"

"Zachary, that's enough," Gabrielle said, looking sternly at him.

"I'm sorry. I know I shouldn't keep saying that. But the thought of a man, any man, being violent to a woman causes my blood to boil." Zachary balled his hand into a fist and punched it down into the air.

Gabrielle stood up and rubbed Zachary's back. She knew he was not only thinking of her mother, but his sister who had been beaten and died after her boyfriend set her on fire. Her father was bringing up all of the thoughts and emotions Zachary was trying so hard to keep buried regarding his sister's death that had eventually caused Zachary to become a burn specialist.

Bennie came and stood face to face with Zachary. "Son, I was wrong all those years ago. I've come to a place in my life where I openly own what I did wrong. I was sent away to prison, away from everything in my life that I held dear, the most important being my baby girl here." He nodded toward Gabrielle, and then turned back to Zachary. "I had anger issues that have since been resolved. Not through counseling, although I did get that. But through getting to know the greatest Being who ever walked on the face of this earth: Jesus Christ. The one who died on the cross for my sins before I ever even committed them. The one who was buried in a borrowed tomb. The one God raised up from the dead that Sunday morning and who now sits at the right hand of the Father making intercessory on each one of our behalves."

Bennie placed his hand on Zachary's shoulder. Zachary instantly turned his head toward his hand. "I'm not the same creature I was. I'm not. Granted now, I'm not all I desire to be. But I thank God I'm not what

I used to be, do you hear me? I'm trying to live my life for the Lord. Whatever I can do to make things right, I'm trying to do that."

Gabrielle was sniffling at this point. Bennie turned to her and, putting his arms around her, pulled her close to him. "I can't bring your mother back, baby girl. Believe me: If God told me that I could trade my life and He would bring your mother back to you I would do it in a heartbeat. I mean that. But that's not going to happen. So all I can do is try to make things right for you now. Understand?"

Gabrielle nodded. Zachary slowly shook his head. This was hard for him. He knew Gabrielle wanted nothing more than to believe her father, believe he truly was a different person. Zachary understood that much. But if trusting a person was the only way one could tell if one can trust a person, he wasn't sure that Bennie wouldn't hurt Gabrielle again.

Bennie pushed Gabrielle away from him slightly and looked into her eyes. "If you want me to leave, I'll pack my things right this second and like smoke in the wind be gone. So don't you be worrying about me. I'm going to be all right. I didn't come here to cause you any more pain than I've already done. I appreciate you allowing me to stay

149

these three weeks. I've been trying to find work, but it's not easy out there for someone with my kind of record."

"I know, Daddy. I know. And with the economy already a wreck, too, I know."

"Yep. And for whatever reason, society says you may have paid your debt by being locked up, but we're still not going to give you a break once you come back out amongst us. Nobody seems to want to hire an ex-con." Bennie shook his head. "But I'm not giving up. I don't mind sweeping floors, cleaning toilets, digging ditches —"

"They have machines to dig ditches now," Zachary said clearly frustrated.

"Yeah. I've been reading the flying rolls."

"Flying rolls?" Zachary said.

"Yeah, you know . . . scrolls. It's like the handwriting on the wall. I'm not equipped to work, but if I don't have a job I can't support and sustain myself. So then what am I left with?"

"That's why it's fine that you stay here while you get yourself together," Gabrielle said.

"But if it's going to cause you problems or stress," Bennie said to Gabrielle before turning to Zachary, "or you *distress,* then I'll get my stuff and move on. I asked my sister about possibly staying with her, but she shut me down before I could get the words out of my mouth good. But there are other places."

"Of course," Gabrielle said. "Aunt Cee-Cee and the whole gang were trying to stay here with me last year at one point."

"Yeah, she did sort of mention that, inferring that you're somewhat not appreciative of all she's done for you," Bennie said.

"More like *to* her," Zachary said. "What they did *to* Gabrielle." He held his hands up in surrender. "I'm sorry. Some habits are just hard to break."

"I'm sure Aunt Cee-Cee called me an ingrate," Gabrielle said. "I try to forgive, but I'm not going to just lie down and let folks step all over me. If you knock me down, I'm going to get up and stop the spiking of the heels."

"You *are* your father's daughter," Bennie said with a chuckle. "That's the Booker blood in you. But I'm not going to do anything to hurt you ever again, not if I can help it. So if I need to go to a homeless shelter while I get things together, I'll do that."

"If *I* might interject," Zachary said. "I don't feel comfortable with you being here. I've offered to let you come live at my house."

"And I've told him that won't be necessary," Gabrielle said, giving Zachary *the eye* before pivoting back to her father. "You can stay here. I have the room and you are my father."

"I appreciate that," Bennie said. He took her hands and held them.

Zachary came and took Gabrielle's hands out of Bennie's. "I do have one other possible solution." He stood squarely in front of Gabrielle. "The other house that's presently in your possession."

Gabrielle frowned. "The other house? Are you talking about Jessica's house?"

"Yes. It's vacant. There's furniture in it. We could have the utilities turned on and it would be perfect for Bennie."

"I can't do that," Gabrielle said, taking her hands out of Zachary's.

"Why not?"

"Because, Jessica left that house for Jasmine. I'm merely the guardian."

"Yeah. And Jasmine has a home here with you. And after we get married" — he touched her face with his right hand — "you both will be living in my house with me, which will effectively become *our* house."

"I'm not trying to be any trouble. I'm sorry this has turned into that," Bennie said.

Zachary threw a hard glance Bennie's way,

almost appearing to tell him to shut up while he and Gabrielle were discussing this.

"I don't think it would be right for me to use the house in that way," Gabrielle said. "It's Jasmine's house. I'm just keeping things for her until —"

"Gabrielle," Zachary said with a grin. "Jasmine is nine years old. I think there will be plenty of time for her to have the house even if you did something with it right now. It's not good for a house to sit unoccupied. At the very least, Bennie here" — Zachary nodded toward Bennie — "would be helping out because he could maybe clean things that need cleaning. You know: Get the spider webs out and things like that. I wouldn't doubt if Benjamin has some handy traits lurking in him where he could fix some things that may need attention."

"I can do that. I've always been good with my hands. If you'd like me to go somewhere and do something, I can do that. No problem," Bennie said.

"I don't know. You being here so far hasn't been a problem, either," Gabrielle said to Bennie.

"Well, whatever you want, I'm with it. I'm just thankful not to be out on the streets right now. There are many in my predicament who are not as blessed," Bennie said.

153

"For now, I think it's best that you stay here. But I may get you to help me do some things over at the other house," Gabrielle said to Bennie. "I do need to do something with that house to ensure it remains in tip-top condition for Jasmine."

"Did somebody call my name?" Jasmine said, skipping into the den.

Gabrielle hugged Jasmine when she came over and stopped.

"Girl, you need to slow your roll," Miss Crowe said. "I've told you I'm not as young as I used to be. I can't be running and skipping and stuff." Miss Crowe placed her hand on her chest.

Bennie hurried over to Miss Crowe, beating Zachary to her. "Let me help you, Esther." He walked with her over to the couch, where she slowly lowered her body down. "I don't know why you be perpetrating. Talking about 'slow your roll.'" He giggled slightly. "You know you have plenty of pep left in your step."

Miss Crowe looked up at him without cracking a smile. "I've told you not to bother trying to sweet-talk me. I'm not falling for it." Miss Crowe adjusted her body better. "Zachary, I need you to find something to do."

"You're getting rid of me, Aunt Esther?"

Zachary said.

"Yes, I am. And take Casanova Lite with you. We womenfolk have some business we need to take care of," Miss Crowe said to Zachary, then winked. "Miss Jazz, come on over and bring that folder so we can show your mother what we've found thus far for the wedding."

"I know I've not said this, and I certainly have not been asked, but I pray you'll allow me to attend and possibly give you away at your wedding," Bennie said.

Zachary quickly looked at Gabrielle. "Come on, Bennie. Let's leave them to their business. Are there any more chicken wings left?"

"Yes," Miss Crowe said. "So go on in the kitchen and knock yourselves out."

Zachary stood at the entrance of the den. "Bennie, come on. Let's go."

Bennie walked over to Zachary.

"After you," Zachary said, allowing Bennie to go out before him.

CHAPTER 14

Shake thyself from the dust; arise, and sit
down, O Jerusalem: loose thyself from the
bands of thy neck, O captive daughter of
Zion.

— Isaiah 52:2

"Miss Jazz, let's show your mama what we
got done with that computer of yours," Miss
Crowe said. "I'll tell you what: that Google
is a wonderful thing. We were able to put in
what we wanted and, voila, there it was. Jasmine was a huge help, showing me how to
do all this stuff. You know I've been completely out of the loop since my accident.
Ten years ago we didn't have stuff like this
at our fingertips. We did things like using
the telephone and shoe leather. This child
started speaking all this foreign language to
me talking about Bing, Yahoo, and Google."

"I know. It's great, isn't it?" Gabrielle said.

"She says she has officially taught me how

to surf the Web. I told her that was nice because that was the closest anyone was ever going to get me to surf anything. But we found some of the most gorgeous wedding dresses," Miss Crowe said.

"I told you now. I don't want this wedding to be *too* over the top," Gabrielle said.

"Oh, hush up! This is *our* wedding and you're not going to deprive us of *our* dreams." Miss Crowe smiled.

Gabrielle laughed. "Well excuse me. And to think I thought *I* was the bride."

"You are," Miss Crowe said. "But this will be a time when Cinder meets Ella and becomes a *real* Cinderella."

"I *love* Cinderella! Miss C says we're going to bring it all to life, in living color," Jasmine said.

"No." Gabrielle shook her head. "All I want is a simple dress —"

"Well, you can forget that because *that's* out of the window," Miss Crowe said. "I'm buying the dress, and Miss Jazz and I just so happened to have found the perfect one."

"You're not buying my dress, Miss Crowe. I'm not going to let you do that."

"Let me? I tell you what: Try and stop me." Miss Crowe pulled out a printed photo. "I don't have my own daughter to go over the top with for a wedding. You're like my daughter. I have some money stashed away and can spend it on whatever I like and fortunately, or unfortunately according to how you look at it, for you, you can't tell me what to do with it. Therefore, we *will* have this Cinderella wedding, over the top and all. And you're going to stop causing us problems. Now look at this picture and tell me and Jasmine what you think." Miss Crowe handed the photo of a wedding dress to Gabrielle.

Jasmine quickly kneeled down beside Gabrielle and grinned.

"Oh, my goodness! This *is* gorgeous!" Gabrielle said. "But it has to cost an arm and a leg."

"Nah. Just one leg," Miss Crowe said teasingly. "But seriously, nothing is too much for you."

Gabrielle slowly shook her head in amazement. "This is absolutely stunning."

"That's the one we liked, as well," Miss Crowe said. "Jasmine was the one who picked it. As soon as she saw it, she started ooh-ing and ahh-ing."

"Well, I absolutely love it!"

"Since we printed them, we'll show you the others we also considered, although I believe we have a consensus that this is the one," Jasmine said.

"Consensus," Miss Crowe said with a giggle. "You are just too grown for your britches. Don't you love how smart this child is? Now what nine-year-old do you know who goes around using the words considered and consensus?" Miss Crowe turned her attention to Jasmine. "I really don't see any reason to look at any others. Turns out it was a waste of ink printing them. But since they're printed, we might as well show them." She handed five more sheets to Gabrielle, who went through them pointing out three others that she thought were also lovely.

"Miss Crowe liked this one, too," Jasmine said, pointing to the ballroom gown that most resembled ones portrayed in Cinderella books and on television.

"I liked it because I was looking for a real Cinderella dress. But when I saw this one" — Miss Crowe pointed at the one they had all agreed was *the one* — "there was no contest. I love that when you wear this one, you're going to set another idea of what a version of Cinderella can look like."

"Gabriella," Jasmine said.

"Excuse me?" Gabrielle said.

"If you're going to start your own fairy tale, then you need your own character name. Instead of Cinderella you'll be Gabriella. Gabrielle and Ella makes Gabriella"

Everybody laughed. "Okay. I'm not going to argue with either of you. I'm just going to let you do what you're going to do no matter what I say." Gabrielle continued to look at the dress they'd decided on with an enormous smile.

"So we're agreed then?" Miss Crowe asked. "We have a consensus." She smiled, then winked at Jasmine.

"It looks that way," Gabrielle said.

"Wonderful! Daughters of Zion activate!" Miss Crowe said, holding her arm in the air.

"What?" Gabrielle said. "Daughters of Zion? I see you both are in rare form tonight. You, Jasmine, calling me Gabriella. And you, Miss Crowe, calling us Daughters of Zion."

Miss Crowe began to wipe her eyes. "I'm just so happy. Go get me some tissue, will you please, Miss Jazz?"

Jasmine jumped up and left out.

"I love you, Gabrielle, do you hear me?" Miss Crowe said.

Gabrielle hugged her, tears pooling in her eyes. "I love you, too."

"But listen: You and I have enough folks to fight these days. Leslie is still adamant that she's not coming to the wedding. She says it's nothing against you personally; she just doesn't think you and her son should get married just yet."

"I know. I hate that. But I love Zachary."

"I know. That's why we're going to put our full attention on happy things. Jasmine is so excited about you and Zachary getting married, as am I. I have an amount I plan on spending on your wedding."

"But I —"

"Did you not just hear what I just said to you? I'm going to do what I want to do for you regardless of anything you say. I don't want to have to fight you. And that little girl . . . she is so happy about this upcoming wedding. If you won't let me do this big for you and Zachary, will you at least allow your daughter this fairy tale wedding? Can you do that for her? I didn't have a big wedding, so can you also do it for me?" Miss Crowe covered Gabrielle's left hand with hers and patted it.

Gabrielle nodded. "Okay."

"So no more arguing unless you just absolutely don't like something. If we find a cake, I don't want you to say anything against it because of its price. Now, if you don't like it, then that's different. But I don't want to fight with you. I want to pick out what we want and cross it off the list.

Your wedding is June eleventh. We're in the middle of February. We don't have much time left before you'll be walking down that aisle. All right?"

Gabrielle nodded as tears rolled down her face. She and Miss Crowe hugged.

"Oh, my goodness!" Jasmine said. "Are you two hugging? Again. And are you both crying? Again."

Gabrielle released Miss Crowe and smiled at Jasmine.

"Whelp, it looks like we're going to need a lot more tissues." Jasmine stood with tissues in her hand, shaking her head.

Miss Crowe and Gabrielle laughed. "Come here," Gabrielle said to Jasmine, who promptly came over and flopped down between them. "I love you," she said to Jasmine.

"I know." Jasmine grinned. "I know."

CHAPTER 15

And if a house be divided against itself,
that house cannot stand.

— Mark 3:25

Darius was living pretty well at this point.
Him having met Divine at the moment he
had truly had been "divine." He smiled
every time he thought about it.

There he was, completely homeless and
without hope. Nothing was going right for
him. Paris Simmons-Holyfield was trying to
pin a pregnancy on him. He was not hearing that, not at all. He'd specifically gotten
Tiffany to have her tubes tied so he wouldn't
have to deal with any more crumb-
snatchers. Paris wasn't his wife and the last
thing he wanted or needed was to be in
court on some paternity question.

He felt pretty good that he had shut that
whole talk down. Deep down though, he
felt the baby most likely *was* his. Paris had

told him how long she and her husband had been trying. If the man was swinging and striking out for essentially four years, which is how long Paris had confessed she'd been trying, although Andrew only thought it had been two, the odds were not in his favor that during the exact time he and Paris had connected in that way her husband would finally hit a home run.

But Darius figured Paris should actually be thanking him for his contribution. He was familiar with sperm banks. A lot of women paid top dollar for the privilege of finally being able to get pregnant. He had apparently contributed to Paris's success for free. In fact, if he wasn't in a much better place right now, he might have thought about charging her for real.

Of course, if he *had* come back to Paris talking about money, she surely would have taken his gesture as some sort of blackmail. That was the problem with everybody. Whenever a businessman came along and wanted to be paid for certain services rendered, folks wanted to scream you were blackmailing them or doing something unethical. But he knew Paris wasn't going to get much out of him for child support even if it turned out conclusively that he was *indeed* the father. Her best shot was to hang in there with her husband, who had money to do right by the kid.

And what her husband didn't know *certainly* wouldn't hurt him. Darius was in such a good mood these days that he was even willing, maybe in a year or two, should Paris need it, to make another contribution toward one more child. After all, no child should grow up being an only child. There should always be two just to keep the one from growing up to be a completely spoiled brat. Yes, he would do that for Paris, if she should desire another one. The upside to that would be the children would at least look like siblings since they would have the same mother and father.

He walked up to the door of what used to be his house. It was March 29 and Tiffany had sent word several times in the past two weeks by Big Red that she needed to see him. He had been so caught up in having fun and making money with his new venture with Divine that he hadn't thought much about Tiffany *or* his children, for that matter. He was sure she was trying to find him because she needed some money. Fortunately for her, he had plenty of money these days. Yes, life was definitely good now.

He rang the doorbell. Tiffany answered it. "Hi," Tiffany said. She'd lost weight. She looked good. "Come on in."

Darius scanned Tiffany from the back as he followed her. Yes, she was looking *real* good. If he didn't already have a good-looking woman right now, he would definitely be trying to get back with Tiffany. But Dee Vine had turned out to be the perfect woman for him. He could be faithful to one woman. *Who knew?*

They sat down together on the sofa. "Where are the kids?" Darius asked.

"They're with Fatima."

"You and Fatima have certainly become tight. If I didn't know any better, I might ask what's going on between the two of you. But I know that Fatima is not into women —"

"Darius, I didn't ask you here for that," Tiffany said.

"Sorry. I guess I'm still so comfortable with you, I just open my mouth and what comes up, comes out still." He crossed his leg and leaned back. "So what was the bat signal you were sending out all about?"

"I hadn't heard from you since Valentine's Day."

He uncrossed his leg and leaned forward, glancing at Tiffany with a smirk. "Oh, how sweet. So you were worried about me?"

"Darius, you're still my husband. You're

the father of our children. Of course I care and of course I still worry about you."

"Well, you could have fooled me."

"I thought you were going to get with Pastor Landris and try to work on things between us so we can get our marriage and family back on track," Tiffany said.

"Is that what you thought?" He chuckled. "Well, I guess you *thought* wrong. Just like you thinking putting me out of my own house was a good idea. So how's that working out for you?"

"I wanted you to know I was serious this time," Tiffany said. "No more games."

He nodded. "I'll give it to you. You almost brought me down to my knees with this last action. I almost hit rock bottom. Almost. But you see, Tiffany, the Lord knows my heart. He knows I'm a good man whether you want to recognize it or not. And you know what else: the Lord *always* takes care of His own. And as you holier-than-thou folks like to put it: 'What Satan meant for bad, God used it for good.' "

"Darius, what are you talking about? You were the one having affairs on me. You were the one lying to me. I asked you if you'd cheated on me recently and you denied it."

"So what are you saying?" Darius said. "That I cheated on you recently? Did someone tell you I cheated on you recently?" Darius's mind quickly turned to Paris. Had Paris told Tiffany about their night together and about her possibly being pregnant by him?

"No. But then, I'm not out there trying to find out who all else you've been with. What I was praying is that you would see where you've been wrong and that you would come back home with a made-up mind to do right from here on out," Tiffany said as she looked sternly at Darius.

"No, what you were doing is a form of witchcraft," Darius said.

Tiffany pulled back. "Witchcraft? What are you talking about, witchcraft? I haven't done any such thing."

"Not the hocus-pocus voodoo kind of witchcraft. But you were trying to manipulate me into doing and being who and what you wanted. Well, guess what, Tiff? Your plan backfired. You were trying to saw this family in half and make me do what you wanted, and now all you've ended up accomplishing is a house divided. And you know what they say about a house divided? It can't stand. Thus, all of this is about to come to a close real soon."

Tiffany stood up. "What do you mean?"

Darius stood and smiled. "I mean, I'm

going to do what you so far have been too chicken to do. I'm going to file for divorce. I don't want to come back here with you. I don't want to be married to you anymore. I'm sick and tired of you, so I'm going to do what we should have done years ago and cut these chains from around my neck."

"What about our children?"

"What about them? They'll be all right. People divorce every day. No big deal."

"But they need a father in their life."

"I said I'm divorcing you, not dying. As long as I'm still alive, they'll have a father in their life. I just won't be conveniently available to be kicked around by you anymore." Darius looked hard at her.

Tears started to roll down Tiffany's cheeks. "I don't understand you. What has happened to you?"

"I hit rock bottom. It was the end of January. And when I was at my lowest point and flat on my back, I looked up and there was Divine."

"You're saying that you saw the Lord?" Tiffany shook her head. "But you're talking crazy. We need to work things out, Darius, if for nothing else for our children. They miss you. They miss having you in their lives."

"Well, you should have thought about all

of that before you kicked me out. Amazing the clarity a few months can bring. When I left here, I was determined to win you back and make my way back home. I asked you to let me stay here while we worked things out. But I suppose you were too busy listening to your buddies Fatima and Gabrielle, as well as Pastor Landris and his wife. I'm sure they've all been spewing something or other in your precious ear gates when it comes to me."

Tiffany touched his arm. "Darius, this is not what I wanted at all."

"Well, it looks like it's what you've ended up with." He reached into his pocket and pulled out his wallet that bulged with money. Peeling off one-hundred-dollar bills like leaves on a head of lettuce, he stopped, folded them, and placed the ones he counted off into her hand. "That's two thousand dollars. That should just about catch me up on what I owe when it comes to our children's support. No matter what you might think or try to tell them different, I still care about them."

"Two thousand dollars?" Tiffany said, looking down at the wad of money. "Where did you get all this money from?" She looked up at Darius.

He put his wallet back in his pocket. "Like

I said: What Satan may have meant for bad, God used it for good."

"Darius, I hope you're not doing anything illegal. If you are, I don't want any part of this money. And if you are, then you need to stop before something bad happens to you. I'm telling you, Darius. I'm getting a sick feeling here. Don't you be playing with God out there."

"Of course, you're getting a sick feeling. And that feeling is knowing that you just lost the best thing you ever had. That sick feeling is realizing that you were trying to bring me to my knees, but it looks like I'm riding high with plenty of money to boot."

Tiffany placed her hand on his arm again. "Darius."

He leaned down and gave her a quick peck on her lips. "I'll be filing those divorce papers most likely tomorrow or sometime thereafter. Now, we can do this the easy way or we can do it the hard way. Personally, I prefer the easy way myself because I'm ready to move on with my life."

"Darius, you don't want to do this. Apparently, you've gotten caught up in some fantasy world and you don't know what you're getting yourself into," Tiffany said. "Now, let's you and I sit down and talk about what we need to do to bring our family back together. Let's pray —"

"I'm sorry, but I'm all prayed out. I reached my limit when I was outside of my own house back in January sitting in the freezing cold trying to get you to let me in. I'm all prayed out from having had a job that was shipped overseas, to getting another job that didn't pan out, to praying and asking God to help me get something so I could take care of my family only to have you throw some old affair in my face that didn't amount to a hill of beans. Heck, now you and the woman I had the affair with are best of friends, so much so that when I come over today, my children are not here because they're with her. I'm all prayed out with going to see our pastor only to learn that it's almost impossible to just walk in and get instant help directly from him. And when they *do* try to help, they make like everything has got to be my fault, as though you, my dear Tiffany, had no misstep or hand in what happened wrong between us."

"I never claimed I was perfect, Darius."

"Yes, I know. It was just living with you made me feel like I was always wrong, always a loser."

"I never made you feel like you were a loser. Darius, I loved you with all of my heart. You know that. I've put up with so much when it came to you. And when you messed up and I found out about your affair that first time, I forgave you. We worked on things and moved on."

"Well, this last affair you found out about, you didn't try to work it out. In fact, you moved me out. But as I have said: It's all good. In fact, I should thank you. Because if you hadn't put your foot down like you did, if you had let me in to stay that night back in January, my life would *definitely* not be on the upswing as it is right now. So, thank you, Tiffany. Thank you."

"You've found another woman, haven't you? Is that it? Is that why you're talking like this?"

"You mean like you've found another man in Brother Clarence Walker?"

Tiffany folded her arms. "I told you there's nothing going on between me and Clarence. He's only been by here to do what he can to help. He's been great about doing things that have put a smile on the children's faces, your children."

"Yes. A divorce is going to be great for the both of us. That way I can move on with my life and you and Clarence can explore more with each other." He grinned. "I'm not going to contest anything with the house if that will speed things up with the divorce.

We'll come up with an agreement for child support as long as you don't try to get crazy about how much you think I should be able to afford. I still don't have a steady job. And I still have to live, too. And without a home to call my own, I have to pay for somewhere to stay."

"Darius, I don't understand. Why are you doing this?"

"It's like I told you when this all first started happening. We needed to be in the same house to work things out. You saw things differently and you put me out. I suppose you can thank whose ever bright idea that was to do that. You'll be hearing from my lawyer soon. I figure after I file, it will take about two months, tops. Then we'll be legally and finally free. And let this be a lesson to you: a house divided cannot stand." He leaned down, gave her a quick peck on the cheek, and left.

CHAPTER 16

They are all plain to him that understandeth, and right to them that find knowledge.

— Proverbs 8:9

With the precision of a cat burglar, Paris quietly walked into the house. Her mother-in-law, Paula Holyfield, was in there with Andrew. She'd seen her car parked outside. Paris knew it was wrong of her, but she'd deliberately not parked in the garage because she didn't want Andrew or her mother-in-law to hear her come in. This was the only way for her to hear what they were really talking about, as she knew once she entered, whatever private conversations they were having would instantly cease.

Paula was not a bad mother-in-law per se. But she definitely wasn't Paris's biggest fan. She'd been against Andrew marrying her from the start, which was not a surprise considering most mothers of sons seem to think their precious little boys are too good for whichever woman they choose. And it didn't help any when Paris let Paula know that she had no intentions of getting pregnant anytime soon after they married. It wouldn't have been a big deal except Andrew really wanted a family and, knowing that, Paula felt Paris was totally disregarding his feelings when it came to things in a marriage.

Andrew had been great at shutting his mother down when she said something that he knew would upset Paris. But Paris knew the two of them were close and still talked. Andrew loved his mother and valued her opinion. Paris was pretty sure Andrew had told her when they were trying to have a baby and she certainly would have noted they hadn't been successful, at least not until eight months ago.

Paula had made all the right moves and said all the right things, but she could see that Paula wasn't quite buying into everything that had to do with this pregnancy. All of that would have been fine except Paris knew there was a grave possibility this baby really wasn't Andrew's. Maybe she was being paranoid or maybe the guilt was getting to her, but she just felt Andrew's mother was suspicious of this child actually being his. So what better way to find out what they were really saying behind closed doors than to stand behind it and listen? And just as she suspected, they were discussing her and the baby.

"Mom . . . Mom," Andrew said. "You need to stop. I've told you, Paris is not the way you perceive her. You've never given her a chance and now you're *still* not being fair when it comes to her."

"Drew, you can take up for her all you want. But I'm telling you, deep down in my soul, something doesn't feel right," Paula said, calling him Drew, the name she generally called him unless she was purposely being formal.

"But what you're implying would mean that my wife would have had to have cheated on me."

"And — ?"

"And that's not possible," Andrew said in a matter-of-fact tone.

"What are you talking about *not* possible? Do you have some kind of lock on her or something? Was she wearing a chastity belt and you were the only one with the key?"

"No. It's called trust. And I trust my wife. I have never had any reason not to or to believe she would cheat on me."

Paula released a low slow chuckle. "Famous last words. Drew . . . Drew, do you think that when someone is having an affair they tell the person that's what they're doing? Come on, now. I know you're smarter than that. And I've just never been convinced that Paris truly loved you, not the way she should. It's like she was looking for a great opportunity and you came along."

"I can see that you don't think very much of me," Andrew said.

"Oh, I think the world of you. In fact, I wanted nothing more than for you to meet a nice girl and settle down. Someone who didn't mind riding in your beat-up old car and not be ashamed when she was with you because being with you was all that mattered to her."

"Okay. But Paris rode in my beat-up old car with me," Andrew said.

"One time before she insisted she do the driving and drove you right to a car dealership and helped you pick out a nice new car that you *didn't* need and couldn't afford just yet," Paula said.

"Well, all of that is in the past. And the woman you seem to always find fault with is about to become the mother of my child, and subsequently, your grandchild. You're finally getting that little grandson or grand-daughter you say you've been praying about," Andrew said. "So you need to move on and get with the program. And the current program involves the coming of a baby in roughly two to six weeks."

"I thought you said her due date was April twenty-eighth?"

"It is. But as you are already aware, a baby can come two weeks early or two weeks late. It's the end of March now. April twenty-eighth is four weeks away," Andrew said with a smile in his voice. "Two weeks early could be April fourteenth. And we are *so* ready for this baby to get here. The nursery's all done. Paris has had two baby showers with so much stuff we could actually open up our own baby store."

"Sounds like this baby is going to be good and spoiled, just like his mother."

"Mom, I'm not going to tell you again. I'll not let you disrespect my wife."

"I'm not disrespecting her. Speaking the truth has never been disrespect. And you and I both know your wife is spoiled as they come. Her folks pretty much gave her everything she wanted. Then you continued the tradition by giving her everything she wants now. I seem to be the only one who recognizes her for the person she really is. And I'm telling you, Drew, Paris is keeping something from you. I'm telling you, she's hiding something. I don't know why, but God has been showing me there's something going on with this baby she's carrying."

"You're seeing what you want to see and you're trying to validate it by bringing God into the picture. But it's not going to work. That baby is mine, and that's the end of any crazy talk."

"Okay, but just one more thing, and I'll leave this alone. Don't you find it sort of strange that you two had been trying for years to have a baby and nothing? But then she's gone from home with a new job, out all times of the night with who knows who and bam! Baby's on board. It's like some miracle took place or something."

"All right. The reason we were having such a time in the first place is because, yes, Paris really didn't want a baby at first. Originally, she was doing things to keep it from happening. After that, she had to get those pills out of her system. Ask any obstetricians, and they'll tell you. Then there's the anxiety that comes with trying to make it happen, which can cause stress that keeps one from getting pregnant. Paris just became more relaxed after she started working outside the home. And she really loved what she was doing."

"And she was hanging out with some guy who probably helped the two of you out when it came to her getting pregnant," Paula said. "All I'm saying is that you should ask her if anything happened while she was out there 'working' and 'loving' her job."

"Oh, yeah. That will work out great. 'Honey, I know you're pregnant and all. But I just need to make sure that the baby you're carrying is really mine. Oh, no real reason. It's just my *mother* believes in any marriage it's standard operating procedure to ask.' You talk about me and you both not getting to be in the baby's life after that. That will do it for sure."

"All I'll say to you, because you know I'm going to be doing it, is to make sure when that baby arrives, you check to see if the baby resembles you anywhere. And I don't mean telling me the baby has ten fingers and ten toes, just like you. I'm talking about we need to see something of *us* in that child, or else I'm going to want a paternity test done."

"Mom, do you want to be there when the baby comes?"

"Yes, of course I do. What kind of a silly question is that to ask?"

"One that will determine whether you be

there or not by you stopping all of this nonsense talk. I'm telling you, Mom, if you keep this up I'm not going to call you when Paris goes into labor. And you might end up not seeing your grandchild until he or she can call you by name. Got it?"

"Fine. Fine. I'll not say another word on the matter. But if down the road it turns out I was right, don't say I didn't give you a word of knowledge beforehand."

Paris tiptoed out of the area and back out to her car. She quietly closed the car door, let up the garage door, and drove in. She had to figure out what to do. She'd talked to Johnnie Mae Landris a few months ago about what she should do. Johnnie Mae's advice had been to come clean to her husband, but she hadn't been able to bring herself to do that.

In her mind, she thought she could pull this off. Barring anything weird happening, no one had to know she'd ever been unfaithful to Andrew. And, if she was right in the way she believed, this baby would come out looking like Andrew spit him or her out himself. The baby would be the spitting image of Andrew.

She walked into the kitchen, where Andrew and Paula had now moved, undoubtedly after hearing her car drive inside.

"Hi, honey," Andrew said when Paris stepped inside. "How was your day?"

"It was really good," Paris said, closing the door between the kitchen and the garage. "Hi, Mama Paula. What a delight to see you here!"

Paula and Paris hugged. "I know. I just had to come by and see my baby boy. He's so excited about the pending arrival." Paula looked down at Paris's stomach. "He showed me the nursery. It's so lovely. Well, it definitely won't be much longer now." Paula smiled.

Paris placed her hand on her stomach and smiled back. "No, it most certainly won't. And Andrew is going to make the best father, I just know it. I'm sure you're going to be the best grandmother this child could have as well. We are *so* blessed! All of us. Don't you agree?" Paris tilted her head with her gaze fixed on Paula.

"God is good!" Paula said. She looked down at Paris's stomach again. "It's a boy."

"Well, we won't know until the baby gets here."

"I'm telling you. I can see it just as clearly: it's a boy." She held her hand in the air above Paris's stomach. "May I?" she asked permission to place her hand on Paris's basketball of a stomach.

"Sure," Paris said, looking as Paula gently placed her hand on her stomach.

"Yep. A healthy baby boy. I'd say he'll be seven pounds, eight ounces."

Andrew laughed. "I'm surprised my mother didn't make you do the thing with the needle stuck in the eraser of a number two pencil suspended by a piece of thread as she holds it over your wrist or stomach, watching it go sideways to indicate a girl, and back and forth to indicate a boy."

"Oh, we can do that now," Paula said. "I have a number-two pencil and a sewing kit in my purse."

"I'd rather not," Paris said.

"Yeah, that's why I've never suggested it. I figured you'd 'rather not.' " Paula grinned. "Well, son, I'm going to get on down this road. Everything looks wonderful. Paris, let me know if you need anything. I'm sure I'll see you soon and if not, I'll see the three of you at the hospital on delivery day."

"Oh, you're planning on being there?" Paris said.

"Absolutely. I wouldn't miss it for the world. Unless, of course, I don't get a call to let me know." Paula looked slyly at Andrew, bending her head down slightly.

"As long as you behave yourself, I'm sure you'll get a call," Andrew said.

Paula hugged Andrew, and then hugged Paris. "See how he treats his old mother. Well, I'm off. Ta-ta!"

"Oh, yes. I see," Paris said with a sly grin of her own. She wanted so much to finish the rest of the sentence that formed in her mind. "Oh, yes. I see that you're . . . off."

Andrew walked his mother to the front door. Paris went and sat on the couch. "Please, God. Please . . . let this baby be Andrew's. Please. That's all I'm asking. Just let this baby be his."

CHAPTER 17

Then said Boaz unto Ruth, Hearest thou not, my daughter? Go not to glean in another field, neither go from hence, but abide here fast by my maidens.

— Ruth 2:8

"Okay, Gabrielle," Zachary said as they walked in the park together, grabbing a little alone time together. "I know we've talked about this and you've let it be known that you're fine with it, but I'm still having a hard time about your father."

"Has he done anything to validate your concern?" Gabrielle asked.

"Not really. But he came here around the end of January. It's now the twenty-ninth of March. That's been two whole months he's been at your house."

"I know," Gabrielle said. She then looked up at Zachary and smiled sheepishly. "To-morrow is Jasmine's birthday, and I'm so excited! She'll be ten. Can you believe it? Can you believe all that's happened in a little over a year and a half? Last year coming up to this time we weren't sure she'd even *see* nine. And this year, she's turning ten and we're all together." Gabrielle released a happy sigh.

"And we're also getting close to our big day. Two and half more months to go, and we'll legally all be one happy family," Zachary said.

"Yes." Gabrielle smiled. "And I know you're not sure about my father or his motives. To be honest, I didn't know what I'd do if and when I ever came face to face with him again. It's hard to explain. I hated him for so long. Early on in my life as a child, I *hated* him. How could he kill my mother the way he had? How could he take someone else's life as though it was his to take? How he ruined my life. I absolutely despised him. And I missed my mother. Then to have to grow up with folks who treated me as though I didn't matter. But there he was, standing in my doorway. I can't fully explain it, but I couldn't just turn my back on him. I just couldn't."

"Well, while we're being completely transparent, I'll be honest with you," Zachary said. "I don't believe I could be as gracious as you. I don't think I would have let him in my house, let alone back in my life. I guess you can see that I'm not quite there yet in my walk as a Christian. Your father didn't even do those things to me, and I'm having a hard time forgiving him."

"Well, he seems to me to be really trying. He's looking for a job with nothing available to him. I sort of feel sorry for him. Here he is a changed man —"

"So he says," Zachary said.

"I've been around him these last couple of months," Gabrielle said. "I've observed him. He reads his Bible daily. I even caught him praying for Jasmine when she didn't know he was doing it. He rests his hand on her head and closes his eyes. One time she looked up and saw him with his eyes closed and asked him if he'd fallen asleep while he was standing."

"I hear you. But I've not been comfortable knowing he was at your house alone on most occasions with my aunt and then with Jasmine when she comes in from school. I've been doing a lot of praying, making sure everybody in that house is covered by the blood of Jesus. I've called angels to be stationed around them. I would have felt better if he was at my house or somewhere else entirely. I told you I was even willing to pay for an apartment for him if that's what it took."

"Yes. I know. The apartment was your *first* suggestion the day after he arrived. And as you remember, I shot that down," Gabrielle said.

"Yes, you did. Pretty quickly, in fact." Zachary helped her as she walked up the steps on the path back to the car.

"And just in case you think I don't know, my father did tell me how you've given him a 'piece of money' each week. That's how he said it, that you give him 'a piece of money.' I was trying to give him something to help out as he's searching for work, but he won't take any money from me. He says the piece of money you've given him has been more than enough to do what he needs to do," Gabrielle said. "He's really a proud man, in spite of everything. You can't help but feel sorry for him and proud at the same time. The last thing I want to do is kick him while he's down."

"Aunt Esther says your aunt Cee-Cee has been by a few times when you're not there," Zachary said. "Has he told you what she wants?"

"Yes, Miss Crowe tells me everything that goes on. She's keeping a really good eye on things. And no, my father hasn't told me what Aunt Cee-Cee wants, but when it comes to her it generally boils down to one thing. She's always in need of more money. The thing is: There's nothing my father can do to help her when it comes to that."

Zachary nodded. "Aunt Esther believes your aunt is trying to get your father to somehow influence her into dropping the charges against her for stealing your Juilliard money. Aunt Esther says that's *never* going to happen. She's still upset about what was done to you — your aunt taking that money from you that way."

Gabrielle laughed. "Yeah. Miss Crowe has made it abundantly clear, even if I wanted her to, she's not going to let Aunt Cee-Cee off the hook. I believe her words were something to the effect of she will when Hades freezes over."

Zachary opened the car door for Gabrielle to get in. He closed the door and walked around, getting in on the driver's side. He buckled his seat belt. "Okay. Where to now?"

"Home. I have to get up really early for work tomorrow. I plan to get off early for Jasmine's birthday." She clapped.

"Are you glad you went back to work or would you prefer to be staying at home now?"

"Is this a trick question, Zachary?" Gabrielle smiled.

"Whatever do you mean, soon-to-be Mrs. Morgan?" He grinned. "Wow, I love the sound of that. I can't believe we're almost there and then I can drop the 'soon to be' entirely."

"Almost is still a long way away. You and I both know from experience a lot can happen between now and then," Gabrielle said.

"Please don't. Don't speak things like that into the atmosphere. Aunt Esther and Jasmine are working overtime to make this day huge," Zachary said, looking at her. He hadn't cranked the car yet.

"The two of them are so cute." Gabrielle grinned. "I think they're having more fun together than either of them have been having with me. Miss Crowe loves Jasmine and Jasmine positively adores her. I don't know what we're going to do after this is over and Miss Crowe goes back to Chicago."

"Maybe we can talk her into staying. I mean, think about it. She can be there for Jasmine, the two of them continuing to get into mischief together," Zachary said. "And she would be around to help out with the babies."

Gabrielle shrieked and released a short laugh. "Babies! What babies?"

"All the babies we're going to have, one

right after the other," Zachary said. He took his hand and gently moved a strand of hair out of Gabrielle's face and lovingly tucked it behind her ear.

"So you want to ask Miss Crowe to stay after the wedding so she can help take care of all the babies, plural, that you and I will be having? That's the plan?"

"You got it. And before you think I'm being chauvinistic, Aunt Esther told me the other day that she would love to stay here and help if we were planning on having more children. My aunt *loves* children. You know that."

"I agree. But I don't know about us having babies one right after the other, though."

Zachary smiled. "Well, just being able to be your husband and Jasmine's father will be more than I could ever hope for . . . for the time being anyway." He raised his eyebrows several times successively. "You know what I'm saying? You know what I'm saying?"

"Yes." Gabrielle placed the palm of her hand lovingly on his cheek.

He grabbed her hand and pressed it closer to his face. "I'm going to take care of you. I know you're more than capable of taking care of yourself, but —"

"We'll take care of each other," Gabrielle

said. "And I look forward to being there right by your side for whatever life has in store for us."

"Now, you're talking. June eleventh can't get here fast enough for me!"

"Have you spoken to your mother since the other day when you told me she called?" Gabrielle asked.

His face showed his defeat. "I have, and she's saying she's not budging on her decision."

"So she's still not planning to come to our wedding?"

"That's what she's continuing to say. But she's going to cave. I know my mother. She wants her way when it comes to making me do what she feels is right for me. She believes her refusing to attend will make me back down until she decides to give her blessing. But I've told her that I love you and we're getting married whether she's here to witness it or not. I suppose she can always see it on video. But everyone else in the family have already bought their airline tickets and made hotel reservations. We're going to have a great time. And Aunt Esther and Jasmine want me to wear something they call the Prince Charming tux with gold military-looking tassels on each shoulder with a gold diagonal sash."

Gabrielle laughed. "They're taking this Cinderella theme seriously."

"Well, if I get what I want, which is to be married to you," Zachary said. "And they get what they want, which is a fairy tale wedding —"

"But Miss Crowe is spending way too much money accomplishing this."

"So? Let her," Zachary said.

"That's what she told me. But I still don't feel right about it. After all is said and done, this wedding — taking months to plan and put in place and great funds being shelled out — will be over in a few hours and that includes the reception."

"No, we'll get more than that out of the wedding," Zachary said. "We'll get memories. And although memories *can* cost as little as nothing and carry the same weight as those things that cost a lot, at the end of *this* day, at the end of our wedding day, I believe we're all going to walk away with something that can never be taken away by anything, with possibly the only exception being Alzheimer's."

"How depressing," Gabrielle said with a frown. "Alzheimer's? You didn't have to bring up that." Gabrielle shook her head.

"Well, people used to say there were certain things they would never forget as

194

long as they live. But we know Alzheimer's can indeed rob folks of even those precious memories, no matter how well a stated intention otherwise. So let's allow everybody to do what they feel is right for them, including my mother if, in the end, she denies herself the privilege of seeing me pledge my heart to the woman I love."

"Ohhh." Gabrielle said it like a purr.

"I mean it. I'm going to marry *my* girl. Aunt Esther and Jasmine will get the wedding they're dreaming of. And you —"

"And *I* get to know what true happiness looks and feels like because I'll have you to wake up to each and every day of my life, for the rest of my life, until death do us part."

Zachary nodded, biting down on his bottom lip. "Yes. Until death do us part."

CHAPTER 18

And at evening let them return; and let them make a noise like a dog, and go round about the city.

— Psalm 59:14

"Honey, I'm home," Darius said as he stepped into the house and made his way upstairs to the bedroom two steps at a time. "Divine . . . are you up here?"

She held up a finger to silence Darius. "Yes, dearest, I understand," Divine said to the person on the phone.

"Sorry," he whispered as he walked over and gave her a quick kiss on the cheek.

Divine moved the phone to the side where he'd just kissed. "I'm working on it. Yes, yes, I'm looking to hire a few more people to handle that. It shouldn't be too difficult in this economy. Yes, dearest, I'll get back with you soon. I promise. Okay. Bye now." Divine clicked her cell phone off and looked at it before setting it down on the coffee table in the bedroom.

"You have *got* to be the hardest-working woman in the state of Alabama," Darius said. He began to massage her shoulders.

"Oh, that feels *so* good," she said, slowly lowering her body down to sit on the sofa in the bedroom as she kicked off her leopard heels.

Darius sat down on the floor and, picking up her feet, placed them in his lap. He began massaging one and then the other.

Divine slouched down and laid her head against the back of the sofa.

"You like this?" Darius asked as he smiled.

"Oh, yes. But I can't play for long. I have some pressing business vying for my attention."

"Yeah, I heard you saying you needed to hire some more people," Darius said.

"Yes. We lost a couple of folks in that little mishap the other day," Divine said. "And wouldn't you know, we have an order to fill with a huge payoff."

"So what qualifications are you guys looking for?"

Divine sat up and began sliding her feet back into her heels. Darius helped slip them on. "If one can cook and follow instructions, they pretty much have what we're looking for. Why? Do you have someone in mind?" She stood up.

"I could possibly help if you're in a real jam." Darius stood to his feet.

"Nope. I don't want to take any chances when it comes to you. Some parts of this business can be pretty dangerous, as you've now heard. I won't *ever* be putting you in that position."

He grabbed her around the waist and drew her close to him. "Would you like me to see if I can round up a few folks in need of a little extra change?"

"If you could, it would certainly help me out. But you know how careful we have to be when it comes to recruiting folks. Our operation is being tracked pretty closely lately, too close for comfort."

"Well, I know how to be discreet *and* do a good job at the same time."

"I don't doubt your abilities. You've caught on to the business better than I would have ever imagined. I confess: I didn't bring you home with me that day thinking I'd let you in on this part of my world," Divine said with a flirt and a smirk.

"Is that right? Then why *did* you bring me home with you that day?"

She flicked her hair to the back. "I guess you can say I felt sorry for you. It was obvious you were sleeping in your car. You were all scraggly looking. And that pillow in the backseat with the blanket . . . a dead give-away."

Darius rocked her sideways as he wrapped her tightly and securely in his arms. "Is that right, Sherlock?"

She looked up at him with a sheepish grin. "Yes, Watson, that's right." She smiled for a few seconds more, then turned and faced him. "So, what all did *you* do today?"

"Oh, you know: the normal stuff — me and the gang of six hitting up drug stores for the behind-the-counter golden meds containing our favorite ingredient."

"Did you go across the state line this run?"

"Yeah. That's where we're getting the best bang for our bucks. We can buy it without having to show IDs. Although I hear there's talk about more states enacting stricter laws to curb the problem. If too many more neighboring states keep this up, our time may require some overnight stays since I'll likely have to go farther away."

"We certainly wouldn't want that, now would we?"

Darius kissed her. "No . . . we wouldn't, especially not me. I'd miss you too much."

"So is that all you did today? Went and got a stockpile of Sudafed?"

"I did drop by and see my wife," Darius said. "Or as I informed her, my soon-to-be-ex-wife."

Divine broke from his embrace. "You're planning on divorcing your wife?"

Darius grabbed Divine back and locked her in his arms, pulling her closer to him. "Yes."

"I don't know about that," Divine said. "Divorce. That's a really big step."

"I know. But I feel I'm ready to make it. It's time."

Divine placed her hand on his chest. "Listen, Darius. I don't want you divorcing your wife because of me. You know I'm not one looking to settle down or anything. You have a family. I believe you need to think about this a little more."

"I *have* thought about it. I've thought about it since you and I had breakfast together that first morning that changed everything for me."

Divine shook her head slowly. "We don't know each other all that well. It's only been two months."

"Two glorious months," he said. "Two months of you and me opening up about everything. Two months of me finding out what it's like to be with a woman who is *all* woman and not all the time having to be hassled about every single little thing."

"So you're saying you're a man who likes to be taken care of and not have any responsibilities?" Divine pressed her lips tightly together.

"No," Darius said with a puckered smile. "I'm merely saying that I really enjoy my time with you. And as you can see, I'm not at all allergic to hard work if it's required. I would get out there and dig ditches . . . for you."

Divine tilted her head to the side. "Is *that* right now? Ditches?"

"Oh, Miss Divine, that *is* right. Don't believe me? I'll walk away right now, go out and find me something to do, and return and take care of you."

Divine broke out of his embrace. "I don't think you can find a regular job that can take care of me in the way I've grown accustomed. As you've noticed, I have quite expensive taste. I love the finer things of life, and I'm a subscriber of the good. I love good food, good wine, and good company. The company part, you can handle with no problem. Providing me with all the other stuff, including the mortgage on this house" — she looked around her large black-and-white-color-schemed bedroom — "well, let's not pretend. You and I both know that's not something you can handle."

"So what are you saying? You don't want me around?"

"I just told you I love good company. And you, my dearest Darius, have succeeded when it comes to fitting that bill beyond my wildest dreams."

"So if I can come up with a way to provide for you in the way you've grown accustomed, you'd consider spending the rest of your life with me?" Darius asked.

Divine smiled, then winked. "Fortunately for both of us, I'm not looking for anything beyond the here and now. And for now, Darius Connors, you're perfect for what I need."

He grabbed her by the hand and entwined his fingers with hers. "So tomorrow, should someone better come along, what would that mean for me?"

Divine glanced down at his hand locked with hers, then back up to his eyes. She rose up on the tips of her toes and gave him a peck on his lips. "Tomorrow will take care of tomorrow. Today . . . we enjoy today." She gave him a long, passionate kiss. "And right now, I'm starving! What say we go to my favorite restaurant and get something fabulous to demolish?"

Darius grinned. "I'm going to win you

over completely, do you hear me? I refuse to allow what we have to come to an end. You're the best thing that's ever happened to me. And I have no intention of losing you. Ever. So whatever it takes to keep you —"

"Change into your dark lavender shirt and those black pants I bought you the other day. I love seeing you in that shirt," Divine said, before turning and strolling away.

Darius watched her walk away with a full grin on his face. "Ruff, ruff!" he said, barking like a dog. "Ruff!"

She turned around and smiled. "Meow. Bow-wow," she said.

Chapter 19

Folly is joy to him that is destitute of wisdom: but a man of understanding walketh uprightly.

— Proverbs 15:21

The most popular restaurant in town these days was packed. Andrew had called ahead and made a reservation because he knew how long he and Paris would have to wait otherwise. She was too close to her due date that he definitely didn't want to put her through any more stress than necessary. And after his mother left the house, he could see Paris was really down. He was just thankful Paris hadn't heard any of the things his mother had said prior to her entering the house earlier that day.

He couldn't believe how much his mother didn't trust Paris. The idea that the baby she was carrying might not be his was absurd. They'd been trying to have a baby for over two years now. Of course, Paris wanted to get pregnant. Sure, she'd been really busy during the time she'd finally conceived. But everything had worked out. She'd found out she was pregnant and lost her job at the same time. Andrew couldn't have been happier. Now he was determined to show Paris how much he loved her. And he was not going to allow his mother to ruin things. He was not going to let the negative thoughts she was attempting to plant take root in his head.

Fifteen minutes after arriving, the head hostess showed them to their table.

"Thank you *so* much for bringing me here," Paris said. "I absolutely love this place! I'm just glad we didn't have to wait as long as some of those other folks are having to."

Andrew touched Paris's hand. "You know I'm going to take care of you and our baby. I know how hard it is for you if you have to stand or sit for too long."

"I really do appreciate it. You've been absolutely perfect ever since you learned I was pregnant."

Andrew chuckled. "Perfect, huh? Well, I don't know about all that. I did sort of pick you up and swing you around when I first found out the news until it hit me that doing something like that might not be the best thing for a developing baby."

"I'm pretty certain the baby enjoyed it. I can already see you swinging him or her around when he or she gets big enough to beg you to," Paris said.

The waitress came to take their order. As she was writing, someone bumped into her, almost knocking her flat onto the table.

"Oh, I'm sorry," the man said, helping to upright the waitress. "Forgive me."

Paris and the man's eyes connected immediately. "Paris?" he said.

"Darius?" Paris said.

Andrew looked from Paris up at the man. "This is Darius?"

"Hey, man. Darius Connors." Darius held out his hand to shake Andrew's. Andrew stood up. "It's good to finally meet you in person."

"Yes, it's nice to meet you." Andrew shook his hand. "I know we said we would do this sometime last year, but it never happened. Now, here we are."

"Yes . . . here we are," Darius said, looking at Paris. "Finally meeting."

Andrew looked at the woman standing beside Darius. "Hey, if you two would like to sit with us, Paris and I wouldn't mind. It's just the two of us. I'm sure the establishment would appreciate it since they're so crowded. It would free up an extra table and give us an opportunity to do what we planned to do last year."

Paris plastered a smile on her face like a plastic doll. "Honey, I'm sure the two of them don't want to —"

"Sure," said the woman standing next to Darius. "We'd love to."

Darius looked at the woman, then pulled out her chair. They both sat down.

"So you're Tiffany, right?" Andrew said, extending his hand to the woman.

"Oh, no," Darius said. "This is not Tiffany. This is Delilah . . . Delilah Vine."

"But everybody calls me Divine," Divine said, shaking Andrew's extended hand, after which she reached over to present her hand to Paris.

"Divine, huh?" Paris said, giving her the ends of her fingers to shake. "Is that like how the regular divine is spelled?" Paris's nose turned up slightly. Andrew could now see that Paris wasn't happy about any of this. He regretted asking them to join them. But how was he to know that woman wasn't Darius's wife?

"Actually, I go by Dee as in D-e-e. My last name really is Vine. But it's just easier to go by Divine, D-i-v-i-n-e so I just go by

Divine."

Darius chuckled. "Cute, huh?"

Paris grunted, then picked up her glass of water, tilted it, and took a few swallows.

"So, in asking you to join us, I didn't interrupt a business meeting or anything did I?" Andrew asked Darius.

"Oh, no. Our visit here is totally personal," Divine said.

"So, Darius," Paris said. "Are you and your wife, Tiffany, divorced?"

"No. But if you must know, we're headed in that direction," Darius said. He then turned to Divine. "Paris and I worked together last year for a few months. Her father is . . . oh, I'm sorry . . . *was* an Alabama congressman. You may have heard of him: Lawrence Simmons?"

"Oh, yes. In fact, he was my congress-man," Divine said. "I'm sorry to hear he had to drop out of the race so abruptly. Although I admit, I wasn't planning on vot-ing for him anyway. I don't care for a man who switches parties or partners in the middle of a game. I can't feel that you'll be loyal to me when you do something like that. It's like you have no real core or true value. I prefer to be who I am and if you don't care for me, then your loss. You understand where I'm coming from?" Divine said, addressing Paris.

Paris leaned in as much as her protruding belly would allow between her seat and the table. "Oh, absolutely." She smiled.

"I see that you're pregnant," Divine said. "Congratulations. Babies aren't really my thing. But I'm always happy for those who want them."

"Thanks," Paris said, then just as quickly turned a hard gaze at Darius.

"Darius, if I remember correctly *you* have three children," Andrew said.

Darius looked behind him for the waitress. He beckoned for her to come over before turning back to Andrew. "Yes, I do — two girls and a boy."

The waitress came over. Darius and Divine gave her their order.

"Will this be on a separate ticket?" the waitress asked no one in particular.

"You can add it to mine," Andrew said, then looked at Darius. "I planned to invite you to dinner last year. So let me do this now since we're all here."

"Oh, I'm sure Darius would rather take care of his own dinner since he's on a date," Paris said. "Wouldn't you, Darius? That's the kind of man Darius is . . . one who's not afraid to show how much of a real man he is."

Darius stared hard at Paris. "She's right." He then chuckled. "Real men don't have a problem with showing who they are." He turned back to the waitress. "Why don't you put their order on my ticket?" He then turned to Andrew. "My treat."

Divine touched Darius's arm. "Sweetheart, why don't we just pay for our food and let them pay for theirs? I mean —"

"No. I have money," Darius said. "This is nothing." He looked up at a now confused waitress. "Put it all on mine, please." He turned to Andrew. "I'll let you pick it up the next time."

Paris placed her thumb under her chin, her index finger on her lips as though she were telling someone to be quiet. As much as Andrew was trying to do something good, it was obvious to him that he'd messed up royally and Paris was clearly agitated.

Paris took her hand down. "So, Darius, it appears you've managed to land squarely on your feet since last we spoke. You must have a terrific-paying job."

"Oh, it's been rough now," Darius said. "I'm not going to sit here and front. After your father let me go, my wife became so despondent that we began having major problems, which led to me leaving my home for the sake of peace and the sake of our children. Not having a job caused me to have to live off the generosity of others. Yep. It's been rough for sure. But God . . ." Darius shook his head as though thinking about the goodness of God was causing him to become emotional.

"Yeah, Darius. I'm sure it's been *real* hard," Paris said, rolling her eyes with a sprinkle of sarcasm. "I'm sure your wife was all that you say she was during your *difficult* time. But just look at you now. You seem to have moved right along with your life . . . doing rather well, too: designer clothes, a charming woman on your arm, a job that apparently pays mega bucks."

"I don't know about mega bucks," Darius said, chuckling. "But I'm finally getting my footing on solid ground. I still have goals to reach, but I'm on my way." He leaned in. "So, when is your baby due?" he asked Andrew.

Andrew couldn't help but smile. "April twenty-eighth. In another two weeks if the baby comes early. Four weeks if the baby is on time like its father —"

"And six weeks if the baby turns out to be like its mother, arriving two weeks *after* the due date," Darius said with a contrived chuckle. He sat back against his chair shaking his head. "Come on, Paris. You know

I'm right. You know I *know* you. We worked together. There were plenty of times you were late. Andrew, you remember."

Paris picked up her glass of water. "Well, you know what they say: better late than *never.*" She tilted her glass his way almost like a toast.

The waitress brought their food and drinks.

"I'm sorry," Paris said, grabbing hold of Andrew's arm. "But all of a sudden, I don't feel so well. Can we get this to go? I'm sorry, dear. I was so looking forward to this night out."

Andrew looked at Paris. She did look a bit flushed. He turned to the waitress. "Would you please take my and my wife's plates back and make them to go?"

After their meals were ready, Andrew and Paris said their good-byes to Darius and Divine. . . . Well, *Andrew* said good-bye as they left.

But not before Darius said, as they were walking away, "Take good care of that baby now. You hear?"

CHAPTER 20

We have sinned with our fathers, we have committed iniquity, we have done wickedly.
— Psalm 106:6

Paris went to her parents' house the day after her disastrous dinner run-in with Darius. She was glad her mother was gone and her father was there alone.

"Okay, I know something's up, Paris," Lawrence said. "Your mother is worried about you. I've tried to reassure her, but it's obvious something is wrong. Now, I know you generally share things with your mother and not me. Whatever is going on, you're not even talking to her about it. So I need you to talk to me."

Paris started crying. "Daddy, I don't know what to do. I've talked to someone about it and her advice was for me to tell Andrew. But I can't. I just can't."

"Tell Andrew what? What's so awful that

you have to keep it in and it's clearly tearing you *up* inside. I've never seen you like this before." Lawrence took his daughter's hand and held it. "Your mother says your sudden outbursts of tears are likely hormones and connected to the changes babies can cause. Now, I do have a little experience when it comes to being around a pregnant woman considering your mother blessed me with three beautiful children, one of them sitting before me right now."

"Oh, Daddy," Paris said. "You always know what to say to make me feel better. I just don't know if you can fix this. I messed up. And I can't seem to bring myself to tell you, Mom, and especially not Andrew. I'm just so ashamed."

Lawrence chuckled. "Excuse me, but are you saying this to the ultimate mess-up in town? In case you haven't heard, which could only mean you've been living under a rock somewhere, but I have a child out of wedlock that caused me to have to give up one of the things I love doing the most: being a congressman."

"Daddy, I don't mean to be cruel, but you were going to lose your seat anyway. You didn't have a chance of winning as a black Republican, not in Alabama, and you know it."

"See, it's small-minded people like you that see things that way. White folks really liked me. And contrary to what people think, they would have voted for me even though I was black. And right now, there are more whites voting than blacks."

"Daddy, I truly don't want to debate or rehash politics today. I'm so *sick* of it," Paris said.

"You're right. I'm sorry. I was only trying to address the point that I've messed up myself, that I know what it feels like to have done things you don't want anyone to know," Lawrence said. "That's where I was going. Do you think I wanted to ever tell your mother or even you children, for that matter, that I'd not only had an affair essentially with a teenager, albeit she *was* eighteen and an adult at the time, but a child out of wedlock? Do you really think I was on my head to ever tell *that*?"

Paris rocked as she lowered and nodded her head. "I know. And I understand a lot better how you felt and what you must have gone through." She looked up at her father. "I do. And even though I was the first to judge you, I've discovered we really need to be careful in doing things like that. Because we *just* might find ourselves in the same or a similar predicament where someone is now in a place to judge us."

"It's like that scripture that talks about not judging because the same way we judge, we'll be judged. You know I'm not the best when it comes to quoting scriptures, but I'm sure you know which one I'm referring to," Lawrence said.

"Imani is the one who knows the scriptures like the back of her hand. That girl kind of scares me, but in a good way. If I didn't know any better, I would wonder if she was adopted; she's nothing like any of us." Paris chuckled a little.

Lawrence smiled and nodded. "So, baby girl, I need you to come clean with me. You know I love you, right?"

Paris squinted her eyes as she smiled. "Of course, Daddy. I know."

"Okay, then. Let's have a judge-free zone right here, right now. You tell your old daddy what's going on, and I promise it won't go any further than between the two of us. I won't even mention a word to your mother if you don't want me to. I promise. And who knows: Maybe I can shed some light and we can make it right."

Paris released an exasperated sigh and took her hand out of her father's. "This is between you and me and you and me only, right?"

"Cross my heart," Lawrence said as he made a cross over his chest where his heart resided.

"You know what they say about like father, like son?"

"Yeah."

"Well, I have a new one for you. How about like father, like daughter?" She forced a smile.

"Okay, I know folks say you and I are alike in more ways than probably either one of us cares to admit. Although, I'm going to say right here that I'm proud you're so much like me. It makes me feel good to know you've taken after me, at least with some of my better traits."

"Yeah, well, it's not just the better traits. It looks like you and I have other traits that neither of us is all that proud of." Paris looked up sheepishly at her father.

He nodded. "Just tell me, and we'll go from there."

"I cheated on Andrew." There, she said it.

Lawrence continued to nod without any physical outward reaction.

"You don't appear at all surprised by my revelation," Paris said.

Lawrence stopped nodding, smiled, and looked deep into her eyes. "Do you honestly think I didn't know that already?"

Paris continued to look at her father. Tears rolled down. She tried to smile, but the corners of her mouth trembled. "I suppose I didn't. You never said anything."

Using both thumbs, Lawrence wiped the tears from her face. He got up and brought over a box of tissues. "I think I should buy stock in these things," he said referencing the box of tissues. "Looks like somebody is always crying these days."

Paris yanked several tissues from the opening of the box. "I know I certainly have. And I know I've caused more than a few people to cry. I guess I'm merely reaping now what I've sown."

"We all make mistakes. It's part of life. It's part of being human." He gathered her up by her shoulders. "You understand? None of us is *always* going to get it right. Not me, not your mother, not you . . . not even that little one you're carrying. That's how life is. We're in it and we just have to deal with it the best way we can. But for sure, none of us is going to come out of this life without something or other we regret doing or having done."

Paris nodded as she dabbed her eyes. "So how long have you known?"

"Pretty much the morning after you and he slept together."

"Then you also know it was Darius?"

He snickered. "Daughter, please. I saw that train wreck coming a mile away. I was hoping you would come out unscathed, but you're grown. And you sure didn't want to hear *or* listen to anything I was trying to tell you during that period of time."

"No lectures today. Okay?"

"This is not a lecture. What I'm saying is that I knew Darius was no good. I probably share the blame because I was so desperate to try and tamp down both you *and* your efforts against Gabrielle that I placed you in the position of eventually finding yourself this way."

"Like you could have kept me and him from destroying ourselves," Paris said as she turned squarely to her father and grabbed both his hands. "Look, Daddy. I was determined to have my way. Darius was there willing and able to help me in any way that he could. Had we not worked together for your campaign, I was going to find a way, and he and I would have been together working on what I wanted regardless. Working for you likely slowed the timetable of when I was set to self-destruct."

Lawrence shook her hands along with his. "You're being a bit hard on yourself. You thought you were doing something right and noble. You thought, as it turns out rightly so, that Jasmine was my daughter. You wanted our family to stay intact, even knowing that one daughter of mine was illegitimate. How can I be mad at you for that? It's actually the kind of woman your mother and I raised you up to be."

Paris pressed her lips together as she shook her head. "No," she said. "That's not a completely accurate description of me or my actions. I wanted to get back at Gabrielle. I hated her so much, I wanted to make sure she didn't end up with that little girl, whether Jasmine was your daughter or not. In truth: if there had been indefensible proof that Jasmine was not your child, I still would have gone hard after Gabrielle to try and take her away. That was despicable of me. And in the end, my hate and pettiness has done more damage than I ever could have imagined."

Lawrence nodded. "I'm not going to lie, now. There was some true fallout that came from all that you did. Had you just walked away like I asked . . ." He let that train of thought go. "Hey, who can really say what would be different now? It is what it is. Now we just need to see where we are and where we need to go. Okay, so you and Darius slept together. It happens. Have you asked

God to forgive you?"

Paris laughed. "Yes, Daddy. Did you ask God to forgive *you*?"

He laughed. "Yes, daughter. And I asked your mother and you and your brother and even Imani, who still doesn't know that Jasmine is her half-sister."

"You know you're going to have to tell her, and soon. You don't want her to find out from some other place," Paris said. "There have been too many secrets surrounding all of this as it is. Imani will never forgive you if she finds out some way other than from you and Mom."

"I know. But Imani is sixteen, a lot younger than you and your brother. She may not take it in the way the two of you did. And Imani put herself out there for Jasmine in a way that neither of you did — she gave bone marrow to Jasmine," Lawrence said. "If she finds out she did that essentially for her half-sister and not just some stranger, you know she's going to want to go to her immediately and start up a sisterly relationship."

"I know. We've had this discussion as to why you can't do it now. I'm just telling you of the disaster that lies in wait if Imani finds out some other way."

"Well, right now I'm adhering to Gabrielle's wishes. She wants to wait until after her wedding in June. She says Jasmine has endured a lot these past two years and your mother and I agree with that. Jasmine was extremely sick. Her adoptive father died. She had to fight for her life. When she finally gets a reprieve with a bone marrow transplant that still put her out of commission as her body and immune system mended, her mother, or the only mother she knew, is diagnosed with cancer and dies. Then the poor child had to deal with being an orphan, only to learn that she was originally adopted and that the person stepping up to adopt her was her birth mother."

"Go ahead, Daddy, and say it. And I made things worse by being the villain to tell it so she could overhear that her birth mother, as I said it so clearly, didn't want her and essentially threw her away. *I* did that. *I* shattered that little girl's world. And why? Because I hated Gabrielle just that much. And I hated her even more when I discovered that my wonderful and devoted husband, who wouldn't stand by me as I launched my heroic crusade against the evil queen — the ex-exotic dancer better known as Goodness and Mercy — to rescue a damsel I perceived to be in distress, was legally representing *her* against *me.*" Paris nodded and dabbed her face with a dry tissue. "Well, I guess I showed everybody, didn't I, Daddy?"

Lawrence grabbed her hand and squeezed it. "Paris, I have to ask this. You know what I'm about to ask, don't you?"

She leaned her head back, then straightened it again. She nodded. "You want to know if there's any chance this baby I'm carrying is not Andrew's but Darius's."

Lawrence grabbed hold of her other hand and held them both.

Paris looked at her father as tears slid down her face. "Yes, Daddy. Yes, there is a chance. And I'm terrified that this baby is really Darius's and Andrew is going to find out the truth. Then he's going to leave me and the baby. And after everything that I've done, my child and I will be left all alone merely because Darius is a jerk. He now ignores the fact that there's a chance he might be the father —"

"So you've talked to Darius about it already?"

"Yes." She frowned. "Within the first few weeks of me learning that I was pregnant. I asked him to participate in a procedure with a short window where a paternity test could have been done. It's called prenatal paternity. But to do it, the father has to contribute his DNA. As you can imagine, I couldn't go to Andrew and ask him to participate to confirm that he was the father without him figuring out what was going on. Even if it the results had confirmed that Andrew definitely was the father, there would have been a lot of tension following that entire revelation."

"That's putting it mildly," Lawrence said. "Although Andrew really loves you. I'm sure the two of you would have worked through it though."

"Yeah, but too much stress during pregnancy is not good on a developing baby. I can't say for sure how Andrew would have reacted. He might have turned into a totally different man if he knew what I'd done," Paris said. "So I couldn't involve him at that point. I did, however, contact Darius and inform him of all that was going on. I asked him to submit to the prenatal DNA paternity test."

"And he wouldn't cooperate," Lawrence said, scooting back onto the couch.

Paris shook her head. "No, he wouldn't. And if he had, we could have eliminated him as the father, and since Andrew is the only other person I was with, I would know for sure right now that this baby is his."

"So why wouldn't Darius agree to do it?"

Lawrence asked. "I would think he would want to know early on himself."

Paris readjusted her body, placed her hand behind her back and arched it.

"Getting uncomfortable?" Lawrence asked as he watched Paris.

"A little. It gets like this when I don't move around." She stood up and arched her back again. "That's better." Paris looked down at her father, who leaned forward, crossed his leg, and locked his fingers around his knee. "One of the reasons he likely balked about it was the cost. I told him I would put in half. But when you're talking two thousand dollars and it comes to a cheapskate like Darius, you can forget it."

"Yes, he's definitely not one to pay for anything if he can manage to get it for free or manipulate someone else into footing the bill." Lawrence leaned back, his fingers still locked around his knee. "We call those kinds of people moochers."

"Oh, but last night at the restaurant he was Mr. Moneyman," Paris said as she gently and slowly eased back down on the couch next to her father.

Lawrence released his locked fingers and planted both feet squarely on the floor. "Mr. Moneyman? Last night? Restaurant?"

"Yeah." Paris smiled. "Andrew took me to that expensive restaurant out on two-eighty; you know the one you and Mom like to patronize a lot. I'm not even going to try and pronounce the name of it, but you know the one I'm talking about."

Lawrence chuckled. "I know which one. I'm with you; I let your mother say it and leave it alone. She's the one who knows French in the family."

"Anyway, Andrew took me there and who comes strolling in, and almost flattens our waitress by knocking her down, but Darius. And he's with some woman."

"Some woman? But he's married with children," Lawrence said.

"Apparently that's about to be all over soon. The woman he was with is named Dee Vine, but she combines the two names and calls herself Divine," Paris said. "He must have been trying to impress her or something because when Andrew offered to pay for everyone's meal, Darius decided to trump Andrew and pay for ours. He is *such* a *jerk*!"

Lawrence reached over and patted her hand. "Calm down now. Don't let this upset you."

Paris frowned. "Daddy, he made me so mad that I got sick just being in his presence. He was throwing off about my baby. He knows it's possible the baby might be his, so he was trying to toy with me and, on the sly, mess with Andrew." Paris released a sigh. "So that's where I am right now. I'm pregnant with a baby me and my husband have been praying for, and I'm not sure now that it's his baby. I talked with Johnnie Mae —"

"Johnnie Mae? Who is Johnnie Mae?"

"Our new pastor's wife. Remember, I told you that Andrew and I joined Pastor George Landris's church?"

"Yes, yes, you don't have to remind me. I'm still praying you and Andrew will come to your senses and come back to the church you grew up in and where you belong."

"Daddy, we're not coming back. Spiritually, we weren't growing there."

"Fine. Fine. But you're telling me that you've actually spoken to someone outside the family about what's going on with you and *this*?"

"Yes. I had to talk to somebody. And at the time, I didn't feel comfortable telling you or Mom the truth about what was going on. I sure couldn't talk to Andrew about it, although Johnnie Mae says I need to tell him the truth. She says the truth always has a way of coming out eventually. And that it's better when you're in control of it instead of leaving it in the hands of others who don't have your best interest at heart." Paris looked toward the ceiling. "I wanted to tell Andrew. In fact: I tried." She shook her head and looked directly into her father's eyes. "I just couldn't do it. It's so hard to get the words out when you don't know what will come next."

"I don't know if I agree with the advice your first lady gave you. She may have good intentions, but I see no good to come out of telling Andrew this without knowing for sure," Lawrence said. "I mean what if Andrew *is* the father? Why put yourself through something for nothing. I'd say just let things play out, for now. Andrew is ecstatic about this baby. Why go and ruin things for him at this juncture?"

"So you're saying I *shouldn't* tell him? Not even after the baby comes?"

Lawrence grabbed her hands again. "Let's say the baby *is* Darius's. Do you really think Darius will step up and do right by this child? The man's a playa minus the *e-r.* He has three children now, that we know of, and you've seen firsthand how good of a father he is to them."

"I don't know. He seems to be great about his children. It's his wife he didn't seem to do right."

"Okay. Maybe it's not fair to say he's not a good father. Maybe he has been and maybe he is now. But he's demonstrating to you already that he doesn't care anything about the baby you're carrying."

"That's true. But I'm praying that the baby I'm carrying isn't his, so it won't matter."

"On the other hand, Andrew wants this baby more than anything, right?" Lawrence asked.

"Yes. Absolutely," Paris said.

"Then even if the baby is *not* his biologically, why would you hurt him by taking this child away from him?" Lawrence forced a smile through his frown.

"Because I would feel like I'm lying to both of them. Andrew deserves to know the truth, doesn't he? Then he can decide what he wants to do from the side of truth. If he still wants to be the baby's father, at least I'll know he's doing it from the right place. I don't want this baby to not be his and, God forbid, something happens down the road and he discovers the truth. What if after learning the truth Andrew decides to walk away? How would that affect my baby then?"

"You're right. It's a difficult decision and

a difficult call to make," Lawrence said. "And I'm probably the wrong person to be giving advice since I messed up so royally when it came to my own call when faced with the same issue. Maybe that's the cautionary tale for you, daughter. Maybe that Johnnie lady was right. Maybe the best thing *is* the truth and to just let the chips fall where they may. But I'll say one more time: If it was me, I'd probably wait until *after* the baby is born. Maybe there's a way for you to find out the paternity after the baby arrives without Andrew ever knowing what you're up to. You're a smart girl. You're a Simmons."

"Maybe you're on to something, Daddy. You know they *do* have these home DNA kits now." Paris's face lit up. "I could swab the inside of Andrew's cheek while he's asleep maybe. Take some from the baby. Send it off. Get back a definitive answer. And if the baby *is* Andrew's, I can drop all of this and we can carry on with our lives as though nothing ever happened."

"See, now you're thinking like a *true* Simmons," Lawrence said with a slight laugh behind his words.

"But if the baby is *not* Andrew's, I'm going to tell him the truth," Paris said with a sigh and a determined look.

"Sounds like a game-winning plan to me." Lawrence stood up and opened his arms as he waited for Paris to fill them.

Paris stood up and allowed her father to totally engulf her with a nice warm hug. "Thanks, Daddy. Who would have ever thought you'd be so much help with this."

"Yeah, I know, right? That's always been your mother's department. But maybe I was better equipped to handle this one because I've been where you are now." He kissed her on the top of her head, lingering a little longer than necessary. "I love you, cupcake. You hear me? And if you need someone to talk to about this later on, you come to me. You don't need to be putting your personal business out there to some stranger like that Johnnie Mae lady. We're family. I'm here for you. I mean that."

"I know." Paris hugged him back tightly. "I know. And I love you, Daddy." She began to cry again.

"And I love you. So stop all this crying. You hear me?" He held her now with tears in his eyes. "I love you, baby girl."

CHAPTER 21

Then Naomi her mother-in-law said unto her, My daughter, shall I not seek rest for thee, that it may be well with thee?
— Ruth 3:1

"Gabrielle," Miss Crowe had whispered over the phone when she'd left the message on voice mail. "I don't mean to bother you, but something is going on here at the house and I think you need to get here as soon as you can. Jasmine is fine, so it's not anything to do with her at all. But if you can, hurry and get home."

Gabrielle had gotten the message and left work an hour earlier than she'd originally planned, thankful that being the dance director at Followers of Jesus Faith Worship Center allowed her to do things like this.

"Thank the Lord, you got my message," Miss Crowe said, greeting her before she got in the house good.

"Yeah, I got it. What's going on? You say Jasmine is all right?"

Miss Crowe kept her voice low. "Yes, of course. You know if it had been anything to do with Jasmine directly I would have told you that on the message. I wouldn't dare have you to worry like that." Miss Crowe looked back. "But your aunt Cee-Cee is here with one of her sons. They're in there with your father, and I'm not liking what I'm hearing coming from that crew."

"What did you hear?" Gabrielle whispered back.

"It's that boy mainly. Well, I suppose you can't actually call him a boy anymore, but it's the son who's doing most of the selling. I think his name is Jesse?"

"Yes, Jesse would be right. What's he trying to sell? But even if he has something to sell, it's not like my father has any money to buy it."

"I suppose selling is a figure of speech and a bit misleading. Jesse's trying to get your father to go work for this place, but it's not adding up. The troubling part is that your father seems interested and your aunt isn't helping as *she's* pushing it, too. You know if she's pushing something, there *has* to be something not right about it."

"I'll check and see what's going on," Gabrielle said.

"I hope I didn't sound an alarm for nothing," Miss Crowe said. "But I have a bad feeling about all of this. I didn't think it was my place to butt my nose in it. So I decided to call you and let you. I wasn't sure if you'd be able to get home in time, and maybe I should have waited for you to arrive normally and tell you —"

Gabrielle touched Miss Crowe's hand. "No, you did the right thing. I'm with you when it comes to both my aunt *and* my cousin Jesse. I'm not saying my father is not street-smart if they're trying to finagle him —"

"But he also may be primed to get involved with the wrong thing."

"And he's still on probation. He's been a bit dejected lately with the job prospects not panning out and the fact that no one seems to want to give an ex-con a chance. He might be easily talked into doing something he shouldn't do."

"My sentiments exactly," Miss Crowe said.

"Where's Jasmine?"

"I made her go to her room and read a book as soon as your father let them in and led them into the den, where he and Jasmine had been watching the Disney Channel."

Gabrielle took a deep breath. "That's good. I told my father I would prefer my aunt not be here when I'm not at home."

"Yeah, I heard you when you told him that. I probably wouldn't have called you, but, like I said, I didn't care for what I was hearing. If they're in the process of doing something illegal, directly or not, I don't want you involved in *any* way."

Gabrielle shrugged. "Well, I suppose I'll go see what's up." Gabrielle stepped away, then came back over and kissed Miss Crowe on the cheek. "Thank you. You are such a blessing."

"Yeah . . . well . . . right back at you," Miss Crowe said with a wink. "Now go on and handle your business. And if you need me, just know I have my ears tuned and I can move a lot faster than folks think. I'll be in there in a flash."

"I'm sure I'll be all right." Gabrielle touched her hand, then left and headed for the den. She stood outside the entranceway and listened in a minute. Just as Miss Crowe had said, Aunt Cee-Cee and Jesse were there with her father. She walked in. "What's going on in here?" Gabrielle said.

"Hey, there, Gabrielle." Bennie stood up,

walked over, and gave Gabrielle a quick peck on the cheek. "Look who stopped by unannounced."

"Yes, I see."

Aunt Cee-Cee gave Gabrielle a quick nod of acknowledgment. "Gabrielle. How are you?"

"Hey, cuz!" Jesse said as he jumped up and hurried over to Gabrielle, wrapping his arms around her and giving her a bear hug. "What's poppin'?"

Gabrielle instantly could tell that Jesse was on something, some kind of drug. He couldn't be still for more than two seconds. He was bouncing around almost like his pants were full of ants.

"Jesse, come and sit back down," Aunt Cee-Cee said, patting the couch cushion. "I'm sure Gabrielle doesn't want you all over her."

"Sure, Mom. Sure," Jesse said. "So Uncle Bennie, what do you think? Are you interested? I'm telling you, there's some real easy money to be made."

"What does he think about what?" Gabrielle asked Jesse.

"Jesse, please come and sit down next to me." Aunt Cee-Cee patted the couch cushion again.

"I'm cool, Ma. I'm good. I've got all this

energy. I need to burn it off."

"Jesse . . . what opportunity are you talking about?" Gabrielle asked again as she directed her full attention to her cousin, who was only a few years younger than her.

"Hey, cuz! Come to think of it, you might be interested in getting in on this yourself. Everybody can always use some extra cash."

"Jesse! I said to hush up and come sit down!" Aunt Cee-Cee said.

"Why don't you want me to tell Gabrielle? She could likely use some extra money just like Uncle Bennie here. Didn't you say she was getting married soon? She might be interested in becoming a smurf or a cook." He twitched and scratched. His face had visible burn-looking marks and scars in several places.

"Jesse!" Aunt Cee-Cee said as she stood up and hurried in front of him to block him from Gabrielle. "I told you to hush up!"

"Mom, I'm just trying to get as many people in this as possible. The more smurfs we can get, the more —"

Aunt Cee-Cee pressed her hand against his mouth. "Shut . . . up! Now!"

Jesse stepped away and did a quick dance. "Why do you want me not to tell Gabrielle what was all right to tell Uncle Bennie?"

"Yes, Aunt Cee-Cee," Gabrielle said, turning her attention to her aunt. "Why might that be?"

"Because this is menfolk business," Aunt Cee-Cee said.

"You're here," Gabrielle said. "And if I'm not mistaken, this *is* my house."

"Okay, Gabrielle. I know you don't care for me. But my brother is living here and I have every right to come by and check on him."

"Cee-Cee," Bennie said. "That's enough. It's time for you and Jesse to go."

"But Angie is not due back to pick us up for another hour," Aunt Cee-Cee said to Bennie.

"Well, you need to call her and tell her to get back here so she can take you home," Bennie said.

"So you're just going to put us out? Just like that?" Aunt Cee-Cee said to Bennie. "We're family and, once again, we're getting dissed just like before. Nobody would believe all that I did for you, Gabrielle, and for you, dear brother, when I took your child into our home and gave her shelter and fed her hungry mouth."

Gabrielle raised her hand. "Please don't attempt to go there, Aunt Cee-Cee. I really don't want to hear it. Not today."

"Of course, you don't," Aunt Cee-Cee

said with a jeer.

"So, Cee-Cee, get on your little phone and call your daughter to come and get y'all," Bennie said.

"It's not going to make any difference. I can call Angie now, but I can pretty much say that it will still likely be an hour before she gets here. That's how Angie is."

"Well, then perhaps I can help you," Zachary said, strolling into the den.

Gabrielle turned and looked his way. "Zachary." She smiled and released a sigh of relief.

He strolled over and kissed Gabrielle on the cheek. "Is there a problem here?"

"No," Aunt Cee-Cee said. "No problem. My son and I came over to see my brother and it appears we have overstayed our welcome."

"Well, fortunately for you, I have my car right outside, and I'll be more than happy to drive you home."

Aunt Cee-Cee twitched her nose. "We wouldn't want to put you out. Angie will be back shortly."

"Tell you what," Zachary said. "Call Angie and tell her not to bother coming. I'm taking you home. It will be my pleasure."

Jesse's head was twitching repeatedly to one side.

Zachary looked at Jesse. "Hey, my man, what's up with you?" Zachary asked.

"I'm good. Just came to help my uncle out, that's all." He scratched his chest.

Zachary walked over to Jesse and looked him over. "What are you on? What have you been taking?"

Jesse laughed. "On? Taking? Man, I'm good. I'm a giver, not a taker."

"No . . . you're not good," Zachary said.

Jesse suddenly started backing away from Zachary as though he was frightened of him. "Who sent you to spy on me?" He squatted down a little and looked around. "*They* sent you, didn't they?"

"They who?" Zachary said, looking around as well. "Who sent me?"

"Those people who are always following me. You know who. You're part of them, aren't you?" Jesse began to slap his own face.

"Jesse! Jesse! Stop that," Aunt Cee-Cee said, grabbing his hands and holding him still. She then turned to Zachary. "He's ADHD. He needs medication. But without a job, he has no insurance so he can't get the medication he needs. He'll be all right."

"So he's self-medicating?" Zachary said.

"Man, I don't believe in medi . . . cation," Jesse said. "You can't trust these doctors.

They'll experiment on you and you won't even know it," Jesse said.

"That's not true," Zachary said.

"Oh, yeah, yeah, right." Jesse bounced around. "I keep forgetting you're one of them. You're a doctor. You're in with them, so of course you're going to deny it. But I know about the Tuskegee experiment with those men that time." Jesse scratched his chest. "I know all about it."

"Listen, you need help," Zachary said. "You've been smoking meth, haven't you? You have all the signs."

"Man, you're crazy. I don't *do* drugs. My mama just told you that I'm just hyper or I have attention problems. And there are all of these bugs that keep crawling all over my body biting me. They're making me itch. It's where we live now. Everybody ain't able to stay in a fancy house like my cousin here." He turned to Gabrielle. "Ain't that right, cuz?"

"Jesse, Zachary is right," Bennie said. "You're on something, and it's messing with your mind in a bad way."

"You know what, old man? Forget I came over here to help you. Mama told me you were in need of a job. I came over here to try and help you," Jesse said. "And look how you're turning on me." Jesse turned to Aunt

Cee-Cee. "Come on, Mama. We don't have to stay around here and take this. Let's go."

"We can't go. Angie's not here yet," Aunt Cee-Cee said to Jesse.

"I told you I'd be glad to drive you home," Zachary said.

"Man, we ain't going nowhere with you. You'll probably try and take me to a hospital or worse, the police station. I know you're with them people who are out to get me. But I'm not going to fall for it." Jesse turned to Aunt Cee-Cee. "Come on, Mama. We can walk and Angie can pick us up along the way. But I'm not going to stay here with these crazy folks."

Bennie came over and placed his large, worn hand on Jesse's shoulder. "You need help, son. You're going down the wrong road. If you're not careful, you're going to find yourself locked away. I've been there. And believe me: You don't want to go there. You hear?"

"Yeah, yeah, yeah," Jesse said. "I hear you. But I have no intentions of killing anybody, least of all my wife like you did. So I'm good, old man."

"Jesse! That's enough!" Aunt Cee-Cee said. "Come on, we're going." Aunt Cee-Cee grabbed Jesse by the hand and pulled him. He yanked his hand out of hers and picked up his backpack off the floor by the couch. Aunt Cee-Cee grabbed him by his wrist again and continued out of the den.

Zachary walked behind them. "I'll drive you —"

"No thank you," Aunt Cee-Cee said, continuing to drag Jesse along. "We'll be fine. We don't need your help or anybody else's for that matter." Aunt Cee-Cee threw a nasty look Gabrielle's way.

"Cee-Cee, please don't be like this. The boy needs help," Bennie said.

"We'll be fine, Bennie. We've managed fine all this time without you. We'll manage fine now." Aunt Cee-Cee stopped and looked hard at Gabrielle. "And you don't have to worry. I won't be gracing your precious little front door again."

"Cee-Cee!" Bennie said.

"Good-bye, Bennie. When you find another place to live, somewhere your family is welcome, then let me know and I'll come see you there." Aunt Cee-Cee stomped hard, dragging Jesse to the front door as she shoved him out first, then slammed the door behind them.

Chapter 22

And when the barbarians saw the venomous beast hang on his hand, they said among themselves, No doubt this man is a murderer, whom, though he hath escaped the sea, yet vengeance suffereth not to live.

— Acts 28:4

"Mr. Booker, what are you doing?" Zachary said, clearly frustrated with all that had just gone down with Aunt Cee-Cee and Jesse.

Bennie looked at Zachary. "I knew what was going on. You think I just fell from the sky the day I showed up here at this house?"

Zachary put his hands on his hips. "No. But you know you're on parole. I'm sure when your sister and that son of hers showed up here talking about some kind of work, you should have figured out he was trying to rope you into something illegal. Do you realize they will throw you right back in prison for doing anything you don't have any business doing?"

Bennie stared hard at Zachary. "You know, you haven't liked me since the first day I stepped foot in this house."

"I don't like *or* dislike you. I really don't know you, to be honest. I only know that you're a mur—"

"Zachary!" Gabrielle shouted, then shook her head.

"It's okay," Bennie said. "Let him get everything out. Then maybe we can move on. I'm a murderer. That's what you were about to say."

Gabrielle placed her hand over her mouth.

"I just don't understand how you could do something like you did," Zachary said. "Then you just show up on the doorstep of the very person you hurt the most with your actions. And Gabrielle has such a kind, forgiving heart; she wasn't going to turn you away." Zachary put two fingers up to his forehead and shook his head. Taking his hand down from his head, he entwined his fingers, pressing the remaining two index fingers together and his two thumbs and bringing his index fingers up to his lips. After being quiet for a few seconds, he took his hands down and merely shook his head. "How? That's what I still can't wrap my head around. How?"

"I loved my wife," Bennie said.

"And I love your daughter," Zachary said. "And the thought of me *ever* putting my hands on her to hurt her in any way . . ."

"To be honest with you," Bennie said. "Were you to ever put your hands on my daughter to physically hurt her, I'd likely be going back to prison for sure."

"Yeah," Zachary said. "That's what I mean. You feel that way about *your* daughter, but you didn't feel that way about someone else's daughter? I'm not trying to browbeat you on this. It's just — I'm sitting back trying to keep my mouth closed and let Gabrielle run things the way she thinks is right. And you're doing stuff like having the very person who has done nothing *but* hurt Gabrielle come in her house while her meth-head son is apparently trying to bring you into the business of doing what?"

"He was saying I could be a smurf, which I only remembered as being those little blue cartoon characters that came on television when Gabrielle was a baby," Bennie said.

Zachary nodded. "Well, I hope you know that a smurf, in today's terminology, especially on the streets, is a person who buys things from the drugstore with pseudoephedrine — that's a decongestant found in cold medicines as in Sudafed. You buy the pills and sell them to folks who have meth labs so they can cook up meth."

"That was the other thing he was telling me these folks were in need of: a cook," Bennie said.

"Of course," Zachary said. "Because people who are cooks in the meth kitchen produce a higher rate of turnover in the 'business.' That's because when you don't mix the recipe just right, you tend to blow up the lab and yourself along with it. I'm a burn specialist and a good many of my patients these days are the few who manage to survive a meth lab explosion, if you want to call it surviving. They bring patients to us from all over Alabama. They've passed laws here in Alabama to try and curb meth sales and meth making. But mostly what they've done is made the ones determined to make it find other ways to get the ingredients they need. Therefore you end up with a need for a lot of smurfs, folks who use their now-required government-issued IDs to purchase what is presently a nine-gram limit of behind-the-counter medicine for the month."

"Nine grams?" Bennie said. "I'm sorry, but everybody didn't go to college and get a degree like you."

"Nine grams is about seventy-five pills of the twelve-hour dosage package," Zachary said. "If they can get enough folks to go in and buy the pills and sell those pills to them, then they can manage to work around the law."

"Well, I used to hear folks talking all about this when I was locked up. But after I gave my life over to the Lord, I really didn't care to be around much talk about stuff that I knew I'd never be interested in," Bennie said. "Say what you want, but even before I went to prison, I was never dumb enough to want to do drugs or get involved in selling the stuff."

"So did you know what Jesse was trying to get you into?" Gabrielle said.

Bennie looked at her. "I knew something was going on with the boy. I knew he needed help, and quick. And it was obvious to me the first time my sister came here to see me that she's all about what will benefit her. But, she's still my sister. I'm trying to live godly." Bennie turned to Zachary. "So when I saw that young man twitching, jerking, and scratching like he was doing, I knew something was going on with him drug-related. If you had asked me to name the drug of choice, I wouldn't have said meth. But I knew it was something. I was trying to gain his confidence."

"Is that what you were doing?" Miss Crowe said, stepping into the room. "Really now, Bennie?"

Bennie turned to Miss Crowe. "Esther, I swear to you, that's all. I know you might have heard some of what they were saying and you thought I was going along with them. But as I just said: I was trying to gain Jesse's confidence so I could try and talk some sense into him." Bennie then turned to Gabrielle. "You believe me, don't you?"

"Of course, she believes you," Zachary said, still clearly frustrated. "You're her father. She wants to believe you're on the right side."

"I'm not running any con here," Bennie said. He continued to look at Gabrielle. "I promise you, I would never do anything to hurt you. We've managed to move *somewhat* forward in our fragile relationship. I'm not going to do anything, if I can help it, to break the tie we're beginning to forge. You believe me, don't you, Gabrielle? Please tell me you believe me." Bennie touched the elbow of her folded arms.

Gabrielle looked up at him and twisted her mouth a few times. "I asked you not to have Aunt Cee-Cee in my house when I'm not here. I know you think you can handle her, but you don't know her, not the way I do."

Bennie nodded. "You're right. You did ask that of me. And I was wrong to have let her in. It won't happen again. But I need to know that you believe I wouldn't do anything to hurt you. I need to know that you know I love you."

Gabrielle looked at him, then suddenly ran out of the room.

Zachary ran after her. She was in her bedroom crying.

"I want to believe him, Zachary," Gabrielle said. "But what if he's just playing me? What if he and Aunt Cee-Cee are in cahoots together? I mean they *are* brother and sister. But he's my father. I want so much to believe he loves me and that I'm enough."

"Gabrielle, you don't need his approval. You *are* enough. In fact, you're more than enough. I promise you." Zachary lifted her off the bed, where she was lying face down, and he held her together by her shoulders. "For me . . . for Jasmine . . . for all the folks who have been blessed to cross your path in one way or another, you *are* enough. Your aunt Cee-Cee was a jerk. If you ask me, I say she still is."

"And my father?"

"Your father *appears* to be sincere. My problem with him is probably colored by his past. I'm more on alert when it comes to you and him because I want to protect you. And if he's really as slick as the devil, then I know I need to have my eyes wide open to pick up on any clues, no matter how subtle. If you ask me what I think after these few months of him being here, I would say he really cares and he's trying." Zachary smiled. "But when it comes to protecting the women in my life, the women I love, which includes you, Jasmine, and Aunt Esther in this house, then I'm going to stay on post. Understand?"

Gabrielle nodded, then hugged Zachary and held on to him for dear life.

At eight-forty-five, Miss Crowe rapped lightly on Gabrielle's bedroom door. "Gabrielle, I just want you to know that I've put Jasmine to bed and the kitchen is all cleaned up. Good night, dearest. And good-bye to you, Zachary."

Zachary and Gabrielle both snickered. Miss Crowe didn't have to worry about Zachary staying the night there. The two of them had made a commitment to God, and they were holding firm to it no matter how much there was the opportunity to give in.

"I suppose I should go and let you get

251

some rest," Zachary said.

"Could you hold me for just a few minutes more?" Gabrielle said. "It's so peaceful right here. When you're gone, all I'll be left with are my thoughts. And for just a little longer, I'd rather not be alone with them."

Zachary hugged her. "You haven't said anything but a word." He continued to hold her. She began to drift off to sleep.

CHAPTER 23

As obedient children, not fashioning yourselves according to the former lusts in your
ignorance.

— 1 Peter 1:14

Bennie left early that morning (after Jasmine was off to school and Gabrielle was
off to work) telling Miss Crowe he had an
important appointment he had to make. She
heard the horn blow outside and Bennie
open the front door as he yelled back toward
the kitchen that he'd see her later.

Miss Crowe didn't care since she liked being in the house by herself. She had calls to
make for the wedding, mainly to find out
when she could expect the invitations to arrive since there would be two hundred of
them to properly address and mail. Jasmine,
a little computer whiz, had helped her
design things right on the computer. They
were able to print off what they'd done and

get Gabrielle's final approval before commencing mass printing. Miss Crowe couldn't believe how much technology had changed things. Back in her day, you had to visit a shop, tell them what you wanted, wait for them to order it, and hope it was what you desired.

With this new computer technology, you could design what you wanted using the online company's graphics and templates while being able to make it personal, even incorporating your own photos if you liked. She and Jasmine had had magnets made up with Gabrielle and Zachary's engagement photo (which Miss Crowe and Jasmine had to force them to take with the photographer they'd lined up). The magnets were four by six inches and were created to put on the refrigerator to remind folks to save the date of the scheduled wedding. Miss Crowe had loved the idea when little Miss Smarty Pants Jasmine suggested it.

"This way people will know not to make plans for that day because they'll be getting an official invitation for it in the future," Jasmine had said.

It was ingenious! Miss Crowe knew etiquette, and that invitations generally have a specific timeline to be sent out. The problem was with people having so much going on these days; there were times when people would miss a wedding because they didn't know an invitation was on the way. This way they'd know.

Still, Miss Crowe didn't quite trust everything, so she'd written down the toll-free number of the company where the invitations were being shipped from just to make sure the notice they'd received the day before stating the invitations were en route was accurate. After pressing one for this and two for that, Miss Crowe was thoroughly frustrated in the lack of another human on the other end.

But she got a lot done before Jasmine came home from school so she was happy.

"Miss C! Miss C!" Jasmine said as she burst through the front door. "The ice-cream man is coming! I saw him. He's just down the block. May I *please* have some Popsicle money? Please, please!" She used her prayer hands and melting smile.

Miss Crowe chuckled. "Of course, you can. Let me get my purse real quick."

"Hurry, hurry! I don't want him to leave before I get back out there."

Miss Crowe laughed to herself. "It's not like we don't have ice-cream goodies and Popsicles in the freezer here," she yelled back as she went into the den and found her purse where she'd left it yesterday after she'd put the twenty dollars she'd gotten Gabrielle to bring her the day before from the bank. She took out her wallet, wishing she had a five-dollar bill so she wouldn't have to send Jasmine out there with her only twenty. But a twenty was all she had so she would have to emphasize to Jasmine to bring her back her change.

She opened the part where she put her paper bills. It wasn't there. She looked again as though by magic it would somehow appear. Empty. She then looked in other places, wondering if her mind might be slipping and she'd not remembered her normal routine and stuck it somewhere else. It wasn't anywhere in her wallet. She distinctly remembered: she had asked Gabrielle to cash a check for twenty dollars and bring her the cash. Gabrielle had cashed it and given her the money yesterday before she left for work, having forgotten to give it to her when she came home the night before. She had taken the twenty and promptly walked into the den, where she'd left her purse the night before when she and Jasmine had placed an online order.

"Miss C! He's here! We're going to miss him!" Jasmine yelled, obviously half inside and half outside the door.

Not wanting Jasmine to miss out, Miss Crowe looked in her change pocket and counted out three dollars' worth of change, hoping that would be enough for *something* on the ice-cream truck. Back in her day, a quarter was plenty, but definitely not these days.

"Here! Here!" Miss Crowe said walking to the front door. "Run!" She stood at the door and watched as Jasmine jumped up and down to get his attention as he had just driven by. Thankfully, he backed up and Jasmine came back in the house with a chocolate candy-covered vanilla ice-cream bar.

"Thank you, Miss C! You're the best!" Jasmine said.

"Yeah, well, we can't be doing this every day now. I'm sure your mother won't appreciate you having too many sweets like this."

"I told you she doesn't care. She wants me to be happy." Jasmine grinned. "So, you didn't want anything?"

"No, darling. We have plenty of ice cream in the freezer. In fact, I think we have a whole box of what you just bought from him. And they're a lot cheaper than you most likely paid for that one."

"Oh, yeah," Jasmine said. "I almost forgot." She held out her hand that had a small trace of vanilla ice-cream on it now. "Here's your change."

Miss Crowe looked at the coin in her hand. "A quarter? So that one little thing was two dollars and seventy-five cents?"

"Yep," Jasmine said, popping her *p*.

"You can buy a whole box of those things for two dollars and seventy-five cents. And if you buy the store brand, it's even cheaper than that."

"Yeah, but there's just something different about getting one from the ice-cream man." Jasmine bit into her ice-cream bar.

Miss Crowe nodded. "Yes, there is. And as long as you enjoy it and don't drip it on everything, we'll all be fine. Now go on in the kitchen and finish it at the table."

Jasmine went in the kitchen and finished her ice-cream bar as she was told. She went in the half-bathroom and washed the stickiness off her hands. "Can I watch *Finding Nemo* before I do my homework?"

Miss Crowe tilted her head slightly and cracked a little smile. "*Can* you?"

"Okay. I know. Yes, I can. *May* I watch *Finding Nemo* before I do my homework?"

"You watched that DVD yesterday. How many times can a person watch something before you get tired of it?"

"I don't know. But when I discover the

number, I'll let you know."

Miss Crowe put her hand on her hip. "You're a little smart one, aren't you?"

"That's what everybody keeps telling me. I'm just trying to live up to the words spoken over my life. That's what Pastor Landris said. He told parents and other folks that they need to be careful of the words they speak over others, especially their children. Because people are speaking blessings or curses according to what comes out of their mouth. Everybody keeps saying how smart I am, therefore I am."

Miss Crowe shook her head. "Well, since you've been such a huge help to me and we both know you're going to get your homework done, then you *may* watch your little DVD. But after it goes off, I want you to do your homework. Okay?"

"Yes, ma'am," Jasmine said with a giggle. "It's not a lot of homework anyway. I'll be through in less than thirty minutes."

"That's good." Miss Crowe smiled.

Jasmine ran over and hugged her. "Miss C, I love you! I'm so glad you're here with us. I hope you decide to stay after Dr. Z and my mom get married."

"I don't know about all of that. But I'm here for now. So we'll just make the best of our time together. That way if for whatever reason I'm ever not in your life, we'll always have our memories. That's what happened with your mom and me. I got hurt really bad and couldn't get back to her. But she always had the memories we created together. And ironically, I had the memories of her with me. When I *did* see her again, everything clicked. I got well, and here I am — down here planning the biggest day this town may ever see."

"Dr. Z says we're being too dramatic about everything," Jasmine said. "He and Mama say we're going way over the top with this wedding and Mama keeps saying she's getting nervous."

Miss Crowe laughed, throwing her head back. "Isn't it grand when you have your own money and you can do something for another, going as far over the top as your heart desires, and no one can really stop you."

"I suppose," Jasmine said. "I don't get over-the-top money. I only get lunch money and five dollars a week for an allowance, a dollar of which I always take out and put in church."

"I'm sure the Lord appreciates your heart. I know some grown folks that don't put a dollar a week in church. But the Lord does love a cheerful giver." Miss Crowe became somewhat solemn as she thought about her missing twenty dollars. "Miss Jazz, by any chance did you see a twenty-dollar bill lying around in the den anywhere?"

"No, ma'am," Jasmine said wobbling her head back and forth. "Mama, I'm talking about my first mother this time . . . the one who got cancer and died before Miss G came along and became my mother. Mama always said we don't find money in the house. If we see it, it doesn't belong to us, and we need to find the true owner."

"That's right." Miss Crowe nodded. "Well, you go on in and watch your movie while I finish up supper. We're having meatloaf, mashed potatoes, spinach, and candied yams."

"I used to not like spinach. But the way you cook it, it's one of my favorite things now," Jasmine said.

"Is that right?" Miss Crowe said. "Well, it's likely because I use fresh spinach, not that canned kind which has a completely different taste from fresh. And" — Miss Crowe leaned down to whisper it as though someone might overhear her, even though she and Jasmine were the only two people in the house — "I put real butter in mine." She winked.

Jasmine smiled.

"Okay, go on. Your mother will be home soon. This is her day to get off early."

Jasmine skipped into the den. Not even a minute later, Jasmine called out to Miss Crowe who rushed into the den.

"What's the matter? Why are you hollering for me like that?" Miss Crowe asked with a frown, her hand holding her heart.

"The DVD player is gone," Jasmine said.

"What do you mean *gone*?"

"I mean it's not here. It grew legs and walked away," Jasmine said.

"I doubt that it grew legs and walked anywhere. Maybe your mother moved it upstairs to her room for some reason."

"I doubt it. She has one in her room."

"Well, maybe something happened to the one she has in her room so she unplugged the one down here and took it upstairs," Miss Crowe said.

"But my *Finding Nemo* DVD was still in it. The DVD holder is right here." Jasmine picked up the empty case. "One thing I can tell you about my mother is that she hates when folks take a DVD out and don't put it back in its proper holder. She thinks it will get scratched if it's unprotected."

"Yeah, that's what used to happen with our forty-fives," Miss Crowe said.

"Forty-five what?" Jasmine said.

Miss Crowe chuckled. "Sorry. I keep forgetting that I'm antique around here. A forty-five was a record. They call them vinyls now, I think. We had records with record players that required a needle and some-times the needle would scratch the record or if you laid it down, it might get scratched up. When a record is scratched, it doesn't play right and tends to get stuck and repeats itself in one spot until you move the needle."

"That's what some DJs do to records on purpose. They call it scratching," Jasmine said.

"Yeah, okay. I think my head is starting to hurt now."

Jasmine giggled. "You always say that when we start talking about the difference in what was and what is now."

"Yes, I do because it makes me dizzy hear-ing all this stuff."

"I'm going to check in Mama's room to see if the DVD player is in there."

"Okay."

Jasmine ran up the stairs. She came back five minutes later and stood in the kitchen.

Miss Crowe looked up. "Did you find it like I told you you would?"

"Nope," Jasmine said.

"What do you mean, nope?"

"I mean no, ma'am, it wasn't up there.

Her player is there though."

"Well, I know it's not in my room. If I want to watch something I just go in the den and get you to turn it on for me," Miss Crowe said.

"Maybe Granddaddy took it," Jasmine said.

"I doubt it. He's just about as inept when it comes to these electronic gadgets as I am. It took him forever to learn how to answer and dial out using the cell phone your mother gave him so he'd have a sure way for a potential employer to reach him should one call."

"He might have taken it and put it in his room," Jasmine said. "You never know. I can run and check."

"No. You don't need to be going in his room when he's not here. That's not polite."

"I'm sure he won't mind. He and I have bonded. We're buddies. He calls me his BLB: brilliant little buddy."

"Yeah, okay. But still, we respect other people's space and property, and for now, that room is his and you shouldn't be just going in there without his permission. So we'll wait. And I suppose that means you can do your homework now since the DVD is no longer on the agenda."

Jasmine stomped away.

"I know you'd better not be walking away like that," Miss Crowe said. "We don't walk away with attitudes when an adult tells us something to do that we disagree with. Understand?"

"Yes, ma'am."

"Now, where's my beautiful little Jazzy smile?"

Jasmine looked at Miss Crowe, smiled, then burst out laughing when Miss Crowe came over and hugged and tickled her.

CHAPTER 24

Wickedness is in the midst thereof: deceit and guile depart not from her streets.
— Psalm 55:11

Gabrielle came in the house, glad to be home. She could smell the food cooking in the kitchen and allowed her nose to lead her.

"This smells so good!" Gabrielle said to Miss Crowe.

"Thank you," Miss Crowe said. "And your timing could *not* have been better. Everything is ready and you *know* how I love for folks to eat while it's hot."

"I'm starving and truly ready to eat. I skipped lunch today to make up for the time I cut short yesterday when I came home earlier than planned," Gabrielle said.

"Sorry about that," Miss Crowe said as she turned off the eye with the candied yams. The cinnamon and nutmeg truly made the house smell like a home. "I guess I kind of jumped the gun yesterday evening."

"No, you didn't. You were right to call me like you did. Who knows what really would have happened had I not come in and interrupted? I know my father *said* he wasn't falling for any of it, but I'm not totally convinced. It's possible he said what he did to me and Zachary because he wanted to throw us off the trail. Where is he, by the way?"

"Your guess is as good as mine." Miss Crowe took the yeast rolls out of the oven and rolled butter on top of them.

"Is he here at all?" Gabrielle asked as she picked up one of the rolls and, realizing just how hot they were, just as quickly dropped it back onto the pan.

Miss Crowe ripped loose a paper towel and picked up the roll Gabrielle had tried picking up. She placed it on a saucer and handed the saucer and paper towel to Gabrielle. "Here you go."

"Thanks." Gabrielle smiled like a little girl. "So is my father here in the house?"

"He left right after you did this morning. I haven't seen nor heard from him since."

"Hmmm, that's kind of odd. Usually he tells me when he has someplace to go and even then, most times, he's back before I get home, for sure." Gabrielle pulled a piece of the roll off — the steam rising into the air as though a spirit had been freed.

"I didn't ask him where he was going. He's grown and can come and go as he pleases as far as I'm concerned."

"If I know you, you were just happy he was gone," Gabrielle said, then put the cooled-down piece of her roll in her mouth.

"You know me: I live and let live. If you don't bother me and mine, I won't bother you and yours. But if you're foolish enough to mess with me or mine, you need to sleep with one eye open and one eye closed because I'm coming for you."

Gabrielle chuckled. "Miss Crowe, you know good and well you're not going to hurt anybody. You just be trying to talk like you're big and bad."

"Ask your aunt Cee-Cee how much I just be talking," Miss Crowe said as she walked over to the kitchen table and sat down. "I'm tired. But I got a lot done today."

"Speaking of Aunt Cee-Cee, you think maybe that's where my father went? I mean, I was a bit hard in telling him I didn't want her over here again. Maybe he went to see her. I do know he seemed really concerned about Jesse."

"That young man is definitely on something, and whatever it is, is not good. And I'm going to tell you, if he rings the doorbell and you're not here, he won't be stepping foot in *this* house," Miss Crowe said. "Not with me and Jasmine here."

"Well, I suppose Daddy will be back when he gets back." Gabrielle pulled another piece of the roll off, able to hold it in her hand now that it had cooled. "So is Jasmine in her room? No, wait! Let me guess. She's in the den watching her newest favorite DVD, *Finding Nemo.*"

"She would be if the DVD player was in there and the DVD wasn't missing," Miss Crowe said.

"What do you mean 'if the DVD player was in there and the DVD wasn't missing'?" Gabrielle sat down at the table next to Miss Crowe.

"The DVD player is missing. At first I thought you might have taken it to your room, but Jasmine checked —"

"I didn't take it," Gabrielle said.

"That's what I was about to say. And you know *I* don't have it," Miss Crowe said.

"So where do you think it is?" Gabrielle asked.

"I don't have a clue. Jasmine thinks maybe your father has it in his room —"

"I doubt that. He would have asked — at least I would think he would," Gabrielle said.

"My sentiments exactly." Miss Crowe rubbed her leg.

Gabrielle looked down as she did it. "Is your leg bothering you?"

"Not really. I guess it's a habit I have when there's something I have to say and it pains me to have to say it," Miss Crowe said.

"Okay. Let's have it."

"You remember that twenty dollars I asked you to get for me the other day?"

"Yeah. I ended up forgetting to give it to you that night and gave it to you yesterday morning before I left for work," Gabrielle said.

"Right. And then I took it in the den and put it in my wallet in my purse. Well, it's not there. And before you ask, I'm certain I put it in my wallet in the place where I always put all my dollar bills. I'm not crazy. I'm not getting senile. I'm sure I put it in my wallet in my purse that was in the den."

"So it's likely my father may have taken your twenty dollars *and* the DVD player." Gabrielle shook her head with obvious disappointment of her conclusion. "I was *so* hoping he was being sincere about having changed. I'm sorry, Miss Crowe. I'll replace your money. Did you notice anything else missing from your purse? Credit cards . . . your license, anything like that?"

"You know, I didn't even think about checking any of those things. The only reason I realized the money was gone was because Jasmine wanted something from the ice-cream man."

"Oh, no," Gabrielle said. "Don't tell me they've already started their run?"

"You know you can hear that sound all the way on the other street. It's like the Pied Piper charming the children out onto the streets and the money out of our pockets. Did you know a chocolate candy-covered vanilla whatchamacallit cost two dollars and seventy-five cents these days?"

Gabrielle laughed. "Well, we both know it's the experience the kids are paying for. Plus the ice-cream man still has to buy gas. And gas ain't cheap."

"Yes, I know. And don't you dare worry about that twenty dollars. But I do need to check my other things. I used my credit card night before last when Jasmine and I were ordering some stuff for the wedding."

"The way you and Jasmine are ordering stuff, we can have *three* weddings with stuff left over," Gabrielle said.

Miss Crowe got up and went to her room

where she'd put her purse. She came back down to the kitchen. "Everything seems to be there. Just the twenty dollars is missing."

Gabrielle went up to Jasmine's room to check on her. Jasmine was still upset about her DVD. She'd taken it over to her friend Jade's house a few times. But it had definitely been in the player yesterday so she was certain it was in the player now.

Gabrielle told Jasmine to come on down for supper. As they descended the staircase, the front door opened.

Bennie looked troubled. "Oh, hello, Gabrielle. I didn't know you were home already."

"Trying to beat me here, were you?" Gabrielle asked. "Jasmine, go and help Miss Crowe in the kitchen, will you?" Jasmine nodded, hugging Bennie as she went. Gabrielle turned her attention back to Bennie. "So were you trying to beat me home?"

"Not really. I just finished up some business today." He started sniffing into the air. "Something smells mighty good around here. That friend of yours, Esther Crowe, knows she can burn in the kitchen. That woman can throw down."

"Daddy, did you happen to take the DVD player out of the den, possibly to your room last night?" Gabrielle asked as unaccusingly as possible.

"DVD player? Honey chile, I wouldn't know a DVD player if it came and bit me on the foot."

"You've seen it. We play movies on it. It's that thin black box in the den."

"I've seen the movies, sure enough. But if you asked me to put a disc in and get it going, I'd look at you like you'd just told me to translate Russian," Bennie said.

"So you didn't take it to your room?"

He shook his head. "Nope. Perhaps it was Chef Esther Mae. That woman knows she can put her foot in some food. Did you check with her?"

"Of course, I checked with Miss Crowe."

"Well, you don't have to get testy about it," Bennie said. "I was just asking."

"Daddy, I'm going to ask you something and I need for you to tell me the truth. Did you go in Miss Crowe's purse and take twenty dollars out of her wallet?"

He held up his hands in surrender. "Hold on, hold on. I don't go in women's purses now. You can accuse me of many things, but the cardinal rule clearly states that a man never — I don't care if the woman tells him to do it — he never goes in her purse for *nothing*. If she wants something from her purse, you bring the whole purse to her and let her get it herself."

"But if you were stealing from it, you'd have to go in it, wouldn't you?"

He frowned. "You think I stole money out of her purse?"

"I don't know. I'm asking. She said she asked Jasmine and Jasmine didn't take it. I didn't since I was the one who brought it to her. The only person left is you."

"And naturally, since I'm the ex-con, it had to have been me."

"That's not what I'm saying, Daddy. The DVD player is gone as is the twenty dollars, and ironically, you've been gone all day today. So where did you go?"

He nodded. "I'm telling you that I didn't steal anything: not from Miss Crowe, not from you, not from this house, not from anybody, not ever."

"Then where were you today?"

He released a loud sigh. "If you must know, I got a call for a temp job and they let me start today."

"A temp job, huh? Where is this job? Doing what?"

Tears filled his eyes. "You don't believe me. After everything I've tried to show you since I arrived here and you don't believe me."

"I want to believe you, Daddy; I do. I'm

just scared that if I let myself go and fully trust you, you're going to let me down." Gabrielle was crying now. "It's been hard trying to pick up the pieces you left me with."

"But you're strong," Bennie said. "You've more than proven that. What would have crushed others merely brought out the true fragrance of who you really are. And that fragrance fills a room when you enter it. *I* messed up. *I* was wrong." Bennie wiped his eyes. "Nevertheless, look what God has birthed out of both our pain. I'm trying to walk the right path now. I told you I don't want to do anything to hamper the progress we've made over these past three months."

He went to Gabrielle and hugged her. "I didn't do it. Please . . . please, I need to know that you believe me. Tell me that you believe me."

Gabrielle pulled away from his attempt at a fatherly embrace. Miss Crowe was standing in the foyer now with her hands clasped together as though she was praying. For what, Gabrielle wasn't sure.

Gabrielle looked up at her father; his face worn, (far older looking than his actual age of only forty-eight) from the years incarcerated life had taken on him. His eyes spoke to her. She saw deep into them, past his soul, that he really did love her, and he really was sorry for all the pain he'd caused. She saw that much.

"I believe you," she finally said a little above a whisper. "I believe you."

The phone rang.

"I'll get it," Miss Crowe said, exiting the area as Bennie grabbed Gabrielle and broke down completely.

He was sobbing heavily now. As he knelt down, he was crying and began lifting his hands as he thanked God. Gabrielle couldn't help herself; she knelt down alongside her father and the two of them were praising God together. Miss Crowe eventually came back and joined them along with Jasmine. They were on their knees, all four of them, giving God praise.

The doorbell rang. Miss Crowe struggled to her feet and answered the door. It was the police.

CHAPTER 25

Evil pursueth sinners: but to the righteous
good shall be repaid.

— Proverbs 13:21

"I'm sorry to bother you at this obvious dinner hour, but we're looking for Gabrielle
Mercedes," one of the police officers said.

Gabrielle heard her name and made her
way up and over to the door. When she saw
the police, she glanced back at her father,
who was making his way to a standing position with a little help from Jasmine.

"I'm Gabrielle Mercedes. How may I help
you?"

The other officer with a badge that said
HOLMES stepped forward. "We'd like to
come in for a minute if you don't mind."

"What's this about?" Gabrielle asked.
Miss Crowe stepped up to stand closer to
Gabrielle, demonstrating a unified front.
Jasmine was now there under Gabrielle,

who instantly placed her hand on top of her head to make her be still.

"We were wondering if this is yours." Officer Holmes held up a DVD.

"My *Finding Nemo!*" Jasmine said with pure joy in her voice. "Where did you find it?"

"So, this *is* your DVD?" the other officer asked.

"Yes, it is," Gabrielle said, taking the DVD and looking at it. "That's the label I put on it in case my daughter happened to forgot it somewhere. Where did you find it?"

"May we come in?"

Gabrielle opened the door wider to allow them both to pass.

Officer Holmes nodded to Bennie, who nodded back. "Evening, sir."

"Evening, officer," Bennie said, then bowed his head again.

"Miss Mercedes or is it misses?"

"It's miss," Gabrielle said.

"For now. In a few more months it will be Mrs. Morgan," Jasmine said. "Mrs. Gabrielle Mercedes Morgan."

"Jasmine!" Gabrielle said with a playful roll of her eyes. "I'm sure these nice officers don't care about any of that."

"Well, I care!" Jasmine said as she twisted from side to side.

"We won't hold you long, miss," said the other officer whose name tag read PHILLIPS. "We received a call from a pawn shop about the sale of some questionable items. You know there's a law that pawn shops can only buy things from folks they know are not stolen, which is not always easy to ascertain, for sure."

"But in your case," Officer Holmes said, "there was this DVD inside of a DVD player someone was attempting to sell with your name, phone number, and address on it. Were you aware that your DVD player was missing or did you intend for it to be sold to a pawn shop?"

"We noticed it was gone today when I went to go look at *Finding Nemo*," Jasmine said.

"So it *was* stolen?" Officer Phillips said. "Is that what you're telling me?" He was looking at Gabrielle for an answer at this point.

Gabrielle had to think quickly. If she said yes and it turned out her father had taken it and sold it, they would surely arrest him on the spot. She knew the pawn shop kept a record of people who sold them a particular item. But if she believed her father didn't steal it, she could comfortably say it had been stolen and know that her father wouldn't be in trouble. She thought about looking at him to see if he was attempting to give her some kind of signal, but if she did, it would be relaying to him that she wasn't sure he hadn't stolen it.

"Yes," Gabrielle said. "It was stolen."

Gabrielle heard Miss Crowe release a sigh that sounded like relief.

Officer Holmes nodded a few times. "Have you noted any other items missing from your home?"

"Not right off the bat. But then, it appears we weren't robbed in a conventional way. Our robber seems to have just taken a few items in hopes of them not being noticed," Gabrielle said.

"Like?" Officer Phillips asked.

"Like Miss Crowe's twenty dollars," Gabrielle said.

Miss Crowe waved it away. "Not something I would call the police and report, that's for sure."

"Well, Miss Mercedes," Officer Holmes said. "We will have your DVD player down at the station as soon as we wrap up the investigation on this case, first being to arrest the perpetrator. Your DVD player wasn't the only thing brought in by this apparent thief. Fortunately for us, you had this DVD in the player with your name on it assisting us in catching him red handed. And I have a feeling the haul he brought in today will turn up a lot of other stolen property, hopefully things reported."

"So we can keep my DVD?" Jasmine asked Officer Holmes.

"Yeah," Officer Holmes said. "We're going to process the DVD player for evidence, but I have a feeling you'll be getting that back in a few days as he'll likely cut a deal and plead guilty. We have your contact information. We'll call you if we need anything more. But hopefully, it'll be for you to come down to the station and claim your stolen property."

"Well, thankfully, we have another DVD player here," Gabrielle said. "But this *Finding Nemo* DVD would have made me have to go out and purchase another one if you hadn't located it."

"Do you mind telling us who the suspect is?" Miss Crowe said.

"He hasn't been formally charged as yet," Officer Phillips said.

"The reason we'd like to know is because we believe it has to be someone we know. We'd just like to protect ourselves," Miss Crowe said. "You understand?"

"Yeah. I do. I can't tell you *on* the record, but off the record, it looks to be one Jesse

Murphy. Does that name ring a bell?"

It was only then that Gabrielle looked over at her father. She saw him shaking his head, then holding it down in what appeared to be total dejection.

CHAPTER 26

And we know that we are of God, and the whole world lieth in wickedness.

— 1 John 5:19

Zachary passed the policemen as they were leaving. He looked at Bennie as though he was asking what he'd done now.

Gabrielle closed the door and they all laughed. Zachary looked from one to the other. "What did I miss?" he asked.

"Here's your DVD," Gabrielle said to Jasmine as she handed it to her.

"I'm putting it in its case right now," Jasmine said, skipping toward the den.

"Why were the police here?" Zachary said, this time to Bennie exclusively.

"Zachary," Gabrielle said. "Those fine men in blue came by to bring Jasmine back her DVD."

"Okkkaaaay," Zachary said with a sing-song to it. "So policemen not only get cats out of trees but they bring back little girls' lost DVDs? Is that what I'm hearing here?"

"What police have you ever heard that got a cat out of a tree?" Miss Crowe said. "That's pure Mayberry stuff, made for sixties television shows." She shook her head. "Goodness gracious. You're almost as much of a throwback as me."

"Will somebody just *please* tell me what's going on around here?"

"The food I cooked is getting cold," Miss Crowe said. "That's what's going on around here. I hate when that happens. All my hard work for nothing."

"Microwave, Aunt Esther. That's why we have microwaves," Zachary said.

"Well, I'm going in the kitchen to see what I can do to salvage things."

"Aunt Esther, we'll just fix our plates and stick them in the microwave. But I want somebody in this place to tell me why the police were here and why nobody is apparently talking," Zachary said. "Bennie, were they here because of you?"

"Oh, noooo," Bennie said, shaking his head. "I've been thoroughly vindicated, thank the good Lord for His mercy and His grace." Bennie turned to Miss Crowe. "Why don't I go with you so I can get started on warming up my plate? I'm starving. I worked today, but without money for lunch, and only corn flakes for breakfast, I'd eat the food cold and be as happy as a tick on a dog."

"Of course, you would. You are one eating man; I'll give you that," Miss Crowe said.

"That's because you can cook, Esther Mae," Bennie said.

"That's just because you ate prison food and you probably don't know what good food tastes like," Miss Crowe said with a giggle. "And don't ever call me Esther Mae again or I promise you: It won't be pretty if you do."

"All right, Esther Crowe. I won't make that mistake *ever* again. And I know good food. And like I said to Gabrielle earlier, to which I'm sure you were likely listening in on, with your eavesdropping self, you can throw down in the kitchen."

Miss Crowe pretended to hit at him as they disappeared toward the kitchen.

"Okay, Gabrielle. What all did I miss?" Zachary said.

"Let's see now," Gabrielle said with a grin as she recapped all the things that happened, including how her cousin Jesse had apparently stolen from them.

"Wow. So while he was here in the den, I suppose, he must have figured out how to hurry and get the DVD player unplugged. I wonder why that's all he took?"

"Probably because that was all he could get in his little backpack without drawing too much attention to himself," Gabrielle said. "Maybe he'd planned to do more and either my father spoiled his plan or your aunt. And when Miss Crowe called me and I got here, that pretty much nipped all the alone time he and Aunt Cee-Cee had in here." Gabrielle shook her head. "I still can't believe that boy had the nerve to come up in *my* house and steal from me in broad daylight, no less."

"So you say he went in Aunt Esther's purse and stole twenty dollars?"

"Yes," Gabrielle said. She still couldn't believe his boldness in doing that. "I'm just glad he didn't take any of her credit cards or her ID. Then again, it very well might have been my aunt Cee-Cee who took it. Who can say?"

"It was probably him. He was likely just looking for something easy to get to and easy to get rid of so he could get enough money for his next purchase of meth," Zachary said. "We really do need to try and get him some help. I hate seeing our young men go down the path of destruction the way some of them are doing. And it doesn't matter how much you try and warn them, they always think they're the exception to the rule when it comes to getting caught or caught up. Then they're left trying to school the next ones to come along who, just like them, won't listen."

"Well, it sounds like what Jesse stole from here isn't all he took. He's likely about to go to jail. Maybe he'll get some help now because of this," Gabrielle said.

"Maybe. We can only pray for him at this point. But I have a feeling your aunt is going to be none too happy with you about this," Zachary said.

"Not happy with *me*?" Gabrielle pulled back. "What did I do?"

"You had this stuff here and it was your house. When the police showed up, you had the nerve to admit something had been stolen," Zachary said. "See, your fault."

Gabrielle nodded. "Oh, yeah. I see it clearly now. The whole world lies in wickedness, but somehow it's the fault of those who are trying to follow God. Got it." Gabrielle began to wipe tears.

Zachary grabbed her gently by her shoulders. "Gabrielle, what's wrong?"

She nodded, then looked up at Zachary who was staring intensely down at her. "My father. He told me how much he loved me and he wanted nothing more than for me to believe him when he said he didn't take those things."

"And — ?"

"And" — she placed her hand up to her mouth and covered it to hold in a pending cry — "and, I did." She looked up at Zachary and smiled. "I believed him."

Zachary hugged her. "I'm glad, Gabrielle. I'm glad. I suppose fathers are more important to a daughter's life than most of us give them credit for, huh?"

Gabrielle nodded. "I didn't even know *just* how much. Until tonight, I didn't know."

"Well, I don't want to be the one to bring this up. But you know" — he paused a second — "Jasmine might want to know about her biological father, too, don't you think?" Zachary looked decisively at Gabrielle.

"I'm going to do it. I just want to wait until after our wedding," Gabrielle said, fidgeting a little.

"And why might that be? Have you really thought about what difference it would make whether you did it now or after our wedding? And is that fair to Jasmine? Is it even fair to Lawrence, who has said he wants to meet her and introduce her to her other sisters and brother? Are you ducking from what you need to do, Gabrielle, putting it off from one major event in our lives to the next?"

"I don't know, Zachary. Maybe I'm just a coward. Maybe I want to have this fantastic wedding without having any possible fallout or drama before it comes. Am I wrong for wanting something to go my way for a change? Am I? I don't have a clue how Jasmine's going to react when she hears this. If I knew, I would know if the right time was now or if waiting is better. Then again, the last time I waited, things blew up in my face. I don't want that to happen again." Gabrielle sighed. "So are you saying you think I should do it now . . . before the wedding? What?"

"I just see how much you've been affected by your own father, and I'm saying for you not to deny your daughter what you have — good or bad. But that's something you'll need to pray about and be led by God on," Zachary said.

Gabrielle wrapped her arms around Zachary's waist. "Miss Crowe is going to be mad at us if we don't come on and eat." Gabrielle chuckled.

"Yeah, you're right." He kissed her on her head. "I'm still here with you, Gabrielle. I'm not going anywhere. We can do all things through Christ Jesus who strengthens us. You're going to make the right decision. I just know you are."

Gabrielle nodded.

CHAPTER 27

That our sons may be as plants grown up
in their youth; that our daughters may be
as corner stones, polished after the simili-
tude of a palace.

— Psalm 144:12

"Daddy, where are we going?" Darius's
second child, eight-year-old Dana, asked.

"I told you," Darius said. "You're going to
my house for the weekend."

"We're going to celebrate my birthday,"
Jade said in a satisfied tone. "I'm ten.
Double digits. Count them. Ten."

"Yes, we are, and yes, you are, Jade,"
Darius said.

"But her birthday was last Friday on April
the eighth," Dana said. "Why is she getting
another birthday party? Mom gave her a
party last Saturday. Jade always gets to have
all the fun. Me and Junior hardly ever get
anything. It's not fair." Dana folded her

arms and began to pout.

"I had a birthday for my birthday," four-year-old Junior said with a smile. "My birthday's in November."

"Junior, everybody has a birthday for their birthday," Jade said, laughing. "You meant a birthday party for your birthday, which you did have. But it's *my* birthday now. So let's stay focused, people," Jade said.

"My birthday was on February second," Dana said. "You missed my birthday, Daddy."

"Not really missed it," Darius said. "I called and told your mother to wish you happy birthday for me. And then I came over on February fourteenth and brought you something."

"Not for my birthday, you didn't," Dana said. "That was for Valentine's Day. And you didn't give me anything for my birthday. You gave all of us a box of candy, so that doesn't count as a birthday present just for me."

"You're absolutely right, Dana," Darius said. "So let's say this weekend, while you're with me, that we're celebrating both *your* birthday *and* Jade's."

"Why does she always have to get what I'm getting?" Jade said, folding her arms and pouting now.

Darius smiled as he watched them all from his rearview mirror. "We're going to have a good time this weekend. And believe me, there's going to be more than enough celebration for everybody. So let's not get upset. And Jade, I need for you to unfold your arms and to unbutton your lips. Okay?"

Jade unfolded her arms and relaxed her pout.

"That's my girl," Darius said with a grin. He pulled up to the gate of the house.

"What's this place?" Jade asked. "It's huge, whatever it is."

"Yeah," Junior said. "Huge."

"Junior, you're just like a parrot. All you do is say what somebody else says," Jade said.

"I do not. *You* say what somebody else says," Junior said.

Darius pulled up into the driveway and then into the garage. "We're here."

"Here? Where is here?" Dana asked, looking out of the window at the large fully finished garage.

"This," Darius said as he looked at his children, "is where Daddy lives now."

"Whoa!" Junior said.

"Wow," Dana said, opening her car door and stepping onto the red painted concrete floor.

They went inside, which impressed the three children even more.

"Daddy is living large and in charge," Dana said. "This is like a palace. How did you get all of this, Daddy?"

"Hi there," Divine said.

"Hi," Junior said, quickly attaching himself to his father's leg like Velcro.

"Girls, did you hear her speak?" Darius said.

"Hi," Jade and Dana said in dry harmony.

Divine smiled. "Let me guess: You're Jade, you're Dana, and you" — she leaned down to Junior and smiled — "are almost the spitting image of your father, which makes you DJ."

"Nobody calls him DJ anymore," Jade said, rolling her eyes. "His name is Junior."

"Same difference," Darius said. "His name is Darius Connors Jr. I still call him DJ sometimes."

"No you don't, Daddy," Jade said.

"Well, Junior," Divine said, still bending down to his level, "it's nice to meet you. My name is Dee Vine, but everybody calls me Divine."

"What's the difference?" Jade said. "It sounds like the same thing to me. You just said it like it was two words the first time, then one."

"I totally agree," Divine said, standing up and looking at Jade. "I can already tell we're all going to get along splendidly." She smiled.

"You're pretty," Junior said.

"Shut up, Junior," Jade said.

"But she *is* pretty," Junior said.

Divine smiled. "Okay, what say I show you three to your rooms while you'll be staying here? Jade and Dana, I put you two in a room together."

"Figures," Jade said under her breath.

"That's fine," Darius said. "I'm sure Jade will appreciate this much better than sleeping out in my SUV. Isn't that right, Jade?"

"Oh, yes, sir," Jade said with a fake spunk to her voice.

Darius narrowed his eyes at her to let her know he wasn't going to put up with her foul attitude too much longer.

"DJ . . . I mean, Junior, you get a room all to yourself."

Jade rolled her eyes. "And when are we going back home?"

"Sunday afternoon at six o'clock," Darius said.

"But we're going to have such a great time this weekend. I promise you that," Divine said. "Your father and I have lots of exciting things planned. He's so happy to have you here with him. That's all he's been talking about all week long."

Jade moved her head from side to side while twisting her mouth in mockery of Divine. Darius looked at her and she instantly stopped.

"She's okay," Divine said. "I've dealt with people like Jade before. Jade is just being protective of her mother. I like that. Well, Jade, I want you to know that I have no intentions of replacing or taking the place of your mother."

"Like you actually *could*," Jade said, again under her breath.

"Oooh," Dana said.

"Jade, that's enough now," Darius said. "Miss Divine has bent over backward to make things wonderful for all of you. I've missed spending time with you. If you want to be upset with someone, then direct your nasty attitude my way. But you will *not* disrespect Miss Divine in her own home. Have I made myself clear?"

"Yes, sir," Jade whispered.

"I'm sorry, but I didn't quite hear you," Darius said.

"Yes, sir!" Jade said louder.

"Now, I want you to apologize to Miss Divine."

Jade looked at Divine. "I'm sorry."

Divine smiled. "I accept. Now, let's go upstairs and check out your *rooms*!"

They went upstairs. And as much as Jade may not have wanted to be, she was blown away by the room Divine had fixed up for her and Dana. Darius could see it all over her face.

The rest of the weekend went off without a hitch. Divine had successfully orchestrated a birthday party for all three of the children, including Junior, whose birthday was another seven months away. She'd made each child feel special, with a birthday celebration catered specifically to them. She'd showered them with clothes, jewelry, electronics — it was unreal, which was precisely what Tiffany said when they hauled most of their newfound loot home.

"What on earth?" Tiffany said. "What is all of this?"

"Mom, we had the *best* time with Dad!" Junior said. "Look at all the stuff I got."

"I see. We're going to need a bigger house just to have somewhere to put all of this stuff." Tiffany looked at Darius, who merely shrugged.

"Miss Divine was great! She is *so* nice," Junior said.

"Miss Divine?" Tiffany said. "Who is Miss Divine?" Tiffany turned to Darius.

Darius smiled. "Her name is Dee . . . Vine. Divine is just easier for everybody, so that's what she goes by."

"Yeah, okay," Tiffany said, her hand suddenly pressed onto her hip.

"Mom, Miss Divine gave me a birthday party," Dana said.

"She did? But your birthday was in February," Tiffany said.

"I know," Dana said. "Wasn't that great of her? Jade had a birthday party and Junior did, too. We all did, and all at the same time. It was so awesome! There was a real pony there. That was in my party area. And a magician —"

"The magician was for me," Junior said. "I loved it! I want to do it again."

"Wow, that's wonderful," Tiffany said. "And what about you, Jade?"

Jade tried not to smile. "It was nice."

"Just nice?" Tiffany said.

Jade shrugged. "Yeah. We had karaoke for my party. Then we got to dress up, which was kind of fun. Miss Divine invited some other children over for the party, which made it even more fun even if we didn't know any of them."

"So this Miss Divine really showed all of you a great time," Tiffany said.

"Dad had a *little* something to do with it,"

Dana said with a grin.

"Thank you, Dana," Darius said. "I was starting to get my feelings hurt." He smiled.

"Okay, so take your things up to your rooms, and I'll be up to see everything later."

"Do you want us to put our clothes away?" Junior asked.

"No, Junior. Just put the things on your bed. I want you to show me everything you got," Tiffany said. "Okay?" She bent down and gave him a quick tap on his nose.

"Okay, Ma," Junior said.

The children took their things and left.

"I had such a great time with them this weekend," Darius said with a small grin. "I'll be getting them more often now. Maybe every two to three weeks."

"What do you think you're doing?" Tiffany said with a scowl on her face.

"I'm being a father to my children."

"You took my children to somebody's house named Divine? With a name like that, does she slide down a pole or something equally as athletic?"

Darius raised one hand. "No, no, you will *not* insult Dee in that way. Dee is a hard-working woman who was kind and gracious enough to have our children, not just yours or mine, *our* children into her home and

299

treat them as though they were her own. Now if you're having a hard time with the fact that the children went and came back liking someone you were secretly hoping they'd hate —"

"What are you talking about, someone I was secretly hoping they'd hate? I didn't know you were taking them around some other woman, let alone to some woman's house." Tiffany huffed. "You *took* them to another woman's house?"

"It's my home now. It's where I live. I have every right to see my children and to bring them to my home, Tiffany."

"How long have you known this . . . person?"

He shrugged. "What difference does how long I've known her make?"

"It makes a lot of difference, Darius! You can't take our children around just anybody. We have two girls and a little boy. Don't you pay attention to the news and see all of the things happening with innocent children?"

"The children were with me. They were in my possession and sight the whole time. They were never in any danger. And the best thing is that they seem to like the woman who adores me."

"So when and where did you meet her?"

"If you must know, I met her one day back in January, the second day you refused to let me come in *our* house out of the cold."

"January of *this* year? January of two thousand and eleven?"

"Yes."

"So is she the reason you decided to completely abandon our marriage?"

Darius lifted one hand as he shook his head. "No, you're not going to pin this all on me. I was trying to make things work. It didn't, so I'm moving on."

"I thought you said you were going to file for a divorce. You haven't done it, so whether you realize it or not, you're still legally married. Which means you living with this woman is committing a sin. You're committing adultery, Darius."

Darius chuckled. "Newsflash, Tiffany." He moved his face in closer to hers as he smirked. "I was *sinning* when I was living here with you. Yes, that's right. And it wasn't just the two times you think you know about. This is just the first time I'm living openly, truthfully, and free about it. You see, Divine doesn't nag me like you. Divine knows how to take care of her man, unlike you. Divine is —"

"Stop! I really don't want to hear any more. Fine, you want to be with someone else, fine. It's on your head, Darius. You'll have to answer to God for what you're doing."

He laughed. "Yeah, just like you. And don't be trying to act like you're not swooning all over dear, sweet Clarence."

Tiffany shook her head as she frowned. "I'm not. There's nothing going on between me and Clarence. So you can try and make yourself feel better by telling yourself that lie all you want. But God knows the truth. I've been faithful to you *and* our vows. I took it seriously when I said I would give myself to you and you only."

"Well, I'm happy. And it looks like things are going wonderfully for me."

"So does this mean you plan on paying child support to take care of *our* children?"

"That's the only thing you really care about, isn't it, Tiffany? You're just looking for a paycheck. Well, you know what: I'm going to make sure you get money to take care of the children. And I'm going to file those papers for a divorce. Are you happy now? Now that you know you're going to get a paycheck for the kids."

She shook her head as she wiped the tears from her eyes. "It costs money to take care of children. You know this. Our children are not a 'paycheck' to me. But I'm not going to allow them to suffer, to be here without food, a roof over their heads, or the threat of being without utilities to prove anything to you. I'm not. So say what you want, but I love my children."

"Yeah, okay. Listen: I'll hit you up the next time I want to get them." He started toward the door, then turned around. "Oh, and I did check on a divorce. And the lawyer I spoke with says they have an economy special that would save us money. If you and I agree on how everything will be divided upfront without having a long, drawn-out court battle, we can use the thrift plan. I know you used to clip coupons; I assume you still do. I know how much you love a good bargain. So I say we go for the economy deal. What say you?"

Tiffany slowly shook her head and as she frowned at him, one tear made its way down her face. "You truly *are* a despicable person. I can't believe I never saw just how much you were before now. I'm going to pray for you," Tiffany said.

He laughed as he opened the front door. "Oh, please do. You know I can use all the prayers I can get." He winked, then left, gently closing the door behind him.

CHAPTER 28

And said, Whose daughter art thou? tell me, I pray thee: is there room in thy father's house for us to lodge in?
— Genesis 24:23

The Saturday following the children's visit with their father, Tiffany allowed Jade to go to Jasmine's house to play. As was now their custom, the two girls hugged at the door, giggled, then ran up to Jasmine's bedroom.

Miss Crowe and Jasmine had just finished putting a batch of homemade chocolate chip cookies with pecans in the oven. When they were ready, she decided to carry some up to them.

Gabrielle met Miss Crowe on her way toward the stairway. Grabbing one of the cookies off the plate, she took the plate. "You're carrying these to the girls? I'll do it for you."

"Okay, Gabrielle. Just make sure that

plate, along with at least most of the cookies on it, makes its way up to them." Miss Crowe smiled. "I know you."

"You know how much I love your chocolate chip cookies hot out of the oven," she said. "And you put pecans in these. I hope you have some more you're putting in the oven now."

"I do. So give the girls those and you can come in the kitchen and have all you want."

Gabrielle loved smelling the cookies as she walked with them up the stairs toward Jasmine's room. The door was slightly opened, but Gabrielle didn't want to barge in without knocking first. She felt she owed Jasmine that level of respect. About to knock, she could hear that Jasmine and Jade were in deep conversation. She wasn't really trying to eavesdrop, not on purpose. But she overheard Jade say something to Jasmine that made her stop and listen in.

"I had such an awesome time with my father last weekend," Jade said. "I went all set to not like it and to let him know just how much I didn't like how he'd left us like he did."

"Why do you say he left y'all? Your mom and dad are separated. He didn't leave y'all," Jasmine said.

"Yes, he did leave *us*. You can't just leave

our home without leaving us too," Jade said. "So my sister, brother, and I made a pact when our mother told us he was coming to get us to spend the weekend with him that we would make the weekend miserable for him."

"That doesn't make sense," Jasmine said. "That seems like it would make him not want to get y'all again *or* come back home."

"No, you don't understand. We were going to do that so he would feel really crappy about having left us. You know — he would have felt guilty. And maybe that would make him think about what he was doing, then he would come back home and work things out with our mother," Jade said. "My mother has been praying so hard for him. I hear her; she really loves him and she does want him back. When I said something to her about it one day after he first left, she said she wanted him to come home, but she wanted him back like God intends for him to be."

"That sounds like grown folk speak to me," Jasmine said with a short laugh. "You know how when they don't really know the answer, they put everything in God's hands and on Him. My mother says we're to pray about things, but God is also looking for us to do our part."

"So what are you trying to say?" Jade said. "That my mother's not doing her part?"

"Oh, no. That wasn't what I was saying at all. You have an awesome mother. I love coming to your house. I just wish there wasn't always so much fighting going on with grownups. You know grown folks fuss at us about getting along, but they don't always set great examples. Again, I'm not talking about your mother at all. That was just a general observation."

Jade laughed. "You're going to be a professor or a scientist or something smart like that when you grow up, aren't you? I mean you're not like normal people your age."

"Let's not go there," Jasmine said. "Finish telling me about your visit with your father. Did your plan work? Did he end up feeling bad about being gone? Are your parents getting back together now?"

"It was only one visit. In fact, we've barely seen him since he left last year around September. He came to the house back in January acting like he was ready to come home for good. He didn't look so hot that time. He looked like a homeless man. You know the ones you see staggering around and sometimes begging on the streets?"

"Really? He was that bad?"

"Yeah. He was pretty bad. He wanted to

stay the night, but I heard Mama tell him he couldn't. I think she should have let him stay. That might have helped bring them back together. When I told her what I thought the next day, she said I don't know all the facts and that I should stay —"

"Out of grown folks' business!" Jasmine chimed in with Jade. They both laughed. "Grown folks' speak."

"They do all say that, don't they?" Jade said. "It's like they don't think we children have an opinion about anything. But we see stuff. We hurt just like they do."

"I know. There are some things I don't tell my mother because I know she won't really hear me. She wants to protect me, and she thinks she's doing what's best for me. So to cause her less stress, I just keep a lot of things to myself," Jasmine said in a solemn voice.

"Like what?"

"Like I know I was adopted. I know the Nobles were my adopted family. I now know, although I would have much pre-ferred hearing the news in a different way, that Gabrielle was actually my birth mother, the mother who gave me up for adoption. But . . ." Jasmine's voice trailed off.

Gabrielle moved closer to the door, afraid whatever Jasmine had just said had been missed completely because it had been spoken so quietly.

"But what?" Jade said.

"But now I want to know who my real father is. I want to know whose daughter I am."

"It won't be long now before Dr. Z will be your father. I'm so excited about the wedding. I'm glad I'm going to be in it. We're going to be junior bridesmaids!"

"Yeah, I'm excited about Dr. Z and all. But he's not my *real* father. I want to know where I came from."

"Then why don't you just ask your mother?"

"Because she has to know already that I want to know. If she's not voluntarily offering to tell me then that means, in her head, she thinks she's protecting me."

"But if you tell her that you really want to know, that will free her to know you're interested. What is she going to say if you want to know?" Jade said.

Jasmine sighed. "There's one other problem my asking could bring up. What if she doesn't know who my father is? What if she doesn't know whose daughter I am?"

"Do you think that's the case?"

"I don't know," Jasmine said. "But you know Mindy at church?"

"You're talking about Drawing Mindy that likes to draw all the time?"

"Yeah. Well, I heard her telling another girl that her mother didn't have a clue who her daddy was. She said her mother needed to go on that show where they bring on possible fathers to see which one, if any, is the father. She said she would be embarrassed if her mother brought like three men on and none of them turned out to be her father. That would mean her mother was something she called her that's not a word I'm allowed to say."

"I know what word that is. I'm not allowed to say it, either. But it's not a very nice word to say or be," Jade said. "So are you thinking Miss Gabrielle might not know who your father is and that's why she hasn't said anything to you about him?"

"I don't know. I just know right now it's safer if I don't say anything," Jasmine said. "I've learned that sometimes the answer is worse than the question. And with all I've been through, I'm not sure I'm up to being hurt much more. Imagine if I learn that my birth mother can't tell me my birth father's name."

"If she *does* know and *can* tell you, would you want to meet him?" Jade asked with a touch of enthusiasm in her voice. "I mean if he's still alive, of course."

"I would so *love* to meet him. I'd love to find out if I have any sisters and brothers. I'm like an only child right now, which has been okay. I mean, I have you, and you're like a sister."

"Believe me, having a sister and a brother is not all it's cracked up to be," Jade said.

"Oh, you know you love yours," Jasmine said, giggling.

"I do," Jade said with a hint of resolve. "But sometimes they get on my *last* nerve! Like last weekend when we went to our father's new place who, by the way, lives in a mansion with the prettiest woman I've ever seen in my life."

"Prettier than your own mother?" Jasmine asked.

"You know what I mean," Jade said, deflecting the question. "Her name is Dee . . . Vine but she goes by Divine, like it's one word instead of two. Well, when I saw her, I was determined I was going to make her regret the day she ever came between my parents getting back together. I mean — I truly believe had he not met her and ended up at her place, he and Mom would be back together already. I heard my mother tell someone on the phone the following day after he asked to stay at the house back in January that she could tell he was at his breaking point and ready to do right. She said it was just a matter of time. But I guess after that, he must have gotten with Miss Divine and he's not studying *any* of us now, especially my mother."

"So you like this Divine woman?"

"I didn't want to," Jade said. "But she's a pretty nice lady. She had rooms decorated as though she knew us personally. She said the rooms would be ours whenever we came over. Of course, she put me in the room with Dana, which I hated. I'd prefer my own room all by myself. Miss Divine has some more rooms in that mansion. So who knows? Maybe I'll ask for a room of my own the next time I'm there. That's if she and Daddy stay together. My mother told someone on the phone that Daddy has commitment issues. Whoever she was talking to must have called him a dog because my mother quickly came back saying he wasn't a dog; he was just confused."

"You sure do overhear a lot around your place," Jasmine said.

"Oh, if you learn to be quiet and sit perfectly still when you're in the room with adults while they're talking, you'll find that they forget all about you being there, and you can learn a lot you otherwise would

312

never know. But I think people who sneak up and listen in on closed doors aren't people with integrity. That's just being sneaky and deceptive, and I don't do that." Jade laughed.

Gabrielle glanced down at the plate of cookies, tiptoed back to the top of the stairs, then made a lot of noise as she came back to Jasmine's bedroom.

"Knock, knock!" Gabrielle said. "Sorry to interrupt, but Miss Crowe made —"

"Cookies!" both girls shouted in unison and sprinted toward Gabrielle.

Jasmine grabbed the edge of the plate. "Are all of these ours?"

"Yes, ma'am," Gabrielle said releasing the plate to Jasmine. "They're all yours. Miss Crowe has probably pulled out a fresh batch by now." Gabrielle tilted her head slightly. "So, what are you two girls up here talking about with the door pretty much closed?"

Jade looked at Jasmine, who quickly eyed her.

"I was telling Jasmine about my visit last weekend with my father," Jade said.

"Oh, yes. Your mother told me the three of you went to stay the weekend with him," Gabrielle said. "So how was it?"

"It turned out nice. As much as I'm mad at my father on one hand, what I learned in being with him last weekend is how much a father really means, especially when you're his little girl. I'm just glad I, at least, know who *my* father is."

Jasmine kicked Jade on the sly, obviously telling her to cool it. "Thanks for the cookies, Mama." Jasmine smiled and cocked her head to the side.

Gabrielle grinned. "Okay, I can take a hint. I suppose that's my cue to stay out of your business and that I can leave now and go take care of my own."

"Not trying to hurt your feelings," Jasmine said. "But we don't have a lot of time together before Jade has to go home."

"And you'd prefer not having me waste any of that time talking about stuff you don't want to talk about." Gabrielle raised her hands as a sign of surrender. "I got it." She started toward the door, then turned around. "Oh, if you want milk, you'll have to go to the kitchen and get it yourself." Gabrielle stopped at the door. "You want the door open or closed?"

"Open is fine," Jasmine said.

Gabrielle left the door open and walked out. She had a real decision to make at this point. Zachary had just said something about it, and now she'd heard it from her own daughter's mouth: Jasmine wanted to know her birth father. She wanted to know whose daughter she was.

CHAPTER 29

Behold, thou desirest truth in the inward
parts: and in the hidden part thou shalt
make me to know wisdom.

— Psalm 51:6

It was Sunday afternoon, April 24, 2011,
the start of the week when meteorologists
were predicting possible tornadoes across
the South, including Alabama. Gabrielle
hadn't intentionally chosen this day for this
to go down in anticipation of impending
bad weather (she'd set the date well before
the forecast). She just knew it was time.

Time for Jasmine to know the truth about
her birth father. Time for the family to
finally meet. Time to get everything totally
out in the open. Time to move forward.

She hadn't been certain of precisely how
she should proceed. Whether she should tell
Jasmine everything first, then see what Jasmine desired from that point. Or merely

bring them together and lay everything out there. It was a choice between slowly and carefully pulling off the Band-Aid and ripping it off quickly.

Miss Crowe believed she should tell Jasmine everything with just the two of them present and see what Jasmine wanted to do after that, since the birth father had already agreed to go along with whatever Gabrielle decided. Always the one to stand by her side no matter what, Zachary offered that Jasmine was still a child and putting such a decision solely in her hands was not the way parents should parent.

Lawrence let it be known that he preferred being present when Jasmine first learned the news because he didn't want her to have time to hate him before he could show her he really did care. Deidra, Lawrence's wife, felt the whole family should be present for that exact same reason. In the end, Pastor Landris offered a powerful prayer and advised Gabrielle to wholeheartedly allow the Holy Spirit to lead and guide her.

So here they were, Gabrielle and Jasmine, in the car, just the two of them on their way to meet people who, for better or worse, were about to become Jasmine's soon-to-be-newfound branch in her family tree.

Gabrielle only told Jasmine that they were

going to meet some people after church and for her to pick out whichever dress she wanted to wear. Jasmine picked what Miss Crowe called her "Sunday Best" — a pretty yellow dress with daisies on the bottom and a long, white linen coat. It had been her Easter outfit and was now her favorite go-to apparel.

Zachary wanted to come, but Gabrielle told him, on this one, it was something just the two of them needed to do. It would be hard enough with merely the key players involved. She didn't want to add any unnecessary tension to the mix.

And the way Zachary rose up to protect both her and Jasmine, she could just see something jumping off and Zachary pouncing, beating somebody down, even if all he was using to do it were words.

So no, he wasn't allowed to go.

Gabrielle pulled up to the house, walked to the front door, and rang the doorbell. Answering the door, Deidra led them to the den (an area large enough to hold everybody comfortably). She invited them to sit on the couch.

Paris was there, looking like any minute she might grab her stomach and say something to the effect of "It's time," and everybody would be left scrambling to get her to the hospital.

Gabrielle couldn't help but think with her and Paris's history, which appeared to have settled down after the last fiasco Paris had caused, Paris just *might* go into labor just as things were being laid out. She didn't believe Paris would do that on purpose, not at this point with things as they were. But still . . .

Andrew was also there along with Malachi, Lawrence's twenty-seven-year-old, debonair son.

"Dinner is ready," Deidra Simmons said, looking at her diamond watch. "Imani should be down in a few minutes. She wanted to change into something more comfortable, getting out of her church clothes into what we used to call play clothes when we were growing up. I told her she was fine, but you know how sixteen-year-olds are."

"Imani?" Jasmine said, turning and looking at Gabrielle with a huge grin on her face as things were beginning to click before turning to Paris, who she obviously still hadn't quite warmed up to. "Yes!" She did a victory fist pull down. "The Imani who was my bone marrow donor." There was a glorious twinkle in Jasmine's eyes.

Paris smiled and nodded.

They all had agreed that the less said until everyone came together, the better.

Imani came in and saw everybody seated and waiting. When she saw Jasmine, she immediately hurried over to her though the little girl was already running to meet Imani. The two of them hugged and started squealing with delight as they jumped up and down.

"Mom, why didn't you tell me this is who our company was going to be?" Imani said, looking at Deidra. "Oh, my goodness! Look at you! Look at how long your hair has grown." She picked up Jasmine's hair and let it drop. "And you've gotten taller. I almost didn't know who you were. Why didn't someone tell me Jasmine was coming?"

"Don't feel bad," Jasmine said. "My mother didn't tell me where we were going, either. Had she told me, I probably would have been beside myself to get here. I guess that's why she didn't." She hugged Imani again, and the two of them did their celebratory jumping ritual all over again.

"Come and sit by me," Imani said as she and Jasmine found a place on the couch together. "You look wonderful. I can't believe how great you look. Oh, my goodness!"

Lawrence looked at Gabrielle, wondering what the plan was from this point. It had been agreed that Gabrielle would take the lead.

Gabrielle stood up and cleared her throat. "I have something I need to tell you," Gabrielle said, looking at Jasmine. "Can you please come here with me?"

Jasmine giggled, no doubt thinking of the many times Miss Crowe had made a big deal about using the words "can" and "may" correctly, with *can* meaning able to and *may* being will you.

Jasmine came and stood next to Gabrielle, whose look was staid as she kneeled down, causing the two of them to be eye to eye. Gabrielle smiled nervously. She glanced sideways at Lawrence, who was making his way over to stand next to them as Deidra, touching the rose pendant dangling from her necklace, got up and sat next to Imani, putting her arm around her.

"What's wrong?" Jasmine asked. "Why are you crying?"

Gabrielle hadn't realized tears were flowing down her face. She wiped the tears that had managed to squeak out and forced a smile. "Nothing's wrong. In fact, I am soooo happy for you."

"If you're happy, then why doesn't it feel

like that?" Jasmine said.

"Jasmine . . . honey, you know how much I love you, right?"

"Yes. I know." Jasmine nodded, and then glanced up at Lawrence, who was now standing beside Gabrielle. "No! Don't say it." Jasmine began to shake her head quickly. "They're taking me away from you, aren't they? Something went wrong and you're losing me!" Jasmine threw her arms around Gabrielle and clung to her as if it was for dear life. "I don't want to live here! I don't want to leave you! I want to stay with you, Mama! I want to stay with you and Miss C and after June eleventh, Dr. Z! Please don't let them take me from you. Please —"

Gabrielle pushed her back to look in her eyes. "No, Jasmine. Nobody's taking you away from me. You've gotten it all wrong."

Jasmine was crying hard now. "Then why are we here? Why did you tell me to wear my favorite dress? Why is the whole family standing around looking at me like they are?"

Gabrielle knew at this point it was best to just rip the Band-Aid off quickly. "Jasmine, I want you to meet your father."

"What?" Jasmine wiped her eyes with her hands.

"What?" Gabrielle heard an echo of that

322

same word, only it was coming from Imani.

"What do you mean?" Imani said, turning to her mother.

Lawrence stepped forward and kneeled down before Jasmine. "Hi, Jasmine." He gave her a warm inviting smile. "I'm Lawrence Simmons. I'm your father."

Jasmine looked at him, then at Gabrielle, who was now standing and really crying with her hands clasped tightly across her mouth.

"My father?" Jasmine began backing away from him.

"Her father?" Imani said, now on her feet.

Lawrence stood up, grabbed Jasmine, and hugged her. "Yes, your father."

"Daddy," Imani said as she came over to them. "What's going on? Daddy, what are you talking about?"

Lawrence reached over and pulled Imani into the group hug, although Jasmine seemed to be trying hard to break loose. Lawrence took both of them by the hands, and again dropping to his knees, he said, "Imani, I want you to meet your sister. Jasmine, I want you to meet *your* sister. You two . . . are sisters. And I . . . I am both your father."

"We're sisters?" Imani said, looking at Jasmine. "I'm not just your bone marrow donor but your *sister*?"

Jasmine was wiping her eyes. Gabrielle was on her way to pull Jasmine safely into her arms, but Imani beat her to it.

"You're my sister," Imani said to Jasmine with a jubilant smile. "You're my *sister*!"

Jasmine was nodding while being tightly embraced by Imani. "Sisters."

It wasn't long before Imani must have realized she was the only one of her siblings reacting to the news. With one arm still around Jasmine, she looked at her sister and brother. Paris was wiping tears and nodding. Malachi was sitting with a big grin on his face but saying nothing.

"Why aren't either of you surprised?" Imani directed her attention first to Paris, then Malachi. "Did you already know about this?" She looked at her mother. "Am I the only one who didn't know anything?" Tears rolled down Imani's face.

Deidra rushed over and hugged Imani. Jasmine ran into Gabrielle's awaiting arms.

"I'm sorry, Imani. I'm sorry. But we couldn't tell you until now," Deidra said. "It was best this way."

"Best?" Imani said, pulling away from her mother's embrace to look her in the eyes. "Best for whom? Best for Daddy? Best for our family? Oh, I'm sorry. Everybody in the

family apparently except for me. So what does that say about me? How long have you known? How long has everybody known this, *except* me?"

"It's been a few months," Deidra said. "That's all; only a few months. We always planned on telling you. We just had to wait for the right time."

Imani broke away from her mother and went over to her father. "Why couldn't you tell me? If you could tell Paris and Malachi, then why not me? Is it because you thought I couldn't keep it and I might somehow ruin your reelection chances? Oh, wait. You dropped out of the race around the first of September. So what would have been the reason for you not telling me after that?"

"Imani, we didn't tell you because we were well aware of the special bond that exists between you and Jasmine, and I'm not just talking about the incredible gift of bone marrow you so unselfishly gave," Lawrence said. "There was something between you two. We were certain if you knew the truth, you'd want to be with Jasmine more and you'd have a hard time keeping the secret until it was the appropriate time to disclose it. Understand?"

Imani didn't say anything. She merely stared at her father with a hurt look.

Paris went over to Jasmine. "Hello, little sister. Welcome to the family." She hugged Jasmine.

."Thank you," Jasmine said.

Malachi grinned as he stepped up to Jasmine. "Hello, little sis. I'm your big brother." He bent down and hugged her. "I'm the one you can come to if you need me to beat up some boy who might not be doing right by you." He laughed. "But seriously though, I'm your big brother so know that I'm here for you, and that I've *always* got your back. Ask our other sisters; they'll tell you."

"Oh, yes," Paris said, laughing. "Malachi has your back all right. And he'll be the first one to throw you under the bus if it suits his agenda. But he's really a great brother and he really will be there for you when you need him most."

Malachi grinned as he looked at Paris. "Well, thank you, sister dearest. I'm truly touched." He placed his hand over his heart and winked at Paris.

"So I have two sisters and a brother now?" Jasmine said, looking at Gabrielle, who was battling hard at wiping away her flowing tears.

Gabrielle nodded. "Yes, you do," Gabrielle said.

Andrew brought in a box of tissue and began servicing everyone in need of them. Gabrielle yanked out a few and smiled as she gave him a quick nod of appreciation. He smiled and gave her a quick nod back.

There was a lot of hugging exchanged that afternoon. They then went into the dining room for dinner, sat down, and went around the dining room table stating what all they were thankful for. Everyone with the name Simmons anywhere in their name stated how glad they were to have Jasmine now as part of the family.

They ended with a prayer led by Lawrence before digging into food that had been made to nourish their bodies but was somehow becoming the bridge that also blessed their souls.

CHAPTER 30

Better is the end of a thing than the beginning thereof: and the patient in spirit is better than the proud in spirit.
— Ecclesiastes 7:8

Just after everyone had eaten and gotten full, Paris grabbed her stomach. "Whoa," she said. "Now, that didn't feel good *at all.*"

Andrew came over. "What is it?"

"I'm not sure, but that was uncomfortable and a little bit of pain for sure," Paris said.

"Do you think you might be going into labor?" Andrew asked.

"She just probably ate too much," Malachi said. "Paris *was* sort of putting down the food like she was eating for three."

"Well, there's only one other in this body besides me, so I assure you it was just for the two of us."

"We need to monitor you," Deidra said. "And if you have another pain, we'll see how far apart they are. It could just be you ate too much, but it could be labor."

Gabrielle was glad she and Jasmine were already in the process of leaving before this all began. She would have hated to announce their departure at this juncture. Knowing Paris, she'd likely take it the wrong way. She could only hope Paris had turned the corner with her past attitude. But when it came to Paris, Gabrielle knew it was best to keep a guard at the post at all times.

"Okay," Paris said. "I think we need to make our way to the hospital."

Deidra rushed to her side. "Was that another pain? That soon after the one you just had?"

Paris shook her head quickly. "Nope. Not another pain. But I think my water just broke."

"You're having the baby? Today? The baby is coming now?" Imani said. "But the baby isn't due until Thursday."

"Well, some babies prefer to choose their own dates and couldn't care less what a doctor marked on the calendar," Paris said. "Because this one here" — she pointed at her stomach — "appears to have decided to make an early debut."

"But your stuff is at the house," Andrew

said. "We're not prepared for you to go into labor while we're away from home."

"Sweetheart, we can get my bag later. In the old days, you needed a packed bag," Paris said to Andrew. "Today, hospitals pretty much have everything you need, which at this point, will most likely merely be a birthing gown."

Andrew nodded quickly. "Yeah, you're right. It's time." He looked at Deidra. "It's time! Oh, my goodness, we're having a baby! I need to call my mother. I'm about to become a father!"

"And *I'm* about to become a grandmother!" Deidra put her hand up to her mouth. "Granny. Granny Dee. Grandmother. Oh, my goodness. It's time to decide."

"And we," Imani said, hugging Jasmine, "are about to become aunts!"

"An aunt?" Jasmine said. "Me? I'm going to be an aunt, too?"

"Yes," Imani said with a laugh. "You're going to be an aunt, too."

"Wow," Jasmine said. "I arrived here as an only child, and I'm leaving with a new father, a stepmother, two sisters, a brother, a brother-in-law, and now I'm about to be an aunt, too? Whoa, Nelly!"

Everybody laughed.

"What do you know about 'Whoa, Nelly'?" Lawrence said to Jasmine with a grin. "That's *way* before your time."

"Oh, I guess you haven't heard," Jasmine said. "But everybody says I'm smart beyond my years."

"That what you just said," Lawrence said as he hugged Jasmine, "was more than just smart beyond your years. That was old soul smart. That was something my grandmother used to say back in the day."

"Yeah, back when they had horses," Malachi said with a chuckle.

"Can we please table this conversation?" Paris said. "I don't want to make it seem like everything is about me. But at this moment . . . everything really *is* about me and this baby who's definitely coming *pretty* soon, I'd say." She let out another half scream.

"I'd say your pains are about ten minutes apart," Deidra said. "Anybody who's going to the hospital with us had better make your way to my car."

"I'm taking Paris in my car," Andrew said to Deidra.

"I know. I wasn't talking to you and Paris. I was talking to anyone in my family who's planning on going. Because I'm not going to miss one minute of this. In fact, unless you want to fight me for it, Andrew, I hope I can cut the baby's cord."

"Mom . . . Andrew," Paris said, waddling quickly toward the front door. "Can you two talk about this *after* I get to the hospital?" Paris said.

"Come on, baby, let's get you to the car." Andrew helped her. "I'll call my mother after we get to the hospital. You know she wants to be there, too."

Paris let out a moan and looked at Andrew as though she wanted to make a comment. But Gabrielle decided that possibly it was just the pain she was experiencing, although that one wasn't ten minutes from the last time.

Gabrielle and Jasmine left along with Paris and Andrew. But not before Imani and Jasmine got in two more hugs, promising to keep in close touch from here on out.

CHAPTER 31

But this is a people robbed and spoiled;
they are all of them snared in holes, and
they are hid in prison houses: they are for
a prey, and none delivereth; for a spoil,
and none saith, Restore.

— Isaiah 42:22

Paula had been present when the baby was
born, a little boy (just as she'd predicted),
at a healthy seven pounds eight ounces
(again right on the money as she'd said).
She wasn't in the birthing room when the
baby was born even though Paris's mother
was. In fact, Paris's mother got to cut the
umbilical cord, which Deidra commented
was the highlight of the morning, after seeing the baby being born.

Paris had gone into labor on Sunday
night, but didn't deliver the baby until six-
seventeen on Tuesday morning, April the
twenty-sixth. It was a long, hard labor. But

Andrew was right by her side, holding her hand and feeding her ice chips. Deidra had sent her family home early Monday morning without her. They returned that afternoon with Lawrence bringing Deidra her requested change of clothing. He and Imani left that night, only to get a call at five-thirty Tuesday morning, and they were able to make it back just in time to hear the glorious proclamation that the baby boy was here.

Ironically, it was as if the baby knew something in advance of his original April 28 due date. As though the baby knew that even Wednesday wasn't the best day to make an entrance. Because on Wednesday, April 27, the worst devastation Alabama and other states had ever seen or experienced, weather-wise, hit.

Several tornadoes touched down, killing people in Tuscaloosa, Pratt City (which was only thirty minutes, if that much, from where the baby was born and forty-five minutes from his new home). A tornado touched down in Cullman, a town that always seemed to receive its share of tornadoes. Black folks with knowledge of Cullman's history when it came to black folks (a board advising them not to let night catch them there) had their own theory about why that might be. But the destruction every-where was devastating.

Just before 6 AM (even before the second wave of tornadoes touched down, the ones that arrived after two o'clock that after-noon), a brewing storm knocked out the power around Birmingham and surround-ing cities stretching more than forty miles in each direction. Most who called to report the outages heard the recorded message stating outages were known and would be fixed no later than eleven that morning.

Well, that didn't happen. And most who had no power and no other backup method to get news reports had no idea what was about to hit next. Fortunately, hospitals had backup generators. Paris and her newborn were in the best possible place since their home didn't have electricity, as was the case at both Paula's and her parents' houses.

In fact, the power was off from Wednesday to Friday morning at Paula's house. Paula told Andrew her power was back on and they were welcome to come there with the baby when they were released since their power was still off. But Paris was set on the first place she'd be taking her baby being her own home. And Andrew, the ever duti-ful husband, and now proud papa, was determined that Paris would have her heart's desire. So he managed to borrow a small generator from a coworker (the only one he could find available to him in the entire state, it seemed) with the hopes that the electricity would be back on no later than Friday evening.

Well, he, his wife, and son were left without power until Sunday night at around 9 PM. Paula knew all of this because Andrew had kept her informed of all that was going on after Paris and the baby went home from the hospital Friday morning. Certainly not the homecoming they'd planned or envisioned. Andrew was shouting about how God's hand was in all of this because their power did miraculously come on just as the television networks were promoting the President of the United States's pending special announcement, which turned out to be that Osama bin Laden was dead.

Paula had intended on being at the house to help Paris during her first days of being home. But Paris insisted they were fine. So most who stopped by to visit only stayed about an hour so as not to cause them undue hardship. The generator was only a tiny help. Andrew told Paris, "We can only plug in a few things so we need to decide which electrical appliances are the most important to have." He was praying that things would be back to normal soon. Sunday night was a good first step.

But normal, during these times, appeared to be overrated. People didn't have food because, after three days without power, even a freezer with built-up ice (because the freezer wasn't one that self-defrosted) couldn't save anything.

However, a month later, things had indeed settled down. Pretty much most everyone's power had been restored and there was a plan to restore some of the loss of food many had incurred because it had taken longer than ever expected to get the power back on.

Andrew told his mother he'd learned many of those who'd lost power hadn't even been from the deadliest of the tornadoes (the one that hit in the afternoon when most of them had no power to even hear what was coming). It had been because of a transformer that had been picked up and blown so far away early that morning that the power crew couldn't find it and it couldn't be easily or quickly fixed. That's why it was originally believed things would be restored sooner until they saw they didn't possess what they needed. Then after the other tornadoes touched down, it was too much, too overwhelming, definitely one for the record books.

Paris never seemed to miss an opportunity to tell Paula how much certain things about the baby were so much like Andrew. The baby's nose, the way the baby smiled. Paula didn't believe it much since, in her experience, babies didn't possess the motor skills to smile as early as Paris was trying to say theirs was. Paula got so tired of Paris saying that about the baby smiling that she just told her it was most likely gas the baby was expressing.

Paula noticed how much Paris tried to get her to agree with her on the things she said were like Andrew. But truthfully, and it could be that it's just really hard to look at a newborn and honestly find things that match an adult unless you're already inclined to do so, even if there were things one could link to baby pictures. But Paula didn't see anything that indicated in the *least* that this baby was like Andrew.

But she also knew she wasn't going to push things too far by insisting to Andrew, as she'd done a few months ago, that he have a paternity test done. She'd said it already. Andrew had flat-out rejected the notion. So she would just pray that if there was even a remote chance she might be right, the truth would somehow come to light and save her son from possible deeper heartbreak down the road.

But for now, she couldn't honestly say, not with certainty, one way or the other. So she was going to just keep her trap shut.

CHAPTER 32

Behold, ye trust in lying words, that cannot profit.

— Jeremiah 7:8

By May 17 — three weeks after giving birth to Braylen Ryker Holyfield (two first names that had left her mother-in-law scratching her head as she wondered aloud and to their faces why she and Andrew had decided to name their son that), the originally light-skinned little boy was quickly turning darker shades of brown. Paris knew she had to do something to quiet even her own thoughts that were beginning to scream doubts about her baby's paternity who was no longer the color of she and Andrew but increasingly closer to Darius's dark-brown skin tone. She needed to get a DNA home kit in a hurry.

With her mother-in-law visiting that day, she decided to run to the store, telling Paula she had to go pick up something important.

"Back in my day, older women wouldn't even let us go out of the house until our babies were at least a month old. Most times they insisted it be six weeks," Paula said, cradling an almost sleep Braylen in her arms. "My mother used to say we young folks were going to catch it when that stuff caught up with us in our old age. I'm seeing some of those older folks were right."

"I'm not going to be gone long. I just have something I absolutely have to get," Paris said, car keys in hand as she headed for the door to the garage.

"I told you that's what I'm here for. I don't mind going and getting whatever you need. Just make me a list, and I'll be happy to get it and bring it back," Paula said, glancing down at the baby as she spoke softly now.

"I'm not sure which one I want," Paris said, being as evasive as possible. She wasn't *completely* lying. She'd checked online to see which DNA kit was recommended and rated the most reliable. If she was going to do this, she needed to make sure the results would be of the highest standards available. She'd thought about asking her father to pick up the kit for her since he was the only person who knew the truth (other than Johnnie Mae, who she didn't count in the number since she'd only gone to her for counseling), but she knew he wasn't good at finding things in a store which he considered women's work. Besides, she'd hate for that kind of news to get out if someone saw him purchase the kit and report on it. It was her father who'd suggested something like this. For now, it seemed to be her best shot with the least amount of casualties.

Paris left, only picking up that one item so she wouldn't be out in the air for too long. She didn't need Paula saying anything to Andrew to cause him to grill her about her little rendezvous outside the house.

Honestly surprised Paris had been gone for only twenty minutes, Paula said, "What happened? Did you get out of the driveway and change your mind?"

"No. But I do respect your words of wisdom and opinion. I told you I wasn't going shopping; I just needed to pick up something important."

"I still don't understand why you just didn't let me run and get it for you. But that's young folks for you," Paula said. "Well, the baby is asleep. So if I were you, I'd try and sneak me in a little nap as well. I'm out of here." She hugged Paris and left.

All of the kits sold for around thirty dollars, but that was just the cost for the kit. If she wanted fast results she'd have to pay an additional cost to send it overnight as opposed to using the preaddressed envelope provided using standard delivery. She would also have to pay an additional one hundred and thirty dollars for the lab fee, and that was if it wasn't a rush job. If she used a credit card to prepay or sent a money order, she could expect the results in about seven days. If she chose any other way, like writing a personal check, she was looking at a turnaround of three to four weeks.

The good part was that she had the option of them sending the results (discreetly of course) back by mail or going online if she set up an account with an ID and password. She could also call a number and, using a special code, be told the results over the phone. The kit contained three swabs: one for the subject in question (in her case, her baby boy), one for the father, and if desired, one for the mother. She saw no reason to swab her own cheek and waste money when she knew she was the mother.

Now she just needed to decide whether she should contact Darius and get him to agree to this DNA test. If she did it that way, they could prayerfully disqualify him, which would only mean that Andrew was without a doubt Braylen's father. But the mere thought of Darius caused her stomach to turn. He was such a jerk. And knowing him, he most likely wouldn't agree to it even though this was much cheaper than her earlier idea of a prenatal paternity test, and decisively cheaper than going to court, where he'd likely have to pay for the whole test, which was triple this cost.

Wanting to skip the drama at this point, she made a decision. She would swab Braylen's cheek. And when Andrew came home, she would . . . she would . . .

What? What would she do? Ask him to let her swab the inside of his cheek for fun? Like he'd actually fall for that. He was a lawyer, for Pete's sake. He knew the process used in DNA testing. He'd immediately know what she was up to. Then everything Paris had heard his mother say to him would flood into his mind. And he would know that even *she* had at least some reason to question the paternity of her child.

So for Braylen's sake and Andrew's she couldn't do that to either of them. If Andrew was to ever hear the truth, it would be *the truth* and not just a need to know what the truth *might* be.

After Andrew came home and held his son, after he'd told Paris just how happy he was, and how much he loved her. After he vowed that he would always do what he needed to take care of the two of them. After he'd fallen sound asleep and Paris felt pretty sure that nothing would likely awaken him, she took the Q-tip swab provided in the DNA kit and swabbed the inside of his right cheek.

And if anybody were ever to say that she wasn't sorry for any of her past actions, they didn't see how caring and patient she'd been in pulling off this feat, all because she didn't want to unnecessarily hurt her husband if she didn't have to.

After she finished, she quietly slid out of the bed with the swab in hand and placed it in its own plastic bag labeled for the father. She put the two individual bags with the DNA of child and potential father inside the pre-labeled package. She sighed, knowing she was closer to putting the question of Braylen's paternity to bed.

She put the package somewhere safe until it could be sent off in the morning, then quietly crawled back into bed and laid down just in time for Braylen to cry and cause her to have to get up again.

And through all of that, Andrew never moved, not even once.

CHAPTER 33

The letter which ye sent unto us hath been
plainly read before me.

— Ezra 4:18

It had been a week and Paris was looking
for the DNA results to arrive by mail (as
she'd checked off) no later than May 24. So
after two days of it not being there, she
called to follow up on it.

It took a few transferrings of her calls, but
she finally reached someone who could help
her. Yes, it had indeed been mailed, and
should have arrived on Monday as their
turnaround had been two days after having
received her package. A woman named Marie reminded her that the outside of the
envelope would be plain as to be discreet
and wouldn't contain any identifying words
to tie it back to their company, just in case
she'd received it and mistakenly trashed it
as junk mail.

Paris thought back, but there hadn't been anything that had come resembling what the woman was describing. Still, she decided since she hadn't thrown out any junk mail yet, she would definitely go back and check. She asked Marie if she could be given the information over the phone now and was told because she'd originally checked for mail only and had specifically requested it be disclosed that way, she *could* request it differently but there were safety measures she'd have to go through in order to do that.

"If you'd like to give it a few more days and then if it doesn't arrive, we'll be happy to proceed with the required paperwork to disclose the information in a different manner than originally selected," Marie said.

At first Paris was put out at possibly having to jump through hoops to get the results she'd paid for. But when she calmed down and thought it through, she could see where that was a necessary level of protection for someone who might try to deviously circumvent the process. She would give it another week, and if it hadn't arrived by then, she'd feel confident something had happened and initiate necessary steps to receive the results another way.

Tuesday, the following week, she had an appointment for her six weeks' checkup. It was hard to believe Braylen was already six weeks old. He was growing up so fast. Paris's mother was supposed to come over and watch Braylen while she went to the doctor, but her mother woke up with a sore throat and a slight fever. Paris told her not to worry, she had another alternative, and asked her mother to take care of herself and get well soon.

Paris called Andrew, but he couldn't get away. So she decided she'd just take Braylen with her. The doorbell rang just as she was rushing to get him ready.

"Paula? What are you doing here?" Paris asked her mother-in-law as she held Braylen securely against her shoulder, bouncing him to keep him quiet as she spoke.

"I hear you're in need of a babysitter for a few hours. I'm here to offer my services," Paula said.

"Andrew called you?" Paris said. "He shouldn't have bothered you."

"Why not? You need someone to watch my grandbaby while you go to the doctor for your checkup, and I was free to come over." Paula reached over and lovingly took Braylen from Paris. "Look at Grandma's big boy. Look at you," she said to Braylen. "Such a big boy! Such a big boy! Yes, you are!"

"Are you sure about this?"

"Of course, I'm sure. You just go on and don't worry about me and Braylen. We're going to have so much fun. Aren't we, Braylen? Aren't we?" She held him up in the air and smiled as she twisted his body from side to side. He smiled. "Look a' there," she said to Paris. "He just smiled at me."

"I told you that he smiles, but you didn't believe me. You said it was gas." Paris closed the door.

"Okay, Paris." Paula grinned.

"I'm running late, so I'm really glad you came. It's not as easy as it looks trying to get yourself ready and a baby, too. And I didn't even get to the putting him in the car seat part and having to take him out when I arrive. You're a lifesaver. I truly appreciate this. I just need to run and get my purse, and I'll be out of here."

Paris trotted up the stairs and just as quickly returned with her purse on her shoulder. "I'll be back as soon as I'm done!" she yelled as she disappeared to the garage.

Paula walked around the den with Braylen, singing several rounds of "Old Mac-Donald Had a Farm." She was on the "quack, quack" part when the doorbell rang. "Now who do you think that could be?" Paula said as she and Braylen went to answer the door.

"I have a package for you," the postwoman said. "It appears one of our machines mangled the original envelope so we had to put it in this one. It was apparently already late and a trace had been placed on it stating it was urgent. So I was asked to personally deliver it to this address."

Paula took the envelope. "Thanks. I'll be sure and tell them. I'm grandma here babysitting my new grandbaby."

"Oh, he's a cutie," the postwoman said, leaning in closer to Braylen and smiling. "Who does he favor? His mother or his father?"

"Thank you. I suppose if I was pressed, I'd say he *sort* of favors his father's father a little. They're closer to the same skin tone and maybe have a similar nose," Paula said, looking down at Braylen and seeing possible hints of Andrew's father, who'd left them high and dry back when Andrew was a mere baby.

"Well, you two have a good day."

"Same to you," Paula said, baby in her arm while holding the white envelope addressed to Holyfield in her other hand.

Three hours later, Paula heard the garage door rise and then go back down.

"That must be your mother coming back,"

Paula said, standing up with Braylen and going into the kitchen to greet Paris.

The door from the garage to the kitchen opened and closed. Andrew strolled in with his briefcase in hand.

"Hi, Mom." Andrew leaned down and kissed her on the cheek. "Hi, there, Braylen. How's daddy's little man? Did you have fun with Grandma today? Did you?" Andrew set his briefcase on the floor, carefully took Braylen from his mother, and placed him on his shoulder. "Paris's car isn't in the garage. Did she go somewhere after she came back from the doctor's or has she not gotten back yet?"

"She hasn't gotten back yet."

"How long has she been gone?"

"I guess three . . . maybe four hours, but who's counting? You know how it can be with doctor visits. And when it's a doctor who's on call to deliver babies at any moment, a doctor's visit can be a true nightmare. You may be there in the waiting room, and the doctor either has to cancel or postpone your appointment to take care of a patient who's not planning on waiting for the next available time slot on schedule. I wouldn't worry too much, though. I'm just glad you called me to come over and take care of little Braylen. I'd hate for him to have had to be there all this time."

"Well, I thank you for being there when I called and willingly agreeing to come do this." Andrew glanced down at a now sleeping Braylen. "He's out like a light."

"Yeah, I suppose I wore the little fellow out. He'll probably sleep a couple of hours."

"I'm going to go lay him down." Andrew walked slowly and carefully and went and put Braylen in his crib.

When Andrew came back downstairs (minus his suit coat now), his mother had her purse on her shoulder and was standing at the front door. "Well, I'm out of here, unless you have somewhere you need to go, in which case, I can stay longer."

"Oh, no. I'm good. I'm home for the rest of the day. Do you know if Paris got the mail before she left?"

"I don't. But, there was a special package brought to the door." Paula went and got it and handed it to him. "A postwoman — I love saying that — said their equipment chewed up the original envelope so they had to put it in a new one."

He turned the large white envelope over in his hand. "Is that why there's no return address information on the outside envelope?"

"That's what I got from her. I think it was

nice of them though to send someone out special to deliver it. Whenever something like that has ever happened with *my* mail, they just stick it in the mailbox with a stamped message that the original enveloped encountered 'machine' problems. I suppose that's the difference between living in a nice neighborhood and where we came from: They send a postal worker to bring one piece of mail they feel might be important when they mess up." Paula grabbed Andrew by his collar and pulled him down toward her, giving him a quick peck on the cheek, interrupting him just as he was peeling back the gummed flap of the envelope.

Standing upright now, he stopped and looked hard at the information he'd pulled out of the envelope. "Mom, hold up a second."

Paula frowned, tilting her head trying to see. "What is it?"

Andrew was also frowning. "This." He was scanning the chewed-up envelope that had no identifying relevant return address markers on the outside of the original envelope. But because part of the envelope was ripped away at the top, it exposed the letterhead to the contents inside the mangled envelope.

"What about it?"

"First off, this isn't addressed to me. It's

addressed to Paris."

Paula shrugged. "I didn't know. It just had Holyfield on the outside. So you can give it to her when she gets here and tell her what the postwoman said."

"Are you sure a postal worker brought this? This isn't some kind of joke or something is it?" Andrew asked.

"Well, she was wearing an official post-office-looking shirt. However, I didn't ask her for any ID or anything. And she *was* driving a compact white car that looks like the ones I've seen some postal workers drive, when they're not delivering neighborhood mail, that is." Paula moved in closer. "What is it?"

"A part of the envelope was torn off and is exposing the company where it seems to have come from."

She frowned. "And — ?"

"And it appears to have come from, of all places, a DNA company."

"Well, maybe Paris is doing some research on her roots or something. You know, like that professor Henry Louis Gates did on PBS with famous people like Oprah and those others. A lot of people are doing that these days, you know."

Andrew shook his head. "She's never said anything about wanting to do that nor shown any interest. Mom, months ago, you brought up the idea that the baby Paris was carrying might not be mine. I scoffed at that. But truthfully, on that same day you also said the baby was a boy and that turned out to be true."

Paula hunched her shoulders. "Well, I had a fifty-fifty shot of being right."

"That's true. But you also said he would weigh seven pounds eight ounces. Now that's not something one can predict so accurately, but you were right on the money," Andrew said.

"It was a number that just popped up in my head." Paula sighed. "Listen, Drew. I know I was the one who raised the question about Paris and the baby, but —"

"Do you think Braylen looks like he's my child?"

"Andrew, I know you're upset right now —"

"You're absolutely right, I'm upset right now! I wasn't supposed to see this package at all. This was addressed to Paris Holyfield. Do you really believe she was intending to share whatever is in here with me?" Andrew said.

"I don't know. I suppose you'll just have to ask her yourself?"

"Ask me what?" Paris said, walking toward

Andrew.

"You're home. I didn't hear the garage door go up or come down. Why didn't you bring your car into the garage?" Andrew asked Paris.

Paris tilted her head slightly. "What?"

"I said why did you *not* drive your car into the garage?"

She shrugged. "It's no big deal, Andrew. I was merely in a hurry to get in the house to see the baby, that's all."

"So you parked your car outside and came in through the side door?" Andrew asked with a frown. He shook his head. "That doesn't make any sense."

"I didn't think it would be a big deal, Andrew. In fact, I didn't even know you were home. Is there something wrong?" She looked at Paula. "Is Braylen okay? Did something happen while I was gone? The doctor got called away to deliver a baby and they gave us the option of either rescheduling or staying an hour or two longer. I figured since I was already there and you'd been so kind as to come over and help me out, I'd do better to just stay and see if he'd be back soon as he expected he would."

"Braylen's fine. He's sleeping. And it wasn't a problem at all," Paula said. "In fact, I was prepared to stay as long as I was needed."

Paris looked at her husband. "So why are you upset, Andrew?"

"I'm upset because I'm trying to figure out what *this* is all about." He held the mangled envelope out to Paris and shook it toward her.

Paris took it. Her hand visibly began to shake as she saw the DNA return info from the now exposed letterhead.

"What is this?" She tried to laugh it off. "It's likely nothing, probably just junk mail some company sent trying to get me to do something like search for my roots."

"Sure, Paris," Andrew said. "Then why don't you open it."

"Okay," Paris said. "I'll do *just* that. But not right now. Right now, I'm going to check on my son."

"He's asleep right now. And my mother's here. If he wakes up, I'm sure she'll be happy to get him for us. So why don't you open that now, and if it's junk mail, we can deep-six it. Go on, Paris. It's already close to being opened. Rip off the rest of the envelope and let's see what it is."

"I'm not going to bother playing these games," Paris said, opening the trash can and dropping the envelope in it.

"Oh, so you don't want to open it?"

Andrew asked her.

"No. I told you. I don't care about junk mail. And I'm not interested in tracing my roots or whatever they might be pushing."

Andrew opened the trashcan and reached in.

Paris looked horrified as her eyes opened wider. "What are you doing?"

"I'm taking it out of the trash," Andrew said, pulling the envelope out.

"Give it back," Paris said, reaching for it.

"If you don't want to see what's in it, then I'll be happy to see."

"No! Give it back!" She turned to Paula. "This is all *your* doing. Are you satisfied now? Huh? Are you?"

"My fault?" Paula looked puzzled. "What do *I* have to do with this?"

"You're the one who has been putting all of these crazy ideas in Andrew's head," Paris said as she kept her eye trained on Andrew's hand holding the envelope.

"What ideas?" Paula said. "What are you talking about?"

Paris turned to Paula. "You've been trying to get Andrew to believe our baby isn't his. I guess you finally succeeded."

"I don't know what you're talking about." Paula shifted her weight to her other leg.

"About three months ago, you don't

remember standing right here in my house telling Andrew he needed to get a paternity test after the baby was born to be sure the baby was his?" Paris slammed her red Chanel purse down on the counter.

"What are you talking about, Paris?" Andrew asked.

Paris turned her attention back to Andrew. "Oh, don't try and play dumb with me! I heard you, both of you! You didn't know I'd come in and heard you talking."

"So you came home and I was here, but I didn't hear the garage door raise and lower or hear you come in?" Andrew said. "Is that what you're contending?"

"You didn't hear the garage door raise and lower because I didn't drive my car into the garage that day," Paris said. "I came in through the front door."

"And the reason you wouldn't have come into the garage when you knew my mother was here is *why* now?" Andrew asked.

"You know why," Paris said with her hand on her hip. "You know your mother has never liked me."

"That's not true," Paula said, shaking her head in denial. "I like you fine."

"Yes, it *is* true. And you were in here filling Andrew's head with ideas that I may have been with someone else just because I was working outside the home. I found that appalling and you should be ashamed of yourself."

Paula shrugged. "Well, it *is* true: I've never said you were a saint now."

"You know what? I don't have to stand here and be insulted in my own house." Paris turned to Andrew. "May I have my envelope back please?"

"But you threw it in the garbage."

"Which didn't mean it was okay for you to take it out and keep it. So, please give me *back* my envelope." Paris held out her hand.

"I'll tell you what: Why don't we open it together and see what's in here. And if it's merely junk; I'll apologize. Deal?" Andrew said, extending his hand to shake.

"You know," Paula said. "I'm going to go home now and leave the two of you to work this out without a third party hanging around." Paula turned and left without her customary good-bye or kiss to her son's cheek.

Andrew stared intensely at Paris. Braylen woke up, his cry blaring over the baby monitor in the kitchen. Andrew held the envelope in the air, shook his head, laid the envelope down next to Paris's purse, then left out of the kitchen and went and got

Braylen as Paris stood looking up at the ceiling with tears streaming down her face.

Chapter 34

Who can understand his errors? Cleanse thou me from secret faults.

— Psalm 19:12

Paris walked into the nursery, where Andrew sat rocking Braylen, humming a soothing song to him. She gently took Braylen from Andrew's loving arms and laid the sleeping baby back in his crib. She then walked back over to Andrew and kneeled down before him. Reaching into her pocket, she unfolded the still unopened envelope that was the cause of contention between them, and held it out to him.

"What?" Andrew said quietly.

"Take it," Paris said.

"For what?"

"Because I want you to have it in your possession."

Andrew took it and, tilting his head slightly, clenched his jaw. "What do you want me to do with it?"

"I want you to hear me out. And after I finish, if you want to open it then I want you to open it." Paris swallowed hard.

He shrugged, giving her permission to continue on with what she wanted to say.

"He's a beautiful baby, isn't he?" Paris said, glancing over at Braylen in his crib.

Andrew's face softened, only nodding, appearing to be close to tears as he looked adoringly at his son.

Paris continued to kneel with one hand touching Andrew's knee. "Andrew, I love you. I know I don't say it much. And my actions are often far from demonstrating just how much, but I do. I love you." Paris looked affectionately at him. Andrew was rigid with her.

Andrew shrugged.

Paris pressed her lips together, then nodded. "Back in July, I cheated on you."

Andrew twisted his mouth and began to nod profusely. "So my mother was right?"

Paris took her hand away from his leg and sat back on her heels. "No, your mother wasn't right. I didn't have an affair."

"Cheated . . . an affair, I'm sorry, but I fail to note the difference."

Paris stood to her feet. "The difference, at least for me, is what I did wasn't because I wanted to be with someone other than you. It wasn't a heart or a love thing between us. It was one time. It was a mistake. It didn't mean anything."

Andrew laid his head back on the back of the rocker and released a few quick chuckles. "Oh, that makes it all *so* much better. You had sex with another man . . . at least I take it that it was another man. Of course. It would have to be a man for there to be a question of paternity. How silly of me."

"Please don't be ridiculous," Paris said with a scowl. "Yes, it was with a man."

"Well, I suppose if you were going to cheat on me, I can be thankful it was with a man. So should I thank you now, or wait on you to finish your little story?"

"Andrew, this is hard enough. Can you please not be sarcastic?" Paris said.

"Forgive me if I'm not reacting to all of this in the way you'd like." Andrew sat up straight and looked down at the envelope he held in his hand.

"Andrew, it was one time. I had been drinking —"

Andrew began to chuckle again, then stood to his feet. "Maybe we should leave the baby's room. We wouldn't want little Braylen hearing all about his mother and her antics." He walked out of the room with the envelope still in hand.

Paris followed Andrew to their bedroom. "Andrew, it didn't mean anything."

"I think you've said that already. So you slept with another man back in July because of . . . why was that now?" He tossed the envelope onto the bed. "Oh, yes! That's right! You got plastered and are thereby relieved of any responsibility for any and all subsequent actions. Similar to the drunk driver that causes an accident. Why should he or she be responsible? After all, they didn't know what they were doing. Right?"

"I'm not trying to make any excuses, Andrew." Paris walked over and touched his hand. He quickly moved his hand. She nodded. "I just want you to know the truth."

"Well, I appreciate you at least for that much . . . finally."

"Since I'm telling the whole truth, I got drunk because I'd just found out that you were representing Gabrielle against me."

He nodded with pursed lips. "So you were upset with me."

"Yes, I was upset with you." Paris paced a little. "You chose Gabrielle over me, your own wife. You were not only supporting her; you were defending her. How do you think that made me feel?"

"I suppose, although I'm just guessing

now, but mad enough to get drunk maybe?"
Andrew said.

She turned and scowled at him. "It's not
funny, Andrew! Do you have any idea how
much that hurt? I was drinking because I
didn't want to feel the pain."

"Okay, so you got drunk —" He stopped
and frowned. "Was this that night you called
me and pretty near cursed me out?"

Paris gently closed her eyes, painfully
recalling that night. "Yes."

"So who is he, Paris? Or do I even need
to bother to ask? Who's the man you decided to sleep with who didn't mean anything?"

"I didn't *decide* to sleep with him," Paris
said, flopping down on the bed. She covered
her face with her hands.

"All right, then. Who did you sleep with?"

She looked up at Andrew, tears streaming
down her face. "You already know, so stop
pretending just to torture me."

"Good old co-worker Darius Connors."
Andrew nodded. "And that's why when you
saw him the other month you didn't want
him sitting at our table. That's why you
wanted to leave so early after we arrived. It
was because you'd slept with him. And if
I'm following all of this to its logical conclusion, what with" — he picked up the enve-

lope — "this and it seeming to have something to do with a DNA test, it means you're not sure who Braylen's father is."

Paris jumped to her feet and went to Andrew. "He's our son, Andrew. I believe that with all of my heart. Braylen is *your* son and mine. I just know he is."

"Then why did you need to do this?" Andrew waved the envelope in the air. "Why did you need to even do this? And what is it exactly? Did you get Darius to agree to a paternity test so you'd learn the truth that way?"

Paris looked down at the dark blue carpet, then back up at Andrew. "No. I took a sample from your cheek while you were sleeping."

"You did *what*?" Andrew said, recoiling. "Did you know doing something like that could be considered a crime? It's called stealing. You can't do something like that without either permission from the owner or a mandated court order."

"Andrew, cool it with the lawyer stuff, okay? I'm your wife. I love you. You know I love you. And Braylen loves you."

"So what was the plan?" Andrew said. "Before our good old postal service kind of messed things up for you by mangling this?" He shook the envelope.

"I was going to find out that you were really the father and that would have been the end of that."

"Oh, so, let me get this straight. You had an affair, oh, I'm sorry; I meant an accidental one-time encounter that didn't mean anything. You and I had been trying for a couple of years to have a baby but weren't having much success at it. The same month, apparently, you and your cohort 'accidentally' ended up in bed together — a night I'm sure you'd swear you don't even remember, which should be insulting not only to you, but to him. And then you miraculously end up pregnant. And *yet*! Yet, there's a *good* chance that even though all of these things came together at the same time, *I* managed to be the one who produced our beautiful baby boy." Andrew swallowed hard, then clamped his hand over his mouth. "How was *that* for a closing argument?"

Paris wiped her tears. "I'm sorry, Andrew. I know it looks bad. But I'm coming clean with you about everything now because I love you. And I don't want to lose you. I don't. We can get through this, I know we can."

"You're coming clean with me because of this envelope that has come into our lives and you feel you don't have any other choice now *but* to tell me everything. If I hadn't somehow managed to see this, which I probably wouldn't have had you been home today when it arrived, none of this would be being disclosed right now. I would still be the happy camper going around thinking that there's no way Braylen could be anyone else's *except* mine. I would have defended you to the very end against any and all accusations that you ever cheated on me. Which as my mother likes to point out, you can never put past anyone, no matter who they might be."

Paris wiped her tears and touched his hand, which held the envelope. "I want nothing more than for Braylen to be your son. You're the only father he knows —"

"He's only six weeks old," Andrew said with a shrug. "He's only known me for six weeks."

"He's known you for almost eleven months. He's known your voice since the first day I conceived him."

"Unless, of course, I'm not his biological father," Andrew said.

"When I came home the day after that *thing* with Darius, you were the man I came home to. It was *your* voice our baby heard on that first day."

"Yes, and if memory serves me, that was the same day you accused me of representing Gabrielle, and then you somehow found out that she was Jasmine's birth mother and had given her up for adoption. The day you took it upon yourself to blow up their lives without any thought or regard for what would come next," Andrew said.

"I confess, Andrew, I messed up. In getting drunk, I messed up. In sleeping with Darius that one time, and that's all it ever was and ever will be, a one-time error in judgment, I messed up. I messed up by going off the handle and being so bent on hurting Gabrielle that I went to her house and blurted out stuff that wasn't my business or my place to do it." Paris shook her head as she wiped her tears hard.

"But what I didn't mess up with," she continued, "was knowing what a wonderful husband I have and trying, after all of that, to do everything I could to make things right. What I didn't mess up was having that beautiful child who has done *nothing* wrong. Nothing, do you hear me, except be born into a world of sin. A world he didn't make; a world he didn't ask to come to."

Andrew frowned. "I know this. And you know I love that little boy more than life itself. I would give my life for him, and you know it."

Paris nodded. "I do. But that was when you didn't have any doubts that he was your son. So, after all is said and done: we're at a place of decision. My secrets are pretty much out there now. I ordered that DNA to put to rest the question of who's Braylen's biological father. I don't know what that piece of paper inside that envelope says. You have the answer in your hands now."

"So you're trying to put everything back on me, is that it?"

"I'm just saying to you, you can open it now while we're here and we can find out once and for all. I pray it says you *are* the father." She shook her head. "But if it doesn't, you'll have to decide if it's a deal breaker for you when it comes to being Braylen's father. You'll have to decide that even if he's not your biological son, he's still your son. I want nothing more than to make our marriage work, Andrew. I sinned. Me . . . Paris. I asked God to forgive me a long time ago. I've now confessed everything to you. I don't know what else I can do." She wiped her face, then walked over and yanked a tissue from the brass box on her nightstand.

Andrew held the envelope in the air. He could open it right now while she was there and get it over with. Then he would know for sure and could decide what step to take next. But he loved that little boy. What difference should it make whether his DNA helped to create him or not? Braylen was here now. Paris had changed so much over these past months. They were in a new church being fed the unadulterated Word of God by an anointed man of God.

How would opening that one envelope change things? But more importantly: Would opening that envelope destroy them all?

CHAPTER 35

The wind bloweth where it listeth, and thou hearest the sound thereof, but canst not tell whence it cometh, and whither it goeth: so is every one that is born of the Spirit.

— John 3:8

"It's almost here," Jasmine said to Gabrielle as Miss Crowe looked on with a smile. "Your wedding day is tomorrow." Jasmine stood and started doing a dance called The Running Man.

Miss Crowe laughed. "Go on, girl! Do it. Because I sure can't do that."

Jasmine giggled as she danced, then stopped. "One more day." She held her index finger in the air. "One more day! One! One! One!"

"My goodness, you'd think this was *your* big day or something," Gabrielle said as she bent down and gingerly kissed her daughter on her nose.

"It is," Jasmine said. "Miss C and I have done our parts. We've put together everything we could think of to make this a grand day."

"That's for sure," Miss Crowe said. "And after this is all over, I'm going to find myself a nice cave, crawl up in it, and sleep for days."

"Well, I can't wait until tomorrow. It feels like Christmastime. Dr. Z and Mama will officially be joined together in holy matrimony as one. And I can't wait!" Jasmine jumped up and down.

"You sure do have a lot of energy," Miss Crowe said. "I remember when I could jump around like that."

"Tonight is the rehearsal and after that, the rehearsal dinner," Gabrielle said. "I just hope everybody makes it."

"I talked with Jade last night. She said they were going over to her father's this weekend," Jasmine said.

"But they're all in the wedding," Gabrielle said. "If they go with him this weekend, how are they going to also be in the wedding?"

"Jade said her father was going to bring them to rehearsal tonight and home for the wedding tomorrow," Jasmine said. "But it was his weekend to get them so even though

Miss Tiffany wasn't happy about it and tried to get him to change his time to next week, Jade said he wasn't budging and they were still going with him."

"Maybe you should call Tiffany and see what's going on," Miss Crowe said to Gabrielle. "Everybody has had June tenth and eleventh on their calendars long enough that she should have fixed this problem before it became one."

Gabrielle nodded. This was exactly why she didn't want to have a big wedding. There were always so many moving parts and too much on tap for something to go wrong. Even though she wasn't doing as much of the planning as Miss Crowe and Jasmine, who were coming up with all of these elaborate ideas and had finally been convinced to enlist the planning services of Melissa Peeples, she was still feeling some stress and pressure.

Gabrielle called Tiffany, who, although herself frustrated about Darius's latest antics, assured Gabrielle he'd promised to bring the kids to the rehearsal even if they didn't stay for the dinner and to have them at her house at ten o'clock in the morning, long before the official three o'clock wedding hour struck.

Tiffany got out a little bit of her fury

about Darius and all the crazy stuff he seemed to be doing these days. He'd filed for divorce over a month ago, which Tiffany admitted she really hadn't wanted. He was with some woman named Divine who all three of her children were crazy about, which she wasn't *as* upset about. If Darius was going to be with someone, she'd prefer it be someone her children liked being around and who would treat them right. But still, she was having a hard time accepting that Darius cared so little about them that he'd moved on as easily as he had.

Gabrielle didn't want to be insensitive, but she had enough on her mind thinking about all the things that could go wrong with her wedding tomorrow. She still wasn't sure Zachary's mother, Leslie, was going to show up. Some of the out-of-town guests were either already in town or en route. Zachary was picking up his sister, Queen, and her husband and son from the airport that afternoon as well as his father and brother, who were flying in from Chicago and arriving around the same time. Gabrielle knew Queen (coming in from Florida) had likely planned it that way to help her brother. Queen was detailed like that.

Zachary continued to believe his mother

would change her mind and come. Miss Crowe had given Leslie more than a piece of her mind about her foul attitude and selfish actions. Gabrielle just felt bad for Zachary. It had to hurt knowing that your own mother was going to deliberately miss out on your only wedding. And that's what Zachary said it would be. He said after marrying Gabrielle there would not be another wedding ceremony for him unless he and Gabrielle were renewing their vows in the future. But to know that his mother hated the woman he'd chosen to marry so much that she'd refuse to come and witness it had to hurt.

Rehearsal went beautifully. Darius kept his word and brought the children to the rehearsal as promised. He did bring his new girlfriend with him, which was a bit awkward for Tiffany, who was trying hard to act like it wasn't getting under her skin.

Jasmine and Jade were junior bridesmaids. Dana was the flower girl with Junior as the ring bearer. Tiffany, Queen, and Tameka (another friend from church) were Gabrielle's bridesmaids. Zachary's older brother Yancey, his cousin Michael from Toledo, Ohio, who also flew in earlier that day, and a colleague named Peter, were Zachary's groomsmen, also assigned to escort the bridesmaids out when they exited after the ceremony. Three months pregnant now, Fatima Adams Howard was Gabrielle's matron of honor, and Zachary's father, Zechariah, (who everyone called Zachary) stood as his son's best man. There were ushers and greeters, and instead of getting friends to be hostesses and have them serve food at the reception, Miss Crowe made sure the caterer hired enough people to serve the hundreds of expected guests.

Benjamin "Bennie" Booker would be escorting his daughter down the aisle, giving her away. He couldn't have been more humbled that Gabrielle had asked him.

Bennie had thought for sure Gabrielle wouldn't want him anywhere near her wedding, let alone standing next to her, walking with her to meet the love of her life. But Bennie had proven trustworthy since his arrival back in January. He'd secured a full-time job, thanks to a wonderful program Pastor Landris and Followers of Jesus Faith Worship Center sponsored. And he'd defied his sister Cee-Cee, convincing Jesse to make a change in his life, starting by admitting he had a problem, then accepting the help being offered him by the church. Cee-Cee may have been the same Cecelia Murphy, but Bennie was proving he was a different Benjamin Booker than all those years ago.

"I'm moving forward, and I'm not going back," Bennie had said when giving a testimony a month ago. "If God can save me, if God can change me, if God can love me, if God can forgive me, then what are you waiting on to give your life to Him? All you need to do is take one step, that's all. Step out on faith and watch God work a work in you and your life. I'm not telling you what I've heard; I'm telling you what I know!"

After his testimony, five people came up to him and asked what they needed to do to be saved. And this was not even in a church. Bennie was in the store being measured for his tux. Zachary couldn't stop talking about how powerful and moving that was, even for him. When he and Bennie were riding home, Zachary said he asked Bennie to forgive him for the way he'd acted toward him.

"Your father told me if God could forgive him for what he'd done, there's no way he could ever deny forgiving anyone else for anything they may have done to him," Zachary told Gabrielle. "That Jesus had gone through way more than he ever had and Jesus continues to forgive. Your father then said, 'I'm following Jesus just like the name of my new church says. I'm a follower of Jesus, faith and worship center in the flesh.' I told him he definitely was that. He actually prayed the prayer of salvation for folks in a tuxedo rental store. If *that's* not being a faith worship center, I don't know what is. Your father then said, 'Well, it's like Pastor Landris said last Sunday. *We* are the church. Wherever we go, there should the church be also. Those men wanted to know what they needed to do to have what I have. At that moment, all I could hear was: The doors of the church are open.' "

Zachary laughed recounting that to Gabrielle. She'd almost cried seeing how far God had brought not only her, but her father. She could have turned him away and who knows what might have happened. But she'd prayed about what to do. And as always, the Holy Spirit had led and guided her. She could say without a doubt: God had not failed her yet. Even when it looked like it, hanging in there and trusting God proved out the faithfulness of God. There was truly something about the Spirit of God that just changes things.

Gabrielle looked out as everyone was eating. People were laughing and talking, having a great time of fellowship. And this was just the rehearsal dinner. She couldn't wait until tomorrow when she would walk down the aisle and eventually into the arms of the man who had been like wind beneath her wings. The man who had encouraged her to stretch out her wings, even when the storms came, and soar above the storm. The man who had brought back into her life the woman who was going to stand in as the mother of the bride: Ms. Esther Morgan Crowe, better known affectionately to her as Miss Crowe.

CHAPTER 36

For I am become like a bottle in the smoke; yet do I not forget thy statutes.
— Psalm 119:83

"Happy wedding day!" Jasmine said, jumping on Gabrielle's bed. "It's time to get up! It's a glorious day! The sun is shining and all is right with the world! So wake up!"

Gabrielle laughed. "Girl, I know you didn't come in here and wake me up at" — Gabrielle looked at the clock on her nightstand — "six-seventeen on a Saturday morning."

Jasmine shook her. "Not just any old Saturday morning. It's the start of a new day and a new life with Dr. Z."

Gabrielle threw back the covers, jumped out of the bed, and laughed. "Ha!"

"You're dressed. You have your clothes on already," Jasmine said, noting Gabrielle was wearing her pink summer jogging suit she'd given her for Mother's Day with the assistance of Dr. Z.

"Yes," Gabrielle said. "I've been awake since a little after four o'clock this morning. I couldn't go back to sleep, so I decided to just get up and get dressed." Gabrielle hugged Jasmine and brushed back her bang. "Are you happy?"

Jasmine grinned and kissed Gabrielle nippily on the cheek. "Oh, yes. I'm *very* happy."

"Knock, knock!" Miss Crowe said, rapping her knuckles on the opened door. "Look at you. You're already up and dressed. And to think I didn't want to wake you too early," Miss Crowe said to Gabrielle. "And you, Miss Lady, I see you're up as well."

"I guess that means the Daughters of Zion are all excited today," Jasmine said. "That's what you called us one time. Right, Miss C?"

"I did. And we three indeed have a special bond." Miss Crowe gingerly sat down on the bed between the two of them. "Well, this is the day."

"That the Lord has made!" Jasmine said, taking it over.

"And we *will* rejoice and be glad in it," Gabrielle said.

"That'll preach," Miss Crowe said. "Although when I began by saying this is the day, I wasn't trying to start a praise party here. But I'm down with it, or is it up? But that'll work." She nodded. "So, Miss Gabrielle Mercedes, are you about ready to become Mrs. Gabrielle Mercedes Morgan?"

Gabrielle placed her hand on her heart. "Today *is* the day. And I can say without any hesitation: I am *so* ready. I love him so much, Miss Crowe. I do."

Miss Crowe took Gabrielle by the hand and patted it. "I have something for you." She reached up behind her neck and unclasped the necklace she was wearing. Holding it out to Gabrielle, she said, "Something old and something borrowed."

Gabrielle smiled. "Miss Crowe. It's the necklace you wore in that picture you took with that beautiful dance outfit that time."

"Yes," Miss Crowe said. "You always seemed to love it when you'd look at the picture. I was thinking you might want to wear it today."

Gabrielle smiled and nodded. "Absolutely. I would be honored to. It looked so beautiful on you."

"And it's going to look just as beautiful on you with your wedding dress."

"She's already given you your something new," Jasmine said. "Your wedding dress is new."

"You're right," Gabrielle said. "And I can't wait for Zachary to see me walk down the aisle in it."

"Oh, that poor, man," Miss Crowe said. "He's not going to be able to contain himself when he sees you. He may even tell good old Pastor Landris to skip all the other stuff on schedule and just get to the pronouncement of man and wife part."

Gabrielle laughed. "Miss Crowe."

"I'm serious. Jazz and I have seen you in that dress and you're a knockout. And that was even before hair and makeup," Miss Crowe said. "And, incidentally, your hairdresser will be at the church to style your hair. And I got — wait for it now — the wonderful Jestina to come in with her crew to not just do your makeup, but the whole wedding party."

"Me too?" Jasmine said, innocently and jokingly.

"Your hair? Yes," Gabrielle said. "Makeup? Not on your life."

"Jade's mother lets *her* wear lip gloss," Jasmine said.

"Well, I may let you put on a little lip gloss, but that's it for you, missy." Gabrielle tapped Jasmine on her nose.

"So you have something old, something new, something borrowed, and there's one other thing you're supposed to have." Miss Crowe drummed her fingers on the rumpled up duvet. "What is it?"

"Something blue!" Jasmine said, raising her arm high in triumph.

"Something blue, huh?" Miss Crowe said. "Well, what do we have that might fit that bill? What do we have?"

Jasmine got up and ran out of the room, coming back just as quickly. She held out a small box. "Something blue!"

Gabrielle smiled. She already knew what it probably was, but she played along, taking the box, and opening it. "Oh, look! It's a blue garter."

"I don't know what that thing is or what it's for," Jasmine said. "But Miss C said you're supposed to have one. She said her mother used to wear them for real, but this one is only symbolic."

"Well," Gabrielle said, hugging Jasmine, "it appears I'm all set."

Miss Crowe stood up. "I'm going to fix some breakfast, and then we can make our way to the church. They have private rooms all ready for the women as well as a room for the guys to get dressed. Everybody is to meet us there by eleven o'clock so we can get all dolled up."

Gabrielle put her head down and her

hands up to her face as she began to cry.

"Honey, what's the matter?" Miss Crowe said, hugging Gabrielle.

Jasmine touched Gabrielle's leg. "Mama, why are you crying?"

Gabrielle shook her head with her hands still covering her face.

Miss Crowe pulled Gabrielle's hands down. "I suppose you should get it all out now. We wouldn't want you to ruin your makeup crying later. The photographers are going to be taking lots of pictures after the ceremony, and we don't want to look back at your wedding album and flinch because of a mascara-streaked face."

Gabrielle laughed, and then hugged Miss Crowe. "Thank you. Thank you, so much. You don't know what all of this means to me. My mother isn't here —"

"She is . . . in spirit. I believe she's with you in spirit."

Gabrielle nodded her agreement. She looked in Miss Crowe's eyes. "You . . . have been . . . in my corner for so long. When I didn't feel like I mattered or that anyone loved me, you were there. Then you gave me another great gift: a love of dance. And that gift freed me in so many ways I'll never be able to suitably put into words. I just want you to know that outside of everything you've done for me, not even *talking* about the amount of money you've generously poured into this wedding. You've been like a mother to me. And that's why . . . that's why I couldn't think of anyone, with the exception of maybe Johnnie Mae Landris, I'd want occupying the place my mother would have been sitting if she were here to see me marry."

"Oh, baby," Miss Crowe said, pulling her closer. "And you have no idea how humbled and honored I was when you asked me to sit in the place of mother of the bride. God blessed me to have met you. And whether you realize it or not, you've blessed my life as much as you say I've blessed yours. Therefore, I say we're even."

"Oooooh," Jasmine said. "And I love *both* of you."

Gabrielle and Miss Crowe pulled away from each other and pulled Jasmine into the love fest as they all laughed and hugged.

Chapter 37

Behold, the Lord of hosts, shall lop the bough with terror: and the high ones of stature shall be hewn down, and the haughty shall be humbled.

— Isaiah 10:33

"Are we still going to Gabrielle's wedding?" Paris asked Andrew, who was playing with Braylen in the den.

Andrew's attention didn't deviate one iota from Braylen. "We RSVP'd and said we were, didn't we?" He bounced Braylen up and down on his lap several times making squealing effects of "Weeee!"

"Well, if we're going, we need to start getting ready. The wedding is at three o'clock, but I'm sure it will probably be full by then so we probably need to get there no later than two to get good seats."

"You go on and get started. I'll take Braylen and get him ready." Andrew held Braylen up in the air. Braylen made a gurgling sound as he shoved his whole fist in his mouth, causing a stream of spit to flow down like water poured from a pitcher.

"I put his outfit on the dressing table in his room," Paris said. "Would you like for me to bring it down to you?"

"Nope," Andrew said. "I'll go to his room and dress him there." Andrew stood up. "He needs his diaper changed. Don't you, boy?" he said to Braylen as he placed him on his shoulder, walking past Paris without saying anything more to her.

Paris hated how things had been in their home for the past two and half weeks now. Andrew didn't have much to say to her unless it was absolutely necessary. And the sad part: She wasn't sure if he was treating her this way because she'd told him that she'd slept with Darius that one time and that it was possible Braylen wasn't his son. Or if he'd opened the envelope and discovered the answer to the paternity question and knew for sure that Braylen wasn't his.

That was the thing about Andrew: He was a man of true integrity and fortitude. If he promised you something, he worked to keep that promise, many times at his own expense. That was most likely the reason he'd been such a true and dedicated friend to

Gabrielle, even years later. Not because he'd promised to stick by her when they knew each other all those years ago. But because he wasn't one who believed in throwing people who tried to play by the rules under the bus. He was the one person you could count on to fight for the underdog, those Andrew liked to say he believed Jesus was talking about when He referred to "the least of these."

So Andrew could very well have opened the envelope and knew that Braylen wasn't his. But if he had, he hadn't told her. And if he hadn't read it, and still possessed it, she had no idea where he was keeping it.

All of her haughtiness was definitely gone at this point, no matter how folks in the past might have labeled her so. And it was days like today when she wanted to just find the envelope and force Andrew to open it if he hadn't so she wouldn't have to wonder anymore. If he hadn't seen it, and it said he wasn't the father, she could get a reaction and have a better feel for where she stood with him. Not like it was now.

Now, all she knew was that he didn't have much to say to her. He wasn't being abusive in any way. And in truth: He was doing more for Braylen lately than she could have ever asked of him. He fed him, changed him, and even got up in the middle of the night with him, before she ever even heard him cry.

But they were going to a wedding that she knew she personally wouldn't have received an invitation to were it not, first of all, for her relationship to Andrew, who Gabrielle would never *not* invite after all he'd done for her. And there was that official announcement of Jasmine into their family that was likely the other reason. Her father would be there to see Jasmine's participation in the wedding.

"We're ready," Andrew said. "So you can't blame us if we're late."

Paris nodded, but couldn't help but smile. Andrew had dressed Braylen in his little white tux outfit with the navy blue cummerbund she'd bought him specifically for this wedding and put on his navy blue suit and a white shirt, which was a perfect match.

She went to get dressed, opting to change from the silver dress she'd originally planned to wear to a plainer navy blue so she would better match with Andrew and Braylen.

CHAPTER 38

Hear ye now what the Lord saith; Arise,
contend thou before the mountains, and
let the hills hear thy voice.

— Micah 6:1

The female attendants had their own large
room with dividers for them to go behind
when getting dressed. Gabrielle had a
separate room all to herself with Miss
Crowe in there to help her early on before
she would need to leave and do her other
duty. Melissa Peeples popped in to see how
things were going and if there were any last-
minute changes or instructions. Gabrielle
couldn't think of anything; neither could
Miss Crowe. Everything was pretty much
set.

Tiffany was *past* upset. Darius hadn't
brought the children to the house as he
promised. She'd called and left several messages, thankful at least she had his cell

phone number now. She'd been late herself arriving at the church waiting on him. Now it was two hours before the wedding and she *still* hadn't heard from him.

What was also exasperating was that she didn't know where Darius lived. So she couldn't even go to his house or report him to the police if she had a need to. She was kicking herself even more for not having pushed harder for him to give her his residential address as she'd originally requested. Her only hope was that Jade knew what time they were supposed to be at the church so maybe she'd call and let her know what was going on. She wished now she'd gotten Jade that cell phone Jade had asked for. But Tiffany couldn't see herself giving a ten-year-old her own cell phone; she didn't care how many other children Jade's age had one.

Tiffany was going to have to let Gabrielle know what was going on, but she was trying to put it off until she honestly had no other choice. All three of her children were in the wedding. If they didn't make it, Gabrielle's only flower girl and ring bearer would be missing. Tiffany had their outfits with her. So far, she'd only told Fatima of her worries so Fatima could be praying along with her.

Tiffany called Big Red and asked him to see if he could track Darius down for her, hoping in truth that maybe Big Red had been to Darius's new home and could go over there. Big Red said he'd not been to Darius's new place, but he would see what he could do to find out something and get back to her.

That had been an hour ago. He'd just called and said he'd turned up nothing. With two hours left until the wedding, and not wanting to burden Gabrielle, she went to the area where the men were getting ready, knocked on the door, and asked for Zachary.

"I'm sorry to bother you, Zachary," Tiffany said when Zachary stepped out of his dressing room. "But I need your help."

"Sure, Tiffany. What's up?"

"It's Darius. He didn't bring the children to my house at ten o'clock this morning like he promised he'd do. And he hasn't brought them here to the church, either," Tiffany said. "I've called him more times than I can count and left messages, but nothing." She shrugged as she wrung her hands. "And we don't have but two hours until the wedding. Do you think something bad may have happened? You know, like maybe they were in a car accident or something?"

"If something like that *had* happened, I would think you would have gotten a call," Zachary said.

"Yeah, but what if something like that happened, and they can't call. Or maybe they called but called my house? I only have an answering machine, not voice mail so I can't even check it from here. I never figured out how to check messages when I'm away, although I believe my answering machine has that capability."

"Well, I don't think anything like that *has* happened," Zachary said. "Darius is probably just messing with both you *and* Gabrielle. I know you likely don't want to hear this, but Darius is known to be petty like that. He's most likely doing this to worry you. But if you need to run home and check, you should do that. If there's not a message on your answering machine, I'd forward my home number to my cell phone so at least you'd know you won't be missing any more calls that may come in."

"That's a good idea. I can get home in about twenty minutes if the traffic lights work for me. That's forty minutes both ways plus the time to get in and out of the house. That would give me an hour after I get back before the wedding starts."

"You go and take care of what you need

to at home," Zachary said. "Someone will be here. In fact, why don't you give Melissa your cell phone number and if the children show up while you're gone, she can call and let you know."

Tiffany nodded. "I'll do that. I just didn't want to worry Gabrielle."

"Just tell Melissa not to say anything to Gabrielle about what's going on," Zachary said. "I'm sure everything's going to end up being fine. In fact, I wouldn't doubt if when you get out to the parking lot, you run into Darius along with the children."

"I hope you're right. And I'm sorry to have bothered you. But I needed a sounding board and I didn't want to dump any of this at Gabrielle's doorstep. Not now."

"This was fine." Zachary hugged her. "Listen, it's going to be all right. Okay? We're going to pray and believe that God has worked everything out."

Tiffany nodded, hurried and found Melissa, told her what was going on and what she was doing, grabbed her purse, and left.

One hour and forty-seven minutes left and counting . . .

CHAPTER 39

Let every man abide in the same calling
wherein he was called.

— 1 Corinthians 7:20

Zachary was on his way back to his dressing
room. His beeper was not with him on
purpose as he'd told everybody he wasn't
taking any emergency calls no matter *what*
happened. This was his wedding day and
that was going to take priority over everything and everybody. There were other burn
specialists available, and he expected them
to be fully used on *this* day.

So he was slightly perturbed when his cell
phone rang. He'd been planning to put it
away and only had it on him in case someone from either his family or the wedding
party had a need to reach him for whatever
reason in conjunction with the wedding.

He looked at the caller ID and smiled.
"Hey! What are you doing calling me?

Didn't I tell you I wasn't taking any emergencies? Unless you're calling because you're crashing my wedding and you're trying to find the church." Zachary became quiet as he listened intently to his doctor friend, who was hurriedly telling him about an explosion at a meth lab with multiple incoming casualties and chatter of possible children involved.

"Zachary, we have staff available to do our job. But with the numbers I'm hearing that are being brought in any minute and the talk of children possibly involved, I don't know," Dr. Stephens said. "I told you we had you covered. But you know if this wasn't something of this magnitude and specifically involving children who may not have time to wait, I wouldn't be calling you. I wouldn't."

Zachary glanced at his watch. One hour and forty minutes until the wedding. If he left right now, he could assess what was needed, start administrating medical protocols, leave, get back in time for the ceremony, and after saying his long-awaited *I do* and taking a few pictures, he could zip back to the hospital if necessary, with his new wife's full understanding and most assuredly blessings.

"I'll be there in about ten . . . fifteen

minutes maybe."

"That's good because they're bringing them in even as we speak. In fact, if you could shave some of those minutes off the ten, I'd appreciate it," Dr. Stephens said. "If the police stop you, tell them it's in connection with the meth lab explosion. I'm sure they've all heard about it by now."

"On my way right now." Zachary clicked off from Dr. Stephens. He hurriedly called Gabrielle's cell, praying her phone was on and that she'd pick up so he could tell her what was going on and for her not to get married without him. But seriously for her to know that if he *was* late getting back, she shouldn't cancel or postpone the ceremony because he *was* definitely coming back. They *were* getting married, and it would be *this* day. And nothing and no one was going to stop it.

Gabrielle didn't pick up the call. He hung up and called her number again. Still no answer. Deciding three times would be the charm and would convey to her that this was not just some excited groom who merely wanted to hear his soon-to-be-wife's voice, he called one more time. When she didn't pick up the third time, he left a message on her voice mail.

He'd now lost two of the ten minutes he'd

promised Dr. Stephens. But he had to be sure he got a message to Gabrielle. He turned to go back to the women's dressing area.

"Zachary! Don't you look spiffy," a twenty-something-year-old woman's voice said. She had three children with her. "And you're not even totally dressed yet."

"I'm sorry, but do I know you?" Zachary said, not having time to chitchat. "I'm sort of in a hurry right now."

"I'm Angie — Gabrielle's sort-of sister but actually her cousin. Although you wouldn't know by the way we got dissed for this wedding that she even grew up in our house." Angie was working hard to keep a handle on two of the children, who seemed determined to break away from her grip. She jerked each of their hands, which she held in one of hers. "Be still! I done told y'all! And I ain't gonna keep telling y'all."

She looked back at Zachary. "Sorry. I didn't want to bring these bad kids, but my mother said she wasn't going to stay home and keep them. And I can't afford a baby-sitter, so here we are, on time for a change, which was not an easy feat —"

"Actually, you're closer to an hour and forty minutes early. But listen —"

"Early? I don't do early." She shook her

head. "Somebody must have given me the wrong time. I thought the wedding started at one o'clock, which I guess would actually mean if it did I would have been late then, huh?"

"Yes. But the wedding doesn't start until three. Listen, I really —"

Angie sighed hard. "I guess that's what happens when you up and crash a wedding. You get all kinds of bogus information. I definitely wouldn't be here this early. Not with these rug rats in tow. Oh, well, I guess at least we'll get nice seats. That'll be a kicker if my always-late mother comes and sees us up front."

"Angie, is it?"

"Yeah. We met that time we were at Gabrielle's house for that week or so. You remember, don't you?" Angie popped her gum three times in a row.

Zachary was annoyed after just a few minutes of being around her, but decided she might be of some help. "Angie, I have an important errand to run. Gabrielle and the rest of the women are in a special area getting ready. There's a woman named Melissa Peeples who would also be a great one to tell if you can't get to Gabrielle, although I need this message to get to Gabrielle. Understand?"

"Yeah. Sure. I can deliver it for you. What's the message?"

"Tell Gabrielle that Zachary had to leave for an emergency at the hospital, but that I'll be back, hopefully before the wedding is scheduled to begin. But that if I'm *not* back by then, to *not* postpone or cancel the wedding for another day, but to wait on me to get back because we're going to get married today if there's nobody left here but me, her, the preacher, and one witness."

"Oh, that's so sweet and so romantic." Angie smiled and popped her chewing gum. "That's what happens when you're a doctor on call, right? Emergency calls."

"Yes. But just get that message to her for me. Will you do that for me please?" Zachary was already backing away so he'd be able to redeem the time he'd lost now.

"Will do," Angie said. "You can count on me. I got you, Dr. Zach."

"Thanks! Now don't forget. In fact, go right now. They're that way." He pointed toward the back and to the right.

Angie looked in the direction he pointed. "Count it done!" she yelled. "Bye!"

Zachary turned around and jogged out the door and to his car, which he was planning to let his brother drive to the reception since he and Gabrielle would be riding to the hotel in a limousine. He was glad he hadn't given his brother the key yet.

Now to make it to the hospital in record time and make it back for the wedding in the same.

CHAPTER 40

The voice of my beloved! Behold, he cometh leaping upon the mountains, skipping upon the hills.
— Song of Solomon 2:8

Gabrielle heard her phone ringing as she was getting her makeup applied and was about to reach to pick it up from the table where it lay. They'd eaten lunch around noon, everybody except Gabrielle, who didn't want to eat anything until after the ceremony. Now everyone in the wedding party was getting hair and makeup done.

One concern was that Tiffany's children hadn't arrived yet. Gabrielle wasn't supposed to know this since most members associated with the wedding were trying hard to keep anything negative from reaching her ears. But she'd overheard one of the greeters say that a few of the wedding party members hadn't shown up. The one talking had a problem with that since everybody else had seemingly complied.

But Gabrielle knew the situation likely behind all of that. Darius had the children and was doing this to mess with Tiffany, and even possibly *her* since he didn't care for her much, especially these days. She was more concerned for Tiffany as she knew this had to be tearing her up inside, worrying about what he was up to. She'd wanted to reassure Tiffany but didn't want anyone fussing at her about things they were desperately working overtime to keep from her.

In about an hour and thirty-nine minutes, the wedding would be starting. All of the work and effort put toward this wedding would finally come together and she'd be walking down the aisle on her way to marry her beloved Dr. Zachary Wayne Morgan. She wanted to pinch herself to make sure she wasn't dreaming. But she wasn't, and it was going to actually happen.

So when Gabrielle's phone rang and Sandy (one of two makeup artists sent from Jestina's company and the person working on Gabrielle's face at the time) saw that it was Gabrielle's fiancé, she quickly moved the phone out of Gabrielle's reach so she couldn't answer it.

"Let him just wait until three o'clock,"

Sandy said. "He'll be all right."

"But it might be important," Gabrielle said. "Besides, I'd like to hear his voice. I don't want to make him *just* wait."

"Trust me. I do this all the time. Grooms love to call and hear their bride-to-be's voice just like you're saying you want to hear his. Not giving in will up his anticipation that much more. Listen to me; I know what I'm talking about. You just watch: he's going to call right back. Watch and see."

The phone rang again.

"See, there. What did I tell you?" Sandy said. It stopped. Sandy smiled. "Now if he's really, really in love, and I'm talking about the sick in love, he'll call back one more time."

The phone rang one more time just as Sandy had predicted.

"There you go!" Sandy said after looking at the screen and smiling once again. She went back to applying Gabrielle's makeup, brushing on blush. "He won't call back. He's ready now. And I'm going to have you so drop-dead gorgeous, forget about 'you may kiss the bride.' You just might have to give the man mouth-to-mouth from the start of the wedding just to resuscitate him." She laughed. "That's why I'm going to make sure I reinforce your lipstick so it will

407

last if that ends up being the case."

Gabrielle was hoping Sandy was right and that Zachary hadn't really needed her for anything important. In the pit of her stomach though, she felt something wasn't quite right. Most would have attributed it to possibly nerves, but Gabrielle felt it was something more. She began to pray as Sandy continued working on her face. That's all she knew to do whenever she felt this way. The Holy Spirit knew what was going on, even if she didn't. And all she could do at this point *was* to pray.

But she'd *so* wanted to pick up that phone. And she wanted more than anything to hear Zachary's voice. Sandy, likely knowing what she was thinking, picked up her phone, turned it off, then carefully dropped it in her smock pocket.

CHAPTER 41

The sacrifice of the wicked is an abomination to the Lord: but the prayer of the upright is his delight.

— Proverbs 15:8

Tiffany came into Gabrielle's dressing room. Gabrielle had everything done now (makeup and hair) with the exception of putting on her dress, which they were getting ready to help her do. They were timing putting on her dress just right since she wouldn't be able to sit down to keep it from creasing or wrinkling.

"Tiffany," Gabrielle said with her arms opened. She could see by the look on Tiffany's face things were not good. "What's wrong?"

Tiffany stayed back as she wiped her eyes. "Nothing. Everything's fine," Tiffany lied.

"No, it's not. Come here." Gabrielle beckoned for her.

"I don't want to mess up your makeup or your hair. I'm fine. Really I am."

"Are the children here yet?" Gabrielle asked, letting her know she knew some of what was going on.

Tiffany couldn't hold it together any longer and burst into tears. "I don't know where they are! Darius hasn't shown up with them. I just came from home trying to be sure they weren't in an accident or anything and maybe a call had been left on my answering machine or a note on my door. But nobody's called or come by the house. And I don't know what's going on."

"Well, we have about an hour left to go before the ceremony. I'm sure Darius will be here with them by then," Gabrielle said. "Knowing Darius, he'll swoop in just in the nick of time, on purpose no doubt, to cause us panic, but just in time for the children to get dressed and walk all cute down the aisle. You know your husband —"

"Ex-husband," Tiffany said. "Come Monday my final papers will be here."

"Okay. But you know Darius. This is just like something he'd do. So I want you to settle down. All right? I've already prayed, and I know God is working things out, whatever *it* is."

"I know," Tiffany said, wiping her eyes

with her hands before Sandy handed her a white hand towel. "I've been praying as well. We know God hears and answers prayer."

"Yes, ma'am, he sure does," Sandy interjected her two cents. "Now, I know we had you in a different room to do your makeup. But I can do yours in here if you like," Sandy said to Tiffany. "We need to get you done though. But I can't have you crying and messing up all of my handiwork. So are we done with the crying? At least for now? You can cry all you want after the wedding is over, although you might want to hold off a little longer since there are still wedding pictures to be taken."

Tiffany tried to smile as she nodded. "I'm okay. This is Gabrielle's wedding day, and in less than an hour, we're going to look back and laugh at all of this."

Gabrielle grabbed Tiffany's hand and squeezed it. And for whatever reason, Gabrielle began a quick prayer.

After they finished praying, Sandy wiped her eyes. "That was a powerful prayer. It's a good thing I'm not in the wedding because y'all done gone and made me mess up *my* makeup."

They all laughed.

Gabrielle squeezed Tiffany's hand once more. Tiffany looked at her, smiled, then hugged her hard. Gabrielle nodded. "It's going to be okay. It is. I just know it."

CHAPTER 42

The floods have lifted up, O Lord, the
floods have lifted up their voice; the floods
lift up their waves.

— Psalm 93:3

It was three o'clock, the official wedding
time. Only two hundred invitations had
been mailed. But with family and all their
members, and friends with their family
members (not counting Followers of Jesus
Faith Worship Center members, who, personal invite or not, were in attendance even
if they couldn't attend the invitation-only
reception at the hotel ballroom), the church
that held three thousand people was packed.
People merely wanted to show their love
and support for this couple.

Melissa came in to let Gabrielle know that
Tiffany's children still hadn't shown up, but
they had someone stationed as a lookout
for the moment when they finally *did* ar-

rive. Three-oh-five and the wedding was officially late now. And there was one other snafu Melissa hadn't really wanted to tell Gabrielle if she could avoid it, but now was left with no other choice.

"We seem to have lost the groom," Melissa said. "In addition to the three children not being here, we don't know where Zachary is, either."

"What do you mean, you don't know where Zachary is?" Gabrielle said, her eyes wide upon hearing this news.

"I mean that no one seems to have seen him since, like, around one o'clock," Melissa said. "We don't know what happened to him. He was here one minute and gone the next, and no one knows where he is. His tux coat is still on its hanger."

"So what are you saying? That he got cold feet and bailed?" Fatima asked.

Melissa shook her head. "No. That's not what I'm saying or implying at all. In fact, his father and his groomsmen said it took all they could do just to keep him from putting on his full tux and planting himself in his wedding spot, to wait on the time to arrive. Apparently, he had on his pants, shirt, cummerbund, and tie before he stepped out of the room for some unknown reason. After that, no one has seen him."

"Has anyone checked to see if his car is still here? Called his cell?" Tameka asked.

"Do you know how many cars are out there? And his phone goes straight to voice mail." Melissa said to Tameka before turning to Gabrielle. "I'm sure something must have come up. Everybody knows he was more excited about this wedding than even *you* seemed to be, Gabrielle."

"What's going on?" Miss Crowe said, coming over to Gabrielle and grabbing her hand. "We're out there waiting for things to get started and now it's past time."

"Miss Crowe, have you seen or talked to Zachary?" Gabrielle asked.

"Not since we first arrived. I thought I was going to have to sit on him to make him be still until it was time. He's so eager to marry you. What's wrong? Has something happened?" Miss Crowe asked.

Johnnie Mae knocked on the door and came in. She hugged Gabrielle. "Well, don't you look beautiful! Absolutely breathtaking!" Johnnie Mae covered her mouth with her hand, then took it down. "I was sent to find out if there's anything I can do to help get things rolling. Pastor Landris is ready and waiting, as is a sanctuary full of people."

Tiffany stepped forward. "It's my fault. My children aren't here yet. Darius has

415

them. He said he was going to bring them, but he hasn't come yet. And I haven't been able to locate him although I've called everywhere I know to call."

"Oh, my," Johnnie Mae said to Tiffany.

"And it also appears the groom is MIA," Melissa added.

"The *groom* is missing?" Johnnie Mae said. "What do you mean, 'missing'?"

"No one seems to know where he is, either," Fatima said.

"Well, we know where he's not. And that's run off. So something important must have come up," Johnnie Mae said. "That's the only explanation."

"That's what I said," Miss Crowe said. "Let me go ask Queen if she's heard from him," Miss Crowe said, referring to Zachary's sister, who was also in the wedding but was in the other dressing room at that moment.

"All right," Johnnie Mae said. "So what do you want to do at this point? There's a church full of people out there waiting and wondering what's going on."

Melissa nodded, and then turned to Gabrielle. "Well, if it was just the children who weren't here, we could manage around them. I could give the flower girl's job to Jasmine instead of her being a junior bridesmaid. Or we could have one of the brides-maids or even the matron of honor throw out the flower petals before the bride walks down the aisle and no one would know that wasn't our original plan."

"Yeah, and I think my baby is a girl so we could just think of it as *her* dropping the petals and we both doing wedding duty," Fatima said. "Can't you just see me show-ing her the pictures and telling her this was her first stint as a flower girl while in her mommy's tummy?" Fatima smiled, hoping to lighten the mood.

"See?" Melissa said. "I like that idea." She smiled at Fatima. "I didn't know you were pregnant. Congratulations!"

"Thank you." Fatima touched her stom-ach. "Trent is over-the-moon about it."

"Okay, so we could take care of the flower girl's duty easily enough," Melissa said. "Ring bearers these days are mostly for decoration since they don't actually carry the ring, so we could just cut that part out. Unless we want to give the pillow to the best man and have him place the real rings there, you know, holding the pillow over to Pastor Landris when he asks for the rings."

"Okay, but what about the groom?" Tameka said. "As resourceful as we are to make this work, we can't have a wedding without a groom. And so far, no one knows where he is."

Queen and Miss Crowe rushed in. "I've not heard from him, either," Queen said. "Not since this morning when we first got here."

Melissa nodded. "All right. No groom. And therein is the real rub. So we need to locate the groom, and then we can get started."

Gabrielle looked at Tiffany, who was on the verge of breaking down. "Are you going to be all right?" she asked Tiffany.

Tiffany put her hand up to her mouth, obviously trying not to smear her lipstick, and nodded. "I'm fine. I'm just going to really let Darius have it when I see him. I don't *believe* he did something like this!"

Johnnie Mae reached for Gabrielle's hands and squeezed them. "Okay, so what's the plan now?"

"I plan to get married to the man I love. We just need to find him," Gabrielle said. "So if the wedding is late, it will just have to be late. And if anyone wants to leave, they can. But Zachary and I have come through too much together. I know he didn't just leave me at the altar. Something had to have happened —" She sucked in a quick breath as her face lit up. She pulled her hands out of Johnnie Mae's. "My phone? Where's my cell phone?"

"Why are you worrying about your phone?" Sandy asked.

"Because Zachary called me earlier, remember?" Gabrielle said to Sandy. "Maybe that's why he called three times the way he did. He was trying to tell me something important. Somebody find my phone, please. Sandy, you had it."

Sandy nodded. "Yeah. I put it up for safekeeping. I'll run and get it." She hurriedly left the room.

"That's probably what happened," Miss Crowe said. "He was likely calling to tell you what was going on. Hopefully the answer is on your voice mail."

"That's if he left a message," Gabrielle said as she stood tall, taking in and letting out long deep breaths.

Miss Crowe came over to her and hugged her. "You look so pretty." Miss Crowe shook her head. "I've never seen anything so beautiful."

Sandy rushed back in with the phone in hand. "Here you go." She handed the phone to Gabrielle, who quickly accessed her voice mail, then released a quiet sigh.

"What? Did Zachary leave a message?" Fatima said. "What did he say?"

"There was an emergency at the hospital," Gabrielle said, nodding. "He said he was coming back and under no circumstances was I to cancel the wedding today. He's coming back, and he said we're going to get married today no matter what."

Johnnie Mae smiled. "Then I'll just go let Pastor Landris know so he can announce to the people that there *will* be wedding, although late. But delay is not denial. There *will* be a wedding for those who are willing to wait."

"Now, that'll preach!" Miss Crowe said. "Delay is not denial for those who are willing to wait." Miss Crowe shook her head from side to side. "That will *preach*! I feel a shout coming on! Somebody hold my mule!"

Everybody laughed. Everybody except Tiffany.

Gabrielle went over and hugged Tiffany. "Now, don't you be over here worrying. God has your three children in His hands. You know this. You and I prayed about it, now we're going to act like we believe it's so."

"Faith," Tiffany said. "We have to have faith."

"There you go," Gabrielle said to Tiffany before addressing everyone in the room.

"Well, people, it looks like we're in a holding pattern . . . for now. But we're going to land this plane soon. There may be a storm, but we're flying above it. And we're going to land safely very shortly."

Miss Crowe chuckled. "Now that'll —"

"Preach!" everyone in the room yelled. They all laughed, this time *including* Tiffany.

CHAPTER 43

The Lord on high is mightier than the noise of many waters, yea, than the mighty waves of the sea.

— Psalm 93:4

Thirty minutes past the time the wedding was supposed to begin, there was a knock on Gabrielle's dressing room door. Fatima answered it, and after a few words were exchanged, she allowed the person on the other side to enter.

"Hi, Cousin Gabrielle," Angie said. "I'm sorry to barge in like this and all. Oh, look at you! You look gorgeous! I love that dress! Maybe you can let me use it after you finish with it for when me and my hubby get married."

"If you're married already, why would you need a gown *or* a wedding, for that matter?" Fatima asked, her nose slightly turned up.

"Oh, we're not actually *married* right now. I just call him my hubby until we make things legal," Angie said. "You know . . . faith. But I know I would look *good* in that dress. It looks like it cost a fortune. I bet we can get a lot for it on eBay. I buy things off eBay all the time, and I find some great deals. Although that dress has to have cost thousands, I can tell by all the diamonds sewn on it going down diagonally and the pleats crisscrossing on top meeting up with the diamonds."

"They're not diamonds," Gabrielle said, trying hard to be patient with her cousin, who was getting on her nerves by being her normal superficial self.

"Well, they look like diamonds," Angie said. "All sparkly and everything. Look at the detailed ornate design of each piece. And they're all linked together going from the left side at the top diagonally to your right hip. That's a lot of bling! Even if they're not diamonds, whatever they are, they had to cost a pretty penny. And then there are those pleats going across your waist, then some slanting downward — absolutely gorgeous. And I mean that dress is fitting you, too. You go, girl! Got that swirl going on at the bottom. Zachary is going to pass out right there in front of everybody when he sees you. Oh!" She raised her hand. "That reminds me. That's why I came. Zachary sent a message to you by me."

"When? When did you see Zachary? Is he here?" Gabrielle asked.

"I don't know if he's here or not. But I saw him about two hours ago."

"You saw him?" Gabrielle asked. "Where?"

"Here," Angie said as she unwrapped a stick of gum and shoved it in her mouth. "I had my little crumb snatchers with me. They're with Mama now. Oh, Gabrielle, Mama is out there! She wasn't going to come at first, but she didn't want Uncle Bennie tripping like he's been doing here lately. Uncle Bennie has been trying to get everybody in our house to go to church, to walk godly, get on the straight and narrow. Prison sure can mess a person up. That's why I told Jesse he'd better listen to Uncle Bennie, who knows from which he speaks —"

"Angie, please! I want to hear about Zachary? What did Zachary say?" Gabrielle said.

Angie popped her gum a few times and rolled her eyes. "You don't have to be all rude and everything. I was going to get to it. Dang. And y'all supposed to be the bougie folks. He told me to tell you he had an emergency at the hospital, but he'd definitely be back for the wedding, so if he was late, know that he would be back. Oh, and to not cancel the wedding regardless of how late he might be."

"So why didn't you come and tell somebody that two hours ago when he first told you?" Fatima asked.

Angie slowly turned toward Fatima. "Because" — she popped her gum three times — "I had those bad kids of mine, and I didn't want to be trying to find folks and having to drag them around. So I got in my car and went home. I talked my mother into coming to the wedding, which means I could leave them with her, come back, and find somebody *to* . . . tell. Is that all right with you?" She screwed up her mouth.

Fatima held up both hands, shook her head, and merely walked away.

Angie turned back to Gabrielle. "So I'm going to go back out there and wait for the wedding to start. I sure am glad I went home earlier though. I would have hated to have sat here all this time waiting on some wedding to start. It looks like y'all are just as late starting as people are always accusing my family of being."

"Thank you, Angie," Gabrielle said, rubbing the side of her temple as she tried hard to hide her true feelings.

"Okay then. I'm gonna go now. But don't forget what I said about that wedding dress. And those purple satin gowns y'all bridesmaids are wearing with the rhinestones on the top edge of that one shoulder drop with pleats going diagonally and pleats around the waist are banging, too. Although I like *those* two better" — Angie pointed at Tiffany and Tameka's dresses — "they fit better across the stomach. No offense but you" — she pointed at Fatima — "look like you're pregnant in yours."

"Well, since I *am* pregnant, then no offense taken," Fatima said.

Angie smiled and left with Fatima gleefully closing the door behind her.

After being sure she was out of earshot, Fatima turned to Gabrielle and said, "Is she for real?"

"Yep," Gabrielle said.

"And you grew up with her?" Fatima said.

"For a little over fourteen years," Gabrielle said. "I most certainly did."

"Well, God bless you, child," Fatima said. "Because I think I'd have to hurt that one if she was any kin to me."

Queen knocked on the door and rushed in.

"Why did you knock?" Fatima said.

"Guess who's here?!" Queen said with so much joy everybody knew the answer.

"Zachary," Miss Crowe said to her niece while clasping her hands together.

"Yes! And Tiffany, he's asking to see you," Queen said.

"Me?"

"Yes. And please hurry," Queen said.

"My children?" Tiffany said with complete fear on her face. "Please don't tell me —"

"Just go. He's down the hall a little ways waiting on you. You'll see him," Queen said. "Go." Queen touched Tiffany's hand to calm her some. "Go."

CHAPTER 44

He that hath the bride is the bridegroom:
but the friend of the bridegroom, which
standeth and heareth him, rejoiceth greatly
because of the bridegroom's voice: this
my joy therefore is fulfilled.

— John 3:29

Tiffany closed the door and quickly looked
down the hall. Her hands instantly went up
to her mouth as she ran down the hall, high
heels and all. She grabbed up her children,
wanting to be able to hold each one indi-
vidually and collectively all at the same time.

"You're okay! You're all right!" she said as
she kissed them.

"Yeah, but it was scary," Dana said.
"Daddy went in there. It's bad, Mama.
There were ambulances and bodies being
put on stretchers." She shook her head, unable to say more.

"Scary?" She looked at Dana, then Jade,

and finally up at Zachary, who was standing there looking a little worn out.

"It wasn't scary, scary, Mama," Junior said. "There was an explosion, BOOM! And sirens and policemen and policewomen and about three fire trucks with firemen running around everywhere."

Tiffany stood up straight and directed her complete attention to Zachary. "What?!"

"Dad's girlfriend," Jade said. "Apparently she was running or involved in some sort of a meth lab operation or something."

"What? What are they talking about?" Tiffany asked Zachary as she swiped at her tears, her beautifully made-up face demolished now.

"Darius took the children over to a place where apparently they were cooking up meth —"

"He did what?!"

"Daddy got a call," Jade said. "Well, actually, Miss Divine got a call on her phone, but she was out at the time. Daddy was on his way out the door to bring us home so we could come to the wedding, the wedding I suppose we've missed now."

"I don't think you missed it. They wouldn't dare start without *you*," Zachary said to Jade with a quick wink. "And possibly me." He grinned. Jade grinned back.

"Oh, yeah," Jade said, still grinning. "That's right."

"Back to your father," Tiffany said to Jade. "I don't believe that man. What was he thinking?"

"Daddy doesn't think," Junior said. "At least, that's what Miss Divine said when he showed up at that house with the three of us. She asked him what on earth was he thinking bringing us with him to a place like that. She then told him he doesn't think."

"Junior, I'm sure Mama doesn't care about that," Jade said to her brother.

"Okay, so your daddy answered Miss Divine's phone on his way to bringing you home like he promised," Tiffany said. "So why didn't he just drop you off at the house first, and *then* go do whatever stupid thing he was going to do next?"

"That's also what Miss Divine said to Daddy," Junior said. "Wow, Mom, you and Miss Divine must be twins or something. Y'all say the same things."

Tiffany placed her hand on top of Junior's head, then looked over at Jade. "So he didn't bring you home. Why didn't somebody call me and tell me what was going on? I've been worried sick about y'all for the past six hours. Why didn't you call me,

Jade? Or even you, Dana?"

"I would have called if you would have bought me a cell phone like I asked," Jade said. "Otherwise, what was I supposed to call you with?"

Tiffany nodded. "I know, I know. I'm not blaming you, any of you."

"Anyway, it appears Darius answered Divine's phone she accidentally left at the house. It had some kind of a distress message with an address. He went over there and it turns out it was actually a place where they were cooking meth," Zachary said.

"So my husband . . . their *father* took them to a place where they were cooking meth? Meth?" Tiffany said through clenched teeth.

"In truth, I don't know for sure that Daddy knew that's what they were doing," Jade said. "He told us to stay in the car. Miss Divine must have looked out and seen him when he drove up. She came out to the car and started blasting him for bringing us and saying all those things Junior just told you she said."

"Then Daddy and Miss Divine went toward the house and were about to go inside," Dana said. "And —"

"BOOM!" Junior said. "There was a loud booming noise! It was *so* loud! And the car

431

shook with us in it. So we all jumped out of the car and Jade made us lay flat on the ground."

"The house exploded? Is Darius . . ." Tiffany looked at Zachary, who was using his eyes to point out that the children were there and there were likely some details they didn't need to discuss in front of them. Tiffany nodded that she understood his coded message. "Hey, they're waiting on you so we can have a wedding," Tiffany said to the children. "Do you still feel like doing this or would you rather I take us home?"

"Are you kidding me?" Jade said. "I want to stay and be in the wedding."

"Me too," Dana said.

"Me three," Junior said, causing Tiffany and Zachary to laugh.

"Well, okay then. Let's get you three dressed in a hurry, or should I say four since I think they're also waiting on the groom." Tiffany looked at Zachary and smiled.

"Yeah, I think he might be a *little* bit important," Dana said. "Dr. Z?"

"Yes?" Zachary said.

"Thank you," Dana said, hugging him. "Thank you for everything. I hope and pray that Daddy's going to be all right." She looked up at Zachary, who smiled.

"Yeah, Dr. Z. Thanks for everything," Jade

said. She then looked at her little brother. "Junior."

"What?"

"Don't you have something you need to say to Dr. Z?"

Junior walked over to Zachary. "Dr. Z, can I please go with you to put on my outfit? I don't want Mama to dress me. The mood she's in right now, she'll be kissing me all over my face and treating me like a little baby. I've been in this place before. Please, Dr. Z. May I go and get dressed with you?"

Zachary smiled and placed his hand on Junior's head as Junior looked up at him with his classic puppy dog eyes routine. "Sure. That's if it's okay with your mother." Zachary looked at Tiffany, who tearfully nodded.

"I need to go get his suit and bring it out," Tiffany said. "But we do need to hurry. Everybody has been waiting for a while now." Tiffany put her arms around her daughters' shoulders and walked them to the dressing room. She hurried back out and held Junior's tux out to Zachary.

"Mama, I can take it," Junior said. "I'm a big boy. I promise I won't drop it or anything."

"Yes, you *are* a big boy," Tiffany said, handing the tux to Junior instead. "You most certainly are."

Zachary and Junior left, going toward their own dressing area. Tiffany hurried back inside where the women were still gathered.

Tiffany's children were okay. Tiffany now knew there had been an awful explosion. Darius was hurt but alive. But there was still going to be a wedding.

God had heard and answered everybody's prayers.

CHAPTER 45

Till we all come in the unity of the faith,
and of the knowledge of the Son of God,
unto a perfect man, unto the measure of
the stature of the fullness of Christ.
— Ephesians 4:13

At five o'clock in the afternoon, on June 11,
in the year of our Lord 2011, Gabrielle
Mercedes stood in the hallway as the wedding party began their processional march.

She couldn't see the ones lined up in the
hallway with her after they turned the
corner. But she knew that Pastor Landris
was standing up front with Zachary next to
him, and Zachary's father as his best man
next to him, along with Zachary's brother
Yancey, his cousin, and a colleague in that
order. Zachary would be wearing a white
tux with a purple cummerbund — purple
being the color of royalty and totally Miss
Crowe's choice, although it was the color

Gabrielle had been planning on . . . either purple or a pretty cobalt blue. The best man and groomsmen were wearing black tuxes with purple cummerbunds.

Junior looked so cute in his little all white tux and purple cummerbund. After Tiffany checked on him to be sure he was properly dressed, she came back and said, "That son of mine is as sharp as a tack!"

All the junior bridesmaids, the bridesmaids, and the matron of honor wore purple with the adults' dresses having one side slanted off the shoulder. The children wore more Cinderella-like ballroom gowns, Gabrielle certain that was more of Jasmine's doing than probably Miss Crowe. They were all *so* beautiful. And Dana, the flower girl, was dressed in all white, a miniature version of a bride, only a ballroom-style dress. As an added touch, Miss Crowe had ensured that every female member of the wedding party was sporting a beautiful tiara, though none matched the one Miss Crowe had for the bride. They were like a queen and a court of princesses.

Every person in the wedding on this day had to feel special.

Wanting to have had a hand in *something* with her wedding dress-up, Gabrielle had found a pair of pretty open-toe, white satin shoes with tiny roses on the straps. They were cute. Even Jasmine had said so, although she'd said it with a small giggle.

But Miss Crowe had one more unexpected surprise for Gabrielle, and she'd apparently enlisted Zachary's cooperation in pulling it off. Gabrielle would learn what that was after she made her way to the altar.

The large mahogany double wooden doors opened and Gabrielle and her father strolled in arm in arm down the long aisle. Bennie glanced over at her and, on more than one occasion, was caught wiping away a tear. Then Zachary almost messed up by trying to take possession of Gabrielle before the appropriate time. Everybody laughed and Zachary wiped his forehead, shaking his head as he smiled adoringly at Gabrielle.

"Take My Breath Away" by Berlin played after the traditional wedding march and what most call the "giving away of the bride." Only they'd opted to call it the "presenting of the bride" by the father to the groom. "All My Life" by K-Ci & JoJo was played immediately after the prayer and prior to the lighting of the unity candle, which was followed immediately by a unity sand ceremony that was beyond both touching *and* beautiful.

The unity sand ceremony included a large

heart-shaped monogrammed vase with the letter M, and not just two separate smaller vases with different-colored quartz sand, but four.

"The unity sand ceremony symbolizes what are individuals now coming together as one," Pastor Landris said. "Beginning with the white sand I shall pour first to represent the foundation on which this blessed union is being built: the Word of God and a confession of faith in Jesus Christ." Pastor Landris poured the white sand from his small vase into the larger heart-shaped vase.

"Now I'll ask Gabrielle and Zachary, the bride and groom, to pour their sand along with Gabrielle's sweet little daughter, Miss Jasmine, as an indication of what was separate, now becoming one — never to be separated as, once mixed, grains of sand can not effectively be separated out."

The three of them poured their individual vases of sand at the same time: Zachary's indigo blue, Gabrielle's dark pink, and Jasmine's light pink all flowing and mixing, creating a beautiful work of art in the process. Jasmine had the biggest grin on her face as she watched the sands flow and come together.

After that, the wedding ceremony went

pretty much as most weddings do with the exchanging of vows and declarations to love, honor, and cherish. But then came the one surprise Gabrielle hadn't known about and wasn't expecting. The one she was certain Miss Crowe, and most assuredly Jasmine, had teamed up with Zachary to do.

One of the ushers from the back walked up the aisle with a glass slipper on a beautifully decorated satin pillow. He held the pillow before Zachary and bowed his head as Zachary took the glass slipper off the pillow and kneeled down before Gabrielle. Gabrielle thought she was absolutely going to lose it at that point.

Pastor Landris was in on it as well. He said, "The prince is promising his kingdom to the one whose foot fits this glass slipper. Others have tried and failed. Gabrielle, Zachary is asking you to place your foot in the slipper." Pastor Landris looked at Gabrielle, who was blushing at this point, but also praying that the shoe *would* fit, since she hadn't tried it on prior to this, considering she hadn't known any of this would be taking place. What an embarrassment it would be if the shoe *didn't* fit.

Zachary pulled off the shoe she was wearing on her right foot, then carefully and lovingly slipped the glass slipper, which had an oval-shaped Swarovski crystal the size of two thumbs on the top of it, on to her foot. It went on as though it had been custom made for her. She smiled at Zachary, who stood up and took hold of her hand. Then before she knew anything, Miss Crowe stepped forward, holding out the matching glass slipper inside of a see-through plastic box. Zachary took that shoe, kneeled down again, pulled off Gabrielle's other shoe, and slipped on the matching glass slipper. He took her other shoes and placed them in the plastic box Miss Crowe held. Miss Crowe winked at them and went back to her mother-of-the-bride seat.

"In as much as these two have pledged their love and devotion to each other," Pastor Landris said. "And in as much as the shoe fits" — everybody laughed, interrupting him, although he had to pause because he was laughing as well — "it is with great joy and divine pleasure that I, Pastor George Edward Landris, now pronounce you . . . man and wife." He looked at Zachary and smiled. "I know you've been waiting a long time for me to say this. Dr. Zachary Wayne Morgan, you may *kiss* your *bride*!"

Zachary looked at Gabrielle with so much love in his eyes. He didn't make a joke out of it or anything. And as she looked at him, she saw one single tear making its way down his face. He lovingly leaned in and sealed their love with a kiss.

CHAPTER 46

And the Lord said unto Satan, The Lord rebuke thee, O Satan; even the Lord that hath chosen Jerusalem rebuke thee: is not this a brand plucked out of the fire?
— Zechariah 3:2

Tiffany left quickly, as soon as the wedding ceremony and wedding pictures had been taken. She asked Fatima to watch her children for her since they really wanted to go to the reception.

Zachary had told Tiffany privately, right before the wedding ceremony began, what he hadn't wanted to say in front of the children. Darius had been burned in the fire, plucked from it just in time. He was stable for now, and it appeared he would live. He'd told Tiffany that Darius had been placed in a purposely induced state like a coma for now to keep him from experiencing the intensity of the pain. She could go to the hospital, but Darius wouldn't even know she was there. They would be bringing him out of the coma in the morning to begin the real work that was ahead of him. Zachary assured her there was an excellent team in place working on Darius.

Tiffany didn't know exactly how she felt at this point. Darius had filed for divorce over thirty days ago. In fact, she hadn't contested it, even though she'd considered doing so. Her lawyer had advised her that there was nothing she could really do to stop the divorce, short of the two of them reconciling and dropping the case entirely.

But Darius had made it abundantly clear that he didn't want to be married to her anymore and that there was nothing she could say or do that would *ever,* not in a million years, change his mind. He'd reiterated that anything she did to delay things would be stupid on her part. And it would only be taking money from their children to give to the lawyers and the court, which, in the end, wasn't going to change their inevitable outcome. The final approved paperwork was set to be delivered to her on Monday. But on this day, she believed she still had a legal right to see Darius, as his wife. Come Monday, she wouldn't.

She *was* allowed in to see him without

any problems. He was bandaged up in some places, exposed in most. Darius's doctor said he would have to have skin grafting done. The gory details of what would happen caused her to cringe. She was told recovery would be a long and painful ordeal. But Darius had been one of the fortunate ones, he and the woman he'd protected. In fact, had they walked in that house one minute earlier, a mere sixty seconds, which would have put them closer to the brunt of the explosion, neither of them would be here right now. Two people had already died and two were so badly burned they really weren't expected to make it.

The police were there. And after learning who Tiffany was to Darius, they wanted to question her.

Had she known her husband was into this illegal activity? No. In fact, she wouldn't say that he was, even though he had obviously been there when something illegal was taking place. From her understanding, he was doing a friend a favor and just happened to be there at that particular time. After all, he'd had their three children with him. She couldn't see him doing anything dangerous or illegal knowing that they were that close to something like that.

How long had her husband known Delilah

Vine aka Divine? As far as she'd been able to ascertain, she'd say around the end of January. But since Miss Vine was the other woman in this triangle of her marriage, she really didn't care. Besides, there were those filed divorce papers, his choice not hers, so technically speaking, they were no longer really married and the final papers of dissolve were arriving Monday.

She stopped the questioning by letting them know she hadn't been there, she didn't know anything, and anything she could tell them would only be considered hearsay and not admissible in a court of law.

As mad as she was with Darius for all that he'd done and for all he had put her through, she didn't hate him. And she certainly didn't want to do anything to *deliberately* hurt him, even though she got it from him that, when it came to her, he obviously didn't feel the same way.

"Your husband's going to need a lot of care after this," Darius's doctor had said to her. "He's going to have a long and difficult road ahead of him."

But Tiffany could only think about how he'd treated her over the years, and how he'd utterly mistreated her just over these past months. Come Monday, again totally Darius's choice, she would have a piece of paper that legally declared he was no longer her husband. She could only pray for him and hope that he and Divine (who she had overheard one of the policemen say was in good condition, sustaining only minor burns to her arms and legs since Darius had essentially taken his body and shielded her from most of the fire) would have great support following this.

Tiffany got in her car and drove to the wedding reception at the hotel ballroom. Yes, she would do what she could to help the father of her children by taking them to see him. However, he'd kicked her for the last time. When it came to her being a wife to him, as Darius had so bluntly put it Friday night at the rehearsal dinner, she would no longer stand in the way of his happiness and him having fun. She was only a ball and chain that was holding him back and dragging him down, and come Monday, he would be thankfully and gloriously rid of her.

Yes, she would pray for him, praying also that he get himself together and get right with God. Satan had been rebuked, this time. Darius had been plucked out of the fire, this time. But what he did from here on out, as far as she was concerned, was entirely *on* and *up* to him.

CHAPTER 47

And behold, the veil of the temple was rent
in twain from the top to the bottom; and
the earth did quake, and the rocks rent.
— Matthew 27:51

Andrew and Paris only stayed at Gabrielle
and Zachary's reception for about thirty
minutes. Braylen was worn out and a bit
fussy now, likely from having been at the
church at two o'clock, an hour before the
wedding had originally been scheduled to
start. Well, the wedding hadn't started on
time. And after about a half hour, Pastor
Landris had announced there *would* be a
wedding but, for reasons he didn't disclose,
there would be a delay. Andrew had gathered from all the squirming Paris started
doing an hour *after* that announcement that
she really wanted to go home. But since he
wasn't talking much to her these days, she
must have decided to keep that sentiment

to herself.

Andrew wasn't trying to hurt Paris. But he had never been one to hide his true feelings. He wasn't good at faking it. During a court case, he could do it. But when it came to his personal life, he wasn't good at wearing a mask, pretending something was okay when it wasn't.

And things clearly weren't okay at the Holyfield house. His wife had cheated on him. And he'd been foolish enough to defend her against his mother, who really did have his best interests at heart. His mother only wanted him to protect himself, even in the face of love. He merely wanted to throw caution to the wind and allow the wind to blow as it willed.

He knew what Paris had likely concluded from his quiet demeanor these past three weeks: that he'd opened the envelope and that he knew Braylen was not his.

Paris came into the bedroom after putting Braylen down for the night.

"That was a nice wedding — after it got started, that is," Paris said, then stopped when she saw Andrew holding the infamous mangled envelope in his hand.

"Come and sit, won't you?" Andrew said.

Paris walked over to the bed and gingerly sat down next to her husband. "You haven't opened it yet?"

Andrew shook his head. "Nope."

"So why do you have it with you now?"

"Because I was thinking how beautiful that unity sand ceremony was between not just the bride and groom, but Gabrielle's daughter Jasmine," Andrew said.

"That *was* touching," Paris said. "Jasmine looked so happy. She's a lovely girl."

"It was. And she is." He tapped the envelope on his knee, then looked at Paris. "Jasmine is not Zachary's biological child, and yet, he loves her no less than if she were."

"So what are you saying? That it doesn't matter whether Braylen is your biological son or not?"

Andrew shrugged. "That's why I haven't opened this to see yet; I wasn't sure what I thought. I had to be quiet and talk to God about this. I needed to search my heart and find out just where I was when it came to this, not merely flesh, but spirit."

"So, have you heard from God on it yet?"

"Yes."

"And, what is God saying?"

"He's saying that we've all missed it at some point and fallen short of the glory of God. And that *all* includes me. I love that little boy." He nodded toward Braylen's room. "Whether what's in this envelope says

Braylen and I share the same DNA . . . the same blood, or not . . . we share the same heart. The only blood, in the end, that truly matters . . . is the blood of Jesus. And Jesus' blood covers everything, period, the end of the story."

"So, you're *not* going to open that?" Paris asked, nodding at the envelope.

"Yes," Andrew said, turning it over and sliding a letter opener along the edge to rip it open. He reached in and slowly pulled out the yellow paper. He then read the results, and nodded slowly as he tightly buttoned his lips. With his head still down, tears began to flow. He wiped his eyes and looked up toward the ceiling.

"What?" Paris said. "What does it say?"

He handed the paper to her and stood up as he wiped away the tears. He looked up again, twisted his mouth, and nodded some more. His body began to shake and he fell down on his knees.

Looking at the paper, Paris released a cry, then covered her mouth. "Oh, Lord! Oh, my Lord," she said, walking toward Andrew, who was quaking on bended knees.

He looked up at her as he continued to completely break down. She kneeled down beside him and hugged him as tight as she could.

"He's mine," Andrew said. "He's my son! That confirmed it. Braylen is *my* son!" He cried and hugged Paris back, as they lovingly rocked each other before the Lord.

CHAPTER 48

And I took your father Abraham from the other side of the flood, and led him throughout all the land of Canaan, and multiplied his seed, and gave him Isaac.
— Joshua 24:3

Gabrielle and Zachary were enjoying the reception with family and friends. Her new mother-in-law came over and hugged her.

"Everything was so beautiful," Leslie Morgan said. "I mean *everything* was absolutely beautiful: the ceremony, your dress, all of the attendants' wear, including the men, the decorations for the wedding, and this reception hall." Leslie began to scan the entire area. "Beautiful! And where on earth, pray tell, did you find someone to create that bride's cake table?"

She and Gabrielle were both looking at the bride's cake table now.

"I mean that's a full-size Cinderella coach

made out of clusters of perfectly placed white, light pink, and purple balloons for the pumpkin-looking frame, small gold star balloons stuck to spokes fashioned into the carriage wheels, and on top, white feathers that look like a humongous woman's Sunday church hat."

Leslie then turned her attention to the groom's table. "And instead of just the usual chocolate groom's cake, you have four separate chocolate cakes connected by white bridges decorated with purple flowers, one cake flat on the table with a replica of a bride and groom on it, then two slightly elevated cakes on each side, with all of them leading up to the cake on top sporting a small golden pumpkin horse-drawn carriage parked outside of a gold and purple accented castle with a fountain of water and light underneath it. That's the most beautiful thing, other than the bride's table, I've ever seen, when it comes to wedding cakes. Brilliantly done!"

"I can't take credit for *any* of this or anything that had to do with the wedding, for that matter, at the church or this reception, other than pretty much showing up," Gabrielle said. "Miss Crowe and her little helper, Jasmine, who I'm so very proud to call my daughter, did and arranged absolutely everything. I'm talking everything."

"Well, they did an awesome job," Leslie said. "As well as the people they employed to carry things out."

"Thank you," Gabrielle said with a sincere touch of love laced in her voice.

"Oh, you're welcome."

"No, I mean thank you . . . for being here. You don't know how much your being here means to Zachary."

Leslie nodded. "Well, Zachary made it perfectly clear that he was going to marry you no matter what I said, did, or did *not* do. He then laid Genesis 2:24 on my plate for me to chew on. 'Therefore shall a man leave his father and his mother, and shall cleave unto his wife: and they shall be one flesh.' I suppose we can also thank my late daughter, Xenia," Leslie said, in reference to her oldest daughter killed over ten years ago.

Gabrielle didn't want to push for a further explanation, knowing that any talk of Xenia was still a painful topic for Leslie.

Leslie must have known what she was thinking and voluntarily offered the explanation: "I was trying to control my son and make him do what *I* thought was best and right for him. But this morning, I felt the spirit of my daughter letting me know that what I was doing was no different than what the man who murdered her was trying to do. Then God placed on my heart that we can't go back and experience the times in life we miss, whether by choice or not. If we don't seize those moments when and while they're before us, we just may end up living a life full of regrets later. I didn't want to look back and have to kick myself because I was so bent on having my own way at whatever cost. So I sat down and I counted the cost. And losing out on this time in my son's life, and mine in truth, wasn't worth me proving some idiotic point. The only thing is: I didn't have a chance to get you two a wedding present. But I'll take care of it after I return home."

"Well, I know I was shocked to see you when he and I were leaving from the altar. I could tell he was on cloud nine. Having your presence here was the best gift you could have given him as a wedding present," Gabrielle said. "And you've already given me the best gift you could ever give me: You gave me Zachary."

"Ah," Leslie said with a heartfelt hug. "Now I must thank *you.*"

"For what?"

"For loving my son so much that you'll not allow anyone, including me if that's what it takes, to come between him and his ultimate happiness," Leslie said. "That's what I figured out, albeit almost too late. But thank God for being able to get a flight out from Chicago to Birmingham at the last minute. It looked like I was still going to miss most of the wedding. But wouldn't you know, something happened that caused the wedding to not start on time? And I not only made it in time, but I got to see the pleased look and the big old smile on his face when I came in and lit the candle that represented our half of what would be used to light the unity candle."

Gabrielle nodded. "Well, I can assure you, we had *fully* intended to start on time before a flood of things seemed to unleash."

Zachary walked up to his mother and pecked her on the cheek with a kiss. "Mama, what are you and my beautiful wife over here talking about?" He smiled at his mother, then Gabrielle.

"Oh, just how good God is, no matter how much we may get in the flesh and try to mess things up. God is faithful." Leslie nodded. "He is faithful. He'll definitely bring us over to the other side."

"I love you," Zachary said, hugging her. "Aunt Esther said she was praying for you and she believed there was nothing too hard for God. I'll be honest: I didn't think you were coming, especially after Daddy came yesterday and you weren't with him. I knew then that any hope I still may have held was gone."

"Well, I'm *so* glad I made it. Seeing that surprised look on your face when you saw me walk in was priceless. And then to be here in the flesh to witness such a beautiful ceremony with that sand and the glass slippers —"

"All of that was Aunt Esther and Jasmine's doing," Zachary said with a grin. "Jasmine wanted her mother to have a Cinderella wedding. And it didn't take but one word to convince Aunt Esther."

"Well, looking around, that has most definitely been accomplished," Leslie said. "And where is Esther, by the way? I haven't seen her flitting around in a while."

"I don't know," Gabrielle said, looking around as well. "There are so many people here."

"I know you two are busy," Leslie said. "I'll find her. I'm sure she's around here somewhere. I have to congratulate her on a job well done as well as my new little grand-daughter — Jasmine, is it?" Gabrielle nodded in the affirmative to Jasmine's name.

"Yes, indeed. I must congratulate them both."

The DJ was announcing that it was time for the first dance with the bride and groom as husband and wife, "Dr. and Mrs. Zachary Morgan." A song began, "Happily Ever After" by Case. Zachary held out his hand to Gabrielle and bowed from his waist. Gabrielle smiled and took his hand, and they danced. She felt like someone had actually placed clouds beneath them and they were no longer dancing on hardwood but floating on air.

After they finished, the DJ called for a father-and-daughter dance.

Gabrielle's father came over and took her hand. "I'm gonna warn you. I'm a little out of practice now," Bennie said. "But Esther has been working with me on the side for a few weeks now. So I suppose we'll see just how good of a dance teacher she really is." He started their dance.

"You're doing great, Daddy. I guess this proves Miss Crowe is a great teacher."

"Yep, I guess it does. And today you were the most beautiful thing I've ever laid eyes on. I only wish . . ." He bowed his head and shook it before looking back up. "I'm sorry, Gabrielle. I'm so sorry. I can't tell you enough just how sorry I truly am."

"Daddy, let's not go there. Not today. Okay? I've forgiven you, and it's just no longer me merely spouting the words. That's where we are today — forgiven. Now let's just dance." Gabrielle smiled as her father leaned down and kissed her cheek.

Zachary was dancing with Jasmine until, halfway through the song, Lawrence bowed from his waist and politely cut in. Jasmine was eating it *up*. She had the biggest grin on her face as she had her father dancing a waltz.

After they finished that dance, the DJ announced it was time for the cutting of the cake, and then there was the toasting period. They did the traditional throwing of the bouquet and after that, the garter. Gabrielle was wearing two garters, one lower down her leg for her new husband to remove and throw and the one Miss Crowe and Jasmine had given her that morning. She wanted to keep that one for a keepsake.

The DJ opened the dance floor for everyone. The next slow song that played, Zachary went and asked his mother to dance with him. Leslie cried through the entire dance.

Zachary also wanted to dance with Miss Crowe. Leslie said she'd found her, but that she was a little tired and sitting more in the back and off to the side out of the way of traffic. Gabrielle went to locate her while Zachary danced with his mother.

"Miss Crowe. There you are." Gabrielle kneeled down in front of her.

"You're going to mess up your dress," Miss Crowe said. "I bought you one to change into so you could shed that long thing for a shorter one when you got here. I need to go get it or maybe get someone to get it for me. It almost slipped my mind."

"I'm fine. Don't you worry about a change of dresses," Gabrielle said, grabbing her hands and squeezing them tight. "You've done way too much as it is already. And everything has been so wonderful and so perfect. I couldn't have asked for anything more or better if I had my very own fairy godmother who could have whipped up something like this with a magic wand."

"Well, it came from my heart. And I've learned when it comes to magic, there's nothing more powerful than love. And we all know there's no greater love than the love of God. God's love makes you want to do and not just talk about it. I love you," Miss Crowe said. "I do."

"I know you do. And I love you . . . so much. I wish there were words big enough, grand enough, and powerful enough to express *just* how much." Gabrielle stood up. "Zachary wants to dance with you. And since you're occupying the place of my mother right now, you must oblige the both of us."

"Well, you know me when it comes to dancing now," Miss Crowe said, struggling to stand to her feet. "Show me a dance floor, and I'll show you someone who will cut the rug, as we used to say back in my day."

"Are you sure you're feeling all right?" Gabrielle held her arm to help keep her steady.

"Just a little tired, that's all. But I have plenty of time to rest tomorrow and all next week. Jasmine and I said we're just going to stay in bed until we feel like getting up when you and Zachary are gone on your little Jamaican honeymoon." Miss Crowe laughed, then started toward the front of the room alongside Gabrielle, who continued to hold on to her.

When they reached the dance floor, the DJ said, "Oh, looky, looky now! It looks like Mama Esther is about to show us *all* how this is done. Come on, Miss Crowe. Show them what you can do."

Zachary looked at Miss Crowe and smiled. He bowed from his waist, then held up their hands in the ready, dance position. Everybody cleared the dance floor, surrounding the edges as Miss Crowe and Zachary began their waltz. When they finished, everyone in the entire reception hall, including those sitting at tables, was on his or her feet, clapping.

Miss Crowe took a few gracious bows, waved to the crowd, then collapsed to the floor.

CHAPTER 49

I John, who also am your brother, and companion in tribulation, and in the kingdom and patience of Jesus Christ, was in the isle that is called Patmos, for the word of God, and for the testimony of Jesus Christ.

— Revelation 1:9

Zachary was on the floor giving Miss Crowe CPR. She didn't appear to be responding. An emergency call had been placed. Gabrielle could tell by how frantic Zachary was that she wasn't even breathing.

The paramedics arrived quickly enough possibly because this was a hotel and they were always somewhat on standby. They began frantically working on her. Gabrielle saw one of them covertly shake his head to another one as if to say she was gone, although those words were never audibly uttered. One of them just kept saying, "No change." An ambulance was on the way.

Zachary came over to Gabrielle and held her in his arms. She was crying hard now. How could something like this happen? They were just talking, not five minutes ago. Miss Crowe couldn't be gone. Not now . . . not today. She just *couldn't* be gone.

Gabrielle broke loose from Zachary and kneeled down. "Miss Crowe, open your eyes. Come on now. Please, all you need to do is open your eyes. Miss Crowe, come on. Wake up. You can't leave us . . . you can't leave me. You keep fighting, do you hear me?! Don't you quit on us! We need you. . . . I need you. . . ."

Jasmine came over and kneeled beside Gabrielle. "And I need you, Miss C," Jasmine said. "You know I do. Who's going to teach me how to spell words like Mississippi in the fun way that you do?"

Zachary grabbed Jasmine and pulled her up on her feet. Jasmine buried her head into him as he continued to hold her tight.

"She can't die," Jasmine said, looking up at him. "We're supposed to go over everything that happened today. She promised me we would talk about how great everything turned out. And it *did* turn out great; just like we planned. She can't die. I can't lose anybody else. Not now. I'm just a little

464

girl. I can't lose Miss C, too. Please God, please God. I'm begging you. Make Miss C live." Jasmine put her hands together in prayer. "I thank You for healing her, right now. I thank You for Your mercy and for Your grace. Lord, please touch Miss C's body. Don't let her die. Please, Lord. I'm asking You."

As Jasmine was praying, the people inside the reception hall began to pray aloud with their own individual prayers. Gabrielle had her hands on Miss Crowe's shoulder, trying hard not to be in the way of the ones working on her, although they really weren't working too frantically anymore as they knew she was gone. Gabrielle also began to pray.

But Miss Crowe lay unmoving, peaceful, and still.

CHAPTER 50

I was in the Spirit on the Lord's day, and heard behind me a great voice, as of a trumpet.

— Revelation 1:10

Miss Crowe saw Zachary when he kneeled down and started pumping her chest, occasionally giving her mouth to mouth even though she knew it was said you didn't *have* to do that in order for CPR to work. She could almost hear the song playing that they said you should pump to the rhythm of when giving CPR to get the right pace, "Stayin' Alive" by the Bee Gees.

She saw Gabrielle kneeling down telling her to wake up, to open her eyes, to fight. She saw the paramedics doing all kinds of things. Her heart did go out to little Jasmine when she said they were supposed to recap everything. Jasmine was right; she had promised her that the two of them would do that after everything was over. It broke her heart hearing Jasmine talking about her loss over the years. Miss Crowe was aware that she'd lost her adoptive father in a car accident and her adoptive mother to cancer. Jasmine's world had been turned upside down and turned upside down again only to feel like it had finally been righted in the past six months or so.

Miss Crowe saw the bright light before her. She'd heard about that light, but words couldn't describe *this* kind of light, not this one. Mere words were grossly inadequate! It was so beautiful. She was standing — gliding, more like it — on what appeared to be rows and rows of miles of perfectly uniform clouds. There was nothing but indigo blue and white clouds as far as the eyes could see. She suddenly saw people standing off in the distance waving at her. She felt so at peace, so at home right now.

That was *it.* She felt like she'd returned home from a long journey and a long time of having been away. As she came closer, she couldn't believe her eyes. It was her mother and father . . . together. And as though just thinking a thought made things instantly happen, she was right there in front of them. It seemed they wanted to speak, but there was nothing but love exuding from their mere presence. She glanced out of the corner of her eye and, lo and behold, there was her beloved husband. He nodded, then leaned over and gently kissed her on her cheek.

But it was the light that seemed to be the thing that she couldn't look away from. Inside the light, she saw what appeared to be the figure of a man. But the light was so intense, so stunningly bright, it was hard to completely focus and declare the figure inside of the light for sure. Divine. Yes, divine! That was the best word Esther Crowe could find to describe everything she was seeing and experiencing. It was paradise, a place full of divine divines.

It was then that she knew she was about to cross over. She was leaving the other side and entering pure Divine. She was standing in the presence of what she could only describe as her Lord. She bowed down before the Great Light, which seemed to move closer to her. There was such warmth; there were no words to describe it. Such peace and love she didn't know how anyone could stand after experiencing this and *not* want to possess this always and forever.

While bowed down, she heard voices. Only the voices were coming from the other side, the other side of Divine. And the voices were calling for her to come back. But how could she go back? Why would she even want to? She was home now. This was her home. This was Heaven or, at the very least, the entranceway where she'd step over into it. Then all of her troubles, tears, trials, and tribulations would be left behind.

But then she heard Bennie's voice, of all people. The man who had been filled with such rage and evil at one time that he'd killed his own wife. The man who had gone to prison for that very crime, leaving a beautiful little girl to essentially have to fend for herself. A little girl who would find she'd have to fight for whatever she got and even then, she would be at a disadvantage because she was fighting against folks who had no problem fighting dirty.

Still, Gabrielle had given her life to the Lord, and just *look* at her now. Esther was proud to have played whatever small role she had in Gabrielle's life. But now, all of that was over. She'd run her race. She'd finished her course. Now it was time for her to take her rest.

But Bennie was talking to her. Loaded on the gurney as they were taking her body to the hospital to pronounce her death there, Bennie was jogging beside them talking to her.

"You can't leave now, Esther Mae," Bennie said.

Esther couldn't believe he was calling her Esther Mae! She'd told him twice before that she didn't have a middle name and she certainly wasn't going to be called Mae by the likes of him. She'd told him what she'd do if he ever called her that again.

"My little girl still needs you," Bennie said. "You can't go now. Do you hear me, Esther Mae? Do you hear me, you old stubborn woman!"

"No, he didn't just call me stubborn," Esther said what felt to be within herself. "I have told him I'm not stubborn. I'm set. I'm determined. I'm focused. But what I am *not* is stubborn! Stubborn is what you call a mule."

"Gabrielle needs you. Jasmine needs you. Zachary needs you. Your family needs you," Bennie said. "How are you going to just up and leave them like this?"

But Esther Crowe didn't care what he was saying. *Everybody knows we're not on this earth to stay. They know this place is not our home. They know we're merely pilgrims passing through this unfriendly land. And they know that no one is going to live forever, that we're all going to leave this place one day.*

Well, this is my *day. And I'm fine with it.*

This place where I am now is beautiful. And when I tell you how beautiful, you're not going to believe just how much so.

But then Bennie had to go and say one more thing. One more thing, as they rolled her gurney into the parking lot. One more thing as she could see all of the ones she loved following behind her as they were whisking her body away. He had to speak one more thing he *knew* would likely get her attention.

"Esther Crowe, you listen to me and this is the last thing I'm gonna say to you. Do you *really* want the day Gabrielle and Zachary got married on to be marred by the remembrance of the day that you died? Do you really want to leave that on them as each and every year they celebrate their glorious wedding anniversary they're left saddened because you up and died on the very same day? Huh?"

Esther heard a great voice like a trumpet. She felt heat rush through her body. She looked and saw the One in the Light touch her and shake His head as though He was saying either it wasn't her time to be there or that she had to go back. Maybe the One in the Light knew she was having second thoughts now. And He knew that if He'd asked if she wanted to go back, that she'd say yes. Everything seemed to happen so fast after that, in less than an instant, so she couldn't say how long for sure. All she knew was that she felt pain in her chest from all the pumping and CPR efforts. She saw a man holding two paddles in the air cheering that they had a pulse now and a heartbeat, although faint.

She was back — back on the other side of Divine.

Gabrielle rushed over to her and softly rubbed her forehead. "Thank God, you're alive." Gabrielle was crying, but those were definitely tears of joy. "You came back to us. Thank you. And thank You, Jesus, for hearing and answering our prayer."

They were pushing the gurney into the ambulance now.

"I'm riding with her," Gabrielle said to them. She then climbed in, wedding dress and all.

Zachary knew only one could ride in the ambulance, so he nodded to Gabrielle. "I'll be right behind you." He blew his new bride a kiss. Still holding tight to Jasmine's hand (that had sneaked into his) he said to her, "Do you want to go with me or stay with Miss Tiffany?"

"Yes, Daddy Z," she said. "I want to go with you. Please don't make me stay."

He stopped and looked at her, his head tilted lovingly to the side. "Daddy Z?"

"Yeah. My friend Princess Rose calls her stepfather — that would be Pastor Landris — Daddy Landris. And since I technically just found another father, which is Mr. Lawrence — although I'm still working on calling him Daddy anything, even though he said I could when and if I ever felt like I wanted — I've decided, that is if you don't have any objections, to call you Daddy Z."

He picked her up, hoisting her in the air. "I would be honored and love nothing more," Zachary said. "Me, you, and your mother are officially family now."

"Yep!" Jasmine said. "We've mixed our sand together and there's no separating them back out, not now, not ever. That's what Pastor Landris said."

"That he did." Zachary was on his way to his car until he remembered he'd let his brother have it as he and Gabrielle rode over in the limousine Aunt Esther had for them after the wedding to bring them to the hotel's ballroom.

"Looking for this, little brother?" his brother Yancey said as he tossed him the key. "You go on. Your car is right over there." He pointed where he'd parked. "You go on after your woman and take care of

Aunt Esther until we get there. Both of those women are one of a kind."

Zachary nodded. He located his car, made sure Jasmine was buckled up, and went to the hospital, where he found Miss Crowe had experienced a heart attack. She was doing okay right now, as it appeared there had been a blood clot that had caused it, and the clot seemed to have passed.

CHAPTER 51

Write the things which thou hast seen, and
the things which are, and the things which
shall be hereafter.

— Revelation 1:19

Miss Crowe told of all that had taken place
over the time when it appeared she'd died.
She told them about this place she'd heard
of, the place she was looking forward to going back to again someday, now that she'd
gotten as far as the door and gotten to peek
in. A place of love and peace and Jesus, His
arms open wide.

The doctor told her she really hadn't gone
to the place she called Divine, but that it
was merely her brain shutting down after
her heart stopped. As for the light she
described, he attributed that to the firing of
lights in her brain. Yes, clinically speaking
she *had* died, for a good amount of time.
And what she experienced was something

many have said actually happened, but he was skeptical.

"I'd like another doctor," Miss Crowe said to Zachary and Gabrielle as soon as he left the room. "I don't want any doctor working on me who doesn't believe in God or the afterlife waiting once we leave this place."

"Aunt Esther, are you serious? He's really a great doctor," Zachary said. "One of the best around."

"He can be great and the best all he wants," Miss Crowe said. "But I know what I believe, and I can tell you what I saw. You can't tell me I didn't see and experience something when I know that I did. I told him everything I saw when I was declared dead even by their standards, didn't I?"

"Yes, ma'am, you did do that," Zachary said with a slight chuckle.

"And didn't you confirm that everything I reported that I saw and heard when I was supposed to be unresponsive . . . dead . . . whatever fancy term anyone wants to call it?"

"You did indeed do that as well, and with shockingly great accuracy," Zachary said, scratching his head. "You've definitely made a complete believer out of me. But if it was as beautiful as you said, I'm even more surprised that you came back. Not that I'm complaining."

"Well, I wasn't going to," Miss Crowe said with a loud sigh. "And you tell your father, Gabrielle, that Benjamin Booker, I've told him not to call me Esther Mae, and I resent him using that guilt tactic that he did about y'all's upcoming anniversaries."

Gabrielle frowned bewildered. "What about our upcoming anniversaries?"

"Well, as crass as Benjamin was, he was right. The last thing I would ever have wanted to do was to blemish the most beautiful day of you two's life with you having to remember it also being the day I transitioned — not died, because I'm telling you there's no death, just eternal life in a different place. This much I know without any doubt now." Miss Crowe tried to sit up straighter. "But know this: I *am* leaving here one of these days. And when I do, I don't want anybody crying for me. You can cry for yourself, but don't cry for me. Because that place . . ." She shook her head. "I can't wait to see Jesus and see what's beyond the light. That's all I have to say. Everybody got it?"

They all laughed. "Yes, ma'am. Maybe we'll just throw you a New Orleans-style home-going fully equipped with the horses and band and all," Zachary said.

Miss Crowe nodded with a smile. "There you go! That's the idea. Just don't get some cheap band to play. If you're going to get a cheap band, then don't even bother. And just know, if you try it, I'll likely see what you did. And when you get to Heaven, we're going to have a nice little chat. Oh, yes!"

"Well, we're going to go now. The doctor said they're going to keep you and run some more tests while they monitor you. But you should be home Monday if everything pans out as I suspect it likely will." Zachary hugged Miss Crowe.

Jasmine walked up to the bed. "I'm so glad you're all right. We still have to do our recap, but it can wait until you're better." She hugged Miss Crowe.

"Well, that will be on Monday when I come home. So get ready. Because that wedding you and I put together and attended was off the hook!" Miss Crowe smiled. "We threw down!"

Jasmine laughed and hugged her again, then whispered, "Get well. I love you, Miss C. And thank you for staying here and deciding not to leave us. I know just how beautiful a place it was." She smiled. "Thanks for coming back."

Miss Crowe winked at Jasmine as she stepped away.

"We'll be right outside," Zachary said to Gabrielle, who was still wearing her wedding gown. Zachary and Jasmine left.

"You were the most beautiful bride I've ever seen in my life," Miss Crowe said. "And I know I've said it before, but I want to say it again. I love you with all of my heart."

"Miss Crowe . . ." Gabrielle started to cry.

"Don't you dare. Don't you do that. I'm fine. You see that I'm okay now."

"But I thought I'd lost you," Gabrielle said, wiping away the tears. "You just did too much. You overdid it. So when you get home, I'm going to take care of *you* for a change. And you're going to let me. You've taken care of me for too long, and so many times. Now it's my turn to make sure you're all right."

"I *am* all right. You're correct. I just overdid it, that's all. But I'm finished with everything now, so I'll be fine from here on out," Miss Crowe said. "But you and Zachary were supposed to leave for your honeymoon on Monday. Listen: Your flight doesn't leave until the afternoon. I'm sure they're going to release me first thing Monday morning. Jasmine and I will be fine together. So —"

"We're not going on a honeymoon."

"Oh, yes, you are!" Miss Crowe sat up

straight. "I'm not going to allow you to put off your honeymoon because of me. I'm not. I wanted everything to be perfect. You and Zachary have tickets and reservations and you're going to use them. If you don't, then why did I come back from the other side?"

Gabrielle laughed. "We're not going. And that's that. I'm sure Zachary agrees with me. Until we know you're okay, the honeymoon can wait. Because you know what?"

"What?" Miss Crowe said.

"I'm married now." She held up her hand with her ring finger and twisted it in the air. "And I married the man of my prayers and my dreams. I had a wedding I thought I could only fantasize of having someday. But because of you, a dream world stepped right out of a fairy tale book and became a reality for me, little ol' me. And so, I have everything I need right here in good old Alabama. My husband, my daughter, and now my new aunt. So, *Aunt* Esther, stop arguing with your new niece."

Miss Crowe smiled and smiled some more.

Gabrielle hugged her. "I love you, and there's nothing you can do about it."

Miss Crowe didn't want to let go. "I love

you, too. I love you, too. And there's nothing you can do about *that,* either."

EPILOGUE

Blessed is he that readeth, and they that hear the words of this prophecy, and keep those things which are written therein: for the time is at hand.

— Revelation 1:3

A year later, much had happened in the lives of Zachary and Gabrielle, the least of all being the new baby that arrived on March 30, 2012, the exact same day as Jasmine's birthday. When the baby boy made his screaming debut on that day, Gabrielle was a little concerned with how Jasmine might take having to share her birthday with a new baby brother.

"Are you kidding me?" Jasmine said. "My baby brother was born on *my* birthday. Now how awesome is that?! And you want to know what else?" Jasmine had said in the hospital room on her eleventh birthday, holding her little brother as Gabrielle sat on the couch with them.

"What?" Gabrielle said.

Jasmine looked down at her brother as she spoke. "It's really a blessing from God that little Zachary chose to be born on my birthday."

"How so?"

Jasmine looked up at Gabrielle. "Well, my mother, or should I say my adoptive mother, died on my birthday. It kind of made my birthday sad after that. But now, something wonderful has happened. Of all the days that my brother could have picked to be born, he and God got together and decided it would be on *this* day, my birthday. That really says a lot. Don't you think?" She smiled.

Zachary and Gabrielle debated what they really wanted to name their little boy. Jasmine was already calling him Little Zachary, but they weren't sure they wanted to make the baby a junior. But after Jasmine was so insistent that he would be *thrilled* about it, Jasmine decided she needed to help them with their apparent dilemma.

"If you don't want to name him Zachary Wayne Morgan Jr. then what about Zachary Wayne Morgan the Second?" Jasmine stood over his portable crib in the hospital room when she made that declaration. She then grabbed the baby's hand and shook it lightly. "What do you say?" She suddenly bent down with her ear to his mouth. "What's that? You say you like it? What? Ohhhh, I'm sorry. You said you *love* it!" She turned to Gabrielle and Zachary. "He loves it." She grinned.

"Well, then," Zachary said to Gabrielle, "looks like you and I are outnumbered?"

Gabrielle frowned and pulled back a bit. "How is two to two outnumbered?" Gabrielle asked, pointing first to Jasmine and the baby and then her and Zachary.

"Actually, it's three to two," Zachary said. "Jasmine, the baby, and God."

Gabrielle chuckled. "God, huh? Okay. So Zachary Wayne Morgan the Second it is."

Then there was Tiffany, divorced from Darius, now dating Clarence Walker with their relationship appearing to be serious and moving with promise toward a possible wedding altar.

Fatima and Trent's baby girl was born on December 3, 2011, as healthy and as pretty as could be, looking like the both of them.

Darius was still slowly recovering from the burns he'd incurred during the meth lab explosion. He could have gone to jail, but no charges were filed against him or Divine. The four people who died from the fire (two on the scene and the other two in the hospital) were the only ones who could have definitively fingered their true involvement. But needless to say, because Divine knew she was being watched, she'd dropped her illegal activities, which meant she no longer had the money to live in the lifestyle to which she'd grown accustomed. Darius couldn't work because he was recovering. They had been evicted from the mansion and were presently residing in an old run-down house that once belonged to Divine's parents.

From what Tiffany was being told by Darius (who was trying to make up with her and get her to remarry him and throw their divorce nonsense out), Divine wasn't the woman she was when they first met. She didn't take care of him. He was definitely having a hard time. He confessed that he hadn't realized what a wonderful woman he'd had in Tiffany until he'd lost her. Tiffany reminded him that he hadn't lost her; essentially, he'd thrown her away. There was a difference in how those two things were viewed, as one man's loss can be another man's gain. She told him she would continue praying for him and Divine. She even took the children to see him on occasion. After all, he was *still* their father. She would support her children. But when it came to her and Darius? That chapter was over, and she'd already turned the page.

Aunt Cee-Cee was convicted of fraud. But because it was her first offense (that she'd been caught doing anyway), they only made her spend sixty days in jail with three years of probation, and she had to pay back all the money she'd stolen plus a hefty interest. Miss Crowe admitted she'd likely never see a dime of the money. But still, if there was an opportunity to collect any of it, she was going to, and happily so. "People need to learn to stop taking stuff that doesn't belong to them and not caring about how it affects the one they took it from," Miss Crowe said. "I absolutely positively forgive her. But she's still going to pay."

Bennie was now living in the house left to Jasmine by her late adoptive mother. Someone had to keep the house up. Gabrielle had intended to let him stay there for free, but he insisted on paying his way, so she let him. Not because she was greedy or needy for money. But because it allowed her father to be a man, the man he desired to be. He was working full-time at the church and loving it as much as they seemed to be loving him and the work he was doing keeping up the grounds. And of course, the day Miss Crowe came home from the hospital after her heart attack, she blasted Bennie.

"I told you not to call me Esther Mae. I heard you when I was being carted off," Miss Crowe said. "You'd better be glad I was flat on my back or I would have kept my promise and clocked you one."

Bennie grinned because he'd done that on purpose in hopes of causing just the reaction it had: that she would open her eyes and fight.

Paris and Andrew were still together. Gabrielle didn't understand why he felt the need to tell *her* that a month after her wedding. It was as though he was confessing that there was a reason he and his wife shouldn't have still been together. But Andrew loved Paris. And Paris did appear to have changed a lot. Gabrielle attributed some of Paris's transformation and growth to her being a member of the ministry led by Pastor Landris and his anointed teaching.

"I mean, if you can sit under the true Word of God and not see a change in your life," Gabrielle said to Zachary concerning Paris, "then there's something fundamentally wrong with you."

"Or mentally wrong," Zachary said.

Reportedly, Andrew and Paris were actively trying to have another baby.

Lawrence got Jasmine some weekends. They never forced her to go or made her feel guilty if she didn't want to go. It helped that she and Imani were so close. Imani loved her little sister and refused to call her a half-sister.

Jasmine relayed what Imani had said to her the first time she was there for an unsupervised visit. "We have the same marrow, the same blood type, and we're children of the same God. That means: In every sense of the word, we're full-blooded sisters."

Miss Crowe (now Aunt Esther) was doing better than ever. In fact, she was keeping Jasmine and Little Zachary while Gabrielle and Zachary were gone for their one year anniversary. They were finally making good on that honeymoon they didn't get to originally take.

"Just know," Miss Crowe said to Gabrielle and Zachary, "that when you two get back from your little honey over the moon, Jasmine and I are going to Disney World to see Mickey and Minnie and, of course, Cinderella and Prince Charming."

And when the not-so-new newlyweds returned two weeks later, the following week Miss Crowe and Jasmine did just that. The two of them had a special bond indeed.

That Sunday after Miss Crowe's near-death experience, Jasmine had taken a picture she'd drawn and colored to the hospital for Miss Crowe, who looked at it, and nodded. She then grabbed Jasmine and hugged her tight.

"You've been there, too, haven't you?" Miss Crowe said, gazing down at the picture. It was a picture of rows and rows (as far as the eyes could see) of white clouds on top of an indigo blue sky, and a male figure with arms open wide surrounded by a bright light of such magnitude it was difficult to see Him.

Yep, the other side of Divine might not be as great as the actual Divine that for many is to come. But there were always places and special moments where one could experience a little bit of Heaven right here on earth. Amen?

Amen.

A READING GROUP GUIDE
THE OTHER SIDE OF DIVINE

VANESSA DAVIS GRIGGS

ABOUT THIS GUIDE

The questions that follow are included to enhance your group's reading of this book.

DISCUSSION QUESTIONS

1. Miss Crowe is back! Discuss your feelings about her relationship with Gabrielle, Jasmine, and the rest of the people who happen to cross her path.

2. What were your thoughts when Benjamin Booker showed up? Would you have trusted him? Would you have allowed him to stay? Why or why not? How did you feel about the way he and Miss Crowe interacted with each other? What were your feelings about him by the time you reached the end of the book?

3. Discuss the things that happened between Darius Connors and his wife, Tiffany, then with Paris Simmons-Holyfield, and with his newfound friend Miss Dee Vine.

4. What were your thoughts about Miss Divine? What did you think about her when

it came to Darius's children?

5. Paris had a lot on her mind these days, with the baby coming and all. Discuss everything she dealt with. What were you thinking when it came to the baby both before she delivered, then afterward?

6. Discuss the things that went down at Lawrence Simmons's house when Gabrielle and Jasmine came over for dinner. What were your thoughts about that?

7. Everybody seems to need to talk about the various dilemmas in their lives. Touch on the many discussions conducted throughout the book and how you felt about them. To get you started: Johnnie Mae Landris and Paris, Jasmine and Jade, Gabrielle and Zachary (when it came to what she should do about Jasmine and how much she should be told and when), Miss Crowe and Gabrielle, Gabrielle and Bennie, Bennie and Zachary, Lawrence and Deidra, Andrew and his mother Paula, Tiffany and Darius.

8. Discuss Divine, Aunt Cee-Cee, and Jesse and what they were up to.

9. Zachary didn't trust Bennie. What were your thoughts when it came to the two of them?

10. Paula Holyfield also didn't trust Paris. Talk about what was going on with them prior to Paris giving birth. Do you think that at any point Paula was wrong or out of line? What about when it came to the discussions between Paula and Andrew about Paris?

11. The DVD player came up missing. Discuss everything surrounding that incident.

12. Discuss what's going on with Darius and whether or not you agree with the course Tiffany decided to take in the end. Did your opinion of Tiffany change from the first time you may have encountered her? Elaborate.

13. Talk about your favorite part(s) of this story. Were you satisfied with how things turned out in the end? Discuss.

Thank you for going on this journey with me. I hope you have enjoyed this as much as I have enjoyed bringing it. My ultimate goal has and will always be to give you a great reading experience. My prayer is that, as we come to a close, you've felt that here.